WITHDRAWN

EVICTION NOTICE

D0966975

ALSO BY K'WAN

Gangsta
Road Dawgz
Street Dreams
Hoodlum
Eve
Hood Rat
Still Hood
Gutter
Section 8
Welfare Wifeys

ANTHOLOGIES

The Game
Blow (with 50 Cent)
Flexin & Sexin
Flirt

K'wan

EVICTION NOTICE

A Hood Rat Novel

St. Martin's Griffin ❧ New York

This is a work of fiction. All of the characters, organizations, and events portrayed in this novel are either products of the author's imagination or are used fictitiously.

EVICTION NOTICE. Copyright © 2011 by K'wan Foye. All rights reserved. Printed in the United States of America. For information, address St. Martin's Press, 175 Fifth Avenue, New York, N.Y. 10010.

www.stmartins.com

Library of Congress Cataloging-in-Publication Data

K'wan.
    Eviction notice : a hood rat novel / K'wan. — 1st ed.
        p. cm.
    ISBN 978-0-312-53698-5 (pbk.)
    1. African American women—Fiction.   2. Street life—New York (State)—New York—Fiction.   3. African Americans—New York (State)—New York—Fiction.   4. Harlem (New York, N.Y.)—Fiction. 5. Urban—Fiction.   I. Title.
    PS3606.O96E95 2011
    813'.6—dc22

                                                           2011020384

10 9 8 7 6 5 4 3

This story is dedicated to my friend, mentor, and inspiration, Leslie Esdaile Banks, who not only pushed me to succeed but offered me a hand when everyone else offered me a fist. You've done your part so rest easy now. I'll take it from here.

EVICTION NOTICE

This shit is fly," Von said when he stepped into one of the elevators of the Empire State Building, looking around like a tourist.

"You ain't here to sightsee, you're here to handle business," Murder reminded him. He was a greasy-looking dark-skinned dude whose face always seemed to be twisted into a scowl. He had become a local celebrity on the underground circuit, which had brought him to the attention of Don B., the boss of one of the hottest rap labels in the game, Big Dawg Entertainment. Murder thought that since he got signed everything would be roses, but he soon felt the prick of the thorns in the rosebush.

"Murder, I don't know if this is a good idea. The lawyers said they'd handle it," Steve tried to reason with him. He was Murder's right-hand man and manager.

"Fuck you mean the lawyer is gonna handle it? My nigga, we been waiting like three months already and the lawyer ain't did shit yet, so I'm tired of waiting," Murder snapped. He had been trading e-mails and phone calls for too long already with little results, and decided it was time to express himself in person. As insurance he had brought a few goons with him.

They spilled off the elevator and into the carpeted

hallway like gorillas at a zoo during feeding time, startling a young man with an armful of files who had been waiting for the elevator. He tried to skirt around Murder and his goons without making eye contact, but that didn't stop one of them from smacking his files out of his hands, spilling papers all over the elevator floor, and drawing laughter from his buddies. After their shits and giggles they mobbed down the hall to their destination, the office of Big Dawg Entertainment.

The office was nice, but didn't boast the over-the-top bravado that was associated with Big Dawg. The carpet and furniture were all deep red, with posters and plaques of several popular acts adorning the walls. Behind the glass wall of the reception area several men were gathered in a conference room, sitting around a large table. Hunched over the receptionist's desk was a dark-skinned chick with a high weave and a tight blouse.

"Yeah, Shay, the muthafucka had the nerve to ask me if I was sure it was his baby." The receptionist clicked her gum loudly as she spoke into the phone, completely ignoring Murder and his crew.

"Shorty, you just gonna act like you don't see us?" Murder asked.

The girl rolled her eyes and raised her index finger for him to hold on. "Girl, I said the same thing. How you gonna ask me some shit like that just because I slept with his brother that one time? I told him we were twisted and it was a mistake. And then this fool—" Before the girl could finish her sentence, Murder snatched the phone from her and ripped the wire out of the wall.

"Bitch, you keep acting like I'm invisible and the next thing I'm gonna snatch is you," Murder threatened her.

"Damn, you ain't gotta be all violent and shit." The girl snaked her neck. "What you want?"

"I *want* to see Don B.," Murder told her.

"He ain't here." The girl rolled her eyes.

Murder and his crew looked at one another, because they could all see Don B. sitting in the conference room. "Shorty"—Murder leaned forward on the desk—"maybe you don't know who I am, but I'm Murder. Don B. signed me to Big Dawg last summer. Tell Don B. I wanna see him."

"It don't really matter who you are, Don B. ain't taking no appointments," she told him.

"See, you one of them bitches that like to do everything the hard way, huh? Come on, fellas." Murder made his way toward the conference room.

"I wouldn't go in there if I were you," the girl warned.

"Fuck you," Murder spat, and pushed open the door of the conference room.

Don B. sat at the head of the conference table with his white Nike Airs propped on the tabletop. His signature piece, a jeweled rottweiler head, hung from the end of his thick gold chain. His hair was freshly cornrowed into four thick braids that stopped just short of his shoulders. A black-on-black Yankee cap sat ace-deuce on his head, with the brim stopping just short of black sunglasses.

Sitting across from Don B. were Blaze, a young rapper who had earned the Don's favor, and the attorney for Big Dawg Entertainment. Blaze was visibly uncomfortable in the presence of the goons Don B. had looming around the conference room, but he did his best to keep up his gangsta-rap persona. He had been trying to get Big Dawg to sign him for months and his moment was almost at hand. Blaze was well aware of the stories associated with Big Dawg Entertainment, but he was willing to risk it if it meant he would be able to stand next to Don B. and get his piece of the Big Dawg pie. Everybody wanted to get down with Don B.

Don B. was every little ghetto kid's dream come true. He had gone from being a petty crack-cocaine dealer to one of the most successful men in the music industry, all thanks to his brainchild. Big Dawg had initially been a small record company started by two childhood friends from Harlem. In the last few years it had grown into one of the most successful record companies in the business, but also one of the most notorious. Big Dawg had been linked to a dozen high-profile murders, including those of the members of the up-and-coming group Bad Blood and their front man, True, who had been Don B.'s best friend. Though True's murder had come long after the members of Bad Blood's, they were both due to street-related beefs.

Dealing with the deaths of his friends and artists had put Don B. in a very dark place, and had him questioning his love for the music industry. His next group, the Left Coast Theory, had shown great promise, but that fizzled when one of their members had a nervous breakdown and the other was sent to prison. Still, Don B. had found a bright spot in his life when he discovered a talented young man who went by the name Animal. When Don B. had first discovered Animal he was in the streets heavy and had made a name for himself as a strong-arm bandit and killer, but that all changed when his mentor and two of his best friends were gunned down. Their murders and a new love interest caused a change in Animal and he began to wonder how long he could run the streets before his number was called. With little other option than dying in the streets or going to prison, Animal finally ended the courtship between himself and Big Dawg Entertainment and accepted Don B.'s offer to join the Big Dawg roster.

Animal was extremely talented and seemed to be a natural showman once he got into the swing of his new life. For a while it seemed like he had finally broken his ties with the streets, but soon the secret life he had been living under everyone's nose came to light. Animal was arrested and convicted for the murders of several people who had been involved in the murder of his mentor, Tech. To make matters worse, Animal had escaped while being transported to Rikers Island and almost killed two police detectives in the process. The police launched an extensive manhunt for the young killer, but he had simply vanished. Animal's notoriety made his album the biggest release in the history of Big Dawg Entertainment, but it was yet another black eye for the record label.

"Yo, Don, I just wanna thank you again for giving me this opportunity, fam," Blaze said sincerely.

"It's nothing." Don B. made a dismissive gesture. "My mans and them told me you had some hot shit and after listening to your demo I find myself inclined to agree."

"I'm telling you, I'm gonna be the hottest nigga ever to come outta this camp, word to mine," Blaze declared.

Don B. was unmoved by the declaration. "So you say. Well, sign on the dotted line and let's begin laying the groundwork for your legacy." Don B. motioned toward the contract in front of Blaze. Blaze hurriedly scribbled his name and passed the contract to Don B. to sign also. Once both signatures were down, the lawyer slipped it into his briefcase.

"Man, it feels like I just signed to the Lakers," Blaze said excitedly.

"Better, me and mine are like the Bulls when Mike was in his prime. This is a dynasty we're building here and you'll be a part of it, if you're ready," Don B. taunted him.

"On fish and spaghetti," Blaze shot back.

"Good." Don B. steepled his fingers. "Now there's just the little matter of your advance. I was thinking . . ."

Don B. was interrupted when Murder and his crew stormed the conference room. Murder smirked as he knew that they outnumbered Don B. and the dudes he had on deck, but he hadn't accounted for the four guys who came out of a side office, led by Devil, who was Don B.'s bodyguard. Murder and his crew found themselves quickly surrounded and outnumbered.

"Doesn't anybody knock anymore?" Don B. shook his head and got up from the conference table. He crossed the room and stood eye-to-eye with Murder. "I don't recall seeing you in my appointment book for today."

"Fuck an appointment, we got business to discuss about the royalties I ain't been getting on this single y'all put out." Murder was referring to "Real G's," a song that he had put out through Big Dawg that was in heavy rotation all winter.

"Listen, B., I told you before that my accountant will take care of you in a few weeks. Now if you need some paper or something," Don B. pulled a knot of money out of his pocket and started peeling off bills, "I got you." To everyone's surprise, Murder slapped the money from Don B.'s hand.

"Nigga, I don't want no punk-ass sneaker money, I want what's owed to me," Murder barked.

Don B. looked at the money scattered on the floor, then back at Murder, and sighed. "Okay, I can tell you're upset, Murder, but there's no need to get physical. If you look at clause zero-three-one in your contract, then you'll see where Big Dawg stands on this li'l dilemma."

Murder was clearly confused, as he had only skimmed through his contract instead of reading it thoroughly. "What the fuck is clause zero-three-one?"

"Mr. Devil, could you please explain clause zero-three-one to Mr. Murder?" Don B. asked politely.

"No problem at all, Mr. B." Devil stepped forward with a clipboard in his hand and proceeded to slap Murder across the face with it. The clipboard broke and so did Murder's nose. Devil grabbed the taller Murder by the front of his shirt and heaved him through the glass doors leading to the reception area. "That's clause zero-three-one, blood." Devil laughed and spat on Murder.

"I told you not to go in there." The receptionist laughed.

"Anybody else need to go over their contracts?" Don B. addressed Murder's crew.

"Nah, we good," Steve said, backing out of the room. He and Von helped Murder to his feet and out of the office.

Don B. sat back down to the table with a shocked Blaze and folded his hands calmly as if nothing had happened. "Now, where were we?"

Part I

AN INTRODUCTION TO GANGSTERISM

CHAPTER 1

The sky was rich with darkness that night. The meteorologist with the bad hairpiece on the CBS *Morning News* had predicted that the rain would stop by that afternoon, but it was approaching midnight and it was still going. Every few seconds one of the whirling clouds would belch a rumble, followed by bright flashes of menacing lightning. When the flashes of lightning caught them right, they made the thick drops look like diamonds raining over Harlem. If only this were so.

Holiday was slumped in the passenger seat of the gray Dodge Magnum, staring lazily at the smoke wafting from his nose and being sucked out through the partially cracked window. He had a hard face that told the tale of the wars he'd fought in the New York streets and detention centers. Holiday took another deep pull and held the smoke while he took a gulp from the pint of Hennessy that was sitting on his lap. Holding everything in until his eyes were good and bloody from the rush, Holiday finally passed the weed to Baby Doc, who was behind the wheel.

Baby Doc tried his best to look cool when he reached for the bottle and blunt simultaneously, using only his knees to steer, and he almost lost control of the vehicle. Baby Doc quickly regained control of the station wagon and tried to play it off like he was cool, but Holiday had already given him the *face,* that look of disappointment he got from his big homie when he did some silly shit.

Holiday was only three years his senior, but he was *connected,* whereas Baby Doc was still just a wannabe trying to crawl out from under his father's shadow. Big Doc was Holiday's OG and shot caller of their crew. He was a tough old dog who had seen heaven and hell and was still on the block to talk shit about it. Holiday was Big Doc's eyes, ears, and, when necessary, judgment on the streets, and because of this the older heads gave him a wider berth than the rest of the up-and-comers. Baby Doc looked up to Holiday and wanted to walk a mile in his shoes.

A cut Baby Doc liked came through the speakers so he cranked the volume. The bass from the song was so heavy that it rattled the speakers and Holiday's teeth.

"What yo turn that shit up so loud, B.?" Holiday turned the volume down to a respectable level.

"Chill, that's Lord Scientific." Baby Doc readjusted the dial.

"Lord who?"

"Lord Scientific, he's this new cat from outta Jersey. Holiday, this cat is hard, *pause.*"

Holiday listened to the vulgar lyrics about gang banging and murder and found himself bobbing his head. "He's type nice, but I ain't never heard of him."

"That's because you outta the loop, kid. Lord Scientific is all over the Internet and the news," Baby Doc said, filling him in.

"The news, what the fuck is he, one of them new rap celebrities?" Holiday laughed.

"Nah, Lord Scientific is a gangsta rapper, but he's really

off that shit he be kicking. Yo, me and a few of the homies was at this club in Brooklyn a few weeks ago when he came to perform and that shit got super ugly. Some kids tried to snatch his chain in the middle of the performance and that muthafucka went ham! On my moms, Lord Scientific jumped off the stage and outta nowhere bust out with like ten razors. There was so much blood on the floor that I had to throw my Timbs away after that shit."

Holiday shook his head. "Rappers trying to be gangstas and gangstas trying to be rappers, what is this world coming to?"

"Nah, Lord Scientific ain't playing, he's the real deal."

"Baby Doc, you stay on some starstruck shit. What you need to do is turn off that fucking radio ever once and a while and digest some of this game being dropped on you." Holiday shut off the radio. "See, that's the problem with y'all li'l niggaz, you're more focused on shit that goes on outside your world then you are with what's going on in it. The same way you know all these rappers, you need to know the names and faces of every nigga in our organization. This is the trap, li'l nigga, not the MTV awards."

Baby Doc twisted his lips. "Holiday, you need to loosen the fuck up. All you ever talk about is the trap this, and the block that."

"Muthafucka, because that's all I know," Holiday snapped. "I am these muthafucking streets, so I always gotta know what's going on with me. It's this type of thinking that has me sitting on the inside while your ass is still peeking through the window waiting on yo daddy to let you in!"

"Man, fuck you." Baby Doc went back to looking at

the road. He hated when Holiday tried to come at him like a kid, and had a hard time hiding it.

"BD, I know you ain't getting sensitive on me." Holiday pushed him playfully, but Baby Doc was nonresponsive. "Come on, BD, don't act like that. I'm just trying to keep you on your toes, my nigga."

"Holiday, your problem is that you don't know how to talk to people. I know I'm the youngest of the crew, but I'm still a man," Baby Doc declared.

"Is that right?" Holiday looked at him disbelievingly.

"Muthafucking straight. Y'all keep looking at me like Big Doc's kid, but there's gonna come a day when I gotta get my weight up and step outta my father's shadow."

"Baby Doc, there's more to this shit than what you think. It's one thing to get your hands dirty, but when it comes time for you to receive that blemish on your soul . . ." Holiday shook his head. "I don't know many who can carry that load."

"So you think I'm a pussy?" Baby Doc eyeballed Holiday.

"Not at all, BD. I know what your bloodline is so I would never slander your pedigree. All I'm saying to you is that being a part of this family is not something to do, but a way to live."

"Whatever, man, you just don't think I'll pop off. Watch, you're gonna see how I give it up one day."

All Holiday could do was sigh. "Out of love for you and your dad, I pray that day never comes." Holiday relit the blunt, which had gone out. "You've got a lot to learn about these streets, BD. They can be easy lessons or hard ones, that's on you. But as long as you're under me you'll keep your mind on game and off shit that ain't gonna help you, understand?"

Baby Doc nodded, as he had been more preoccupied with a girl crossing the street whose soaked dress was showing her goodies to anyone looking. A slap to the back of the head from Holiday brought him back to attention.

"I said do you understand me?" Holiday barked. Baby Doc nodded. "Good."

When they rolled through the light at the corner of 132nd and Madison, Holiday sat up and peered out the window at a group of young men posted up in front of the corner bodega. "See, it's niggaz like these are a prime example of what I mean about you li'l niggaz focusing on the wrong shit. They're dead foul right now, but floating around like they ain't got a care in the world. Young and dumb."

Baby Doc peered over across Holiday and squinted. "I know them kids, I went to school with the tall one, Buck, but son dropped out last year." Baby Doc pointed to the tall light-skinned kid wearing the green do-rag on his head.

"Well, he should've stayed, because his dumb ass still has a lot to learn." Holiday removed his nines from the stash spot. "Pull over, son."

"Beef?" Baby Doc asked Holiday, ready to get down for his mentor and friend.

Holiday smiled and mushed Baby Doc playfully. "It ain't beef unless both parties are willing to kill." Holiday winked at him and slid from the car. Immediately all eyes fell on the approaching Holiday. Everyone tensed except the kid who had been identified as Buck. Buck folded his arms across his chest and glared at Holiday.

"What you need, son?" Buck asked with an attitude.

"Just a li'l information," Holiday told him.

"Then you need to take your ass to the seventh floor of 100 Centre Street, because ain't no snitches on this corner," Buck capped, drawing laughter from his boys.

Holiday gave him a crooked grin. "You a funny dude, real talk. Listen, I ain't got a lot of time to play with shit birds like you so I'm gonna keep this short and sweet. Whose corner is this?"

"Son, you out here asking a whole lot of questions for a nigga I don't know," Buck said defiantly.

"I'm sorry, where are my manners? My name is Holiday." At the mention of Holiday's name, everyone suddenly got very quiet. Even if you didn't know Holiday by face you knew his reputation. He was the enforcer for Big Doc, one of Shai Clark's capos. "From the look on your face, I'm gonna assume you know who I am."

"Yeah, I heard of you," Buck said sheepishly.

"That's a good thing, so you know how I give it up. Now I'm gonna ask you one more time: whose corner is this?"

Buck hesitated for a few minutes before whispering, "King James."

"Wrong answer." Holiday shot Buck in the thigh. Buck rolled around on the ground whimpering in pain while his crew watched in shock. "Listen to me and listen well," Holiday addressed the horrified young boys. "This shit is property of Shai Clark. If you don't get money for my team then you don't get money for NOBODY. Are we clear?" No one said a word. "I'll take your silence as a yes. Now get this pussy to a hospital because he's bleeding all over my street."

Holiday stomped on Buck's injured thigh for good measure and got back in the whip.

What the fuck was that about, Holiday?" Baby Doc asked when they were safely away from the crime scene.

"That was about me letting niggaz know what time it is out here," Holiday said dismissively.

"I think you did a little more than let him know what time it is. You shot that kid in front of mad witnesses."

"What's your point, BD?"

"My point is, maybe we should've found out more about this King James cat before you popped off. You never know what may come of this."

Holiday gave Baby Doc a disbelieving look. "Li'l nigga, do you hear yourself? This ain't no damn democracy, niggaz violate and they get it and I don't give a fuck who they're connected to if their last name isn't Clark!" Holiday declared.

"Holiday, I was only saying—"

"You wasn't saying shit," Holiday cut him off. "Baby Doc, this ain't like college where shit is decided with student unions, this is the streets and disputes are resolved over pistols. You wanted to be a gangster, right? So stop crying and play ya fucking position."

"Whatever you say, Holiday," Baby Doc told him.

"Muthafucking right. Who the fuck is King James anyway?"

CHAPTER 2

Johnny-O lounged on the velvet sofa with the remote control in one hand and the thigh of a pretty brown thing in the other. The stuffy project apartment was thick with the smoke of purple haze from the Dutch burning between his lips. At the dining-room table bagging up crack were two of the young boys Johnny-O had on his payroll. Once they were finished bagging it up, the crack would be distributed to the night shift when they came on at midnight. The brown fox leaned over and whispered nasty things into Johnny-O's ear, giving him an instant erection.

"Y'all hurry up and finish bagging that shit up. I've got business to attend to," Johnny-O told his workers, never taking his hungry eyes off the girl. He had heard through the grapevine that she was a superfreak and couldn't wait to see if the rumors were true about her not having a gag reflex. There was a knock at the door and Johnny-O cursed, as it was sure to be one more thing delaying him from getting to her sweetness. He gave one of the workers the nod, and with pistol in hand he crept to the door and looked through the peephole.

"It's the nigga Antoine," the worker told Johnny-O.

"Yo, tell that base-head ass nigga to get the fuck away

from this door and cop in front of the building like every-body else," Johnny-O ordered.

The worker nodded eagerly. He had never liked Antoine and looked forward to barking on him. He placed the gun on the table and undid the locks on the door. When the worker snatched the door open, his lips poised to spew venom at Antoine, something smashed into his mouth and cracked two of his teeth. The worker spilled to the ground, holding his bloody mouth and trying to figure out what was going on. By the time Johnny-O even thought to reach for his gun on the coffee table, three masked gunmen had rushed into his apartment.

"G'head and reach for it, sun, so I can open ya fucking melon," the shortest of the gunmen warned, waving a MAC 11 menacingly at Johnny-O.

The girl on the couch began screaming hysterically as the gunmen inched toward her. The lanky robber tried to shush her, but she just kept screaming, so he tried a differ-ent approach and slapped her viciously across the mouth. The girl flipped over the armrest and landed on the floor. The lanky gunman pressed the .38 to her forehead and placed one finger over his lips for silence. Immediately the girl's hysterical screaming was reduced to heavy sobbing. The gunman took her by the arm and tossed her on the couch next to Johnny-O, who was sweating like a runaway slave.

"You niggaz got big balls coming in there like this," Johnny-O said, trying to sound tough. His heart was beat-ing a million miles per minute as he sat there wondering if he was going to die.

"If you open that pretty mouth of yours again I'm gonna

show you a pair of balls that you won't soon forget," the leader of the gunmen said. He was a muscular man holding a dusty-looking .45. "Y'all get the money and the work. If any one of these dizzy muthafuckas move, put the love on 'em." His henchmen hurriedly did as they were told. "Looks like you're doing good for yourself these days, Johnny"— the gunman ran his hand down the terrified girl's thigh— "*real* good."

"Get your fucking hands off her." Johnny-O slapped the gunman's hand away and sprang to his feet. Feeling the .45 under his chin cut his moment of courage short and he eased back down to the couch.

"Tender-hearted ass nigga, you ready to die for this bitch?" the leader asked mockingly.

"Y'all gonna be the ones who die when word that you robbed Born's spot gets out. We're connected to some major players and you just fucked yourself," Johnny-O threatened.

The leader reached into the pocket of his hoodie and pulled out a thick link chain that was stained with blood. Johnny's eyes widened as he stared at the medallion, which was slightly smaller than a saucer. It was the number 7 tucked in a crescent moon, laid over black onyx. Johnny knew the chain well because for the last three years Born had always worn it.

"No," Johnny-O whispered.

"Oh yes." The leader of the invaders removed his mask. For some reason, Johnny-O wasn't surprised when he saw who it was that had come to pay him a visit. The gunman smiled, showing his perfect white teeth, and placed the .45 to Johnny-O's cheek. "It's like I told y'all faggots when I came home: there's only enough room in Harlem for one

king." He squeezed the trigger and put the lower portion of
Johnny-O's jaw on the coffee table.

Yo God, you got blood on my fucking Timbs," Lakim told
King James when they got back to the stash house, which
was an abandoned apartment in West Harlem. After the
murder/robbery they had made a beeline back to the hood
to divvy up the spoils.

"Here, buy yourself five more pairs." King James threw
a handful of money at Lakim and laughed. "You okay,
Fangs?" King addressed the third man who was in the apartment with them. He was sitting by the window, chain-
smoking cigarettes with a worried expression on his face.

"Yeah, I'm good, man. I just thought we were gonna go
in there and rob Johnny-O, not kill him," Fangs said nervously.

King James walked over and placed a reassuring arm
around Fangs. "Sometimes you gotta break a few eggs to
make an omelet, my nigga. No need to worry, because the
blood is on my hands and not yours. But on another note,
you did good with shooting us that info about Johnny-O's
stash house."

This made Fangs smile a bit. "It wasn't about nothing,
I was glad to be able to help out."

"But something has me curious: you been down with
that cat for like a year—didn't you feel no way about giving him up like that?"

Fangs spat out the window. "Fuck him. All this time
I've been working for that nigga and he still ain't trying to
put me in position to see no real bread, so I figured, why
not take it?"

James laughed. "I guess you can't argue with that kinda logic."

"But yo, y'all gonna put me down with the team now, right?" Fangs asked eagerly. He knew after what he had done he would need some type of team behind him to keep him eating.

"True indeed. In fact, I've got something for you to show how much we appreciate you." King James raised the .45 and blew Fangs's face off.

"What the fuck you do that for?" Lakim hopped up off the chair in shock.

"He who recognizes a snake and still invites it into his home is a fool, and I ain't never been no dummy, La. If he turned on Johnny-O, how long do you think it would've been before he turned on us? Fuck him." King James spat on the corpse. "Go get that lighter fluid from under the kitchen sink so we can get rid of this pussy and this crib."

After setting the apartment on fire, King and Lakim hurried back to the car and away from the burning building. Lakim watched in the rearview mirror as the flames came spewing out of the apartment. "Damn, looks like the whole building is gonna go. Do you think we might have overdone it?"

"There's no such thing as overdoing it when you're trying to make a point," King said.

"My dude, it's been a long time since we had a nigga like you on the streets of New York."

"Correction: there ain't never been a nigga on the streets like me and there never will be," King James said confidently as they drove off into the night.

CHAPTER 3

Old San Juan, Puerto Rico

Old San Juan was the oldest settlement in Puerto Rico located in its colonial section. During the day tourists moved throughout the streets of San Juan, taking in the sites and history of the place, but when the sun set, creatures of a more sinister nature roamed its streets, and anything was likely to pop off if you weren't careful.

"Why don't you slow down before you kill us?" Javier snapped at Victor as the beat-up, green military-style jeep bounced over the broken streets.

"Kick back, bro. I know these streets like the back of my hand. Besides, in a little while Poppito's boys are gonna be all over this place and I don't wanna be caught out here alone if we bump into Los Negros Muertes looking for their money."

"You mean our money," Javier corrected him, patting the duffel bag resting between his legs. "Besides, we're the police, remember?" Javier held up the badge hanging around his neck.

Javier and Victor had been on the force for three years, but for the last few months they had been on special assignment working for Captain Herman Cruz, a dirty cop and one of Poppito's top competitors for control over Old

San Juan and its drug trade. Cruz and Poppito had been friends as children but as adults they had become rivals. For the last six months the two had been locked in a bloody battle, with Cruz gaining ground over his enemy.

"Fuck Poppito and fuck Negros Muertes." Javier dismissed Victor's fears.

Legend had it that Los Negros Muertes, *The Black Death,* were a mysterious sect of killers that were whispered about throughout the Caribbean and parts of South America. Some said they were rogue black ops or some other government agency, while the more spiritual aligned them with the devil, with the human soul as the price for their services. No one had ever lived to verify any of the accounts.

"Victor, watch out!" Javier shouted as he spotted something lying in the middle of the road.

Victor yanked the wheel to avoid whatever it was in their path and sent the jeep into a tailspin that ended with the back end crashing into an abandoned car and his head slamming violently into the driver's side window. "What the fuck?" Victor dabbed at the gash that had opened up in his forehead.

"There's something in the road." Javier shook off his dizziness and tried to focus on the object. The small lump seemed to be moving and he could hear soft whimpering. "Shit, it looks like a dog or something."

"You almost made me kill us over a dog? Fuck that dog, I'm outta here." Victor put the jeep in gear.

Javier had a good mind to let Victor pull off, but since he was a kid he'd always had a soft spot for animals. "It's still alive; we can't just leave it there to get run over. I'm gonna at least move it out of the road." Javier got out of the jeep with his machine gun slung over his shoulder.

"Javier, fuck that dog. Let's get out of here, man," Victor called after him, but Javier ignored him and kept walking toward the wounded dog. "This guy . . ." Victor mumbled under his breath and got out to join his partner.

The dog curled up in the middle of the street was a brindled pit bull with a jet-black muzzle. It looked to be healthy, so they doubted it was a stray, but it had clearly been in some fights. There were old wounds covering the dog's front and hindquarter, and an especially nasty-looking scar that went across its back. When the pit bull spotted the two men approaching, it growled.

"We ain't gonna hurt you." Javier eased forward with his hand extended. Victor chose to keep his distance and watch from the sidelines. "Just be easy." He got in closer. The dog placed its chin on the ground and allowed Javier to stroke its head. "That's a good girl," he cooed. His cooing quickly turned into screams when the pit bull locked its powerful jaws around his arm.

"Oh shit." Victor reached for the pistol at his waist, but the press of cold steel against his cheek froze him.

"You weren't thinking about shooting my dog, were you?" a voice breathed in his ear. A hand snaked around Victor's waist and removed the gun. "That's better."

The dog was shaking Javier's wrist violently, but he was able to bring his machine gun around and crack it across the bridge of her nose and free himself from her grip. He staggered backward and went to bring his machine gun around when out of nowhere his body was covered in infrared lights. "Your next move is your last move," a voice called from the shadows. It seemed to be coming from everywhere and nowhere at the same time. Slowly, several men and a woman dressed in all black and holding guns began to step from the shadows.

"Los Negros Muertes." Javier crossed himself. Tossing his gun away, he dropped to his knees and raised his hands in the air.

Victor was shoved roughly to the ground where Javier was already kneeling and instructed to do the same. For the first time he had gotten a good look at the man who had gotten the drop on him. He was tall and built, with a shaved head and brilliant smile. Victor studied him quizzically because he had never seen a man so dark with eyes so green.

"It's okay, everybody be cool. Just take the money and we're straight." Javier grimaced in pain from the dog bite on his wrist, which wouldn't stop bleeding.

"Nice of you to offer something we already *know* we can have." Javier recognized this as the voice he'd heard in the shadows. He was a few inches shorter than the green-eyed man, but stockier. His thick black hair was braided into two ponytails that hung down his back. "We gonna take yo money, fo sho, but we came here for yo life." He raised his gun and shot Javier in the face. When he turned around to pop Victor, the green-eyed man stopped him.

"Chill, leave this one for baby bro. It's about time the li'l nigga busts his cherry."

The cat rocking the braids hesitated. "Chill, K, you already know how son get down. Let me finish this spic off so we can be out."

"It's cool," a soft voice called from the shadows of a doorway. "I can speak for myself." The darkness peeled back and out stepped a youthful-looking man dressed in black fatigue pants and a black thermal shirt. His long, thick hair was pulled back and stuffed under a black hair net. Hanging from his back pocket was a red bandanna, which fluttered in the warm breeze. When he cracked his perfectly bowed lips to take a pull of the cigarette he was smoking, the streetlights kissed his diamond and gold teeth.

"I hear you talking, li'l brother." The green-eyed man tried handing him his gun, but the young boy declined, opting for the two-foot knife that he pulled from the leg of his pants.

"Don't hear me, my nigga, watch me," the youngster said and knelt in front of Victor, who was trembling. The youngster moved close, causing Victor to flinch. "Close your eyes, and be still." He placed his hand on Victor's trembling shoulder reassuringly. "I'll make sure you go quickly." In a sharp movement he pushed the knife through Victor's rib cage and pierced his heart. As promised, Victor never felt a thing.

The green-eyed man clapped his hands and smiled proudly. "Well done, superstar!" he said sarcastically.

"Keep your praises, homie, because I don't want 'em or need 'em. This li'l thing we got going on here is a tempo-rary arrangement and as soon as the opportunity presents itself I'm outta here, so don't twisted like we the best of friends. I ain't my brother." The youngster spat and walked off.

The dude with the two braids placed his hand on the green-eyed man's shoulder. "Don't stress, my nigga."

The green-eyed man raised his eyebrow. "Stress? I'm not stressed, just a little confused. Seeing how I interrupted his trip to the gas chamber, at the very least you'd think he'd show some gratitude."

"I'll talk to him, K."

"You might want to. You're one of my oldest comrades, so you should know better than anyone else how much loyalty means to me," the green-eyed man said and began walking down the alley. "Get at ya li'l brother, Justice. The war is on and it's only two sides, ours or theirs. Anything that ain't a Dawg is in the way," he reminded him before disappearing.

Detective Brown sat behind the wheel of his brown Buick, sipping a cup of coffee. The cigarette in the ashtray had almost burned itself all the way to the butt, but he hardly noticed as his attention was on the papers spread across his lap. There was a series of reports about suspected drug-related executions from every city along the New Jersey Turnpike, but he targeted the especially brutal ones. His brain swirled, trying to find the connection, if any, between the killings.

"Boo!" someone screamed from the passenger-side window, scaring Detective Brown and causing him to spill his coffee on the reports. Leaning in the window, laughing, was his partner, Detective Alvarez.

"You're a fucking dick, you know that?" Detective Brown snapped, looking over his ruined reports.

"My fault, I didn't know you were working on a case." Alvarez slid into the car and began helping Brown salvage what he could from the pile. He looked at one of the reports and saw that it was from an old case they had worked together. It had to do with a teacher who had molested the daughter of a man connected to the underworld. When they found the teacher, his eyes had been removed from his head and delivered to his parents wrapped in a kiddie-porn magazine. It was one of the murders they had been trying to pin on Animal back when they had been building a case against him and his crew. "Dude, this case has been cold for years."

"I know," Detective Brown said, dabbing the papers with a wad of napkins.

Alvarez sighed. "Brown, when are you gonna stop chasing ghosts?"

"When somebody rips that diamond grille out of his mouth and drops it on my desk!" Brown barked.

"Calm the fuck down, I ain't your enemy, bro," Alvarez shot back.

"I'm sorry, J, but I'm still fucked up about all this. We had him, and somebody helps the bastard escape!"

The newspapers called him the Rock Star Serial Killer, but Brown called him trash, and the day he watched a judge convict Animal of his crimes had been one of the happiest of his life, next to the birth of his children. Knowing that Animal was going to die with a needle in his arm made all the shit Brown had to endure over the years worth it, but then the unthinkable happened. As it turned out, there was someone who had a bigger hard-on for Animal than the detectives. The abduction ended with Detective Brown spending three weeks in the hospital and Animal vanishing from the face of the planet. He was on the most-wanted list with several law enforcement agencies, but it had been two years and he was still missing.

"Brown, they got the drop on us and there was nothing we could do about it. Look at it like this: Animal had a lot of enemies and for all we know that could've been somebody he pissed off that came for his ass. Let's just be thankful that we're still alive to argue about it. Let it go."

"You're right, J, I am too wound up about it, but the way it played out between us and them has just never sat right with me. I'd love to know that little shit bird was maggot food by now, but my gut doesn't say so." He picked up a newspaper clipping that had been among the reports and placed it on the car's heater to dry. It was an article about the execution of two police officers in Puerto Rico.

CHAPTER 4

After what seemed like a wave of never-ending rain, the sun had finally decided to show its face. It was only eight A.M. and the weather was already a balmy eighty degrees in New York City. The dry voice broadcasting over the radio on 1010 WINS warned that there would be a heat advisory for that day and people should stay in doors for safety reasons. This might've applied to the squares but it meant nothing to those forced to get it how they lived.

Happy's two-hundred-plus-pound frame sat wedged behind the wheel of his Dodge Magnum; he was sipping McDonald's Sweet Tea from a large Styrofoam cup and eating a jumbo bag of pork skins. Even with the air conditioner on full blast he still found himself sweating. The doctor had diagnosed him with high blood pressure due to his recent weight gain and advised him to start taking better care of himself, but it was a task. Happy had a thing for fried foods, fresh pussy, and money. It was the latter that had him out and about so early in the morning.

For the fifth time in as many minutes Happy looked down at his diamond-encrusted watch, then to the window of the check-cashing spot he was parked across the street from. "What the fuck is taking this bitch so long?" he asked no one in particular.

"I hope she ain't do no stupid shit, you know the bitch is slow," said Levi, who had been sitting in the passenger seat. He'd been so quiet the whole time that Happy had almost forgotten he was in the car. Levi was good at making people forget he was in the room. He took a deep pull from his Newport, killing it and tossing the butt out the window. "It'd be just our luck if she doesn't pop and we miss out on this cheese."

"Man, why you always gotta think negatively?" Happy snapped at Levi. Levi was a true pessimist and rarely had anything good to say.

"Why you getting mad at me?" Levi asked, adjusting his custom Prada glasses. They were black with chrome frames and that bulged out a little because of the one-carat diamonds on the ends. It was rumored that the odd-looking glasses were fitted with small spy-cams that Levi would use to secretly tape women, but he would neither confirm nor deny this rumor. "Just kick back, son. It ain't been that long."

"Dumb bitch." Happy huffed and took another swing of his tea.

"Speaking of dumb bitches"—Levi lit another cigarette—"did I tell you what happened the other night with that one bitch from the strip club?"

"Which one?" Happy raised an interested eyebrow.

"You know the one, the big-butt dark-skinned chick I was drinking with the other night."

"Oh, you mean your new wife?" Happy joked.

"Fuck outta here," Levi said defensively.

"Man, you was up on her so close that at one point I thought you were gonna start tonguing her down."

"C'mon, son, you know better than that. And don't start

acting like you ain't cuff master. It's been a few times when I wanted to go in on something you had and you wouldn't give me the green light," Levi accused.

"Man, them must've been my personals because you know ain't a whore in the world that I wouldn't share with my brother." Happy smiled.

"Whatever, nigga." Levi exhaled the cigarette smoke. "Like I was saying, after the spot closed, me and shorty slid back to the telly and shit. We negotiated everything in the club so it wasn't no misunderstanding. A'ight, so I roll an L and me and shorty have a few drinks, before she stripped down and got real nasty. Shorty is popping herself, giving that porno head and the whole nine."

"Word? Did she spit on ya dick, too?" Happy asked excitedly.

"The spit and everything else. So just when I'm hard as a rock and ready to fuck, this bitch looks at the time and stops."

"Oh hell nah!"

"Word to everything, my nigga. Put the breaks on my whole wave. Now I'm confused because I know she said a buck-fifty at the club and I paid her before we left, so off the back I know some funny shit was going on. You know what this bitch had the nerve to tell me?" Levi gave a dramatic pause. "That she meant it was a buck-fifty per hour."

"Oh hell nah." Happy laughed, slapping his meaty palm against the dashboard. Tears were forming in the corners of his eyes and he was wheezing so badly that he had to take two hits off his asthma pump. "Man, that's some bogus shit. So you just let the bitch beat you outta your scratch?"

Levi looked at Happy as if he should know better.

"Never that. I told the bitch to hang loose while I ran downstairs to use the ATM. Not only did I leave that bitch stranded in the Bronx, but I stole her pocketbook on my way out."

Happy shook his head. "Youz a stone cold dude."

"Nah, the illest part about it is that I taped the bitch giving me head. As soon as I got back to the crib I uploaded her shit to my Web site. I got over fifty thousand hits off that dick-sucking whore." Levi grinned wickedly. "It'll be a cold day in hell before a bitch can put one over on Levi Brown!"

"Church." Happy gave Levi dap. The smile on Happy's face melted away when he spotted the blue-and-white patrol car in his rearview mirror. They rode by slowly, looking into the car, and kept going. Happy breathed a sigh of relief until the patrol car got to the light and made a U-turn, pulling to a stop right in front of the check-cashing spot and going inside. By the time they came out with the girl Happy had sent in, he was ten blocks away.

Damn," Happy cursed as his truck crept through traffic.

"You think they made us?" Levi asked nervously.

"I doubt it; we could've been any two niggaz on that block. I'm just worried about shorty running her mouth."

"How long have you known her?" Levi asked.

"'Bout fifteen years or so. She's my baby mama's oldest daughter."

Levi looked at him in shock. "Hap, you sent your stepdaughter in there to pull a lick?"

"She ain't no kin to me by blood. Besides, I don't recall putting no gun to her head; she came to me wanting to get down. Before me she was selling pussy to them broke-ass niggaz uptown, so if you look at it I was doing her a favor," Happy reasoned.

Levi shook his head sadly and went back to looking for police on their tail. A chick that was crossing in front of the truck caught his attention. She had a mean shape and moved like a stallion, turning the heads of damn near everyone she passed. Her swag was on a thousand, and from all the designer bags she was carrying, Levi knew she was holding. "Hap, pull up on this bitch so I can holla."

CHAPTER 5

Francine, known to her friends as Frankie, pushed open the exit doors of Macy's and stepped out into the warm morning air. She was dressed in a loose-fitting business suit and lightweight Burberry raincoat that matched her heels and sunglasses. She had shopping bags in both hands, which made her stumble a bit, but she still made good time getting as far away from Macy's as she could. She was thinking about hopping a cab, but with the way traffic was she would probably make better time on the subway. After burning down the stores on Thirty-fourth Street all morning, she was anxious to get out of Dodge.

Frankie was a jack-of-all-trades, but her most lucrative source of income was boosting. It was a skill she had acquired at a young age from her now-estranged father. The old con would take Frankie to all the high-end fashion stores and let her explore all the aisles while he plied his trade. Frankie loved the outings and developed an early love for fashion thanks to her father, but not until she was older would she come to realize his motives for taking her. Security in the stores was less likely to watch a dad out shopping with his kid, so Frankie made the perfect front while he relieved them of their goods.

The art of theft was the only thing Frankie's father had

ever given her, and she cherished and perfected her gift. Frankie could make it in and out of a clothing store in less than ninety seconds with hundreds of dollars' worth of merchandise without anyone even realizing she had been there. She was a master thief and it made her very popular in her hood. If you wanted the latest in designer wear, you went to Frankie to fill your order; there was nothing she couldn't steal. She had even pulled off a few armed robberies when the price was right, but there was less risk and less time in boosting so she mainly kept it to that.

A police car bent the corner, causing Frankie to freeze. A lump formed in her throat when the officer on the passenger side looked up at her and studied her for a moment. A part of her wanted to bolt, but she played it cool and just smiled. The officer smiled, then tapped his partner and said something. From the way both of the men smiled, she could only imagine what kind of chauvinistic statement had passed between them. The driver's attention was drawn to the squawking police radio and after listening for a few seconds they threw on their lights and sped off.

"Jesus," Frankie said, sighing when she finally released the breath she was holding. Clutching her bag a little tighter, she made hurried steps toward the train station. Just as Frankie neared her destination she spotted an SUV slowing down to keep in step with her.

"Hey, baby, you need some help carrying those bags?" one of the vehicle's occupants called to her. Frankie kept walking as if she didn't hear him. "Come on, sweetie, don't act like that. I don't bite unless you want me to." Seeing that Frankie still wasn't receptive to his advances, he switched his tone. "Well fuck you then, bitch!"

Not able to stomach the disrespect, Frankie spun on

him angrily. "Ya mama's a bitch, muthafucka!" she spat. She was looking for a bottle or something to throw at the SUV when she realized that she knew the vehicle and the young man hanging out the window disrespecting her. "Levi?"

Levi's squinted from behind his glasses. "Frankie, is that you? Oh shit. Hap, that's Frankie."

Happy leaned across Levi and looked out the window. "Damn, that is Frankie. What's up, li'l mama?"

"Ain't nothing. Where y'all headed?" Frankie approached the vehicle.

"Shit, we about to roll uptown. Where are you coming from?" Levi asked, looking at all the bags. "As a matter of fact, I already know. What you got, ma?"

"If y'all give me a ride uptown I'll let y'all get first dibs," she offered.

"Shit, hop in." Happy popped the locks. Frankie tossed her bags in the backseat and climbed in beside them. "Man, I didn't even recognize you with that weave in ya head," Happy said, admiring Frankie through the rearview mirror.

"Negro, please, you know I don't do no weaves." Frankie pulled the wig off and exposed her shoulder-length black hair beneath, which was neatly cornrowed going to the back. With the wig gone you could see Frankie's face clearly. Cunning brown eyes blended almost perfectly with her cinnamon-brown skin. "I gotta keep 'em guessing so I try to change up my look when I go to certain spots. I just came up on some nice Nautica cardigan sweaters that'll be real wavy with some Nike boots in the winter," Frankie told them, while rummaging around in the bag. She came up with one of the items in question and held it out for them to inspect. "Hap, I don't know if I got your size but

I'm picking up some Air Max tomorrow and I'll hold a pair for you if you want."

"That'll work, baby girl," Happy told her.

Levi reached out to touch the sweater, but Frankie snatched it back. "Nigga, you better move away from my merchandise with that cigarette!"

"Stop acting like that, Frankie."

"I ain't acting like nothing, but this is how I eat and a burnt piece ain't no good to me. Now if you're buying it then you can flick as many ashes on it as you like," she said seriously.

"You know Levi ain't buying shit unless it's pussy," Happy mocked.

"Then I ain't got nothing for him," Frankie said.

"Hap, you gonna cut ya shit, my dude, because I ain't the only one with skeletons," Levi warned. "Man, fuck all that. Frankie, I'll take the sweater. How much?"

"For you . . . give me fifty cash and it's a done deal."

"Fifty?" Levi's voice went up an octave. "How you gonna charge me fifty dollars and we live in the same hood?"

"That's the reason I'm charging you fifty, instead of what I'm hitting everybody else. When I shoot to the Bronx with these later on, I'm not accepting anything less than seventy-five," Frankie told him.

"Y'all muthafuckas be killing me," Levi mumbled while digging around in his pocket. He peeled off fifty dollars and handed them to Frankie.

"You know you love me, Levi." She kissed him on the cheek and tucked the money into her bra.

"I guess Levi gets all the love, huh?" Happy said sarcastically.

"I got love for all my niggaz, Hap. Don't act like that." Frankie draped her arms around him, bringing a smile to his lips. "As a matter of fact, I was gonna go to the face on this but I'm about to share my weed with y'all. Let's stop at one of these stores and get a couple of Dutches so we can burn on the way to the block."

"What you working with, Frankie?" Levi asked.

"Some shit I copped in Jerz called White Rhino."

"They ain't got no good weed in Jersey," Happy added his two cents.

"I used to feel the same way, until I discovered where I had to get some bomb shit. I'm telling you, my nigga, this shit is that fire."

"We'll see," Levi said mockingly. They pulled up at a small newsstand and Levi got out to get two Dutch Masters and two Snickers bars. He placed them on the tiny wooden counter and asked, "How much?"

"For you, seven fifty, my friend," the young Middle Eastern man behind the counter said with a smile.

"Seven fifty?" Levi reeled back, disgusted. "Fam, how much is your candy?"

"One fifty each."

Levi looked at his purchases and did the math in his head. "So you mean to tell me y'all want two twenty-five for a Dutch? Homeboy, what kinda shit is that? My man, a Dutch is a dollar twenty-five uptown."

"Then you should go uptown and buy. Down here the Dutch Masters are two twenty-five."

"This is a fucking rip-off," Levi mumbled and tossed a wad of crumpled bills at the man.

"Have a nice day!"

"Fuck you," Levi cursed over his shoulder and climbed back into the truck, slamming the door.

"Why you gotta do my door like that, man? Niggaz ain't used to nothing," Happy said and pulled off from the curb.

"Yo, play this CD for me." Frankie handed a blank disk to Happy.

"What the fuck is this?" Happy asked.

Frankie shrugged. "I don't know, some kid was selling these in downtown Newark when I was out there boosting yesterday. He looked like he was really on his grind so I decided to support him."

Happy shook his head. "A thief with a heart. I wonder what they'll come up with next."

"Shut up and play the CD." Frankie tossed a balled-up napkin at him.

"You keep tossing shit in my ride and you're gonna pay to get it cleaned," Happy threatened and put the CD in. Surprisingly, the music was pretty good. "This is kinda tight. What did you say this kid's name was?"

"Lord something-or-other," Frankie tried to recall.

"Hold up, was it Lord Scientific?" Levi asked.

"Yeah, that was it. He had a street team out there that was twenty deep and they were flooding both sides of the strip with the CDs and posters. You've heard of him?"

"Yeah, I seen the kid on 106th and Park one day doing the freestyle battle thing. He ate this kid from the Bronx so bad that I felt like crying for him. But Lord Scientific got disqualified because he cursed."

"That's some shady shit," Happy said.

"Yeah it was. I dunno, they say the kid is a hot item

these days, with all the top labels checking him out. I heard even Don B. wanted to sign him to Big Dawg."

"Dear God, I hope he doesn't," Frankie said.

Happy looked at her. "And why the hell not? Them boys over there getting heavy paper."

"You mean *Don B.* is getting heavy paper," Levi corrected him. "C'mon, Hap, I know you're illiterate and all, but at least once per year Big Dawg's name comes up in newspapers and magazines in connection with tragedy. Nobody that has signed to that label his lived long enough to enjoy their success. That whole place is jinxed."

"Don B. is the damn devil and one day he's gonna get what he deserves." Frankie sealed the ends of the blunt she was rolling. "Now enough talk about Satan and his little helpers, let's get fried!"

As she had promised them, the White Rhino was the truth and it quickly turned the inside of the whip into a beautiful bubble of chronic. Frankie was finally able to breathe easy in the comfort of truck and out of Midtown with her haul for the day. Half the stuff she had was sold already, and the other half she knew she'd get off over the next few days. The lick came right on time because she and her roommates were already two weeks back on their rent. She could relax now, knowing that she had her end of it. Frankie leaned back and made herself comfortable, losing herself in Lord Scientific's rant coming through the speakers and the nothingness of her buzz.

CHAPTER 6

By midafternoon the projects were jumping. Grills were set up, card and dice games were going on, and there seemed to be kids everywhere. Everyone was taking advantage of the warm weather. Sahara sat on the bench, fumbling with her BlackBerry and killing time while she waited for her on-again off-again boo, King. He and his partner, Lakim, were both topless and sweating like slaves working overtime as they battled to see who could do the most push-ups. To the victor went an ounce of Kush, courtesy of the loser, so neither of them wanted to lose. Even though both men had been home for a while they still carried themselves like they were on the inside.

Sahara had become a regular fixture in King James's hood. She had an apartment in the Douglass projects that she shared with her roommates, but she been spending quite a bit of time in the Grant projects since she'd started messing with King. The Grant projects were his *court,* as he liked to call it. King James had come home from prison on some real brolic shit and put the smash down on the hood he'd grown up in. King hadn't hit the big time yet, but he was fast on his way and everybody knew it. You either feared King James or you loved him, but either way you respected him.

Sahara's social standing had also gone up a notch or two since she'd started getting noticed around town with the young goon. Chicks hated on her and dudes wanted her. Cats knew that King indulged only in the best, so for him to be with her meant that she was special. King helped boost her value, but it wasn't like Sahara had ever been a slouch. She stood nearly six feet, with a stripper's body, jet-black hair, and skin almost as dark. She was born in Africa but had spent enough time in the United States to catch on to the law of the land, which was *trap or die*. Sahara was about her business, so when King James had opened himself up for her to dig her claws into him, she made sure she dug deep.

With all the shit talking King and Lakim did between sets, it seemed like it was taking forever to determine a winner, and Sahara was getting impatient. "Damn, how much longer y'all gonna be at it?" Sahara asked with an attitude.

"Until I drop or his bony-ass arms break," King capped, flexing the muscles in his chest. Across his chest were tatted the words *Peace God* in a fancy scroll. A heavy gold medallion hung from this thick neck, bearing the crescent moon and a diamond-filled number 7. It was not only a magnificent piece, but a reminder to all who knew its history as to how much of a beast the young man was.

Lakim sucked his gold teeth. "Sun, you bugging. I used to get money in the yard." Lakim flexed his biceps. He was wider than King, but had a potbelly and stood almost a foot shorter. Lakim had a Napoleon complex and stayed caught up in drama, but he would lay down his life for King James.

"Well, I'm about to show you whose yard this is," King

told him before dropping down to do another set of fifty push-ups.

"Yo, speaking of the yard, shit is getting crazy on the other side of town," Lakim said as he planted his hands to do his own set of push-ups. "The li'l nigga we gave that work to got shot."

King James immediately stopped his push-ups and stood to his full height. "Somebody killed one of our people?"

"Nah, sun ain't dead, but he's gonna probably walk with a limp for the rest of his life," Lakim explained.

"What about the nigga who shot him?"

"I heard it was one of Shai Clark's people. Sun came through on some state-property shit and told them li'l dudes that if they wasn't getting money for Shai, they couldn't eat in Harlem."

King James frowned at the news. He knew the Clarks by reputation, but had only actually met Tommy. The two had spoken briefly when King James had first arrived on Rikers Island and Tommy was coming through on a gun charge. Though Tommy Gunz was wild as hell, he was no bully. "Sun, I can't believe that the Clark family is out here on some guerilla shit. I was just a shorty when Poppa was boss and Tommy was running the streets. They definitely had this whole shit in the stranglehold, but they never tried to stop a nigga from getting money as long as they were going about it correctly."

Lakim laughed. "Dawg, I know you've been gone for a while, but Poppa dead and Tommy Gunz ain't even on the radar no more. Shai is running shit, and he ain't built like his bloodline. That nigga ain't concerned with the streets; his mind is on that fucking casino."

"Well then, maybe we need to holla at him and see about getting his mind right," King said seriously.

Lakim smiled. "I had a feeling you would say that so I put one of my li'l homegirls on the job. Word has it that him and some of his peoples are supposed to be in Newark tonight for the grand opening of this spot called Brick City. Shai and the owner are cool, so the king of Harlem is supposed to be coming out to show his support."

King laughed. "My nigga, I keep telling y'all there's only room for one king in Harlem. Holla at the homies and tell them to be ready. I wanna have a talk with this Shai nigga and see where his head is at."

By then Sahara was too through with King, Lakim, and their bullshit and was about ready to leave them to it, but she remembered that King was supposed to lay some bread on her. As usual, King had made her wait for the money, thinking that she was just going to run through it on foolishness like she normally did, and he was half correct. A good chunk of the money was going on a pair of boots that she had seen in this store on Fifth Avenue, but she also had moves to make before the party the following night.

King had been home for more than two years and hadn't had a birthday party since the year before he started his bid, and back then he was still a teenager. His sister and a few of his comrades had decided to throw him a surprise party for his birthday, and Sahara immediately found a way to earn some points with the family by volunteering to coordinate it. Granted, the task took more work than Sahara had anticipated, but it allowed her a chance to get in good with the few people King held dear. Sahara wouldn't have gone as far as to say that she was in love with King James, but there was a deep connection between them. He was a man with stars in his eyes and no fear in his heart, so it only made sense to bet on him.

Sahara dug into her purse for a cigarette and realized that she was out. "I'll be right back, I'm going to the store," she called to King and got off the bench, headed for the store. Sahara scurried across the big street to the other side of Broadway. Instead of going into the store and paying almost twelve dollars for a pack of cigarettes, she went two doors down and paid the old Spanish man eight. As she turned around to go back across the street, she spotted a familiar face coming her way on a bike.

"What it do, ma?" Ashanti asked, bringing the bike to a stop in Sahara's path. He had grown a bit, but he was still the same kid with the high-pitched voice and criminal nature. Ashanti was off the chain, but he was a cool dude.

"Chilling. What's good with you?" Sahara gave him a light hug. "Where you been hiding at? I haven't seen you around here like that in a minute."

"I ain't never hiding, I've just been busy. You know how that goes."

"Fo sho. So what brings you to these parts?"

Ashanti shrugged and raised his shirt so that she could see the nine tucked into his sweatpants. "Trying to see what's for dinner, ya heard?"

"Ashanti, you're still wild as hell. What's up with the rest of ya peeps?"

"Niggaz is out and about doing them. Ima go check Brasco later on, you should come through and kick it." He smiled at her devilishly.

"Stop it five." She put her palm in his face playfully. "I know how y'all niggaz do and I ain't about to have King kill *all* of us."

"Damn, you still fucking wit the god?"

"Off and on, you know how that goes. Ain't too many real niggaz left, so when you get one you hold on to him."

"You ain't never lied," Ashanti agreed.

"Speaking of real niggaz, any word?" she asked. When she saw his face darken she regretted the question, as everyone knew that the disappearance of Animal was a sensitive subject for him.

Ashanti looked at the ground for a few seconds before answering. "Nah, still not a peep. But anyway, let me get up outta here. Tell my nigga King I said *what's good.*" He peddled off on his bike.

Sahara made her way back across the street and spotted a girl named Yvonne that she'd been exchanging dirty looks with over the last month or so, and some of her friends. King had been fucking Yvonne but when he started checking for Sahara he backed up off Yvonne. Instead of her taking up her issue with King, she chose to direct her shade at Sahara. The girls watched Sahara and Sahara watched them as they passed one another. Yvonne rolled her eyes and Sahara laughed, which caused Yvonne to stop.

"Somebody tell a joke that I missed?" Yvonne asked Sahara.

"Nah, it's an inside joke. You probably still wouldn't get it if I told you." Sahara snickered.

"Shorty, you talking real slick to be so far from home," Yvonne told her.

"Baby, I'm comfortable wherever I stomp," Sahara said defiantly.

"Wow, I know you ain't gonna let her talk to you like that," one of Yvonne's friends instigated.

Yvonne took the bait and stepped up. "Yo, word to mine, I'm tired of you li'l bitches from downtown coming up here talking fly and trying to fuck other bitches' men." Yvonne put her hands on Sahara's face. As soon as her finger made contact with Sahara's forehead, Sahara swung on her.

Sahara had a very lean build, but the hate she already had for Yvonne added to her strength and the punch landed with an impact of someone twice her size. Yvonne staggered back and Sahara closed in. One of Yvonne's friends tried to trip Sahara, but she peeped the move and stepped over her outstretched foot, just before she popped her in the mouth. By then all Yvonne's friends had joined in the brawl, and Sahara did the best she could to hold them off.

"Fuck is going on over here?" King stepped into the center of the melee, trying to separate the girls. He was finally able to pull Sahara free and get between her and Yvonne's crew. "Yo, what the fuck is good with y'all?"

"King, you better tell your li'l whore something, because the next time she tries to run up on me, I'm gonna kill her!" Yvonne shouted. She tried to dip around King to get to Sahara, but he grabbed her around the waist and held her.

"That's enough . . . and that shit goes for the both of you!" King barked, and the hostility in his voice seemed to calm both the girls down. It looked like King was finally getting a handle on the situation, but things went from bad to worse.

"Fuck is you doing?" Lamar called from the lobby entrance of 3150. He was short with a bald head and muscles that looked like they would rip through his skin at any moment. Lamar was Yvonne's oldest brother, the one you never got to see in the wintertime because he was always in jail.

"Lamar, chill. It ain't what it looks like, my nigga," King tried to explain.

"Fuck what it look like, I see you over here grabbing on my sister like you her daddy or something," Lamar amped himself up.

"Sun, chill the fuck out. We was just breaking up the fight," Lakim said.

"What, fuck is you to get loud with me?" Lamar peeled off his shirt and flexed his hulking, tatted chest. "Y'all li'l young-ass niggaz think you're hot shit out here, but you better learn to respect the ones who made this possible." He turned to King. "And I don't give a fuck how much time you did, nigga. You still li'l James to me, and that's the only reason I didn't hand you your head when I seen you out here trying to *handle* my sister!"

That was the last straw.

King moved like a blur, closing the distance between him and Lamar in less than a second. Lamar tried to raise his hands but by the time he got them up, King had already blasted him in the jaw twice. "You li'l bitch-ass nigga, trying to come at me like you built." King slapped him viciously across the mouth, drawing blood. He followed up with a nasty hook to the gut, doubling Lamar over. "Sun, gimmie the hammer so I can push this faggot," King ordered Lakim.

"Chill, God, it's mad people out here," Lakim warned.

"I don't give a fuck." King smacked Lamar again, but held him by the back of the head to keep him from flipping over the gate.

"King, please don't kill my brother." Yvonne dramatically threw herself at King.

"Bitch, get off me," he snarled while trying to detach her pleading arms from around his neck. The whole thing had become comical.

It didn't take long for a crowd to gather around the spectacle and of course that led to someone's calling the police. The way King was abusing Lamar was not only embarrassing, it was sad. As the cops were making their way to the brawl, Sahara was making her way away from it. Seeing another grown man get beat like that was more than Sahara could bear. She caught a taxi at the curb and gave the driver her address. Her hair was a mess from the girls pulling it and her outfit was ruined, but outside of that and a few nicks and scratches she was good. The fact that it had been three-against-one and they couldn't do much to her brought Sahara a little joy. Even three-against-one they couldn't see her, and this brought Sahara a little joy. The last thing she saw as they were pulling away were the cops struggling to get King off Lamar.

CHAPTER 7

Porsha made her way leisurely through the aisles inside the Columbus Market, studying the different labels like they were Chinese arithmetic. She hated food shopping, or doing anything domestic for that matter, but it was her turn to cook that night. Porsha dreaded cooking almost as much as she dreaded the feedback she got on the rare occasions when she did cook. But when you looked like Porsha, whether you could cook or not was the furthest thing from a man's mind.

Porsha was a brown-skinned piece who stood around five-seven, five-nine in the right heels. She'd had long, curly hair since she was a little girl, but six months ago she'd chopped it off and now rocked a funky cut that complemented her round face and China-doll eyes. Porsha was a bad chick with a Lil' Kim swag about her that she wore on her sleeve and made no apologies for who she was. But, as with most things, there was more than met the eye with Porsha.

Porsha had watched her mom bust her ass working two jobs to provide for her children while her father came in and out of their lives like bad phone reception. Things had started looking up for them when her mother met her stepfather. He was a slightly older man with a military background and no-nonsense attitude. He and Porsha never quite saw eye-to-eye, but she respected him because he was a good man. Within a few years' time her mother and stepfather had taken them from a tenement in Bed-Stuy, Brooklyn, to a beautiful brownstone on Ninety-first between Columbus Avenue and Central Park West. Both her parents worked every day of their lives to make sure Porsha and her siblings had all the best that life could afford them in an attempt to bury their less-than-pleasant roots. The oldest two, Vanessa and Charles, were the pride of the family, fitting right in with their new Ivy League friends and acting as if they had never spent a day of their lives in the ghetto, but a piece of Porsha's heat would always be in Brooklyn.

Porsha still had aunts and cousins there so from time to time she was allowed to spend weekends in Bed-Stuy. When Porsha got old enough to ride the train by herself, the weekend trips became regular. On those weekends she spent with her cousins in Brooklyn she was free from the restrictions of her parents and she let it all hang out. By the time she was fourteen, Porsha was halfway through her education on boys and blunts and trying to find an introductory course on paper chasing. When her parents got hip they tried to put a tighter yoke on Porsha, but the more rules they set, the more she broke. The summer before she was supposed to leave to start her first semester at Howard came the straw that broke the camel's back. When Porsha told her parents that she was pregnant by a dude who had just gotten sentenced to eight years in prison, her stepfather gave her an ultimatum: terminate the pregnancy and start school on time as if it had never happened, or get out. So Porsha left.

Sixteen weeks into her pregnancy she miscarried and fell into a deep depression and turned to drugs to comfort her. School, family, and even time all became a blur the deeper she sank into her funk. When she finally crawled out of it, a year had passed, she had been living from pillar to post, and school seemed a lifetime away. Porsha was at a low point . . . a point at which the average young woman may have given up and slipped further into oblivion, but Porsha wasn't quite ready to lie down and die. She could've gone home and begged for her parents' forgiveness, but pride wouldn't let her, so Porsha searched for her own way.

Porsha was still as intelligent as ever, but she had been out of the loop so long that she had to crawl before she could walk, so she enrolled herself in a community college. Next, she managed to find a place to lay her head when a friend of a friend was looking for a roommate to share her apartment and bills with. It could be stressful at times with several women in one apartment, but Porsha made the best of it. She tried to find a job, but with the twisted economy and no degree, all she was offered were minimum-wage positions, and her high-end tastes wouldn't allow that, so she turned to *other* ways to make money, capitalizing on the only real asset she had left, her looks.

"Porsha-boo," someone called, snapping her out of her daze. When she turned around and saw Scar peering at her from the end of the aisle, her mood instantly darkened. Scar was a local knucklehead who was always into something. He was a drug dealer by trade, a pain in the ass by nature, and a natural magnet for trouble, which a teenager named Jay who worked for him had to find out the hard way. Someone Scar had run afoul of tried to kill him, and they ended up hitting the boy by accident. Not only did Scar skip the funeral, but he didn't even offer Jay's mother so much as a crumb to bury her son, when it had been his fault the boy was killed. Scar was a bastard and the whole hood either feared him or hated him.

"Hey," she said dryly and continued pushing her cart down the aisle.

"What you got up in there?" Scar caught up to her and snatched a box of rice from the cart. "Let me find out you're cooking us a romantic dinner tonight." He smirked.

"I ain't cooking us shit." She snatched the rice back and kept going.

"I was just joking, Porsha, don't act like that with me," he said, softening his approach.

"That's your problem, you're always playing and never serious about anything."

"I know one thing that I am serious about." Scar touched her arm lightly.

"Whatever, nigga. Dick that has run up in Boots will never run up in me." Porsha rolled her eyes and kept pushing.

Scar was stunned for a second, but quickly rebounded. "Boots? You shouldn't go believing everything you hear, ma." He fell in step with her.

"It ain't about hearing, it's about seeing, because it ain't like y'all got the common decency to put no shade on it. Everybody in the hood except Bernie knows you and his baby mama are fucking, among other things. Now please leave me to finish this shopping so I can get outta here."

"Why don't you let me pay for those groceries for you, ma. Porsha, I know you ain't no hood bitch, so it takes a nigga who can take care of you to even step to you," he said, pulling out a knot of money, spreading the bills so she could see that he was holding.

Porsha looked down at the money and the look on her face said that she wasn't impressed. "Scar, sometimes it ain't about money, it's about class, and right now you're a little short on it, boo. It ain't nothing personal, I just don't feel you like that," she said frankly.

Scar's face melted. "Word?" He shook his head sadly. "All y'all broads is the same. When you first move around you act like your pussy is wetter than the next bitch, but before long you all ask me to be the judge," he said smugly.

Porsha wanted to snap, but she kept her cool and only the half smirk on her face said that she was fazed by the comment at all. "Scar, I almost went there with you, but I know you be on your ignorant shit so I'm gonna let it slide, but if you feel like you gotta come at me sideways, then we don't have to say anything to each other."

"Shorty, you better take that shit back down to Ninety-whatever Street you're from and recognize that this is my hood—"

"My bad, I didn't mean to interrupt." A well-built man, wearing a white shirt under his burgundy smock, stood at the top of the aisle, watching the altercation. He was a handsome brown-skinned fellow who wore his hair cut low and tapered on the sides and in the back. He ran his hand over the top of his hair, lightly disturbing the swirls of thick waves.

"Yeah, we were kinda in the middle of something," Scar said bitterly.

"No, we weren't." Porsha pushed her cart toward the worker, leaving Scar standing in the aisle.

"A'ight, so Ima see you on the block, Porsha," Scar called after her.

"I guess so," she said over her shoulder.

She waited until Scar had disappeared down the other end of the aisle before acknowledging the young man in the smock. "Thanks, Alonzo, that dude was getting on my last nerve."

"Ain't nothing, I peeped ya body language and figured you could use an assist," he told her. "So what brings you into our fair market, and with a shopping cart no less?" he joked.

"I'm cooking dinner tonight," she explained, riffling through the items in her cart, still feeling like she was missing something.

"You should have somebody cooking for you!" Alonzo said.

"In a perfect world." She sighed.

"Hey, it ain't gotta be perfect to be right."

Porsha looked up at him and saw that he was seriously trying to court her. "Alonzo, go ahead somewhere with that Jodeci shit. Right now I come with way too much baggage for a man to deal with."

Alonzo flexed under his fitted dress shirt and showed her all thirty-two of his teeth. "I got a pretty strong back. But on some G shit, Porsha, you ain't never even thought about giving me no play."

"Alonzo, you're fine as hell but there's no way it would work out. I'm moving fast right now, trying to get where I gotta get on the express train, and you're riding the local," she said seriously. Seeing that she had offended him, she explained, "Alonzo, I don't mean that as any kind of slight to you, but I'm into a certain type of dude that's on the same page as me. Working a nine-to-five for as many years as you've been here is beyond impressive, but—"

"But what?" he cut her off. "Porsha, before you give me the 'good kid working in the supermarket' speech, don't forget that working here is one of the only things that are keeping me outta prison," he reminded her. Alonzo had been a notorious stick-up kid in and around the Bronx until a four to nine slowed him down. He started working at the supermarket as a condition of his parole, and by the time he was off parole he was next in line for the manager's position so he stayed on. People often clowned him for working in the supermarket but Alonzo had a plan.

"That shit Scar and them doing," Alonzo waved his hand dismissively, "been there done that, and ain't none of them built like I was when I was popping, but unlike them knuckleheads, I realized that there was more to life than a fucking five by nine and a chow call. This shit," he motioned around the supermarket, "is an ends to a means."

"I hear you talking," she said with a smirk.

"Don't hear me talk, watch me move." Alonzo winked and walked away. "You gonna stop playing with me and act like you know Porsha," he called over his shoulder.

CHAPTER 8

After successfully tackling the grocery shopping, Porsha headed home to catch a quick nap before she started dinner and went to work. She passed Scar and a few of his cronies leaning against he fence in front of the community center, obviously up to no good. He looked at Porsha and smirked, but she just rolled her eyes and kept walking.

To get her mind off Scar's creepy stare, she reflected on her and Alonzo's conversation and it brought a smile to her face. Alonzo was a good dude and a fair catch, but she respected his grind too much to complicate his life with her bullshit. She was a broke college dropout with half a plan and a dream to get out of the hood, and Alonzo looked like he might actually make it, so she wouldn't share her karma with him.

As she was about to turn up the path leading to her building, a cab was pulling up on the avenue and someone was calling her name out the back window. "Porsha, it's me, Sahara. Come here right quick."

Porsha looked to make sure it was really Sahara before approaching the cab and looking at her in shock, because she was such a mess. Her hair was all over the place and there were welts on her dark face. "What the hell happened to you?"

"It's a long story, and I'll tell you all about it, but first I need you to let me hold eight dollars to pay for this cab," Sahara said.

"Shit, where's your money?" Porsha asked suspiciously.

"I left my pocketbook on the bench in front of King's building. Please don't play twenty questions with me right now, Porsha, because I'm not in the mood." Porsha paid for the cab and held the door open for Sahara. When she stepped out, Porsha could really see how much of a wreck Sahara was. Her elbows were scraped and her dress was torn down the back, barely covering her ass. "I swear to God I'm gonna murk this bitch." Sahara smacked her hand against her palm in frustration. She was speed-walking down the path to her building.

"What bitch? What happened? Who?" Porsha fired off questions while trying to keep up with Sahara.

Sahara stopped in her tracks and looked at Porsha as if she were stupid. "Yvonne! Damn, ain't you been listening?" Sahara continued walking, giving Porsha the short version of what had happened.

"Wow, I can't believe that bum bitch tried to frog-up on you." Porsha shook her head.

"That's a'ight, because I'm about to call my bitches from Patterson and let the BX in me be felt," Sahara fumed.

"Well, I ain't no big fighter but I got some wild-ass cousins from Bed-Stuy that'll come up here and get it *way* popping," Porsha offered. Fighting had never been one of Porsha's strong suits, so she generally left it to her cousins, and those chicks were professionals at delivering ass whippings.

When they rounded the corner toward their building

they spotted Happy, Levi, and Frankie on the bench passing around a blunt. There were a half-dozen designer bags on the ground and on the bench, so Porsha knew she had caught Frankie fresh off a lick, which meant she would get the pick of her goods before they made it to the streets to be picked over. Shopping with Frankie as opposed to in the stores allowed Porsha to keep up her high look, on a broke bitch's budget.

As they were closing in on the bench, Boots and Bernie were coming out of the building with three of their children. Bernie pushed the stroller carrying their youngest child with one hand and clutched a brown paper bag in the other. He strode so purposefully and proudly with his family in tow, and it sent a wave of sympathy through everyone watching it. Bernie was an accident that just hadn't happened yet.

Boots was decked out in gray sweats and lime-green flip-flops with a black tank top that struggled to hold in her large breasts and increasingly growing waistline. Boots was a cool chick, but she had some very scandalous ways about her, promiscuity being only one of them. Boots loved to fuck and didn't care who knew it, which probably explained why she had five kids by almost as many dudes.

Bernie was the only one of her kids' fathers who actually stuck around and tried to create a family structure with Boots and her children, but she did him the dirtiest. At one time Bernie had been a promising basketball recruit, but Boots's trifling ways and a patch of ice had ruined all that. Bernie worked odd jobs and sold weed to get by, but he wasn't very good at either so it was always left to Boots to fill in the gaps. By hook or by crook, Boots would go out and get it when her number was called, but how she was getting it was the best-kept secret. Bernie's love for Boots made him deaf to the mocking laughter all around him about Boots and her fucked-up ways.

"What's good, y'all?" Boots greeted everyone and went to lean against the fence.

"I can't call it." Levi shrugged.

"What's popping, Frankie, you on?" Boots asked, trying to peer inside the bags.

"I'm always *on*. What you need?" Frankie opened the bag and slid it toward Boots to examine the merchandise.

"This is nice," Boots said, holding up a stylish leather dress she'd fished out.

"Yeah, that's tight. I wanted to keep it for myself, but I ain't got enough ass to fill it out properly," Frankie joked. "If you want it, I'll shoot it to you for something light. Give me fifty bucks and you can have it."

Boots thought on it for a minute. She had seen the same dress in the window of Level X, so she knew that getting it for fifty dollars was a steal. "Bernie, you got money on you?"

Bernie turned his pockets out. "I'm popped, ma."

"Figures," Boots mumbled. "Frankie, I really want this dress but I'm fucked up right now. If you let me get it, that's my word I'll hit you off when I get my check Tuesday."

"I wish I could, Boots, but I got some people coming through to check me later and I know one of them will give me at least a hundred for it, so I can't miss out on no bread." Frankie plucked the dress out of Boots's hands. "I'll tell you what I can do: I'll hold the dress for you until later on tonight so you can have some time to come up with it."

"That ain't about nothing, ma, we'll come up on fifty dollars by the end of the night," Bernie said as if he were the one who had to hustle it up.

"Yeah, I'm sure ol' Boots will figure out a way to come up with it by then," Happy said slyly.

"What the fuck happened to you?" Levi asked, noticing Sahara's appearance for the first time.

"I don't even want to talk about it." Sahara rolled her eyes. "Can we go now, Porsha?"

"Yeah, I gotta put this food up anyway." Porsha adjusted her bags.

"Hold on, I'm coming up too. I gotta take inventory of all this stuff." Frankie gathered her bags and fell in step with them to the building.

"I'm about to go up the block to the Chinese restaurant." Happy hoisted himself off the bench. "Levi, what you about to do?"

"I'll be right here when you come back," Levi said, thumbing away on his BlackBerry.

"I'll go with you. I gotta get something from the corner store anyhow," Boots said.

"A'ight, we can all walk together," Bernie offered.

"Nah, you ain't gotta have Hassan out in all this heat." Boots adjusted the hood of the stroller.

"Don't worry about it, boo, it ain't even that hot." Bernie pushed the stroller ahead of them.

"This muthafucka," Boots said under her breath and fell in step with Bernie. Happy brought up the rear, laughing at a joke that only he seemed to know the punch line to.

***

The three girls got off the elevator, with Frankie doubled over in laughter about what had happened to Sahara.

"I can't believe y'all were out there scrapping over King's tired ass." Frankie slapped her thigh while trying to catch her breath.

"It ain't funny, Frankie," Sahara snapped, "and we weren't fighting over King, we were fighting because she keeps trying to play me."

"Personally I think it's stupid. Come on now, y'all are making spectacles of yourselves in the middle of the street, fighting like hood rats," Porsha said.

Sahara turned her anger on Porsha. "Excuse the fuck out of me, little princess. I don't know how they do it in la-la-land, or wherever the fuck you're from, but around here bitches get stomped out for disrespecting."

"Slow your roll and lower your tone when speaking to me, because I didn't get stink with you. I was just giving you my opinion on the situation and you can miss me with that *princess* shit, ma. Before my family had money we rested our heads in Bed-Stuy, so you can bet your ass I done had more than my fair share of scraps over hos acting silly. Ain't nobody trying to clown you, Sahara; all I'm saying is that you're better than those bitches so it looks crazy when you stoop to their levels."

"Whatever." Sahara marched down the hall toward the apartment the three of them shared.

"Don't pay her no mind, Porsha, after we put something in the air she'll be back to her pain-in-the-ass self." Frankie laughed. When Frankie and Porsha made it to the apartment door, Sahara was standing as still as a tree with a piece of paper in her hand.

"I can't believe this shit," Sahara said in shock.

"What's that?" Porsha tried to peer over her shoulder.

"I found this taped to the door," Sahara said, holding the paper out for her roommates to see. It was an eviction notice.

CHAPTER 9

The room had gone quiet. So quiet that you could hear the paper from the Dutch Master burning every time Frankie took a pull. The three girls sat around the living room coffee table, staring at the eviction notice like it was a Chinese arithmetic problem. No one could believe it or figure out where it had come from, but they knew they had to deal with it.

"I can't believe this shit." Frankie expelled a cloud of smoke. "Who the fuck gets evicted in 2011?"

"According to the letter, *us.*" Porsha snorted. She hated to laugh, but it was all she could do to keep from crying. She had seen some hard times in her day, but being homeless was something she couldn't even fathom. No matter how close she cut it when it came to paying the rent when she was out on her own, it had never come down to her being tossed into the street.

Sahara ran her fingers through her hair, shaking her head when loose strands came away on her fingers. "This shit couldn't have happened at a worse time. King's surprise party is tomorrow and I got enough shit on my plate to deal with without this adding on to it."

Frankie rolled her neck and looked at Sahara as if she had bumped her head. "We're about to get kicked out on our asses and you're worried about throwing a party for some nigga? Baby girl, you better prioritize and try to help us brainstorm to get this money up."

"Get the money up." Sahara leaned forward in the rickety brown rocking chair. "Why the fuck should I when I've been dropping my portion in the pot for I don't know how long and it ain't been getting to where it's supposed to be? That letter says we're over three months behind and I know for the last few months since I ain't been working I've been giving my money to Porsha as I get it so I'm not tempted to spend it." She glared at Porsha.

Porsha leaned back and eyeballed Sahara. "Don't be looking at me all crazy like this shit is my fault. I've been working all night and sleeping all day, so getting the rent delivered can get complicated with me so I've been giving it to Frankie. And besides, she's always the last one to kick up and we all agreed to the rule, right?" The girls had come to the agreement that whoever was responsible for the rent being late would be the one to drop it off and have to endure the bullshit lecture from the woman who was subleasing the apartment and none of them looked forward to that because Debbie could talk for hours about absolutely nothing.

Frankie flicked the blunt ashes in the ashtray and took in her roommates. "Okay, okay, I'll take responsibility for coming through at the last minute with my portion of the rent, but don't be looking at me like I stole the fucking money. I've been paying Debbie."

"Nobody called you a thief, but I will call you a damn vacuum." Sahara snatched the blunt from Frankie. "Nah, ain't none of us gonna risk being homeless or back living with our parents"—she glanced at Porsha—"so this can only mean that Debbie did some funny shit with our rent money instead of paying Housing."

Porsha shook her head. "Why am I not surprised? Had I heard some of the stories that have surfaced about her before I agreed to move in here, it wouldn't have gone down." Porsha recalled some of the stories she'd heard about Debbie and her exploits. "This bitch think she got more game than a little bit, but we about to show her that this shit is bigger than Nino Brown. Once we go into Housing court and show them the receipts from the money orders proving that we've been paying the rent. Frankie, go get the receipts so we can start getting our ducks in a row," Porsha told her, feeling that it was an open-and-shut case. Frankie didn't move. "Frankie, what's good? You got the rent receipts, right?"

"Not exactly," Frankie mumbled.

"What do you mean 'not exactly'?" Sahara questioned. "Frankie, please don't tell me that you gave Debbie the rent money in cash?"

Frankie looked at the worried faces of her roommates. "Only the last few times, but let me explain—" Frankie began, but was cut off.

"Aw hell nah, tell me you were smarter than that, Frankie." Sahara began to pace and went back to running her fingers through her hair.

"I know I should've just gotten a money order like we normally do, but I've been making crazy moves. Debbie was in the hood a few times so I just hit her with straight bread because it was easier than going to cop money orders. I was just trying to cut a corner to make it easier on us."

"You mean easier on you," Sahara told her. "Frankie,

you know damn well giving Debbie cash is the same as picking a snake up by its tail and not expecting it to bite you. The whole reason we go through the trouble of getting money orders to pay her is so she can't hit us with her *Debbie* shit, because you know how she do."

All Frankie could do was nod because she knew Sahara was right. Debbie was an older chick from the projects who had a Harvard education and a dope fiend's mentality. Her knack for creative schemes made her somewhat of a legend in the projects, but it was her powers of manipulation that made her notorious. Debbie could piss on your head and tell you it was raining and you'd believe it, that's just how good she was. Frankie had had a bad feeling about the offer to sublease Debbie's apartment but she'd been desperate at the time so she'd gone along with it. Staring at the eviction notice on the coffee table, she wished she had taken her chances with the shelter.

"What are we gonna do?" Porsha asked, accepting the blunt Frankie passed her.

"I don't know what y'all are gonna do, but I know what I'm gonna do." She got up and stormed into the bedroom. Frankie came back out holding a pistol. "I'm gonna bust a cap in that slimy bitch."

"Frankie, you can't just go around killing people!" Sahara told her.

"Kill her? A dead bitch can't pay no debts, I'm just gonna shoot her in the leg," Frankie said.

"Frankie, would you stop playing with that gun, this is serious," Porsha said.

Frankie glared at her. "Ain't nobody playing. Yo, I'm out here stealing from sunup to sunup and still barely making ends meet and pay my portion of the rent for this raggedy-ass apartment and Debbie wanna be stealing? Fuck all that, I ain't no punk bitch. She gotta get dealt with."

"I agree, but shooting her isn't gonna help, Frankie," Porsha tried to reason with her. "Before we jump to conclusions, let's give her the benefit of the doubt. For all we know, she didn't steal the money and it was an accident on Housing's part," Porsha suggested. Frankie and Sahara gave her the same blank stare.

Frankie patted Porsha's hand sadly. "Poor thing." This got the girls to laugh for the first time since they'd gotten the notice. "Okay, I promise not to shoot the bitch unless she tries to pop fly when we step to her about the money." Frankie slipped the gun into her shoulder bag, which was sitting on the couch next to her. "But as God is my witness, if Debbie tries to spin us I'm gonna go up top."

"Fair enough," Sahara said as she pulled her hair back into a ponytail. After grabbing her keys, she made her way to the door, with Frankie on her heels. "You coming?" Sahara asked Porsha from the doorway.

"Nah, y'all go ahead." Porsha got off the couch. "I've got some shit I need to do." She headed to the bedrooms.

"And what could you have to do that's more important than going to holla at Debbie about this eviction?" Sahara asked with attitude.

"Trying to get the money up to keep it from happening," Porsha said over her shoulder before slamming her bedroom door.

CHAPTER 10

The setting sun cast a shadow onto the patio that cut down the middle of the marble chessboard on the table. The effect gave the black pieces, which occupied the shaded side, a more morbid appeal, while making the white pieces appear more brilliant. Shai hunched down over the table so far that the crucifix hanging from his neck grazed the board and almost toppled his bishop. He looked like a perplexed child trying to figure out the next move he would try against his cagey opponent. As a rule, Poppa Clark had made sure that all his children were skilled at the game of chess, so Shai considered himself quite experienced, but his opponent had been playing for longer than he.

Sol Lansky sat across from him in a high-backed chair, crossed-legged and completely at ease. Sol was a silver-haired grandfatherly-looking man, but his mind was still as sharp as it ever had been. He watched Shai carefully, anticipating his next move. Lansky had made his bones anticipating people's moves and beating them to the punch. In his old age Sol Lansky was a retired businessman and antique dealer, but his life hadn't always been so quiet. In the fifties and sixties Sol had been in deep with the Jewish syndicate, but as the conflicts with the Italians became more intense, Sol took his business to Harlem and learned to burn the candle from both ends. Sol had been a financial wizard as well as a good friend to both mafia dons and kingpins, including Shai's late father, Poppa Clark. The death of his good friend Poppa Clark had turned Sol off to the game so he stayed away from it, choosing to focus more on his legitimate holdings, but from time to time he would council Poppa's heir, Shai.

"You gonna gawk at the board all day or make a move?" Sol asked in his gravelly voice.

Shai threw his hands in the air. "See, you keep trying to rush me and throw off my concentration."

"What's to concentrate, there's only five moves you can make without me putting you in checkmate."

"I got this." Shai ran his fingers down his goatee and continued studying the board.

Sol laughed.

"What?" Shai looked up.

"It's nothing, it's just that it still tickles me to see you with facial hair. I remember when you were a snot-nosed punk running around dribbling a basketball."

"Everybody has to grow up sometime, Sol." Shai moved his bishop to take Sol's rook. Shai folded his arms and smiled triumphantly.

"Shai, you may have your dad's good looks but you don't have his skill for games of strategy." Sol moved his queen into the spot that the bishop had vacated. "Checkmate, youngster."

Shai was dumbfounded. "How the hell did you . . ."

"Simple, I anticipated your next move. I put the rook out there because I knew you'd be tempted, which you were, and it left your king exposed." Sol picked up Shai's white king. "The king must always be protected."

"Damn, I didn't even realize I would leave myself open like that." Shai studied the board.

"Because you think more in the here and now than the future and that's always been your Achilles' heel. If you don't remember anything else I've told you, remember this: before you do something, always think of every possible scenario so that way your ass is covered, especially when dealing with people. Know what the other guy is thinking and counteract that move even before he makes it. You stick to that kinda thinking and you'll never get caught with your pants down, you hear me, kid?"

"Sol, you know whenever you speak I'm all ears. You been around for a long time so I know you ain't gonna tell me nothing wrong."

"Of course not, Shai, and if you stick to the script, as you guys say, you'll be around for a long time too," Sol told him.

"You guys still going at it?" Honey stepped out onto the patio. Her golden locks were pulled back into a ponytail, showing off her beautiful caramel face. She was wearing spandex pants, running sneakers, and one of Shai's old S.C. sweatshirts. The shirt nearly swallowed her, but you could still see the baby bump in the front. She and Shai were expecting their first child.

"Nah, he kicked my ass again." Shai laughed.

"We'll, you're still a winner in my book, baby." She leaned in and kissed him. "You're gonna stop coming over here bullying my fiancé," she teased Sol.

"Hey, I'm from the school that an ass whipping is the easiest way to teach a kid." Sol laughed.

"Where are you off to, dressed like Jackie Joyner?" Shai pinched her thigh.

"To the gym—you know it takes good to look this good." Honey struck a pose.

Shai pulled her down onto his lap. "No the hell you're not while you're carrying my li'l man. The doctor said no working out."

"She said no strenuous workouts," Honey corrected him. "I'm gonna do some light work on the bike and some curls, nothing major. When are you gonna stop acting like I'm made of glass?"

"The day you push my son into the world."

"And what make you so sure it's gonna be a boy, Shai?" she asked.

"Because he's a Clark, and we don't make nothing but warriors," Shai boasted.

"So what do you call Hope?" she asked, referring to Shai's little sister.

"A fucking headache." Shai burst out laughing as if it were the funniest joke in the world.

"You're such a dick." She mushed him and got off his lap. "If it will make you feel better, then I'll only work out for an hour."

"Twenty minutes," he countered.

"A half hour and that's as low as I'm going so deal with it." She flipped her ponytail and walked back through the glass doors just as Swann was coming out. "Move, punk." She bumped him playfully.

"You need to watch where you're going, pudgy," he teased her.

"That isn't funny, Swann. Don't you know it's rude to tease a pregnant woman about her weight?"

"You know we ain't got no class in the hood." He threw

his hands up in surrender. Honey just shook her head and went to start her workout. "Boss dog, what it is?" He gave Shai dap.

"I can't call it, might spoil it."

"How's it going, Swann?" Sol asked from his corner.

"Mr. Lansky." Swann nodded. "Ay, Shai, I need to holla at you for a minute."

"It must be important if you made a house call instead of hitting me on the jack." Shai picked up on Swann's vibe. They had been down so long that they could reach each other's body languages.

"Hood politics," Swann said simply.

"That's my cue to leave." Sol got up from his chair.

"Sorry, Sol. We'll go another round next week." Shai shook his hand and patted him on the back. "Let me walk you out."

"Don't bother Shai, I know the way. You guys go ahead and take care of your hood politics." Sol laughed. "I swear, I need a dictionary to talk to some of you kids these days. Take care fellas, and Shai, make sure you work on that game." Sol disappeared through the glass doors.

"It went down last night . . ." Swann began, but Shai cut him off.

"Chill, let's take a walk." He motioned for him to follow and stepped off the porch into the backyard. Swann fell in step with Shai and the two of them walked the expansive yard. "A'ight, run it down."

"It's like I was telling you, some shit popped off uptown with one of them li'l hoppers from the East Side."

"How ugly?" Shai wasn't sure if he wanted to know.

"Not super ugly, but ugly enough. Holiday rides down on

these kids about moving a package other than what comes from the Clarks and, long story short, Holiday sent him to the emergency room to get a bullet removed from his leg."

"Fucking Holiday and those guns." Shai shook his head. "Who was the kid working for?"

"From what Holiday said, he was handling for some kid named King James or some shit like that." Swann relayed the story as Holiday had told it to him.

"Who the fuck is King James?" The name wasn't familiar to Shai.

"The hell if I know," Swann admitted. "I asked around about him on the street and the info is sketchy. He supposed to be some kind of jailhouse goon from Grant, but other than that nobody really knows too much about him."

Shai shook his head in disappointment. "Just what we need, another knucklehead who's seen *Scarface* too many times trying to make a name for himself. And that fucking Holiday shooting people left and right doesn't help either."

"You know how it is with the young ones, Shai. They're constantly trying to prove that they can walk a mile in our shoes. Remember how we were?"

Indeed Shai did. He and Swann were constantly into something when they were kids. They would see the kinds of things the older guys who worked for Poppa Clark would do and try to emulate them to get Poppa or Tommy's attention. Of course, Shai proved to be a horrible criminal back then, but Tommy took a liking to Swann and took him under his wing. While Shai went off to college, Swann was in the trap with Tommy Gunz.

"Shai, I was thinking that maybe we should skip the event at Brick City tonight and keep you local until we find out exactly what's up with this situation," Swann suggested.

Shai smiled at his old friend. "You sound like Tommy: *stay off those corners, Shai,*" he said, imitating his brother's voice.

"You know we only wanted to keep you out of the game," Swann said sincerely.

"Well, considering I'm elbow deep in it, I guess you guys made some piss-poor teachers." Shai laughed. "But on the real, I appreciate your concern, Swann, but it wouldn't look good on our part if we didn't show up. Paulie's turning a nice buck for us and his father is connected, so I wanna keep things kosher between us so we can keep eating with them."

"You got that, Shai. But do you think we should take a few extra guys with us tonight?"

"Maybe." He stroked his goatee. "Call Angelo and tell him to come through, and bring that li'l ignorant muthafucka Holiday, too, I need to holla at him. As far as that King James thing, don't stress too much about it. It's a street beef, so nine times outta ten it's gonna stay there, but make sure Holiday has his people tighten the fuck up."

CHAPTER 11

Alonzo took a deep breath when he stepped off the train and onto the elevated platform on 125th and Broadway. He hated riding the stuffy trains, especially in the summertime, but, as high as the gas prices had gone in New York, buying a car was a headache he didn't need.

When he got to the ground level he ducked into the store and grabbed two Dutch Masters and a six-pack before beginning the trek up the hill to his building. He greeted a few heads he knew along the way, but didn't stop to make small talk. All he wanted to do was blow something down and go to sleep. Since being promoted to assistant manager at the supermarket, his pay had increased, but so had his hours. He had to be one of the first in the store and one of the last to leave. That morning he had clocked in at four A.M. to do inventory and still worked a six-hour shift. The long hours were taxing, but it was better than standing on the corner throwing stones at the pen, so he didn't complain.

The fact that Alonzo had a job still tripped him out, considering the fact that it was the first job he'd had in his life. He had been a career criminal who came from a like-minded family of lawbreakers. His father, uncles, brother, and even his mother had been involved in illegal activities at one time or another, and going to prison was like a rite of passage in their family. Alonzo had been locked up before, but it was on his last trip that he had finally hit the big time: state prison. The things Alonzo had seen and been forced to do in order to survive his stay had changed something in him. Prison had made him take a serious look at the way he was living and he'd started to wonder if any of the bullshit was worth it at the end of the day. When he was released, he vowed that he was done with the street life. Of course no one believed him, and everyone was just waiting for Zo-Pound to resurface, but he never did. Alonzo was often teased by some of his old crime partners about his newfound profession, and though it bothered him he never let it sway him from the path he was on. Being assistant manager at a supermarket wasn't the most glamorous gig in the world but it was honest work and he didn't have to worry about police or rival crews trying to force him into early retirement.

As Alonzo neared his building he noticed that the park was especially crowded and there were two police cars parked on the curb. Something must have gone down, which was no surprise because something was always going down in the hood. He thought about simply walking past the police into the lobby, but decided against it because he had weed on him. The police didn't have a reason to stop him, but the NYPD didn't need a reason other than his being young and black to hassle him. He was just about to cut through the path and try to enter the building through the back door when he heard his name being called from across the street.

***

Ashanti sat on a stoop across the street, on the other side of the El, watching the crowd slowly begin to disperse under the direction of the police. The fight that had broken out in front of 3150 provided a good dose of morning entertainment for the hood. King James had beaten Lamar like an unruly child and he deserved it. Lamar was always around the hood flossing like he was the supreme gangsta when in all actuality he was a pussy. The only reason he fronted like he was tough was because he ran with some cats from Manhattanville who were known to lay their hammer game down. As tickled as Ashanti was watching Lamar get his ass whipped, he was sad when the police took him away because he had planned on robbing Lamar that day. With Lamar in custody and the heavy police presence in the hood because of the fight, all the juxes Ashanti had planned were officially postponed until further notice, which didn't sit well with him at all.

Since striking out on his own Ashanti had had to learn quite a few different hustles, and so far he seemed to be best at stealing because it was easiest to do by yourself, which he had been since the dismantling of his crew. Animal had been the glue that held them together and after his disappearance things seemed to have fallen apart. Brasco was locked up, again, on a parole violation for pissing dirty, and Nef had gone out and found a job, which was probably best as he had never really had the heart for their lifestyle anyhow. When Nefertiti had gotten a job with UPS, he tried to pull Ashanti in with him, but Ashanti had declined. He was technically still a fugitive so going legit wasn't an option, and besides that, he had no desire to work a *regular* job. He was married to the streets and divorce wasn't an option.

Ever since he was a shorty, Ashanti had been in the streets, living by his wits. Ashanti's mother had been a junkie who sold his sister for drugs and would've done the same to him had he not run away from home when he was ten years old. He had been an orphan adopted and nurtured by the hustlers of whichever neighborhoods he called home at the time, and family structure was something alien to him, but that had all changed when he came under the wing of Animal and Brasco. Much like him, they had been abandoned by their families and left to fend for themselves in the cold world. From them he learned the lessons of the game and found the love that he had been starved of all his life. They had been a family until the demons of their pasts had broken them up.

When Animal went down they all took it hard, but none harder than little Ashanti. Animal had been his hero and his savior and the thought of his spending the rest of his life in prison had been too much for the youth to bear. During the trial, Brasco and Nefertiti had to keep Ashanti away from the courthouse, not just because he was a fugitive and would run the risk of being apprehended but because he had gotten it in his young mind that they could bust Animal out of jail like an action movie. Brasco had to literally watch him twenty-four hours per day to keep him from trying to execute his escape plan. Ironically, someone else had beaten Ashanti to the punch and made off with Animal.

"Peace." The voice snapped Ashanti out of his daze. Reflexively he spun in the direction of the voice with his gun raised, but lowered it when he spotted Lakim. "What the fuck is good with you, sun?" Lakim raised his hands in surrender.

"My fault, big homie." Ashanti tucked his gun. "You can never be too careful out here."

"True indeed." Lakim gave him dap. "What you doing over here looking like you scheming?"

"Ain't shit, just chilling. I had something I was supposed to do but it's on hold now because of all the heat on the hood. What's up with King, he good?"

"Nah, they locked my nigga up for mashing duke out," Lakim told him.

"Wow, that's fucked up. What is this world coming to when a nigga gotta spend a night in jail over a fight?"

"Nah, they ain't gonna keep the god but a few hours, if that. I already got the lawyer on the case so King should be straight. We got too much going on over the next few days to have my nigga laid up."

"True." Ashanti nodded. "Yo, I heard through the grapevine that y'all niggaz is having a big-ass party tomorrow night?"

"Yeah, we throwing the god a birthday party, but don't tell King because it's supposed to be a surprise."

Ashanti raised his eyebrow. "Ain't y'all niggaz too old for surprise parties?"

"You're never too old for ya peeps to let you know you're appreciated, youngster."

"I hear that hot shit." Ashanti laughed. His eyes zeroed in on a familiar face creeping on the other side of the street. "Ain't that ya brother over there?"

Lakim squinted. "Yeah, that's that nigga. Ayo, Zo!" he shouted, waving his hands so Alonzo could see him.

Alonzo hesitated at first but eventually made his way across the street to where Lakim and Ashanti were posted up. "What's good?"

"You." Lakim hugged his little brother. "What you doing creeping around like you still putting in work?"

"Trying to get past these dicks so I can go upstairs. They got the front of the building on smash," Alonzo told him.

"What, you dirty or something?" Ashanti asked.

"Ain't shit but a few bags of Kush, but it's enough for them to take me through on they bullshit."

"Put it in the air and get ya big bro high, my nig," Lakim said.

"C'mon, son, I know you holding too. Match me," Alonzo shot back.

"Say no more. Ashanti, why don't you run in the store and grab a Dutch," Lakim suggested.

"Why y'all niggaz still treat me like I'm fourteen going to the store for y'all?" Ashanti scoffed.

"Ain't nobody treating you like nothing, God. I know you wanna smoke and you probably ain't got no weed, so make that happen so we can burn," Lakim told him.

"A'ight, but I ain't rolling," Ashanti said before getting off the stoop and going next door to the bodega. Ashanti came out of the store and tossed the Dutch to Lakim. "Where we gonna blow at, because I sure as hell ain't trying to smoke out here with all this *bacon* around."

"My whip is parked around the corner. We can blow it down in there." Lakim led them around the corner to where his black-on-black Durango was parked. He hit automatic locks and climbed behind the wheel while Alonzo got in on the passenger side and Ashanti climbed in back.

"This shit is hard," Ashanti said, admiring the black leather seats.

Lakim shrugged. "It's a'ight. Give us another year and watch how me and my niggaz gonna be rolling."

"Yo, remember when you had the money-green Range on twenties?" Alonzo reminded Lakim as he sealed the ends of the blunt he was rolling.

"You mean the one you crashed." Lakim elbowed him playfully. "Zo-Pound, if you wasn't my li'l brother I would've killed you behind that shit."

Ashanti looked at Alonzo quizzically. "Zo-Pound?"

"Yeah, that's what they used to call me back in the days," Alonzo told him.

"I used to hear Animal and them talking about a kid named Zo-Pound who was doing his thing in the BX , but this kid was supposed to be a certified beast."

"Yeah, that was a long time ago." Alonzo's eyes took on a far-off look.

"Get the fuck outta here," Ashanti said in disbelief. "I can't see your box-stacking ass out here getting it in the trap."

"That goes to show how green your li'l ass still is to this game. Before my brother squared up he was out here laying shit down left and right," Lakim informed him.

Ashanti looked shocked. "Damn, kid, if you was out here getting it like that, what made you square up?"

"Prison," Alonzo said seriously. "I was getting bread out here on the streets but the bullshit I had to deal with wasn't worth running the risk of spending the rest of my life in a cage. There comes a point in every man's life when he looks back on the things he's done and looks ahead to the things he will do and asks himself it it's worth it. For me it wasn't, so I hung up my guns."

"Shit, I ain't never gonna put my gun down." Ashanti patted his waistband. "The only thing that's gonna separate me from my hammer is death!"

"Be careful what you wish for," Alonzo told him.

Lakim sensed that Alonzo was about to start preaching to Ashanti so he changed the subject. "Yo, Zo, what you getting into tonight?"

"My fucking bed, I'm tired as hell."

"Why don't you roll with us to Jersey?"

"What the fuck is going on in Jersey?" Alonzo asked suspiciously, fumbling with the radio dial.

"They got this li'l strip joint out there that we wanna hit up," Lakim said, as if it were as simple as that.

Alonzo looked at him. "La, y'all don't even do strip clubs in New York like that, so why would you wanna roll all the way to Jersey to hit one?"

"Sun, stop being so paranoid. We gonna go out and have some drinks and look at some ass. Besides, me and King got some business to handle."

Alonzo sighed. "Come on, La, you know I ain't trying to get caught up in no street shit."

"Li'l bro, I know you on ya square shit so I wouldn't even do you like that. I just thought that you might wanna come out and have a good time with us. Sun, you go from work to home every day and never have any fun, that shit ain't healthy for a young man of your age," Lakim teased him.

"Fuck you." Alonzo laughed.

"Yo, turn that up," Ashanti said excitedly from the backseat as a familiar tune came on the radio. Alonzo turned the volume up and Animal's familiar voice came through the speakers.

"Who that?" Lakim asked.

"That's my nigga Animal," Ashanti said proudly.

"Damn, I ain't know he was nice like that." Alonzo

bobbed to the beat. "That shit was crazy how he just vanished."

"Word on some Harry Houdini shit," Lakim added.

"I heard Rico sent his peoples to snatch him up and murdered him over them cats he killed," Alonzo said.

"I doubt that," Ashanti said, recalling the look on Rico's face before he had shot him outside the church.

"Niggaz like Animal don't die that easy. Sun is probably on some Tupac shit and hiding out in Cuba," Lakim suggested.

"Lakim, you sound crazy right now. Dude's face was way too known for him to be hiding somewhere. If the police or the feds ain't got him yet, then he's gotta be dead."

"The feds ain't God. Assata Shakur outwitted them so why couldn't Animal?" Lakim turned to Ashanti. "You knew him better than anybody, what do you think?"

Ashanti took a deep pull off the blunt and thought about it for a minute. "Honestly I don't know, but I can't accept the fact that he's dead." Most, including Brasco and Nefertiti, had written Animal off after his disappearance, but not Ashanti. Part of what had kept him going throughout the years since Animal's disappearance was his hope that one day they would be reunited and the team would be back better than ever. It was a stretch, but it was all he had.

Part II

LOVE AND WAR

CHAPTER 12

Old San Juan, Puerto Rico

In the light of day, Old San Juan looked almost serene with its borders of clear blue water, sprawling green hills, and historic architecture. Tourists moved about freely, going in and out of the shops that lined the street and taking pictures near various landmarks, oblivious to the blood spilled on the cobblestoned streets on a nightly basis. Among the tourists and locals, the shadow of death moved silently, lost in his thoughts of yesterday and tomorrow.

In what seemed like another lifetime he had been called Animal, a baby-faced killer who had gone from a thug to a superstar to a wanted man both by the police and by his enemies. When his sins had finally caught up with him in the form of the police, Animal secretly breathed a sigh of relief. Not because he was in a rush to be carted off to prison for the rest of his life, but because he could finally stop running—running from his past and the demons that haunted him every day of his life. Animal was ready to repent and accept responsibility for the things he had done, but fate had another plan.

They came for him in broad daylight, armed assassins who descended on his police escort like dark angels armed with assault rifles, who had no fear of death or the law. At first glance Animal had thought them to be his enemies who had come to settle up for the lives he had taken throughout his underworld career, but he soon learned different. Lying in a pool of blood and glass, Animal looked up into the green eyes of his abductor and knew the truth: they were not angels but demons who had been sent by the devil himself, K-Dawg.

At the turn of the century, K-Dawg and Animal's brother Justice were leaders of a crew called the Road Dawgz, which had conquered the streets of Harlem. Their run was short yet memorable, and under the rule of the Road Dawgz New York had become the murder capital. K-Dawg's tyrannical reign had forced the city officials into action and they closed in on the Road Dawgz. Justice was carted off to prison, but K-Dawg didn't go so quietly. K-Dawg's last stand had made headlines in every major newspaper and been broadcast on every news channel as he held court in the streets. The battle had wiped out not only the rest of the Road Dawgz but an entire city block when K-Dawg blew up their headquarters, killing more than fifty people, including himself, or so everyone thought. The fact that Animal was now a free man wandering the streets of Puerto Rico proved something that most speculated but would not say out loud: you could not kill the devil.

Animal was both shocked and unnerved by K-Dawg's appearance. Like everyone else, he had assumed that K-Dawg had died in the explosion, but his bold rescue was proof that he hadn't. Since his abduction Animal hadn't seen much of K-Dawg, but the kid he'd left to watch over him, Chris, was cool as hell. He did all that they could to make sure Animal felt more like a guest than a prisoner, but even he wouldn't elaborate on K-Dawg's plans. Animal would remain in the dark until they reached a small airstrip in North Carolina, where K-Dawg had chartered a plane to whisk them to Puerto Rico, and Justice was there to greet him.

Animal was overcome with emotions and questions when he saw his brother again after so many years. After his stint with the Road Dawgz, and a short stretch up north, Justice had gone into semiretirement, but ended up catching a body and going right back to prison. It was a self-defense killing, as the victim had been trying to rob Justice and his girl, but a paid informant testified to hearing Justice planning the murder. With the word of the snitch and Justice's reputation as one of the alleged leaders of the Road Dawgz crew, the judge wasted no time in throwing the book at Justice. He was given the long walk, and locked away never to be seen again, but, as with Animal, K-Dawg had intervened and changed his fate.

It was on the plane that Animal learned of the devil's bargain he had unknowingly struck in exchange for his freedom. K-Dawg had gone from hood politics to covert operations, and from the looks of things he was excelling at it. Unlike most, K-Dawg had learned from his mistakes and restructured his operation accordingly. He had assembled a team of wayward souls and molded them into his vision of the chosen army, deadly, merciless, and loyal to none but him. The name Los Negros Muertes was whispered throughout the urban ghettos of the Caribbean as the real power behind several political parties. Justice tried to assuage Animal's apprehensiveness by making it seem like what K-Dawg was doing was done out of love, but Animal knew better. For men like K-Dawg, love was an alien thing, and all that mattered was power. The members of Los Negros Muertes were little more than pawns in K-Dawg's game and Animal didn't plan on sticking around for the final move.

"Hey, mister," a voice called, snapping Animal out of his thoughts. His body immediately tensed in anticipation of combat, but eased when he saw the short and thin Hispanic boy approaching him. "Can I get you to buy some of my jewelry to help me and my family get a hot meal for the night?" The boy held up his arm to show Animal some of the rinky-dink jewelry dangling from it. Most of it was slum, but there was a silver rosary that caught Animal's eye.

"How much for that?" Animal pointed at the rosary.

"An excellent choice." The boy untangled the rosary and placed it in Animal's hand. "Handcrafted and made from sterling silver. This piece goes all the way back to the year—"

"I didn't ask you all that. I just want to know how much?" Animal cut him off.

The boy thought on it for a minute. "For you, amigo, two hundred dollars."

Animal laughed. "Li'l fella, if you're looking to rob me you could've at least brought a gun with you. That old piece of junk don't look to be worth much, especially not the ransom you're trying to charge for it."

"Junk?" The youth frowned. "Sir, this rosary was a gift to Nicolas de Ovando himself on the day of his baptism and has been handed down through his family for years. It's not only an heirloom but a piece of Old San Juan's history."

Animal examined the piece a little more closely. Though the silver was dull and stained, you could see the detailed craftsmanship that had gone into making it. "If it's such a valued treasure, how did your li'l ass come by it?"

The boy thought on it for a minute before answering. "How it came to me isn't important, my friend. What is important is that I am willing to part with it for the sake of making sure my family doesn't go hungry tonight." The boy's voice was quite sincere, but Animal saw the larceny in his eyes.

"I'll tell you what," Animal pulled out a knot of money and peeled off one hundred dollars, "I'll give you fifty dollars for the rosary and fifty dollars for your hustle. If that ain't enough, you might as well take it down the street and try to beat one of these crackers outta their bread, because I ain't going no higher." Animal extended the hundred dollars to the boy. The boy hesitated, but when Animal went to put the money back in his pocket, the boy quickly snatched it from him.

"Sir, it pains me to part with this treasure for so little money but it would pain me more to watch my little brother and sister go hungry for the night." The boy stuffed the money into his pocket.

"You are wise beyond your years." Animal smiled down at him while slipping the rosary around his neck over the gold link chain he was already wearing. There was something calming about the rosary lying across his chest.

"Looks good on you, sir." The boy nodded in approval.

"Yeah, it does look good on you." An older kid came out of the cut. He was flanked by two rough-looking dudes. "Since you're feeling like giving back to the poor kids in Puerto Rico, how about you kick something down to us?"

Animal stepped between the kid he'd bought the rosary

from and the thugs. "Get out of here, kid," Animal said over his shoulder. The boy wasted no time in getting away from the confrontation. Animal now focused on the thugs. "The three of you look able enough, you ever thought about getting jobs instead?"

"Oh, you're a comedian, huh?" the second boy said in a thick accent. His sneer showed off the missing teeth behind his dry lips.

"Nah, funny would be us having to explain to the *policia* why we threw down in the middle of a busy street in broad daylight," Animal said coolly. "Come on, fellas, we ain't gotta do it like this."

The first boy pulled a knife from his pants and brandished it. "You're right, so why don't you hand over the chains and whatever money you're carrying and you can go on your way without getting carved up."

Animal let out a deep sigh, as he already knew how he would answer. "I think we both know that I can't do that, so I guess it's gonna be what it's gonna be, huh?"

By the time the third boy who had been standing with the group tried to blindside Animal, he was already in motion. He dodged the awkward punch and folded him with a hook to the back of the head. The boy was out before he hit the ground. Animal had just managed to draw his pistol from his waist when one of the boys brought a pipe cracking down across his wrist and sent the gun flying. Animal tried to make for the gun when he was bull-rushed by a boy wielding a knife. The boy was good, but Animal was more skilled. When he lunged with the knife, Animal sidestepped it, but not before the blade had cut through his shirt and opened up his side.

Animal locked the boy's arms under, immobilizing him

and leaving him at Animal's mercy. "It's been a while since a nigga made me bleed, but allow me to give you a lesson in suffering." Animal wrenched the boy's arm upward, breaking it at the elbow and causing him to release the knife. Animal caught the blade before it hit the ground and dragged it across his throat. The boy's eyes widened in terror right before blood began to spill from his mouth and throat. Animal tossed him to the ground to bleed out and turned his attention to his last opponent. "What you waiting for, homie?"

The remaining thug croaked out something in Spanish, and the next thing Animal knew, more thugs were coming out of the woodwork and he found himself backed into a corner. They were at least a half-dozen deep and armed. It was about to pop off.

He had been warned: *keep a low profile and avoid causing scenes*. These were the words K-Dawg and Justice had drilled into Animal when he was first introduced to his new life, but their words were drowned out now by the demon whispering in his head that it had been too long since he had fed his cravings. Being confined to boundaries set by K-Dawg was making him feel closed off from his true nature and he needed a release. The thugs had come along looking for a victim, but what they had found was an animal.

"This is your last chance to leave with your dignities and your lives," Animal snarled at the thugs. He tossed the knife from one hand to the other and back again, testing the weight and getting a feel for the weapon.

"We're gonna fuck you up now, bro," the thug who had hit him with the pipe threatened.

Animal nodded. "So be it." He moved with more speed

than any of them had expected, swinging the knife in a complex pattern, causing the thugs to backpedal. One of the thugs felt himself and tried to step in the square with Animal, waving a box cutter. Animal faked high and went low, opening the kid's belly with the knife. When he stooped over to try to stop his guts from spilling into the street, Animal drove the knife into the base of his skull, severing his spine and taking him out of the equation. Another kid swung a bat at Animal's head and ended up connecting with air because Animal was already standing behind him with a fistful of his T-shirt. Animal shoved him into the crowd and bolted for the street.

Animal dodged through the busy marketplace with the thugs hot on his heels. Had he known his little shopping trip would turn into a mad dash for his life, he probably would've stayed at the house. He laughed as he thought about how he managed to end up fleeing for his life no matter what country he was in. A shot whisking past his ear from one of the thugs wiped the smile off his face and brought him back to the reality of what he was dealing with. One of the thugs managed to close the distance and get close enough to grab the back of Animal's shirt. Without breaking his stride, he spun around and cut the thug across his face, which would require almost fifty stitches when he finally got around to getting it treated.

Animal had managed to put some distance between himself and the thugs chasing him, but his pack-per-day cigarette habit was catching up with him. He tripped over a fruit basket, which allowed the thugs to get close enough to try to grab for him again, but fate intervened when a flower cart was pushed out into the street and tripped the thugs up. The boy who had sold Animal the rosary gave him the thumbs-up and motioned for him to keep going. As Animal's lungs began to heave he tired of the game and decided to put an end to it. He came across an alley a few blocks down and ducked into it, determined to bring the chase to a close.

The thug who had hit Animal with the pipe was the first to arrive at the mouth of the alley, with the rest of his mob joining him a few seconds after. He couldn't see much, but he heard Animal moving in the darkness. "Let me get the hammer," he said over his shoulder. After a short conversation about who was armed, he was handed a gun and led his party into the alley. It was so quiet that all he could hear was his heart pounding in his ears. A can rattled somewhere to his left, causing him to fire two blind shots into the darkness. A frightened alley cat darted past him and into the street. When the thug turned his attention back to the hunt, something whistled past his ear, followed by a warm splatter on his face. When he touched his hand to his cheek, it came away slick with blood. He initially thought it was his blood until he saw one of his comrades fall to the floor.

"You wanna play, muthafucka, then let's play." The thug fired blindly into the shadows.

"I sure hope you're keeping track of them shells you're wasting," Animal taunted.

"You stick your ugly face out here and I'll show you just how many bullets are left in this gun!" the thug shouted. He could no longer hide the fear in his voice. There was a scuttling of feet somewhere to his rear. The thug turned in time to see one of his boys swept away by the darkness. There was a bloodcurdling scream and the boy spilled out and collapsed at the thug's feet. His neck was cut from ear to ear. Most of the group hightailed it out of the alley, leaving just the thug and one of his partners, who was too frightened to run.

"You smell that? That's fear, baby boy, sweeter than any drug you can image." Animal cackled.

The thug was now so nervous that his palms were sweating and it became a task just to hold the gun. Something flew at him from the darkness and he fired four times before he realized it was a trash-can lid he'd just mangled. He was so focused on the trash-can lid that he didn't notice Animal standing behind him until he heard his remaining comrade scream. He turned just in time to see Animal gut the frightened young boy like a fish. The thug raised his gun and pulled the trigger, but it clicked empty.

"I told you to keep track of those shells." Animal stalked toward the thug with blood dripping from the knife. The thug was so afraid that he was still holding his gun as if it could save him. Animal smacked the gun away and grabbed him by the throat, pinning him against the wall. He pressed the blade against the thug's cheek and traced a pattern. "You ready to stand before your maker and be judged?"

"Please don't," the thug blabbered.

Animal frowned in disappointment. "Mercy is for God-fearing folks." He leaned in and whispered into the thug's ear, "I fear nothing." Animal had just pierced the tender skin of the thug's throat when he heard a voice behind him.

"For as much as I love a good bloodbath, I think there's been enough killing done for one day."

CHAPTER 13

She was an exotic bronze beauty with eyes the color of mercury and hair that resembled sunset. The cut-off fatigue shorts and black tank top she wore clung to her shapely figure like a second skin. She licked her lips playfully, but the AK cradled in her arms said that she was all business. Watching her back was a tall dark-skinned cat with hawk-like features. Though his guns weren't visible, there was no doubt that he was armed.

"This is no business of yours," Animal said through clenched teeth.

"It becomes my business when bodies line my father's streets." She slung the machine gun over her shoulder and strode into the alley. She made sure to keep a safe distance from Animal, who was still watching her intensely. "Do you know who I am?" she asked the thug Animal had snatched up.

The boy cut his eyes at Animal for permission to speak. When Animal eased his grip, he took it as a yes. "Of course . . . who doesn't know Red Sonja?" he croaked.

"Then you know it was foolish of you to attack one of our guests."

Realizing how deep in the shit he had stepped, the thug

began to tremble. "Sonja, on my mother's eyes I didn't know he was with you guys. We were just trying to roll him for a few dollars," he groveled.

"From all of your homeboys stretched out up and down this alley, I'm guessing it didn't work out too well for you, huh?" Sonja closed the last of the distance between them. "Amigo, I may be able to convince my friend to let you live, but I need to know that this isn't going to turn into a bigger problem in the future."

"No problems, no problems," the thug assured her.

Sonja slowly and cautiously placed a hand on Animal's shoulder. She felt him tense, but eventually he loosened up under her touch. She leaned in close enough for her lips to brush his neck when she whispered, "Poppy, the streets of Old San Juan see how you give it up and the word will be spread. There's nothing left to prove here."

"This pussy tried to take my life, the scales gotta balance out," Animal told her, pressing the knife into the thug's throat again.

"And you have killed at least three of his, from what I can see. Too many bodies in the street lead to too many questions and I think we both know you don't need that right now." She slowly began pulling Animal away. "No more bloodshed today."

Slowly, Animal eased back to the point where he was holding the thug at arm's reach and glaring at him like a hungry tiger. The beast lurking inside Animal cried for more death, and though Sonja's touch was soothing enough to bring about reason, there still needed to be compensation. "Your life is yours for today," Animal told the thug, "but you will be forever reminded of my passing." Animal dragged the knife down the thug's cheek, opening him up.

* * *

At the west end of the island was the Fort San Felipe del Morro. It had originally been built to protect San Juan Bay and the city of Old San Juan from seaborne invaders but had long ago become more of a tourist attraction than an actual military base. People visiting Old San Juan would occasionally venture out to see the fort and its lighthouse, but with the rash of violence that had broken out in and around the village, few dared to venture out that far, which is why K-Dawg chose to make his base in the shadow of the ruined fort.

It was a large farmhouse with a few head of cattle that sat in the middle of nowhere so as to maintain his privacy, not that anyone would be foolish enough to breach the fence that encircled all ten acres of the farm. Vicious guard dogs, bred and raised by K-Dawg, roamed the grounds and would kill without hesitation to protect their master's keep. K-Dawg had many secret hiding places like it, but the farmhouse was special to him because it had been his first real purchase when he was getting money in New York. While most of his comrades spent their money on guns and whores, K-Dawg had been planning for his future.

The farmhouse was safe haven to all members of Los Negros Muertes, but only those closest to K-Dawg actually lived there. When Animal had first arrived in Puerto Rico he'd been offered a place of honor in the farmhouse, but he had declined, opting to make his home in a smaller structure that sat a few yards off from the main house. The small building was said to have once been slave quarters, which struck Animal as ironic considering his current circumstances.

Animal's room was a shadow of his home in Houston or even his apartment in Harlem for that matter. There were no big-screen televisions, no video games, and hardly any electronics at all except for a desk lamp and a satellite radio that sat on his nightstand. On the walls were maps of Puerto Rico and other Caribbean ports marked with red and green thumbtacks that formed strange patterns that only Animal understood. Stacked in corners and scattered on the floor were piles of newspapers and a few magazines. Most of them were New York *Daily News*es, as Animal liked to stay abreast of what was going on stateside. It was one of the few connections he had left to the home he'd been forced to flee.

"Shit, be careful with that thing," Animal said. He was topless and lying on his side across his full-size bed. At his side, Red Sonja sat on a small stool beside the bed with what looked like a sewing needle pinched between her fingers.

"You cry more than a girl. Now quit fidgeting so I can finish," she told him, adjusting the gooseneck lamp so she could see his wound better.

"That sounds familiar," Animal said slyly, which paused her stitching. Animal looked over his shoulder and saw the sadness that had crossed her face. "I was only joking, Sonja."

"Well, it wasn't funny." She folded her arms. Sonja bit her lip in frustration. "Everything is a joke to you, including people's feelings. Ain't you got no heart, Animal?"

He paused before answering. "I used to, but these days I ain't so sure." His answer seemed only to frustrate her more. "Sonja, when you've lost as much as I have, it makes it hard to feel for anything, or anyone. When you're an outlaw, you live in the moment and don't too much worry about tomorrow."

"That's a fucked-up way to live."

"Unfortunately, it's the only way I know how," he said honestly. Since he'd arrived in Puerto Rico, Sonja had been trying to get Animal to open up. She was a good chick and had provided him with comfort when he needed it, but Animal never let it go beyond that. She needed something that he couldn't give so he kept her at arm's length. He could tell by the look on her face that she wanted to press the issue, as she often did, so he changed the subject. "How the hell do you know how to stitch a wound anyway?"

"Well, after I graduated high school I went to the army and got my RN. I did a tour of the Middle East, so that kept my hands full, but after a while it became too intense so I hung it up after my first tour. I ended up working at Cook County Hospital for two years before coming back to Puerto Rico to take care of my father." She went back to threading the needle in and out of his skin expertly.

"Damn, I can't imagine what was worse, the Middle East or South Side Chicago. I'll bet you've seen some shit the way those Folks and Vice Lords be out there butchering each other, huh?"

Sonja stopped her stitching and looked up at him. "It ain't no worse than what the Bloods and Crips are doing to each other in L.A. and New York. What makes your gang holier than theirs when at the end of the day it's all genocide?"

"If that ain't the pot calling the kettle black," Animal capped. "For the time I've been here I ain't seen nothing but Puerto Ricans banging on Puerto Ricans. Fuck how many of these li'l hoppers Poppito had us lay down out here, and he was born and raised in P.R.?"

Sonja thought on it before responding. "The war going on out here is way deeper than what you guys have going on. Even though Puerto Rico is technically a part of the United States, look at how differently we live. The United States is supposed to defend itself from enemies both foreign and domestic, but it's the domestic terrorists like Cruz and his people that are being ignored. Yeah, drugs are what it's about on the surface, but this shit goes *way* deeper. Cruz and his people will run Puerto Rico more crooked than the letter *S* if they're left unchecked," she said heatedly. "I don't agree with the spilling of black or brown blood, but who wants to live under the yoke of somebody motivated more by greed than what's best for the people?"

"If you're against the spilling of black and brown blood, then why play the game for Poppito?" he asked sincerely.

"Because he's my father and the well-being of my family comes before the well-being of everybody, including my country," she said seriously.

Animal quietly drank in not only the weight of her words but the passion in her eyes when she spoke them. Red Sonja was a conundrum to him. She could go from being a socialite princess to a soldier in less than a breath and be believable in either role. Her strong will and no-nonsense attitude reminded him of Gucci, but there was another element to her that was alien to Animal. Had it been another place and another time, Animal would've enjoyed the challenge of trying to peel back the layers of Red Sonja to see what made her tick, but his soul was promised to another, so they would never be more than comrades in the war he had been selected to fight.

"Enough chitchat. I need to finish patching you up so I can get back to my own business. Flip over on your stomach," she told him. Animal smiled back at her flirtatiously. "Let's not go there again for both our sakes. The cut goes around to your back and I just need to finish closing it, so don't flatter yourself. And just because I may bed the *help* from time to time doesn't mean I get caught up with them."

Her remark cut him, but he kept his composure. "Baby, I ain't never helped nothing but *myself* and don't plan on deviating from that, so please don't group me in with the last New York nigga you might've had to stitch up out here. I'm a whole different breed," Animal said with confidence and rolled over so that she could get at the cut.

Sonya straddled his back to get a better angle at the slash and purposely jabbed him with the needle when she went back to her stitching. "Had it been just anybody, they wouldn't have made it out of the town square, let alone have me stitching their wounds. One thing anybody will tell you about Red Sonja is that I don't do something for nothing." She closed the stitch, then leaned in to bite the end of the thread off. As she did so she made sure to press her chest against his back so he could feel her stiff nipples through the tank top. Sonja leaned in and let her soft lips brush against his ear as she whispered, "I see potential in you, gringo, and I think you'll be more valuable to me alive than dead." She slapped him on his ass playfully and rolled off him.

Animal got off the bed and walked over to the dusty dressing mirror. He raised his arm and examined the expert job Sonja had done with his cut. "Damn, you do some good work."

"You don't have to tell me what I already know,"

Sonja said over her shoulder as she washed her hands in the kitchenette sink. "Let me ask you something." She approached him, drying her hands on a towel. "What the hell were you doing wandering the ghettos by yourself?"

"Just taking a walk," Animal said, as if it was just that simple.

"Poppy, this ain't Manhattan, this is the trenches and we are in the middle of a political war. You can't just go for an afternoon stroll like that."

"Why not? We're all children of the ghetto, be it P.R. or N.Y., so why should I have to feel in a way about taking a walk?" he asked.

At first Sonja thought he was being sarcastic but his eyes said he was serious. "You just can't." She sighed. Her answer seemed only to confuse him more and it saddened her. Without meaning to, she reached out and stroked his cheek affectionately. There was such a childlike innocence to Animal that unless you had seen him in action you wouldn't believe that he was a mass murderer. Animal was like a two-sided coin: one side a bright-eyed young man who loved to read and take walks and the other a cold killer birthed in the streets of New York and baptized by pain.

"Is this a bad time?" The voice startled them. Justice was standing in the half-open doorway, watching them with an amused look on his face. He was dressed in denim shorts, white Nike Airs, and a white T-shirt. His long hair was braided into two ponytails that hung down his back. Justice was almost a mirror twin of Animal except his skin was a little lighter and he sported a neatly trimmed beard.

"No, it's cool. I was just patching your li'l brother up," Sonja said. Though she and Animal hadn't been doing anything, the look Justice was giving them made her feel guilty. "I'll catch you guys later. I got some errands to run."

"I'll bet." Justice smirked as Sonja passed him on her way out. He strode into Animal's room, crunching newspapers under his feet. Justice picked one up and glanced over the two-week-old headline about a shooting in Harlem. "Damn, why don't you throw some of these old-ass newspapers away?"

"I gotta stay up on what's going down on the home front," Animal told him.

"I don't know why, it ain't like your ass will be setting foot back in New York anytime soon." Justice laughed, but Animal didn't. "What's good with you and shorty?" He was referring to Sonja.

Animal shrugged. "Nothing. I got into a little scrape and Sonja pulled my ass out of the fire."

"From the look of that beauty mark it looks like a little more than a scrape." Justice nodded at the freshly stitched cut. "But I think you and I both know that ain't what I meant."

Animal pulled a black T-shirt over his head. "If you're trying to ask if I'm fucking her the answer is no." Animal's tone was less than convincing.

"For as much time as the two of you spend together, you should be." Justice laughed.

"You know it's only one chick that'll ever have my heart," Animal said seriously.

"Damn, I was just playing, li'l bro." Justice flopped on the bed. "That Gucci broad must've been a real special lady, huh?"

"You have no idea. Gucci fit me like a missing piece to a puzzle." He closed his eyes and saw her face in his head.

"When you went to prison and Tech got killed I felt like I didn't have nobody, but when Gucci came along, all that changed. I wish you had had a chance to meet her."

"Me too, so I could've thanked her," Justice said sincerely.

"Thank her for what?" Animal was curious.

"Sit down for a second, my nigga." Justice motioned toward the spot on the bed next to him. Justice had envisioned this talk with his little brother a million times, but he suddenly couldn't find the rehearsed words, so he did what he should have done from the beginning a kept it one hundred with his little brother. "You have no idea how much I stressed over you while I was locked up. I left you in a fucked-up predicament and the streets ended up raising you instead of me."

"I think she did okay." Animal brushed his shoulders off playfully.

Justice mustered a weak smile but it didn't take away from the pain behind his eyes. "Tayshawn, you are a master of words with everyone you encounter, but we come from the same womb so I can see through it. Tech taught you the ropes and you became your own man, but you had to give up your childhood for it. Instead of learning how to approach girls, you were learning how to load guns. That ain't no way for a kid to live."

"C'mon, Jus, you're acting like I turned out all fucked up and shit. I've done more in my young life than most niggaz twice my age have even wrapped their minds around. From the trap to the billboards, I did it big! Before I got caught up with all this I had made it out, remember?"

Justice laughed at his brother's ignorance. "Homie, you opened the door to get out, but you ain't step all the way through it. If you'd really made it then you wouldn't be hiding out over here with the rest of us hard-luck-ass nig-gaz. I was beyond proud of you when you was doing the music thing. I used to show everybody the magazines and shit and tell them that you were my brother." He smiled. "That was definitely a great accomplishment, but what I was most proud of you for was being wise enough to fi-nally lay those demons to rest, and I know that's largely in part to Gucci."

"Dude, you're talking some Love Jones shit and you don't even know the Gucci. For all you know she could've been a crab bitch."

"Animal, just because I was locked up don't mean I didn't have eyes and ears on the street. I knew ya chick's résumé from the first time you dropped her name to me in a kite, because that was the first sign that it was getting se-rious, even if your li'l ignorant ass hadn't seen it yet. More importantly, I know you, li'l bro. I don't respect Gucci because she was your girl, I respect her because she was able to help you find something neither Tech nor I was able to . . . peace."

"True," Animal said, looking down at his feet.

"I know is. In a perfect world you and shorty would've been able to make a life together and do something with your success, but shit ain't go down like that. You killed any chance of that happening the minute you set foot back in New York and picked up a gun, and I blame myself be-cause had I been home and on my job instead of upstate, then it wouldn't have played out that way." Justice's voice was heavy with emotion.

"Sometimes shit happens, Justice. I knew that before I even stepped into the arena," Animal said. "Jus, I know I fucked up a great life but I'm thankful that I'm still here to reflect on it. Shit is way complicated for me right now but I know one day I'm gonna get it all worked out. At this point I'd be a fool to think that I can walk back into my old life and expect Gucci and me to pick up where we left off, but I hold on to the hope that if we can't have love we can at least have closure. Fuck, I didn't even say good-bye before I left, and that's gonna haunt me until I make it right."

Justice gave him a serious look. "Homie, if you come within three feet of Gucci the only closure you're gonna have is a coffin lid."

Animal sucked his teeth. "Justice, you know your little brother knows how to conduct himself out in the world." He picked up the pistol that had been resting on the night table and chambered a round.

"Animal, have you forgotten you're a fugitive from justice? You're a convicted murderer, and when them cops went down, that killed any hope you had of ever living a normal life. You are a wanted man, my friend, by the streets and law enforcement. If your enemies don't kill you, the police are sure as hell going to drop you in a ditch somewhere. You touch U.S. soil and you're finished."

"So what do y'all expect me to do, hide out in the jungles of Puerto Rico for the rest of my life?" Animal snapped.

"Nah, man, this shit is way bigger than just P.R. K-Dawg has got some real Poppa Doc shit going on that stretches further than even I'm absolutely sure of. From here we push out to the next port and the next payday. Who knows, maybe we'll land in Europe next and I can finally sample one of those euro devils!" Justice burst out laughing.

"Y'all can do whatever y'all want, Justice, but as soon as the heat dies down I'm out," Animal said.

Justice stopped laughing and became very serious. "My nigga, do you know what it took for K-Dawg to get us our lives back? A few years ago I was lying on my bunk jerking my dick and you were on your way to the gas chamber, but look at us now." Justice pointed out the window to the farmhouse that loomed in the distance. "We're fucking the baddest bitches, smoking the best weed, and driving eighty-thousand-dollar cars. But for as good as we're living, all this shit comes with a price, and in this case the price is loyalty to the man who made it all possible."

"I agree with you on that, but for as grateful as I am to K-Dawg for busting me out of prison, there's only so far I'm willing to go to prove that. I'm gonna thug this shit out with y'all for as long as I need to, but this ain't my life, Justice. I've got things that need to be put in order."

"So you mean to say you'd risk going back to prison or getting killed just to kiss your li'l girlfriend good-bye?" Justice gave him a confused look.

"Better to die in love than in war," Animal told him.

Justice grabbed him in a playful headlock and mussed his hair. "My poor love-struck li'l brother."

"Get the hell off me." Animal pushed him away. "What're you doing out here anyway? I thought you'd have been up in the main house with ya man plotting to take over some third-world country."

"See, that's your problem, you think too damn small. Fuck a country, we're gonna take over the world, but we need all of our Road Dawgz on the same page and this means you too, li'l brother."

"I ain't no Dawg," Animal said sharply.

Justice just smiled. "You're a Dawg, li'l bro, whether you wanna admit it or not. It's in your blood, and no matter what that bleeding-ass heart of yours says, blood is thicker than anything else and you'd do well to remember it."

"Whatever. You still haven't answered my question. What are you doing here?"

"Boss Dawg wants to see you," Justice explained.

"Is that right? And what has ol' Animal done to get an invite to the massa's house?" Animal asked sarcastically.

"Why don't you knock it off with the smart-ass jokes and get serious for a minute. I don't know exactly what he wants, all he said was he needs you to do a favor."

Animal laughed. "The last time he did *me* a favor I ended up a hostage in a third-world country."

"You need to show a little respect to the man who pulled your ass out of the fire." Justice jabbed his finger toward Animal's face.

"And you might wanna watch where you jab that finger," Animal said coldly.

"Or what? Listen, don't play that big-bad-killer shit with me, I used to change your fucking diapers."

"Been a long time since I was in diapers, Jus."

Justice got in Animal's face, but his little brother didn't back down. "Don't test me, Animal."

Animal sized his brother up and for a minute he thought about trying him, but decided to let it go. "Ain't nobody testing you, Justice. I'm just tired of getting my strings jerked like a puppet."

Justice laid his hand on the back of Animal's neck and gave him an affectionate squeeze. "Little brother, I know

this is rough on you . . . it's rough on all of us, but sometimes we have to play the hands we're dealt."

"Even if we didn't ask to sit in the game?"

Justice hesitated. "Yes, even if we didn't ask to sit in on
the game. Now quit with the fucking questions and bring
your ass on. You don't wanna keep K-Dawg waiting." Justice left the room.

Animal didn't move right away. He considered ignoring K-Dawg's summons just to spite him and Justice, but
he knew that would only make Justice mad, which didn't
sound like a bad idea. Justice had been a heavy hitter in
his day, but Animal had killed far more men than half of
the original Road Dawgz put together. Still, in the presence of his big brother, Animal still felt like little Tayshawn.

CHAPTER 14

By the time Animal made it up the grassy path to the farmhouse, K-Dawg was already sitting outside, speaking with some of the others. It was well over eighty degrees, but he still wore a black turtleneck and black fatigue pants over black combat boots. When he leaned in to whisper something to Justice, the sun kissed his bald head and reminded Animal of a Milk Dud.

Sonja sat off to the side in a wicker chair with a toned leg thrown over one of the arms. She was wiping down a long black pistol with a rag, while Sincere hovered near her. From the look on his face, Animal knew he was whispering sweet nothings to her, which he always seemed to be doing. Sonja had confided in Animal that she and Sincere had had a thing for a while, but it was old news. From the way he loomed around her, it was apparent that he hadn't gotten the memo. When Sonja noticed Animal she rolled her eyes and walked into the house. Sincere glared at the approaching Animal and tried to mug him, but couldn't hold his gaze. Sincere was one of the most dangerous members of Los Negros Muertes but he was weighed down by something that would always make him a runner-up when it came to Animal . . . a soul.

"You look well for a man who got carved up like a turkey a few hours ago," Sincere said sarcastically.

"A jury of twelve couldn't take me out, then letting those street urchins do it would've been an insult to my pedigree. Besides"—Animal patted his bandaged side—"Sonja can work magic with those hands." He saw the hurt in Sincere's eyes when he made the statement.

"Yeah, Sonja had to lay hands on me a few times back in the days," Sincere boasted.

"So I've heard, but that girl has come a long way as far as technique." Animal cracked a diamond-toothed smile.

"If you two are finished trying to see whose dick is the biggest, there's a situation that I need to address," K-Dawg cut in.

Sincere continued to glare at Animal like he wanted to do something, but he wasn't fool enough to challenge K-Dawg's authority. "You got that, boss," he told K-Dawg.

"As long as you keep that in the forefront of your mind we'll never have a problem," K-Dawg assured Sincere. "Do me a favor: go get ready for that li'l thing we talked about. I wanna make sure everybody is correct when y'all roll out, feel me?"

"A'ight, Dawg." Sincere addressed K-Dawg but kept his eyes on Animal. "See you around, homie."

"Better you see me before I see you. It'll make it more fun," Animal capped back.

K-Dawg waited until Sincere was out of earshot before addressing Animal. "You two niggaz kill me, out here ready to off each other over a piece of pussy, but nobody's worried about the fact that that girl's daddy will have the both of you clipped if he finds out you're playing hide the salami with his daughter."

Animal raised his hands in surrender. "I have no clue what you're talking about."

"What-the-fuck-ever"—K-Dawg waved him off—"just remember that I warned you. So how've you been holding up out here, li'l bro, everything good?"

Animal made a dismissive gesture. "Outside of the fact that I'm a prisoner on this island, everything is roses."

K-Dawg frowned. "Animal, why are you always such a pessimist? Look around you"—he motioned at the countryside—"beautiful land, the best weed, and your choice of the finest women Puerto Rico has to offer. What more could you ask for?"

"To be free," Animal shot back.

"Listen, kid, I don't know if you got the memo or not but there ain't no such thing as free for you anymore, or have you forgotten about all those bodies you left laying around New York? Animal, out of love for your brother I extend my hand to you, but there's only but so many times I'm gonna let you spit in it."

"K-Dawg, he didn't mean anything by it. Animal is just having a hard time adjusting to all this," Justice interjected.

Animal waved him off. "You ain't no ventriloquist and I ain't no dummy so please stop speaking for me, Jus. K-Dawg, how long have you known me?"

"Shit, all your life. Even when you thought I was dead I was keeping tabs on you and the wild shit you were doing on them streets. Everybody feared the Animal and I had never been more proud of you."

Animal cracked a slight smile at the flattering words. "Thanks, big homie, but my point is: if you know me then you know I'm a man set in my ways. I had a life before you brought me here, Dawg, a life that one day I'd like to get back to or at least as close to it as I can." He thought of Gucci when he said this.

K-Dawg stared at Animal, waiting for the punch line, but his face said he was serious. At that moment K-Dawg didn't see the belligerent young killer but the little boy who used to try to follow him and Justice on capers. "Li'l bro, I know you think I'm being an asshole about all this, but trust me, I have your best interest in mind." He placed a hand on Animal's shoulder and looked at him seriously. "That long, dark road you're just starting down I've been walking on for more than ten years. In the blink of an eye everything and everybody I knew became dead to me, and I had to accept it or spend the rest of my life in captivity. I can't say it was the easiest thing I ever did, but there was only one real choice. If the only way my people can see me is through a glass until the end of time, then I might as well be dead to them anyway."

"Which is why I buried Tayshawn and will forever be Animal, but it's not that easy for some of us to just give everything up like that," Animal told him.

"Unfortunately, you're going to have to adjust. Animal, you walking outta here and risking getting caught not only puts you in danger but my people as well. My men trust me with their lives and I can't put them in harm's way, even for family."

Animal was silent for a long moment. He knew K-Dawg was trying to read him to see how he would react to the proclamation, but Animal was too seasoned to expose his hand too soon. For now he would let diplomacy speak where his guns normally would have. "I hear you, big homie."

"You hear me, but do you understand me?" K-Dawg glared at him.

"Justice said you needed something handled. What's popping?" Animal changed the subject.

K-Dawg peeped his tactic but wouldn't press the issue. "Indeed I do. Now I know you know the skinny as to why we're still in Puerto Rico—"

"Yeah, Poppito hates Cruz and we're here to whack Cruz," Animal cut him off. "We know all this, so let's just kill this muthafucka and move on."

K-Dawg laughed at Animal's outburst as he knew he was getting under his skin. "Animal, for as much as you picked up on the streets, it's amazing how much you still don't know. Political warfare is the real deal, so you gotta make sure you play it right or you'll find yourself locked in some third-world mudhole they call a prison or dead, and dead is lucky when you're playing with these guys. This ain't like capping drug dealers in the projects, so pay attention and you may actually live long enough to see that pretty li'l bitch you're stressing over."

Justice snickered.

"What the fuck are you laughing at?" K-Dawg turned his green eyes on Justice. "How many fucking fugitives do you know that have Facebook pages? I don't know if it's a genetic defect or what, but you and your brother better stop playing and get with the program. Now look: we done got these muthafuckas in check but there's still a move or two to be made before we can move them into mate."

K-Dawg pulled a Polaroid from his pocket and threw it onto the wicker table. The man in the picture was an older gentleman with hard eyes and bulldoglike cheeks. Atop his block-shaped head was a thick nest of salt-and-pepper hair that he wore slicked back.

Animal stared at the picture long enough to burn the image into his brain. "Who is that?"

"The last rook on the board." K-Dawg grinned wickedly. "Cruz pulls the strings because he's police, but it's this piece of shit that the street soldiers listen to."

"This old fuck"—Animal frowned—"he don't look so tough to me."

"That because you're young and dumb, kid." K-Dawg smirked. "In the late seventies and early eighties that nigga had Spanish Harlem rocking until a fifteen-to-life rocked him. He served eighteen on that, then came home on parole and vanished. He's been out here for most of that time, helping Cruz organize his operation. Cruz is the brains but the old man is the finger on the trigger. Cruz is on the ropes right now. The people are starting to call for his head because of the rash of murders, his people are dying left and right, and the Puerto Rican government is about ready to wash their hands of him and his bullshit. The old man is the glue holding things together right now, so if we knock him out we take away Cruz's warlord and his street protection. Once the old man goes, this shit is gonna fall like dominoes and Cruz will have no choice but to try and go into hiding, which is what we want. As soon as he sticks his head out, I'm gonna blow it off."

"Sounds good to me. How soon do we move on the old guy?" Animal asked.

K-Dawg looked at his watch. "In a few hours."

Justice was surprised by the suddenness of the move and it showed on his face. "Forever the impulsive one, huh, Big Dawg?"

K-Dawg sensed his friend's apprehension and it made him smile. "Justice, you of all people should know better than that. I've been planning this hit for a month."

"So why didn't you let us in on it?"

"Because the information was on the need-to-know basis and you didn't *need to know* until now." K-Dawg picked up the picture and flicked a lighter under it. The Polaroid began to crinkle under the heat as the flames licked up the edges. "Besides, this one isn't for you, Justice. I'm putting Animal and Sincere on the case."

"Man, fuck all that, I can handle this on my own," Animal told him.

"I'm sure you can, but I want you to do it with Sincere. He's a good soldier."

Animal frowned in displeasure. "I don't doubt that, but the boy has got a serious attitude problem and I don't need him cramping my style while I'm trying to work."

"Look who the fuck is talking." K-Dawg glared at Animal. "Kid, you've been running around with a chip on your shoulder damn near since you got here, so let's not go casting stones. Now I know you're used to that lone-wolf shit, but you're part of the unit now, so all petty differences go out the window when it comes to business."

"So what's the game plan, Dawg? A dude this high up the food chain ain't likely to be an easy target," Justice said, changing the subject.

"The old man is no fool, so he doesn't have any set routines but one. Every two weeks he gets his hair cut at the same shit-hole barbershop down in the square."

"Why would somebody sitting on all that paper go down to the hood to get their hair cut?" Justice wondered aloud.

K-Dawg shrugged. "He's been using the same barber since he came to the island and refuses to let anyone else touch his hair. Some kinda superstitious shit, but who cares? His superstitious nature is our gain. I want this to be messy. When people hear what happened to that fuck, I want to send a very clear message."

"I'm good at sending messages. I got some preparations to make and I'll be ready to roll in a few," Animal told them and left the two men alone.

"Looks like we're about to wrap this up soon, huh?" Justice asked.

K-Dawg nodded. "As soon as I present Poppito with Cruz's head, we get our bread and we're outta here."

"So where to next—Europe, Asia? I never been to Japan but I heard that shit is popping."

"Your sightseeing tour will have to wait for a while, Jus. I've got some unfinished business locally that I need to wrap up before we move on."

"So we're staying in Puerto Rico?"

"Not exactly. Let's just say that there's a debt owed to me that I plan to collect in the very near future," K-Dawg said and walked into the house, leaving Justice to wonder.

CHAPTER 15

Old man Tony busied himself with sweeping up the excess hair around the two chairs in the tiny barbershop from the few morning cuts he'd administered. Normally at that time of day the shop would've been sprinkled with men from the neighborhood, getting haircuts or swapping stories, but Tony had closed down early to receive his *special* client.

The ringing bell over the front door startled the old man. In walked a heavyset man wearing a gray tracksuit and white running shoes. Flanking him was a round man with a large nose who wore a dead expression on his face.

"Hey, Grovaldo, good to see you." Tony stopped sweeping and walked over to greet the gangster.

"You know you're the only man on the island I'd let touch this pretty mop of mine." Grovaldo patted his high hair. He plopped into one of the chairs and got comfortable as Tony draped a smock around his neck.

"Grovaldo, I'd offer you some coffee but we're all out. I sent my boy home early and didn't have a chance to go to the store myself."

"Don't worry about it, Tony. I'll take care of it. Gino," he said, drawing the soldier's attention from the magazine he was reading in the next chair, "do you think you can pry yourself away from your studies and go grab us some coffees?"

"But the store is like five blocks away," Gino complained.

"It looks like you could use the exercise." Grovaldo laughed. "Now move your ass!"

"Alright, alright." Gino tossed the magazine down and hauled himself out of the chair.

"And while you're down there, get us some of those pastries the old lady makes," Grovaldo shouted after him. "I love those things, don't you, Tony?"

"*Sí.*" Tony grinned and nodded like he always did when Grovaldo spoke. "So, do you want your usual?" Tony began sharpening his razor on the leather strap hanging from the chair.

"Yeah, a little off the sides and clean up this stubble." Grovaldo ran his hand across his chin. "My girlfriend doesn't like the stubble on my face scratching her thighs when I'm going down on her." He laughed.

"Don't worry, your face will be as smooth as a baby's ass when I'm done," Tony assured him as he took the towels out of the steamer. He wrapped one around Grovaldo's face and began mixing shaving cream in a small cup.

"Tony, how long have I been coming to you to get my hair cut?" Grovaldo asked from beneath the towel.

"I don't know, maybe ten years or so. You've been a good customer and a loyal friend. When they rioted in the square back in ninety-eight my shop was the only business that didn't get touched, and I am thankful to have a friend like you."

"As you should be. Señor Cruz and I know how to take care of our friends, not like that Poppito and his bunch."

"We hear many horrible stories about him and Los Negros Muertes, not good at all. But Señor Cruz and his men make the streets safe for an old man like me," Tony lied. In all truthfulness, Cruz and his crooked cops were just as bad as Poppito, if not worse, because they had the government on their side.

"Damn right we do. Poppito thinks he's being cute by bringing blacks to do his dirty work, but we've got a trick for them. Soon there will be no question as to who controls Old San Juan," Grovaldo boasted.

"I as well as the citizens pray for the day when this war is brought to an end," Tony said sincerely.

Grovaldo went on and on, rambling, but Tony was only half listening. All he wanted to do was get the gangster out of his shop so he could go home to his family. He was just about to get started on Grovaldo's grooming when a gust of wind licked his cheek. When he made to turn, a gun barrel was placed against the back of his head. Sincere placed his finger over his lips, warning the barber to be silent, and Tony fearfully complied.

"Yes, my old friend, better days are on the horizon," Grovaldo said smugly as the towel around his face was unwrapped. He expected to look in the mirror and see Tony standing behind him, but instead he saw Sincere and a wild-haired young man standing in front of him holding two knives. He tried to get up, but Sincere yanked him back down with the towel wrapped around his neck.

"*Buenos días,*" Animal greeted him before driving the two knives into his hands, pinning them to the arms of the chairs. When Grovaldo opened his mouth to scream, Animal dumped the cup of shaving cream into it. "We can't have you waking the neighbors now, can we?"

"You cocksucking muthafuckas—do you know who I am?" Grovaldo gasped.

"I sure hope so, because I'd hate to have to do this all over again," Animal told him as he pulled out his Desert Eagle.

"What, am I supposed to be scared now? I've seen the devil and told him to suck my dick, so if you think you two li'l wet-behind-the-ears muthafuckas put fear in my heart, you can go fuck yourself." Grovaldo spat in Animal's face.

Animal calmly wiped the spit from his face with the back of his sleeve. He placed the gun back in his pants. He leaned in over Grovaldo and placed his hands on the hilt of the knives, driving them deeper into Grovaldo's hands.

"You muthafucka," Grovaldo bellowed.

"I've been called worse." Animal busied himself, rummaging through the barber's tools on the counter. When he turned back to Grovaldo he was holding a pair of scissors and tongs. "I was sent here to kill you, but I've got a better idea." He opened and closed the scissors. "You, my bigmouthed friend, will serve as a living reminder to those who challenge the authority of Los Negros Muertes. Now open wide, you little bitch."

The few blocks to the coffee shop and back felt like miles to the heavyset Gino. As he approached the barbershop there was a car pulling off, but he paid it no mind, as that area was high traffic at that time of day. When he entered the shop he dropped the coffee and pastries to the floor. Tony was slumped in one of the barber chairs with a bullet through his eye. On the floor, Grovaldo lay in a pool of his own blood. At first Gino through he was dead, but then he saw the man's leg move.

"Grovaldo." Gino knelt at his side. The blood on the floor seeped through his pants but he paid it no mind. When he flipped his boss over he had to fight the urge to vomit. Both his ears had been sawed off to the gristle, and one of his eyes was missing. What was left of his tongue flapped around in his mouth as he tried to speak, but all that came out was a distorted gurgling. Grovaldo was allowed to keep his life, if you could call the condition he was in a life, but it was just as Animal had promised: Grovaldo would serve as a living reminder of just how Los Negros Muertes gave it up.

When Animal got back to the farmhouse, K-Dawg was standing outside, smoking a cigar. He kept his eyes locked on Animal and Sincere as they came up the path. "I trust everything went well?"

Animal grabbed K-Dawg's hand and placed a small ring box in it. "Just a token of my appreciation, boss dawg." Animal laughed and walked off.

"What's good, everything go down okay?" K-Dawg asked Sincere.

"Man, I don't even wanna talk about that." Sincere ran his hands over his face. "Ya man has got some serious issues, dawg, and you might wanna look into getting that muthafucka into counseling," Sincere gave him dap and walked into the farmhouse, leaving K-Dawg alone with his gift.

K-Dawg opened the box and smiled when he saw what it contained. It was Grovaldo's missing eye.

Animal lay on his bed in his tiny room, waiting patiently for sleep, but it never came. As wired as he was, it'd probably be days before he was able to close his eyes again. For a long while the capers K-Dawg had set up for them felt like a chore, but the more blood he spilled, the more natural it became. He was slipping back into old habits and this worried him. If Gucci had been with him she would be sure to have some calming and reasonable words for him, but he was all alone in the company of sociopaths and a brother too blind to see the forest for the trees. Gucci had always told him that he had a knack for stepping in shit, and her words rang loudest in his ears that night.

"Knock-knock," a voice called from the doorway.

Animal spun with his gun raised, ready to blast the intruder, but his finger froze on the trigger when he recognized the silhouette. "What the hell are you doing creeping around in the middle of the night, Sonja?"

"I wasn't creeping, you were slipping." Sonja stepped into the room. The moonlight shining through the window illuminated her form. She had abandoned her fatigue shorts and tank top for a bathrobe and pajama pants. "Whatever is on your mind, it must be serious for you to let somebody get within ten feet of you and not notice."

"I'm straight, I just got a lot of shit on my mind."

Sonja invited herself to a seat on the edge of his bed. "So I hear things went well earlier?" Animal shrugged in the way of an answer. "I don't know what happened but you've got Sincere rattled."

"He should be. I'm the devil, or haven't you heard?" Animal said sarcastically.

"You ain't tough, Animal, you just act that way, but I can see through you." She touched his side and Animal flinched. "Jesus, I'm not gonna bite you . . . at least not right this second." She smirked. "I see the stitches are still holding." She traced the line where he'd been cut.

"Yes, thanks to you and those skilled hands."

"My hands are good for more than just stitching wounds." She reached down and grabbed his crotch. To her surprise, Animal was as hard as a rock. "Damn, it's been a while since I felt that."

"Stop playing, Sonja." He moved her hand.

"Who said I was playing?" Sonja stretched out next to him so that they were facing each other. "You have the most beautiful lips I've ever seen on a man." She reached out to touch him, but Animal grabbed her wrist.

"Chill, ma. We both know where this is gonna go if we open that door."

"So let's open it already and stop playing this stupid little game. Look, I know when we first started messing around we agreed not to make it more than what it is, but I really like you," she confessed.

"I like you too, Sonja, but there's too much on both of our plates and drama would only complicate things further."

"You're the only one being dramatic about this, Animal. I watch you walking around brooding day in and day out over what you left behind in New York instead of appreciating what you have right here in P.R."

"Ain't shit in P.R. for me but more reminders of why I want to be away from this place and everybody in it." As soon as Animal said it, he wished he could take the words back.

"Even me?" Sonja's voice was heavy with emotion.

"I'm sorry, Sonja, I didn't mean it like that."

"You meant it just like you said it." She sat up and turned her back to him. She felt Animal lay his hands on her shoulders to comfort her, but she didn't turn around. She wouldn't give him the satisfaction of seeing the tears that had welled in her eyes. "So what we shared meant nothing to you?"

Animal turned her around so that she was facing him. By then the tears were rolling down her cheeks freely. He brushed them away with the backs of his fingers. "Sonja, you're a beautiful girl and any man would be lucky to have you, but the things you want I can't give you."

"Can't or won't, Animal?" she challenged.

"Does it make a difference?"

"Maybe not to you, but it does to me. Animal, I know that we agreed to keep our li'l thing simple, but the heart doesn't always agree with what the mouth says. I didn't mean for it to happen, but I've fallen for you and I want to be with you."

For as cold as Animal tried to make himself, seeing Sonja like that tugged at his heart. Animal ran his hands through his hair in frustration. "Sonja, I'm no good for you, ma. There's just so much you don't understand," he tried to explain.

"I understand enough to know that you're still holding

on to the memory of a woman who has written you off as a ghost. I don't see how you keep trying to accomplish something that's impossible."

"That's because you've never been in love," he said sincerely.

"I was in love once, but he didn't love me back." Sonja slid off the bed. "Anyway, I was just coming to check on you. I'll see you tomorrow." She headed for the door.

"Sonja, hold on. Let me talk to you for a second," he called after her.

Sonja hesitated. A part of her wanted to turn around, but it would only make walking away harder. "Nah, I think you've said enough for the night." She walked out.

Long after Sonja had gone, Animal was still staring at the door. He hadn't meant to hurt Sonja, but sometimes the truth could be a painful thing. Sonja was all that a man could ask for: beautiful, intelligent, and dangerous. Animal genuinely cared for Sonja, so hurting her wasn't an easy thing to do, but it was a necessary evil. With the state that his life was in at that point, allowing her to get close to him would only end in disaster. Had the situation been different, he could easily see himself falling in love with Sonja and living out the rest of his days happily on the beautiful island, but his heart was already promised to another.

Just thinking about Gucci made Animal feel nostalgic. He lifted his mattress and pulled out the only piece of his old life that he had left, and old photo of him and Gucci at Baltimore Harbor. They'd driven down to Maryland for the weekend and had a romantic dinner at Mo's Fisherman's Warf. After dinner they'd taken a walk along the harbor and found an old dope fiend to snap the picture.

Gucci looked stunning in a tight-fitting Deréon dress that turned the head of just about every man they passed. Later that night they had blown Kush and made love until the sun came up. Animal was almost tempted to call Gucci and tell her everything, but he knew that would only pull her into the web of bullshit he had allowed K-Dawg and his brother to rope him into, and she deserved better.

"I miss you so much," he whispered to the picture. It wasn't until he saw a droplet of water hit the photo that he realized he was crying.

CHAPTER 16

After riding around for nearly thirty minutes, Gucci was able to find a parking spot on 102nd and Manhattan Avenue. She stood on the curb for a minute, staring up at the tall brown buildings, and a chill ran through her. Though she wasn't from Douglass, it held dark memories for her. Whenever she saw the projects she would think of her lover Animal.

Douglass had been one of many projects to feel the chill of Animal's steel when he was in the streets full-time. He and his crew were known as menaces throughout the five boroughs and anyone with good sense feared them. Animal was bound to the streets, vowing to let nothing ever come between them, until he met Gucci.

They were an odd pair, with both hailing from the streets, but each with different aspirations. Gucci wanted to make it out of the gutter, while Animal's destiny was to die in the gutter. Somewhere along the line the two souls had found a common ground, and good fortune gave Animal a way out. Lending his talent to the Big Dawg Entertainment roster, Animal was on the fast track to stardom, but his inability to let go of old grudges made it impossible to fully make the transition from killer to celebrity. The trail of bodies Animal had left in his wake finally caught up with him and he was sentenced to a lengthy prison term, which he would never have the chance to serve.

While being transported from the courthouse to Rikers Island, Animal's escorts were caught in a vicious ambush that left three dead and nine wounded, including two NYPD detectives, and their prisoner unaccounted for. There was a nationwide manhunt for Animal, but he seemed to have just vanished. The police hounded Gucci for months, but not even she had heard from him. The media came up with a wild story about Animal being rescued by some drug cartel he had been working for, but Gucci knew better than that. Animal had always been independent—even when he was running with Tech, he'd made his own way. What did trouble Gucci was some of the things she was hearing in the streets.

Animal had made some very powerful enemies over the years so it was highly likely that the gunmen had been agents of his enemies who had come to settle up for all the lives he had taken. It had been two years and Animal hadn't tried to contact her or have someone get word to her, which strengthened the rumors she was hearing of his death. Every time she thought about Animal being gone, she broke down into tears, but as time passed, her mind began to tell her what her heart didn't want to hear, that he was dead.

Her best friend Tionna and her mother tried to bring Gucci out of her funk, but she was too far gone in her mourning for Animal. For months she would sit and look out her mother's window, thinking she would see him jump out of a cab and rush up the stairs to tell her that all was well, but he never came. When one year rolled into two, she had to accept the fact that he wasn't coming and try to begin the process of piecing her broken heart back together.

Gradually she began to crawl out of her hole, see what she'd missed while she was away. She had recently started dating again. It felt awkward, like she was cheating on Animal, but a ghost couldn't claim infidelity. Some of the guys she met were cool, but none of them measured up to Animal, so at the end of the day they occupied time, but never a place in her heart.

Gucci's little cousins Jalen and Miles came spilling out of the backseat, carrying on as they had been for the past half hour or so. From the time she had picked them up two days prior, they had been working her nerves. On the first night she had planned to watch movies with them at her mom's house. She sat the kids in front of the television while she went into the kitchen to get their snacks. By the time she came back, one of them had done something to the color on the screen and changed the language to Spanish. It took her three hours and two customer-service calls to get it back to normal. Jalen claimed she hadn't done it, but she was the one holding the remote control. Then there was Miles, sweet and innocent little Miles. For the most part he was pretty well behaved, but he cried over everything. Jada had spoiled him rotten and it was driving Gucci up the wall. She loved her little cousins but this would be the first and last time she offered to keep Jada's badass kids.

Gucci let out a deep sigh. "Can't you guys go at least five minutes without fighting?"

"He started it!" Jalen exclaimed.

"Nuh-uh! She did, because she keeps trying to take my candy," Miles retorted, holding up a half-eaten bag of Skittles, which Jalen snatched.

"If I wanted yo candy I'd take it," Jalen teased while finishing off Miles's Skittles.

"She ate my candy!" Miles started crying again.

"Crybaby, crybaby, stick your hand in gravy," Jalen sang, taunting her brother, causing him to cry harder.

"Enough!" Gucci snapped and grabbed them both by their arms. "Look," she addressed Jalen, "I don't usually beat other people's kids, but I'm about to make an exception. And you"—she turned to Miles—"stop crying for everything, you're a boy so act like one or I'm gonna buy you a jump rope and send your li'l ass to school in a dress! Are we clear?" Both children nodded. "Good, now bring your asses on." She yanked them behind her and entered the projects. When she rounded the corner of 865, she smiled, because she had never been so happy to see her family.

Mookie stood in the lobby of 865, looking suspiciously through the tiny glass square in the steel entrance door. He was dressed in a bootleg Gucci sweatsuit, with a two-tone black and red do-rag tied on his head. Mookie was a man trapped in time. It was more than a decade into the new millennium, but his mind was still in 1989. Mookie was a throwback goon who had at one time been the scourge of the projects and a ghetto superstar on the rise, until the crack epidemic hit. Like a lot of old players from his era, his chase for crack had derailed his chase for paper and he had ruined the empire his brother had built.

When the drug money was cut off, Mookie turned to strong-arm robbery to feed his demon. Friend and foe were all fair game when it came to his trying to score a fix, and only prison had slowed him down. Mookie had been back and forth to various prisons for most of his life, recently coming home from serving five years in Attica. Though Mookie claimed to have changed his fiendish ways, those who knew him knew better. Cats like Mookie never changed, they only got better at hiding their bullshit.

Behind him he heard the staircase door open and close. A skinny woman with bug eyes came speed-walking around the corner with her closed fist clutched tightly to her chest. She gave Mookie a toothless smile and a nod before rushing out of the building and heading up the street. A few seconds later Mookie's cousin and crime partner Fish came around the corner, counting out the crumpled bills in his hand. Fish was a hulk of a man who resembled a mailbox with arms and legs. His pumpkinlike head always seemed to lean to one side, as if it was too much weight for his neck to support. Fish wasn't the sharpest knife in the drawer, but he was deadly and unquestionably loyal to Mookie and the Butler clan.

"What we looking like?" Mookie asked Fish.

"We 'bout done. After these last five bags we'll be all out," Fish said proudly, putting the baggies of small white rocks in Mookie's hand.

"Umm-hmm." Mookie sucked his teeth as if he had something stuck between them. "Let's hurry up and finish them off so we can get outta here. I don't wanna squat for too long and risk getting caught bogus." Mookie shuffled the bags around with his fingers. To the untrained eye the baggies looked like they contained crack, but they were dummies—broken-up aspirin made to look like crack. They had been in and out of different buildings all morning beating the fiends with their imitation drugs.

Mookie and Fish slipped from the building with intentions on going down the block to purchase some *real* drugs and a few beers. The plan was to cop and get low until the sun went down and find another lick to hit, but when Mookie heard his name being called, he knew their plans would have to wait.

"Morris Butler, what the hell are you doing skulking around my building?" Ms. Pat called from the bench where she had been sitting, smoking a Newport and sipping from a Styrofoam cup. A large-brimmed yellow straw hat sat cocked atop her bleached-blond wig to protect her from the beaming sun.

"Hey, mama." Mookie smiled innocently, showing off the gold tooth in the front of his mouth.

"Don't *hey mama* me, boy. Whenever I see y'all two slithering around like *Night of the Living Base Heads* I know you're up to no good," Ms. Pat accused, glaring at the two of them over her bifocals.

"Aw, we wasn't doing nothing, but about to run to the store," Mookie assured her.

Ms. Pat eyed him suspiciously. "Mookie, you don't run to nothing but the rock house, so don't try to play me. I'm telling you, if I find out y'all robbing people in my building I'm gonna call the police on you myself."

Mookie laughed. "Mama, with all the shit you got in your house, you know damn well you don't want the police snooping around here."

"Don't worry about what I got in my house, worry about what I got in this purse"—Ms. Pat patted her shoulder bag, which was sitting next to her on the bench—"and if I find anything missing when I go inside I'm gonna give you a sneak preview," she threatened, causing Mookie to take a cautionary step back. He knew better than most how Ms. Pat rolled and didn't want any part of her infamous purse.

"Hey, auntie." Fish smiled.

"Hey, baby, come give auntie some sugar." Ms. Pat spread her arms.

When Fish leaned in to kiss her on the cheek, he caught a whiff of something familiar. "Auntie, what you got in that cup? It smells like whiskey."

"Boy, you know damn well I can't dance with no whiskey while I'm on these blood thinners. This ain't nothing but a li'l Cîroc." She swirled the ice around in her cup before taking another sip.

"Let me get some." Mookie reached for the cup, but Ms. Pat snatched it away.

"If you try to put your crackish lips on my cup, I promise you I'm gonna take that fake gold tooth outta yo head. Now if you wanna *get* something, why don't you try *getting* away from me?"

Mookie was about to say something, but Fish tapped his arm and drew his attention to Happy, Boots, and Bernie coming up the stairs. "Fresh meat." Mookie rubbed his hands together in anticipation.

CHAPTER 17

Ms. Pat adjusted her glasses and looked at the approaching trio. "Well, if it ain't the good, the bad, and the ugly," she addressed Bernie, Boots, and Happy respectively.

"Ms. Pat, you stay with the jokes." Boots laughed.

"If you wanna hear a joke, wait until they come out with the story of your life on audiobook." Ms. Pat slapped her thigh and roared as if she'd just come up with the funniest joke in the world. "Girl, you know I'm just playing. How the children doing?"

"They're good, the big ones are outta my hair for the day so it's just me and Hassan." Boots nodded to the stroller Bernie was pushing.

"Hey, baby." Ms. Pat pulled the stroller toward her so she could get a better look at the child. "He looks just like his daddy, but I see a little of you in there too, Bernie."

"Huh?" Bernie frowned.

"Nothing, baby." Ms. Pat patted his hand sympathetically, and looked at Boots, whose skin had gone pale. Thankfully, Gucci came walking up with the kids and diverted Ms. Pat's attention. "Hey, my grandbabies." Ms. Pat hugged Jalen and Miles when they rushed to her. "I hope y'all didn't give Gucci too much trouble?"

"Trouble ain't the word." Gucci sighed. "I am so glad I don't have kids, because if I did I'd surely be in the nut-house." Gucci dropped Jalen and Miles's overnight bags next to Ms. Pat on the bench.

"Gucci, what's good, ma?" Boots hugged her warmly.

Gucci's nose wrinkled as Boots was a bit tart, but Gucci didn't push her friend away. For as trifling as Boots was, it felt good to see a familiar face. "Chilling, what's going on with you?"

Boots shrugged. "Trying to get it how I live like everybody else."

"I know that's right." Gucci gave her a high five.

"What up, Gucci, you can't speak?" Happy addressed her.

"Hey, Happy." Gucci rolled her eyes and turned her attention to Bernie and the baby. "What's good, daddy day care?" she teased Bernie.

"You know me, enjoying the square life with my wife and family," Bernie said proudly, pushing the stroller forward so Gucci could see *his* son.

Gucci tickled the baby's plump chin, causing him to giggle and drool. "Damn, he's getting big. When y'all having another one?"

"Shit, I'm five and done. I'm about to get my tubes tied," Boots told her.

Gucci twisted her lips. "Boots, you were screaming you were getting your tubes tied two kids ago and still ain't found your way under the knife, so knock it off. Besides, Bernie is a young man and he'll probably wanna have more kids," Gucci teased her.

"Then he better get one of them mail-order bitches to bear them because I'm done," Boots said seriously.

"Ay, Gucci, what's up with ya girl Tionna?" Happy asked.

"You keep better tabs on her than I do, so I should ask you the same," Gucci shot back.

Happy had been obsessed with Tionna for as long as Gucci could remember, and after Tionna finally let him hit it, the obsession had gone to another level. Happy showered her with gifts, money, and everything under the sun, but there was no amount of wealth that he flaunted that could make her give him her heart, because back then it still belonged to Duhan. Happy turned into a borderline stalker, popping up wherever Tionna was and making trouble. Ironically, it was Happy who had been responsible for Gucci and Animal's meeting.

Tionna and Gucci had been at a Big Dawg listening party when Happy and some of his flunkies showed up. When Tionna slighted him for Don B., Happy tried to cause a scene. He ended up getting his ass whipped by members of Don B.'s entourage, but one of Happy's people had managed to sneak a gun inside the place and when he pulled it, all hell broke loose. When security whisked Don B. and the ladies out of the club, Tionna and Gucci ended up paired off with Animal and Don B. Initially, Gucci couldn't stand Animal, writing him off as just another street cat, but the more she got to know him the more drawn to him she found herself. Tionna and Don B.'s relationship had ended horribly, but for Animal and Gucci it had been kismet.

"Tionna don't want me," Happy said sadly. "I'd be willing to give that girl the world if she just acted right, but she don't see that."

"Money can't buy love, Hap," Bernie said, looking tenderly at Boots.

"It may not be able to buy love, but a damn good substitute," Boots said with a snort, which started a minor argument between her and Bernie.

Happy stood around watching the exchange, laughing, then he suddenly felt a chill down his back. He looked up to see Mookie staring at him. "What's good, Mookie?"

"You tell me, big time?" Mookie sucked his teeth. "I heard you're the man to see, baller."

"You know money makes the world go round, baby," Happy said arrogantly.

"I hear that hot shit. Let ya boy hold something," Mookie said.

Happy shrugged. "I ain't got it."

"You ain't got it, huh?" Mookie looked from Happy's iced-out chain to the nugget ring on his pinkie finger. "Let me find out."

"Well, when you find out, give me a holla," Happy shot back. "I'm out." He waddled down the street. Happy talked tough to impress the ladies, but he secretly feared Mookie. He knew how the old-school gangster got down and didn't want to get caught up.

"Fat muthafucka," Mookie said when Happy was out of earshot.

"Damn, Mookie, you hate everybody," Boots accused.

"Nah, just that muthafucka. He's a piece of shit and a snake that would sell his own mama for a get-out-of-jail-free card."

"Who, Hap? Nah, that's a good dude right there. It's been a few times when I was down he put me on to get some bread with him," Bernie defended Happy.

Mookie looked at Bernie as if he had lost his mind. "You mean get money *for* him. Happy don't do shit for nobody unless it's to benefit his greedy ass. If I were you, I'd steer clear of that muthafucka before you find yourself wearing a charge for him. Come on, Fish, let's boogie. I'm about to go grab a forty and get with this shorty." Mookie started off toward Manhattan Avenue, with Fish on his heels.

"I don't know why everybody always trying to kick Happy's back in; he's one of the realest niggaz out here," Bernie said.

Ms. Pat just shook her head at his ignorance. "The Lord looks out for babies, fools, and dumb animals, and being the good Christian I am, I ain't gonna speculate which category this one falls into," she said under her breath.

"Watch it, that's my baby daddy you're talking about." Boots folded her arms and gave Ms. Pat a stink look.

"What happened, you got some frog in you?" Ms. Pat picked up her purse.

"Auntie, why don't you leave people alone?" Gucci scolded. "Boots, pay her no mind. You know Aunt Pat gets a little crazy when she's off her meds." Gucci tried to laugh it off.

"Niece of mine, you're absolutely right. As a matter of fact, it's about time for my treatment." Ms. Pat fished around in her wig for the joint she'd stashed and placed it between her lips. "One of y'all give me a light."

"Auntie, put that away. You can't get blazed in front of Miles and Jalen like that!" Gucci said.

"Why the hell not? They mama get blazed damn near every night. I guess that's why she keeps getting pregnant." Ms. Pat laughed hysterically.

"Gucci, what does *blazed* mean?" Miles asked innocently.

"None of your business. Don't pay your grandmother any mind." Gucci hugged her nephew to her.

A young man wearing a pair of skinny jeans sagging off his ass ambled over to the bench and waved to get Ms. Pat's attention. "Hey, Ms. Pat, you holding?"

It seemed like everyone, including the children, looked to Ms. Pat for a response.

"Negro, is you crazy, rolling up on me while I'm out here with my fam? I don't play that shit." She hugged Jalen and Miles to her so that their backs were to the young man and mouthed, *Meet me in the lobby in five minutes.* The young man gave her a confused nod and went back the way he had come. "The nerve of some of these young folks, got me out here G-checking mofos and getting all excited. Shit, got my damn pressure up." She fanned herself.

"Auntie, your ass is a trip." Gucci laughed.

"With no luggage." Ms. Pat gave her a high five. "Okay, kids, let me run y'all in the house so I can feed you before ya mama come to pick you up."

"We're not hungry, we had candy on the way over here with Gucci," Jalen told her.

"Well, candy doesn't count as food, so come on." Ms. Pat got up off the bench and started gathering her things. Jalen sucked her teeth. "Suck 'em one more time and I'll bet I'll make you swallow 'em." This quieted Jalen. "I swear you get more and more like ya mama every day."

"Speaking of Jada, what's up with her? Finding her has been like finding Nemo lately," Gucci said.

"I haven't seen too much of her either, thank the Lord. Since Cutty came home from prison she's been staying uptown with him, playing house," Ms. Pat told her.

"More like playing catch-up. I heard she burned him for like twenty stacks and he's making her work it off," Boots said. As soon as the words left her mouth and she saw the glare she got from Ms. Pat and Gucci, she regretted opening her mouth.

"Let me tell you something." Ms. Pat pointed her finger at Boots. "I don't care what you and Jada's differences are, but she's still a Butler so you watch your damn mouth when you're talking about my granddaughter, especially when you don't know what you're talking about."

"I didn't mean no disrespect, Ms. Pat. I'm just telling y'all what the streets are saying," Boots said apologetically.

"The streets say a lot, and if I repeated half of what I hear, yo ass would sure nuff be on the way to the emergency room and ol' Bernie here would be on his way to prison, so let's not throw stones, Boots. And if the streets need something to talk about, tell them this: if anybody is stupid enough to mistreat a member of my family, that iron will sure as hell get their minds right." She patted her purse. "On that note, I'm out. Come on, children." Ms. Pat snatched her great-grandkids by the arms and stormed off.

Boots, you always did know how to put your foot in your mouth." Gucci laughed.

Boots sucked her teeth. "Gucci, your aunt be tripping. I was only saying what's already out there."

"Well, you said it to the wrong person. You know she don't play when it comes to her great-grandkids, especially Jada. She might pop a lot of shit, but that's still her baby girl, crazy-ass baby daddy or not."

"Hey, what's the deal with Cutty anyway? I heard that nigga had a hundred years or some shit like that—how's he home?" Bernie asked.

Gucci shrugged. "Don't start me to lying. Let Jada tell it, he was able to give most of his time back on appeal because of some kind of technicality with his case."

Boots looked at her sideways. "I know niggaz still laying up for drugs because their appeals were denied, so with Cutty having all of them bodies I just can't see him getting off like that. Shit smells funny to me."

"And what do you mean by that?" Gucci asked.

Boots thought about it for a few minutes before answering her. "Look, Gucci, I don't know how they doing it on Fortieth Street these days, but in these projects, snitching has become the new drug of choice and all these niggaz is addicts. Maybe Cutty decided he wasn't built to do life in prison?"

"Hold on, Boots. Now though I ain't no big fan of Cutty's, real recognizes real. Cutty might be a lot of things, but I can't see him being no snitch."

"That's the same thing they said about Rock Head before he got Animal wrapped up." Boots meant it as a joke to assassinate Rock Head's character, but there was no mirth in Gucci's eyes, only fire. "Sorry, Gucci, I didn't mean to bring up a touchy subject."

"Can't be touchy when your spirit is numb, ma." Gucci cracked a half smile, trying to hide her hurt. "My nigga is gone and I'm always gonna miss him, but for the little bit of time we did have together I got to know *true* love. That's something a lot of people will never find no matter how high or how low they look." Her eyes lingered on Bernie, who was playing with the baby. After a few seconds of uncomfortable silence Gucci glanced at her watch. "I gotta get outta here, but it was good seeing you, Boots. You too, Bernie."

"Don't stay away so long the next time." Boots gave her a tight hug.

Gucci held her at arm's length and smiled. "I'm always around, I just ain't here." she looked around at the projects. "Ima see you later, Boots."

Boots stood there watching Gucci stride proudly down the hill toward Manhattan Avenue, letting what she had said roll around in her mind. Gucci had been beaten to the ground by what she went through and still managed to hold her head high and carry on as if nothing were wrong. Boots admired her for her strength and hated herself for not being as strong. She was a settler, in life and in love, and looking at Bernie playing with her son only reminded her of how far down the ladder she was slipping.

CHAPTER 18

The Crazy Horse was one of many gentlemen's clubs located in New York City. On any given night you could find it packed with men and women downing booze and ogling flesh, living out fantasies in their minds and in some cases one of the back rooms reserved for VIP services, but at six o'clock in the evening this wasn't the case. There were a few hard legs mounted on bar stools, watching the two homely girls on stage, trying to make them jump through hoops for the few singles they had to offer, but other than that, the spot was dead that early in the evening.

Porsha strutted across the sticky floor of the main area with her blond wig blowing in the breeze of the tower fans. She wore a black G-string bikini under a sheer robe that tied at the waist. Normally the day shift was reserved for girls who weren't attractive or skilled enough to compete with the nighttime lineup; neither applied to Porsha, but she was on a paper chase and every dollar counted.

Ever since they'd received the eviction notice it had weighed heavily on her. Things had been rough on her for the last few months with paying for school and just day-to-day living, but she had managed to maintain and kept picking up the pieces of her life. Getting evicted would be

a major setback in the grand scheme of what she was doing. If they did get put out, she was sure she would be able
to eventually get back on her feet, but it would take time
and money, meaning that she would have to drop out of
school to work more hours, and that would put her back
at square one. Porsha had worked too hard to get where
she was and wasn't about to blow it all because of someone else's bullshit.

From the beginning she had been apprehensive about
moving in with Frankie and Sahara because of how they'd
all met in the first place. She had known Sahara from her
days dancing at the Golden Lady and had met Frankie
through her. Sahara had a beef with a pimp who was trying to force her to get down with him, so she had started
bringing Frankie with her a couple of nights per week to
watch her back in case he tried something crazy, which he
did. The pimp and Sahara had gotten into a heated word
exchange that resulted in his trying to put his hands on
her, which was a mistake. Frankie broke a bottle over the
pimp's head and the two of them went toe-to-toe in the
middle of the club. Not one to see a man beating on a
woman, Porsha tried to break it up, which prompted one
of the pimp's whores to get into it and all hell broke loose.
The end result was Porsha and Sahara being banned from
the Golden Lady. The girl's having each other's backs during the brawl had forged a bond between them that would
eventually grow into an unlikely friendship.

A hand grazing her arm snapped Porsha out of her
daze and brought her back to the reality of where she was
and what she was doing. He was a young dude of about
twenty or so, wearing gaudy jewelry, sitting behind one of
the small tables on the floor with two of his friends. He

wasn't the most handsome cat Porsha had ever seen but he had a fistful of singles so she went with his advance.

"What's good, ma?" he asked with a smile.

"You," she said seductively. "How about a dance?"

"How much?" he asked.

"Twenty per song."

"A'ight, come on." He pushed his chair back from the table so she could do her thing. Porsha lowered herself onto his lap and began to move in time with the song that was playing. The young man could feel the heat of Porsha's sex through his jeans and it brought him to an instant erection. "Damn," he moaned.

Porsha ground harder on his lap. "You like that, don't you?" He reeked of alcohol but she ignored the stench and kept plucking dollars from him.

"Hell yeah," he breathed. Porsha turned around and grabbed her ankles and began bouncing her ass up and down on his lap. He was in the throes of pleasure when the song ended and Porsha abruptly stopped her grinding. "Shit, why you stopped?"

"Song is over, boo," Porsha said while counting her singles.

"Damn, baby, that was way too quick." He grabbed her arm to try to prevent her from leaving.

Porsha looked at his hand as if it were a rash that had suddenly appeared on her arm. "If you want more you gotta pay for more."

"I can dig it, baby. Money ain't no thing." He fanned out the singles he had left in his hand. "Just let me know what the ticket is?"

"One song for twenty and three for fifty," she told him, eyeing the money hungrily.

The young man thought on it for a minute. "Yeah, all that shit is cool, but what if I wanted something a li'l more intimate?" He was trying to sound suave but the alcohol had his words slurring.

Porsha frowned. "Nah, daddy, it ain't that type of party."

"Not even for two hundred?" he asked.

As bad as Porsha could've used the money, she wasn't about to sell her pussy. "Like I told you, I don't get down like that. If you wanna fuck, then you might wanna get at one of these other chicks to see if they can help you out." She tried to walk away, but he grabbed her again, this time more forcefully.

"C'mon, ma, stop acting like that. I know you could use the paper or else why would you be in here shaking your ass in the middle of the day. Check it, let's not play games. I got a stack for you if you break out with me and my niggaz right now." He pulled a large knot of money from his pocket and set it on the table.

Porsha looked at the money as if it were a steaming pile of shit. "You got me fucked up. I tried to tell you nicely, but let me say it to you in a language that maybe your drunk ass will understand: I wouldn't fuck you for ten stacks, let alone one, so why don't you save that fake baller-ass game for one of these other bitches because I ain't beat." She jerked her arm away.

The young man's friends burst into laughter, which infuriated him. "Bitch, you better act like you know." He lunged at Porsha.

She tried to move out of his reach but her heels affected her balance and he managed to grab a fistful of her hair. Porsha dipped under the smack he tried to deliver and left him holding nothing but her wig. Before he could try to swing on her again, Porsha came up holding the razor she'd had stashed in her purse and opened a gash in his forearm. The young man howled in pain as blood sprayed all over the table.

"I got your bitch right here, you lowlife muthafucka." Porsha swung the razor again. The young man managed to move back in time to save his face but she caught him across the chest. The young man was now as sober as a judge as he watched his blood spill all over the place. Porsha kicked the chair out of the way and charged him, with the razor angled for his throat, but luckily one of the bouncers grabbed her arm before she could connect. While Porsha was being restrained, the young man reached around the bouncer and punched her in the side of the head so hard that she almost blacked out. Before he could swing again, the rest of the bouncers were on him and his crew and proceeded to open up a can of whip ass.

"Oh no, this nigga didn't just steal on me." Porsha checked her head to make sure it wasn't bleeding. She lunged for the young man again, but the bouncer was still holding the hand wielding the razor; however, her legs were still free. Porsha waited until she got a clear shot at his face and drove one of her stiletto heels into his cheek.

"Porsha, chill the fuck out." The bouncer picked her up by the waist and carried her away from the scuffle.

"Fuck that, he punched me. Let me get mine." She struggled against him. Her head was throbbing but her rage made her immune to the pain. She was so mad that she tried to turn the razor on the bouncer, which only made the situation worse.

A stripper named Kat, who knew Porsha, rushed to her

side. She was a tall brown-skinned chick whose body was almost completely covered in tattoos. "Let her go, I got her," Kat told the bouncer while trying to break his grip on Porsha's waist.

By now a crowd had gathered to see what was going on, including the owner, Vinny, and he wasn't pleased by the mess they had made of his club. "What the fuck is wrong with you?" he snapped at Porsha.

"Vinny, chill, it wasn't her fault," Kat tried to explain.

"I don't see anybody else holding a razor and acting like a crazy person," Vinny said. "Porsha, get your shit. You're done here."

"But, Vinny, he tried to swing on her; how you gonna fire Porsha?" Kat snapped.

"Since you wanna be her lawyer, then you can leave with her. Both of you bitches get dressed and get the fuck outta my spot!"

"Fuck you and this whore-shack!" Porsha screamed.

"Don't argue with that bitch-ass nigga, we got too much class for this joint anyhow." Kat pulled her by the arm to the dressing rooms.

"This is some bullshit." Porsha punched one of the lockers in the dressing room.

"Breaking your hand on the locker ain't gonna change shit, Porsha, just let it go," Kat said while pulling her bag from the locker on the other side and digging out her street clothes.

"I am so sick of these hole-in-the-wall clubs." Porsha flopped on the bench and buried her face in her hands.

"Me too, baby girl. When I danced at my brother Marcus's club Shooters, we didn't have these kinds of problems."

"Why'd you stop?" Porsha asked.

Kat shrugged. "When he squared up and married his shorty he shut it down. My brother loved that club, but he loved Billy more."

"Must be nice." Porsha sighed.

"What, dancing at Shooters?"

"No, finding love . . . real love."

Kat laughed. "That shit is overrated, take it from somebody who knows."

"This shit is blowing mine. I was depending on the money I make in here to take care of some things I got going on. What the fuck am I supposed to do now?"

"Porsha, you ain't no stranger to the circuit. In a week you'll be shaking your ass somewhere else," Kat assured her.

"In a week it'll be too late. I need to come up on some paper now!"

Kat could see how stressed out Porsha was and she felt bad for her. "Look, I was gonna keep this li'l bit of info to myself so I could do my thing, but I know a place where you could come up right quick."

"Kat, I ain't selling my ass, so if that's what you're about to suggest you can forget about it," Porsha told her.

Kat laughed. "Slow down, Porsha, I ain't talking about you selling pussy, I'm talking about dancing. There's a spot that's having its grand opening tonight and it's supposed to be a big turnout. The tip out is like a hundred dollars, but from the type of money that's gonna be floating around in there, that ain't shit. Besides, you know them Jersey bitches can't hold a candle to us New York hos."

"True." Porsha gave her a high five. "So what's the name of this spot?"

"It's called Brick City. Now let me give you the rundown." Kat proceeded to tell Porsha all about the Brick City grand opening. By the time she was done, Porsha was convinced that that was the place she needed to be.

"Okay, I'm in, but how do I get out there by train?" Porsha asked.

"Ma, you ain't gotta take the train. My brother Marcus is driving me out there and I'm sure he wouldn't mind picking you up along the way as long as we kick in for gas and tolls."

"That won't be a problem," Porsha assured her.

"A'ight, so I'll pick you up about eight o'clock. Just make sure you're ready because I ain't trying to miss out on none of this paper."

"Me either," Porsha cosigned. "And thanks, Kat. I really appreciate you looking out."

"It's all good, Porsha. Maybe one day you'll be able to do something for me." Kat looked her up and down seductively. It was no secret among the girls that Kat loved pussy just as much as she did dick, if not more so. "I'm outta here, Porsha. See you tonight." Kat winked and left.

Porsha sat there and finished dressing in silence, lost in her own thoughts. Now that the adrenaline had worn off, her head began pounding where the dude had hit her. She looked around the cramped, musty dressing room and wondered what the fuck she was doing there. She decided right then and there that if she was going to continue dancing it would only be at upscale spots, because the hood jump-offs were for the birds. As she put the last of her stuff in her bag and prepared to leave, she wondered if Frankie and Sahara were making better progress than she was in trying to solve their problem.

CHAPTER 19

The hike to Debbie's building was a short one as only six blocks separated the projects from her Central Park West high-rise. The tall building sat on the corner of 110th Street overlooking the park and the newly gentrified Harlem. It was considered prime real estate, but like most of the older buildings that had been renovated with the rest of Manhattan they had to allow a certain number of rent-controlled apartments that they gave away in lotteries or through city-controlled programs. The waiting list for the building was five years, but Debbie had managed to pull it off in under a year. She had been a home attendant for a woman who lived in the building and one day the woman had mysteriously died of a heart attack and Debbie had taken over the apartment. The building's board of directors tried to challenge it, but strangely enough, before the woman died she had added the name of Debbie's oldest daughter, Josephine, to her lease. There was some speculation that Debbie had forged the document but no one could prove it, so they had to let Josephine, and by extension Debbie, stay.

Frankie led the charge, swinging open the glass doors of the building as if she were about to announce the arrival of the president. With her cornrows swinging and her face twisted into a gangsta-ass scowl, Frankie drew quite a few stares as she stormed through the lobby. The doorman raised his hand for Frankie to stop but she ignored him and kept walking to the elevator. Frankie managed to catch the elevator doors just as one of the tenants, who had been watching them, tried to shut the doors in her face.

"Thanks for holding the door," Frankie said sarcastically, looking him up and down. He was an older white guy with thinning salt-and-pepper hair and a beet-red tan. At the end of the studded lavender leash that hung limply around his wrist was a stocky white pit bull with a pink ribbon tied around a tuft of its hair. The dog glared up at Frankie maliciously as she held the door for Sahara. The low growl coming from the pit made Frankie and Sahara back into the far corner.

"So, I don't recall seeing either of you sign the guest's book when you came in." The man looked them up and down as if they had just blown in with the trash.

"That's because we didn't." Sahara rolled her eyes.

"All guests are supposed to sign the book when they're visiting someone in the building."

"That's for the guests who are visiting on pleasure; we're here on business," Frankie told him while tapping the button for Debbie's floor.

"Judging by the floor you're going to, I can only imagine what kind of business it must be." He smirked.

"I don't know what kind of business you think it is, but I can tell you what it ain't and that's none of your business." Frankie laughed and gave Sahara a high five. Their laughter turned into shrieks when the pit bull started barking at them.

"You'd better restrain that mutt or else," Sahara warned from behind Frankie, where she was cowering.

"Or else what?" The man placed a hand on his hip and looked them up and down. "Holly and I are residents and you two are trespassing, so if she decides to take a chunk out of those sweet little asses, the law will be on our side."

"You might have the law on your side, but I've got this on mine." Frankie uncapped her pepper spray and shook the can. "Fuck around if you want to and I'll blind this bitch." She aimed the pepper spray at the dog's face.

"Don't you touch my Holly!" The man jumped in front of his dog. "You would think that for as much as we pay for these apartments we would be able to live without fear of these Harlem bitches terrorizing us night in and night out."

"Bitch"—Sahara looked around the elevator, confused—"I don't see ya mama in here."

"Fuck you, you broke-ass Lil' Kim," the man spat at Sahara and Holly began to bark again.

"Gimmie the spray, Frankie." Sahara grabbed for the can but Frankie held it out of arm's reach. The elevator stopped and the doors slid open. Frankie pushed Sahara out and then backed out slowly, keeping the pepper spray aimed at Holly and her owner.

"This isn't over," the man threatened, staring hatefully at the two girls. "You're all going to burn for this, and that includes that high-yellow bitch you're going to visit. You think management doesn't know what's going on in that apartment? As soon as I get upstairs I'm calling the police and you're all going down!"

"Well then I might as well give them a reason to take

us," Frankie said before blasting the dog in the snout with a stream of pepper spray. Holly let out a bloodcurdling howl as she flapped about, scraping her muzzle across the carpet to get the pepper spray off.

"Holly!" the man yelled before throwing himself on top of the dog as if he were about to take a bullet for her. "Leave us alone, you, third-world savages."

When he opened his mouth this time, Frankie blasted him with the pepper spray, too. Frankie kept her finger on the trigger of the can until the doors finally closed and all that was left of the man and his dog were their painful shrieks, which could be heard throughout the building.

"Elton John–looking muthafucka trying to play us." Frankie gave Sahara dap and they shared a laugh.

"Frankie, that was so foul, but funny as hell. You know he gonna call the police though, right?" Sahara pointed out.

"Please, hopefully by the time he can see well enough to even get into his apartment we'll be long gone. Besides, if Debbie don't have something good to tell us, then they're gonna need some serious police presence in this muthafucka."

The farther down the hall they got, the more potent the smell of weed became. Whoever was smoking tried to mask it with dollar-store incense but the cheap, perfume-heavy sticks only made it worse. When they reached Debbie's door it was obvious where the smell was coming from, not just because that end of the hall reeked of it but because you could almost see the smoke seeping from under the door. It was a wonder that no one had called the fire department on them.

"Damn, they getting blazed in there," Sahara said.

"Curve that shit, pookie, we ain't here on a social call," Frankie reminded her before ringing the doorbell. They waited for a few seconds, and when no one came to the door Frankie rang the bell again. When there was still no answer she knocked aggressively.

"Hold on a damn minute," a deep voice came from behind the door. There were a few more muffled curses before the locks came undone and the door was snatched open, bathing Frankie and Sahara in a cloud of smoke. When their vision finally cleared they were greeted by Debbie's youngest child, Valentino. Valentino looked like a darker version of his mother with his high cheeks and big brown eyes. He was wearing a pair of black Dickies that sagged off his ass and a pair of Scooby-Doo slippers with a blue bandanna tied around his head Aunt Jemima–style. Valentino was barely out of grade school but already looked like a top prospect in the next prison draft. "Oh shit, what's hood, li'l mama? I knew you'd get off that bullshit and come see about a nigga," Valentino cracked, looking at Frankie like she was the last porterhouse steak on the planet.

Frankie rocked back on her heels and looked down at the brown-skinned boy. "First of all, watch ya mouth, and second of all, where's ya mama?"

Valentino sucked his teeth. "She in the back putting in that twirk. Come on in." Valentino stepped back so they could enter. As Frankie passed, he reached out to touch her ass, but she caught his hand in midair.

"If I gotta tell you about these pervert-ass hands of yours one more time, I'm gonna take them from you, feel me?" Frankie said seriously.

"Stop acting like that, ma. Every man wants to test-drive the car before he buys it," he said in a sly tone.

"Valentino, it'll be years before you even come close to being on the radar of a thorough bitch, and even then you'll still be just a li'l nigga trying to play grown-up." Frankie shoved him out of the way.

"Frankie, you're cold as hell." Valentino laughed.

"Valentino, who the fuck did you just let in my house?" Debbie shouted from the back of the apartment. Now that they were inside, they heard what sounded like a large machine running.

"It ain't for me, so why don't you come find out instead of yelling like a crazy person," Valentino shot back and walked off into the kitchen.

"Yo, that's on my moms if you don't stop playing with me I'm gonna bust your shit," Debbie barked as she came down the hall. She looked like a mad scientist, dressed in a white lab coat and latex gloves. She was a big girl, standing around six feet tall and weighting a little over two hundred pounds. When she saw Frankie and Sahara, her eyes went wide, making her look like the cat that had swallowed the canary. "Oh, what's good, y'all?" Debbie quickly pulled the gloves off and stuffed them into the pocket of the lab coat.

"You tell us," Frankie shot back.

"Ain't shit, I was just in here cleaning up a little bit," Debbie lied.

"In a lab coat?" Sahara questioned.

"Oh, that's just to keep that Ajax from getting in my clothes." Debbie brushed the phantom dust from the lab coat.

"That looks like ink, not Ajax," Frankie said upon closer examination.

"There you go on your pet detective shit." Debbie tried

to laugh it off as she slipped out of the lab coat and stuffed it into a laundry basket in the hallway. "Come in the living room, I was just about to light an L."

"We ain't really trying to stay, we just came to holla at you about something right quick," Frankie told her as she and Sahara followed Debbie into the living room. The living room was plush, from the peach carpet to the flat-screen television to the imported suede sofas and the stained-glass lamps in each corner.

Debbie flopped in the high-back chair under one of the lamps and lit the half of a blunt that was resting in the ashtray. "So what's going on?"

"That's what we're trying to figure out. We got home today and found an eviction notice taped to the apartment door," Sahara explained.

"Say word." Debbie's eyes went wide with shock. She was so good at what she did that it almost passed as genuine.

"Word," Frankie picked up. "The notice says that we're behind on our rent and I know that's impossible because we've been paying you every month since we subleased the joint from you last year. So we figured you may be able to help us solve this li'l mystery."

Debbie exhaled a stream of smoke and shrugged. "I don't know, B. When y'all kick me the rent I kick it to Housing, so I don't see what the problem could be."

"Well, have they contacted you about anything?" Sahara asked.

Debbie thought about it for a few minutes and then snapped her fingers as if she had suddenly had an epiphany. "You know what—I did get a budget-adjustment letter in the mail a few months back. They were talking some shit about going up on the rent, but they can't because I get public assistance. I sent them proof of income and all the rest of the shit they asked for to straighten it out. I gave it to Valentino to mail off for me."

"You mean that paper from court you got in the mail?" Valentino asked from the entrance of the kitchen, where he stood eating a sandwich.

"It was not a court paper, it was a budget-adjustment letter," Debbie corrected him. She tried to give him the eye signal to go along with it, but Valentino ignored her.

"The envelope sure looked like it had the housing court as a return address," he said smugly.

"If you could read so good, your stupid ass wouldn't be getting left back again. Now mind your fucking business and go in the room," Debbie barked.

"What-the-fuck-ever," Valentino mumbled under his breath, and did as he was told.

"Stop playing with me before I fuck you up," Debbie shouted after him. "I swear that boy is gonna make me go upside his head. Now, like I was saying: I gave Valentino that paperwork to drop in the mail and his dumb ass probably didn't do it when I sent him to do it. You know how these kids can be, right?"

"No, because I don't have any, and if I did I wouldn't have them handling important business for me," Frankie snapped.

"Ain't no need for the attitude Frankie, it was an honest mistake. I'll get it straightened out, don't worry about it."

Frankie looked at Debbie as if she had taken leave of

her senses. "What the fuck do you mean don't worry about it? Debbie, these muthafuckas are talking about putting us out if we don't pay them that back rent."

Debbie rolled her eyes. "Frankie, you know Housing is all talk and no action. By the time they even get around to executing the eviction we'll have straightened it out. I told you I'll take care of it."

"Oh, I'm sure you'll take care of it, but I'd rather it be sooner than later. Look, if it really went down like you said, then it ain't nothing for us to go to management and get it cleared up. Today is Thursday and we've got roughly until Monday to stop this eviction, so tomorrow morning you can grab whatever paperwork you need and let's shoot down there," Frankie suggested.

"Ah, tomorrow's no good for me. Valentino got suspended from school again so I gotta go see his principal in the morning and I gotta take Lucy to the doctor Monday. Why don't y'all give me a call Monday night and we'll set up a day next week to do it," Debbie said.

"Debbie, we're gonna be in the fucking streets by next week. We need to get this shit done ASAP," Frankie said aggressively.

"Well, ASAP ain't gonna work for me because I got shit to do," Debbie said, matching Frankie's tone. The tension in the air suddenly became very thick and it looked like Debbie and Frankie were gonna go at it, but luckily Lucy came into the living room before it popped off.

Lucy's face was smudged with ink and she held what looked like a bank check in her hands. "Mom, I ran this one through the machine twice but the routing numbers still look like they're lining up wrong. Should we—"

"What the fuck, don't you see grown people out here

talking? Take your ass in the room until I'm finished!"
Debbie roared. Lucy was so crushed that she all she could
do was spin on her heels and run back into the room, crying. "Like I was saying," Debbie turned back to Frankie,
"Housing can't just come and put y'all out into the street
without taking it to court, but it ain't even gonna go that
far, trust me."

"Trusting you is what's got us all fucked up now," Sahara said.

"And what's that supposed to mean? Look, don't be
coming in here trying to pop fly when I was looking out
for y'all bitches by letting you sublease the crib. Shit, I
could've rented it to a cracker and got double what y'all
are paying."

"Yeah, but if you had rented it to somebody white they
would've sued your ass for this fraudulent shit you're trying to pull," Frankie huffed.

Debbie leaned forward and looked Frankie dead in the
eye. "I see somebody ate a bowl of courage this morning.
If that's how you feel about it then feel free to take it to
court, but the first thing they're gonna wanna see is proof
of what you're accusing me of and you ain't got it."

"Bitch, we been paying you rent on the apartment!"
Frankie shouted.

"Yes, and because your ass was too lazy to go to the
post office and get money orders, you've been paying me
in cash. Without receipts it would be your word against
mine," Debbie said with a sly grin.

"Debbie, how you gonna play us like that?" Sahara
asked.

"I ain't trying to play you like shit. Ya homegirl wanna
come in here throwing her ten-dollar words around and

act like I'm stealing from y'all or something. Do you see my crib?" Debbie motioned around at her living room. "What the fuck I look like, doing some crackhead shit like stealing your bum-ass rent money? Like I said, y'all can either wait for me to fix it or get up whatever paper they say y'all owe. From the way y'all came at me, I don't even give a fuck at this point." Debbie flicked the ashes from her blunt and crossed her legs victoriously.

Frankie sat there with her head down, running her fingers through her braids, while Sahara kept trying to reason with Debbie. Frankie thought of all the things that were already going wrong in her life, and the pending eviction was the straw that broke the camel's back. Before she had even realized what she was doing, she was on her feet and rushing Debbie. Debbie tried to pop up from the chair but Frankie cracked her in the jaw and sat her right back down. She managed to get two more punches up before Debbie hit her with a crushing uppercut that sent her sailing across the room. She tried to move in to finish Frankie off, but Sahara tripped her.

"Oh, so you want it too, bitch?" Debbie rushed Sahara. Sahara was a more skilled boxer but in such close quarters she was no match for the brutish Debbie. Debbie wrapped her fingers in Sahara's hair and began using her head to punch holes in the wall. The only thing that stopped Debbie from beating Sahara unconscious was Mookie and Fish coming out of the bedroom to break up the fight.

"What the hell are y'all out here doing?" Mookie asked once they had gotten the girls separated. Normally he would've just smashed on a chick for trying to get at his lady, but he knew Sahara and Frankie from the hood.

"This Alice the goon-looking bitch robbed us!" Frankie raged, trying to get around him to get to Debbie.

"I got your bitch, you fucking dyke!" Debbie spat back.

"Hey, ain't no need for name-calling," Mookie warned both of them. "Come on, y'all got to go." He ushered Frankie and Sahara toward the front door.

"Nah, keep them bitches there, I got something for both of them." Debbie darted into the kitchen. They could hear her rummaging through the drawer for a knife.

"Fish, get her while I get them outta here," Mookie ordered as he pushed Frankie and Sahara into the hallway. "Man, why y'all gotta be disrespecting the pad?" Mookie asked them once they were out of harm's way.

"Mookie, we didn't mean no disrespect, but Debbie is wrong," Frankie said before giving him the short version of why they were beefing.

"Damn, so they trying to put y'all out?" he asked sympathetically.

"Yeah, if we don't get up the money Debbie deaded us on," Sahara said.

Mookie shook his head. "My heart goes out to y'all, but you know I can't let y'all go about it like this. I got a good li'l thing going on with shorty and y'all making my spot hot right now." He looked over his shoulder to make sure no one was listening. "Look, y'all know how Debbie gives it up so you should've known better than to pay her in cash."

"But we've known Debbie for years so we didn't expect her to try and beat us," Sahara explained.

"And that's what makes it worse: you've known her for years and still didn't have the good sense to cover your asses. Y'all ain't new to this so y'all know how the game goes, it's a dog-eat-dog world."

"So what the fuck are we supposed to do now?" Frankie sighed.

"That's a damn good question," he said honestly.

"Mookie, I know you ain't still out there talking to them hood-rat bitches!" Debbie screamed from inside the apartment.

"Hold the fuck on," Mookie shouted back. "Let me go in here and take care of this. I'll holla at Debbie and see what's good when she calms down, but my advice to y'all is to get that bread up or find somewhere else to crash," Mookie told them before going back into the apartment to deal with Debbie.

That amazon bitch is lucky I ain't have my hammer with me, because I'd sure have popped her ass," Frankie said once they were back on the elevator.

"We are fucked with no Vaseline." Sahara pressed her head against the elevator door.

"Don't fold on me now, baby girl. We still got a few days to make something happen, so this shit is far from over. I think I got about three hundred dollars put up. You got anything in the stash?"

"No. I planned to crack on King but never got the chance because them bitches was hating," Sahara said.

"Damn. A'ight, let's get back to the crib and plan our next move. We'll come up with something."

When Frankie and Sahara got off the elevator, they saw that a crowd had gathered in the lobby and a police car was parked outside. No doubt someone had reported the noise coming from Debbie's apartment. They blended in with the crowd and made their way outside. They thought they were going to make a clean getaway until they saw the man they'd gotten into it with earlier talking to one of the officers and motioning in their direction.

"There they are! I want those bitches locked up for what they did to my Holly," he shouted, pointing in their direction. "I told you this wasn't over!"

"Ladies, could you step over here for a minute please?" the officer called to them. They thought about running, but something about the way his hand was resting on his gun made them think it was a bad idea, so they did as they were told. The girls were handcuffed and placed into the back of a patrol car. Settling into the seat to get as comfortable as she could with her wrists shackled behind her back, Frankie spared a glance over her shoulder and saw the man still pointing and laughing.

"This ain't over," Frankie mumbled as the patrol car whisked them away.

CHAPTER 20

Gucci wasn't sure how long she had been sitting in the car with the engine running but it had to have been a while because the sun was starting to set. Her mind was whirling with a million thoughts that she couldn't make heads or tails of but they all came back to the same person, Animal. Her chest tightened with the ball of emotions welling within her and threatened to pop if she didn't calm herself. Tiring of sitting in the shadows of the projects, Gucci put the car in gear and pulled off. She didn't have a destination in mind but driving always helped her to clear her head. She hit Play on her CD player and the sounds of Soul II Soul's "Keep on Moving" filled the car. It was a fitting song, considering the way she was feeling.

Gucci liked to tell herself that she was over Animal, but the truth beneath the lie was exposed every time someone so much as mentioned his name. For, as twisted as it may have sounded, Gucci wished that Animal had gone to prison—at least then she would still have had him in her life, or if his body had been discovered she would've had some kind of closure. Instead, he had vanished without a trace, leaving Gucci with nothing but heartache and questions.

She drove down Broadway, doing a little light window-shopping at red lights, and then cut over and drove up Central Park West. She could remember riding the number-ten bus with her mother as a little girl and marveling at the beautiful park-side real estate. She would close her eyes and imagine pulling up in front of one of the plush buildings and having the doorman open the car door for her. She would ride the glass elevator to her penthouse apartment and look out at the sprawling green trees of Central Park. When she was a girl there were only daydreams, but when she got older the lifestyle had come to fruition.

Gucci's mother had taught her the value of a dollar at an early age, so Gucci made sure she always had a job or a hustle to maintain whatever lifestyle she chose. Granted, she was in no way balling out of control, but if she saw something in the store that she wanted, she would find a way to get it, even if it meant putting it on layaway and paying it off a piece at a time. When Animal came into the picture and landed his record deal, he tried to encourage her to live outside her means, but Gucci refused. It wasn't that she didn't want to burn the malls down on the regular, but because she had been raised to be an independent woman and didn't want to get used to leaning on someone to do everything for her.

Gucci's mother, Ronnie, had always stressed to her the importance of having her own, even when someone else offered her the world. The reason for her thinking this way was that she knew that men came and went, but if you relied on yourself you'd never have to deal with the pain of disappointment when and if the man decided to leave. Animal had always promised not to leave her, but in the end it was a promise that he couldn't keep.

Animal's getting arrested and eventually becoming a

fugitive from justice set off a snowball effect of events. The government had swooped down and tried to freeze Animal's assets because of a law that said an inmate could not profit from his crimes and because Animal's lyrics were a depiction of his capers in the streets. Their claim was eventually thrown out, but because Gucci and Animal had never gotten the chance to get married, she wasn't legally entitled to anything, so everything had been deposited into a trust for his heirs or next of kin—but the only relative he had left was his brother Justice, and he was doing life in prison, or so Gucci had been led to believe. Don B. tried to look out for her every so often, but she didn't like taking money from him. There was something about accepting gifts from Don B. that made her feel like she was making a deal with the devil, so she avoided him as best she could. Once again Gucci was left on her own, but she hardly walked away empty-handed.

Gucci owned an apartment in a nice building on the east side of Manhattan, where she and Animal used to crash when they were in the city. The house in Houston and all the vehicles they'd purchased were in her name. When it became obvious that Animal wasn't coming back, Gucci had sold the house and all the vehicles except the white X5 he'd bought her, which was the car she was currently driving. Her friends had tried to persuade her to keep it all, but to Gucci it didn't make any sense to have five cars when she was only one person. She took all the money she'd made off selling everything and dumped it in the bank with what she'd already saved. One thing about Gucci was that she knew how to squirrel away money. Over the years she had banked all the money Animal had given her, so when it was all said and done, she was sitting on some paper. Gucci might've been a lot of things, but a fool wasn't one of them.

She pulled to a stop at a red light on Ninety-fourth and Central Park West and for the first time noticed that she was in a familiar neighborhood. She looked at the clock on the dashboard and saw that it was after five, so she knew she'd be home from work by then. She coasted through the light just as it turned green and made a left on Ninety-fifth Street. She had some free time on her hands so she decided to pay a visit to the one person other than Animal who could pull her out of her melancholy mood.

I don't know whether to let you in or call security," Tionna said, standing in the doorway and looking at Gucci. She had just come in from work so she still had on her suit skirt and her hair was pulled back into a ponytail.

"Is that anyway to greet your BFF?"

"The same BFF who gets me shot at or arrested every time she shows up on my doorstep? Bring your trifling ass in here and give me a hug." Tionna snatched Gucci inside the apartment and gave her a tight hug. It had been a minute since Tionna had seen her best friend and she missed her dearly. "So what's up, tramp?"

Gucci shrugged and flopped onto Tionna's love seat. "Same shit different toilet, you know how it goes."

"No, I don't, since my so-called BFF never calls me anymore."

"I'm sorry, T, but I've been dealing with a lot lately, so if I don't call as much as I should, blame it on my head and not my heart," Gucci said sincerely. "So how's my favorite attorney been?"

"Ha, I wish. My dumb ass has taken the LSAT twice and failed both times," Tionna confessed.

"You know you never were quick to pick up on anything, T. Didn't you get left back in the third grade? Maybe the third time will be the charm for you on this," Gucci joked, but Tionna didn't laugh.

"I'm serious, Gucci. I went to school all year around, including night courses, and still haven't been able to pass the test, and without that LSAT, all this time I've put in will have been for fucking nothing. I'm starting to feel like it's not in the cards for me," Tionna admitted. The usual bravado in her voice was gone, which worried Gucci.

"Tionna, you're a lot of things but a quitter isn't one of them. I've never known you to put your mind to something and not get it. Remember when we were in the eighth grade and they came out with those short-cut North Faces?"

Tionna's eyes lit up a bit with recognition. "Yeah, I remember Ronnie copped you the pink one and I was tight because my moms couldn't afford to get me one."

"But that didn't stop you from getting one, did it?"

"Hell no, I scraped up two hundred selling weed for Li'l B then gassed his boss Bubbles to trick off on the other four hundred. That was a decent winter for the kid," Tionna laughed. "I bust up in school the following Monday rocking the purple one."

"That's exactly my point. Tionna, one thing that's always drawn people to you was your determination to get what you wanted. From surviving the game, to bettering your living situation"—Gucci looked around the apartment—"you've always made it happen for yourself and this punk-ass test shouldn't be any different," she said seriously.

"Damn, Gucci, you're better than a championship coach!"

"Because all my team does is win." Gucci popped her collar. "A'ight, now that we've gotten that out of the way, let's get into some grown shit. What you got to drink in this piece?"

Tionna looked at her watch. "Damn, lush life, ain't it kinda early to be sipping?"

"Girl, with the way my day has been going I should've started drinking hours ago."

"Oh Lord, I gotta hear this one." Tionna disappeared into the kitchen. She resurfaced a few seconds later, holding a half-empty bottle of Moscato and two glasses.

"What, no yak?" Gucci teased her.

"Bitch, knock it off, you know I can get on my grown shit when I want to." Tionna set the glasses on the coffee table and began rummaging through her purse. "While you're busy running your mouth, why don't you roll this up." She tossed Gucci a bag of weed, followed by a Dutch Master.

Gucci sniffed the bag and frowned. "Smells like you dipped this in diarrhea."

"You know mama smokes nothing but the best." Tionna winked.

Gucci proceeded to roll the weed while Tionna filled their glasses. As soon as Gucci put flame to the L she could smell tart buds burning. It didn't take long before both girls' eyes were hooded, and the stress they'd carried in them suddenly seemed to ease up, as it always did when they were together. Tionna and Gucci had been best friends since grade school and the bond had only gotten stronger with time. From schoolyard fights to Internet sex scandals to happy endings, Tionna and Gucci had been through it all together.

"Damn, I just realized what's wrong with this picture." Gucci looked around the room.

"And what's that?"

"Noise! Where are your big-headed-ass kids?" Gucci was referring to Tionna's sons Duhan and Duran.

"Oh, they're with their grandma. She keeps them for me a few nights per week if I gotta study or work late."

Gucci smiled at the news. For quite a few years Tionna and her mother had had a strained relationship. Throughout most of their childhood Tionna's mother had been on and off drugs, which had contributed to Tionna's spending so much time caught up in the streets. Over the last few years her mother had started to put the pieces of her life back together and rid herself of her addictions so that she could be a better grandmother to her grandsons than the mother she had been to Tionna. Gucci and Ronnie had tried to coax Tionna into reestablishing a relationship with her mother, but Tionna wasn't so quick to buy into Yvette's recovery. The wounds of her childhood were deep and slow to heal, but Gucci was glad to see that they were finally making progress.

"On the real, T, I'm glad y'all are finally making peace. You know Yvette has worked really hard to stay clean for y'all," Gucci said.

"I know, Gucci. It's just that I was so afraid that I was gonna let her back into our lives and she was gonna pull a dope-fiend move that it made me act kinda like a bitch."

"Kinda?" Gucci raised an eyebrow.

"Okay, okay, I was a *super*bitch!" Tionna admitted. "But it feels good to have my mom back in my life."

"Aw, so you guys can do mommy-daughter dates?"

Tionna twisted her lips. "Damn a mommy-daughter date, I'm talking about free babysitting!"

"Tionna, your ass is so trifling." Gucci laughed. "But what good is free babysitting if all your ass does is sit in the crib?"

"I do not just sit in the crib."

"So when is the last time you went out?" Gucci quizzed her.

Tionna thought on it for a second. "I went out last Friday to see the new Tyler Perry movie with Zeda."

Gucci sucked her teeth. "Bitch, please; going to some dry-ass church movie with the dizzy bitches you've taken to hanging with down here doesn't count. I mean go *out*, like how we do."

"I haven't partied like a rock star in a hot minute. But then again, who the fuck am I gonna party with when my BFF is in hiding?" Tionna eyed Gucci.

"Tionna, ain't nobody hiding. I live back in New York now, remember? So I'm always around."

"Gucci, just because you live in New York don't mean you stay in New York. You talk about me not getting out, but you've been harder to catch than a cold. You're either traveling somewhere doing God knows what or holed up in that damn apartment like an old-ass widow."

"See, now you're about to go there," Gucci said as if she was about to catch an attitude, but Tionna didn't care.

"Damn right I'm about to go there, because I can." Tionna snaked her neck. "Gucci, for the last two years I've watched you deal with your grief by running from it."

"I'm gonna tell you like I keep telling everybody else: I'm not grieving." Gucci folded her arms.

Tionna gave her a disbelieving look. "Gucci, I know you better than anyone except probably your mother, so save that tough shit because I ain't buying it. I know you're hurting over what happened to Animal, and there's no shame in that."

"I keep telling you, I'm good. The past is the past and I've moved on with my life," Gucci told her.

"That's what your mouth says, but your eyes say something else." Tionna reached out and placed her hands over Gucci's. "Gucci, I know you're strong, but even the mightiest shoulders get tired after carrying a load for so long, and there ain't no shame in that. I loved Animal, maybe not as deeply as you, but we gotta be real about this, he's gone and he ain't coming back." Gucci opened her mouth to say something, but Tionna raised her hand for silence. "Ma, I'm not telling you it's wrong to miss him, but it's wrong to hold on to him so tight that you begin to fade away with his memory. For you to truly begin to heal, you have to let him go."

Gucci looked up at Tionna and there were tears dancing in the corners of her eyes. "I just miss him so much, T," she whispered before breaking down in tears. She had suffered in silence for so long that a well of pent-up emotions began to pour from her as she opened up to Tionna. "I got so used to having Animal around that I don't know how to function without him."

"Then you learn." Tionna used her thumbs to wipe the tears from Gucci's cheeks. "It's okay, Gucci. I ain't gonna sit here and front like I know what you're going through, but I ain't gonna let you go through it alone."

"Thank you, Tionna." Gucci hugged her tight.

"You ain't gotta thank me, baby. You're my sister and you know how family does for family." She rubbed Gucci's back affectionately. "Now get off me before you get makeup all on my blouse." Tionna pushed her playfully.

"Damn, you could fuck up a wet dream." Gucci mustered a smile.

"As if you'd know about a wet anything when you ain't smelled a dick in years."

"Must your mouth be so vulgar?" Gucci faked embarrassment.

"Bitch, please, like you ain't grow up right across the avenue from me. And you know I ain't said nothing but the truth about you being backed up."

"And how would you know what my sex life is like?"

"Because that cheap-ass foundation can't hide them pimples popping up on your big-ass forehead." Tionna mushed her playfully.

"Don't hate because I ain't loose like you, Tionna."

"I ain't loose, I just know how to have a good time, which is what you need."

"I'm cool." Gucci waved her off.

"The hell you are. Look, my mother is gonna have the kids until Sunday so I say that me and you hit the town and turn it up like we used to do." Tionna snapped her fingers.

"Tionna, I'm too old to be running around to ghetto-ass clubs with your ass. That was so five years ago."

Tionna side-eyed her. "Bitch, knock it off. One of my homegirls from the job invited me to a birthday party she's going to uptown tomorrow night and I just thought it'd be a good idea if we rolled. It's supposed to be really nice."

Gucci looked at her suspiciously. "Ain't nothing nice

going on uptown, especially if one of your hood-rat-ass friends are involved."

Tionna rolled her eyes. "Marlene is one of the partners at the law firm I work for and she's an older chick so she ain't no hood rat."

"Okay, an old-ass educated hood rat," Gucci teased. "Where is this party and what's the lick?"

"It's at the Amsterdam Lounge," Tionna told her.

Gucci twisted her lips. "Oh hell no, ain't that where ol' boy got shot a few years ago?"

"No, it was called something else back then, but some yuppies bought it and cleaned it up. It's a really nice spot now. Anyhow, it's a surprise party for a client of Marlene's fiancé and she invited a few of us from the job to roll out. It'll be a good look for me to get up under some of these lawyers and a good look for you to have some fun, because your sour ass ain't had none in a while. Gucci, come on, for old time's sake."

"Tionna . . ."

"Please." Tionna batted her eyes.

Gucci tried to hold her ground, but looking at Tionna and the silly-ass face she was making reminded her of all the fun they'd had growing up and how much she missed it. "A'ight, T. I'll roll with you."

"Aw, thank you, Gucci." Tionna hugged her.

"Yeah, yeah, yeah." Gucci slapped her hands away. "But I'm telling you now: if this is some ol' hood shit, I'm out!"

"Don't worry about it, Gucci, we're gonna have a grand old time, just like we used to."

"That's what I'm afraid of," Gucci mumbled. "And by the way, whose birthday party is it anyway?"

Tionna shrugged. "Some nigga named King James."

CHAPTER 21

After hours of bullshit and paperwork, the police finally released King James. They were trying to stick an assault charge on him but his lawyer had laughed them out of it. Lamar was a notorious piece of shit who was always terrorizing people in the neighborhood, so the lawyer argued that King had only been defending himself against Lamar and his goons. When it was all said and done, King was released with a desk-appearance ticket for disorderly conduct, which he was sure his attorney would have thrown out at his next court date.

King was glad they hadn't tried to remand him, because he had a million things to do that night. He wanted to go home and wash the jail stink off him and jump into his clothes so that they could push out to Jersey and holla at Shai Clark. Unfortunately, his plans were further delayed when Lakim met him outside the precinct house and informed him of Sahara's getting locked up too. Grudgingly, he got his lawyer to go back inside to see about springing the girl and her friend.

"Fucking chicks," King cursed. He and Lakim were perched on stools at the Jumbo Burgers joint, waiting for the call from the lawyer about the girls. "It's bad enough that I gotta pay this blood-sucking Jew to spring me on a bullshit charge, but I gotta turn around and pay him again to get these bitches out."

Lakim took a bite of his turkey burger and shrugged. "You could've left her in there."

"I started to, but shorty is still useful to me. Sahara is a bonehead but she's a down-ass chick that'll do just about anything I ask her to. How do you think we were able to get rid of that fucking rocket launcher stupid-ass Latif brought to the spot."

Lakim laughed as he recalled the day the little fella had walked into the stash house with the rocket launcher wrapped in a blanket. "Sun was illing for that shit. That joint was mean, but if the police ever ran up and caught us with that, they'd give us like a thousand years in jail, word to mine!"

"That's why I got it up outta there and convinced Sahara to hide it in her crib. That's one of the benefits of fucking with a chick who don't live with her moms," King confessed.

"My dude, you mean to tell me that bitch was stupid enough to let you put that on her?" Lakim shook his head. "If her crib ever get rushed, it's curtains!"

"Better her than us," King said coldly. "But yo, we still good for tonight?"

"Yeah, my peeps said that the owner has already been putting it out to the girls that there's gonna be some heavyweights in the house. Shai and his crew are gonna be there."

"Good. I think it's long overdue for me and Poppa's youngest boy to have a chitchat."

"True indeed. I got the whole squad on deck for this too. We rolling out like three cars on some real heavy shit," Lakim informed him.

King thought about it. "Nah, clip that number by more than half. I don't wanna give Shai the impression that we're coming at him on some beef shit and create an unnecessary problem."

"I don't know if we should roll shorthanded like that. I know Shai is gonna have his whole crew in there, plus it'll be other niggaz in the spot with their teams. We'll be outnumbered if it goes down, God."

"Numbers don't mean shit when you're rolling with niggaz who got heart. We'll go six deep. Me and you will roll in with two of our strongest and have the other two floating around so our backs are covered if it does pop off. I'm on some peace shit, but I ain't stupid either, feel me?"

Lakim nodded. "A'ight, so we'll have Big Dump with us and Zo."

King gave him curious look. "Zo-Pound coming out? I thought that nigga worked like twenty-three hours a day."

"Yeah, Zo is serious about this life-of-a-square shit, but I convinced him to come out with us tonight and blow some steam off with one of these bitches. I'm proud of my baby bro for sticking with this work shit, but I miss hanging out with the li'l nigga."

"A'ight, but as I'm thinking about it, let's bring one more head to stay with the whip in case we gotta make a speedy exit."

"I got the perfect man for the job, li'l Ashanti," Lakim told him.

"You bugging the fuck out, sun. Ashanti is a baby."

"A baby with a serious appetite for blood. All he do is play the block and plot chaos."

"But he's still just a kid, Lakim," King pointed out.

"I hear you, but we were getting into shit when we were

younger than him. King, by the time you were Ashanti's age you was already upstate doing time on a body."

"And it ain't something I'm proud of, La. Sometimes shit happens when you're living the fast life and I ended up getting my lumps and bumps early, but if I had it to do all over again I would've tried to finish school or something instead of getting caught up in this bullshit."

"Me too, but that ain't the hand fate dealt us, my G."

"I hear you talking, La, but what if we try to put him down and he can't handle it. This is grown folk's business, God."

"King, trust me on this one. You know how them li'l dudes was giving it up, running around with Animal and Tech, so I know the li'l nigga is 'bout it. King, I be watching this li'l nigga move and he's seriously about his business. If he's gonna do dirt anyway, why not snatch him up and try to school him instead of letting him fall to the wayside?"

For as much as King hated to admit it, Lakim made a lot of sense. He had been watching Ashanti for years and he just seemed to keep getting worse, especially since his crew had left him on his own. Ashanti was like a rabid dog preying on anything and everything moving, and at the rate he was going, it wouldn't be long before somebody put a bullet in his ass or locked him away in someone's prison until he was an old man. Ashanti definitely needed a guiding hand but King wasn't sure if it was his.

King's cell phone suddenly vibrated on the countertop. He flipped it open, listened for a minute, and hung up. "Let's bounce," he said to Lakim and dropped two twenties on the counter for their food and drinks. "Goldberg is about to pull outside with Sahara and her peoples. Let's get them situated and go handle our business."

"What about Ashanti?" Lakim asked.

King hesitated. "Fuck it, snatch the li'l nigga up, but make sure he understands that he's just a spectator. Him riding out with us to Jersey will give me a chance to pick his brain and see where his head is really at. If he's on some bozo shit, I'm kicking his li'l ass out on the turnpike."

"Say no more." Lakim smiled.

By the time King stepped out of Jumbo Burgers, Goldberg's black Lincoln was pulling up to the curb. Sahara stepped out of the car first, looking a hot fucking mess. Her hair was sticking up on the sides and there were dried tears on her cheeks. She was followed by a thick chick that King recognized as her friend Frankie. He and Frankie had never met in more than passing so this was the first time he had really gotten a good look at her, and he nodded his head in approval.

"Oh, baby, thank you so much." Sahara jumped into King's arms.

"Don't thank me, I should bust you in ya fucking head for getting locked up," King scolded her.

"It wasn't my fault. We were just . . ."

"Save that shit, because I really don't wanna hear it right now." He waved her off and walked over to the car to speak with his lawyer. "Yo, I really appreciate you getting my shorty out, Goldberg."

"No thanks needed, I'm only doing what you pay me to do. Oh, and you'll be getting my invoice in a few days." The lawyer smiled.

"So what was the deal with them anyhow?" King asked.

"Apparently they stormed into a high-rise building and

beat up one of the tenants. The girl wanted to press charges, but apparently she had an open bench warrant that I offered to make disappear if she didn't go through with it. I'll most likely get it busted down to trespassing and the girls will probably have to pay a fine or do some community service."

"Good looking out." King stuck his arm through the car window and shook Goldberg's hand.

"No problem, but let's not make this a habit, James. I make my bones off the big cases and it really makes me look like I'm hurting when my colleagues see me handling project cat fights. The next time one of your little jump-offs gets into something less than a murder or drug case, call the Legal Aid Society because I don't have time for this shit." Goldberg threw the car in gear and sped off.

"Sometimes I wanna slap that nigga's face off," King mumbled as he rejoined the group.

"He does have a nasty-ass attitude. I don't like the way he was trying to talk to us back at the precinct." Sahara folded her arms.

"Shorty, you need to be glad that muthafucka bothered to talk to you at all, let alone get your simple ass outta jail. Do you know how much I'm gonna have to pay that nigga to take care of this shit?"

"I'm sorry, King. We didn't go over there to get into a fight, but the bitch tried to pop off and we had to handle our business," Sahara explained.

"Whatever, Sahara. I got too much going on tonight to be bothered with this petty shit. I gotta go home and get right so me and Lakim can head OT."

"OT?" Sahara gasped. "King, you promised that we would hang out tomorrow night." She was afraid that he was about to ruin the plans by pulling a no-show at his own surprise party.

"Why don't you calm the fuck down. I never said how long I was gonna be gone. I got some shit I need to take care of across the water so I'll be back in time."

"Okay, baby, because you know I wanna make sure I show you a good time on your birthday." Sahara draped her arms around King and planted kisses on his cheek.

"Chill, ma, I don't wanna get none of my jail funk on you." King gently pushed her away. Sahara's breath was on fire but he didn't want to hurt her feelings by telling her. "But on the real, Sahara, you gotta curb some of this chicken-head shit you're out here doing. You can't be a part of the King's court and you out here getting locked up on crackhead-ass charges, feel me?"

"Yeah, and I'm sorry, King. Trust me, this is the first and last time you'll have to rescue me from jail. Isn't that right, Frankie?"

"Yeah," Frankie said, but she was only half paying attention. Her mind was still on how to keep them from getting evicted.

"Shorty, don't I know you?" Lakim sized Frankie up. He had been staring at her the whole time, trying to place her face.

"I don't think so," Frankie said in a less-than-interested tone. Lakim did look familiar, but Frankie had too much on her mind to dwell on it.

Lakim continued staring and flipping through his mental Rolodex. He knew Frankie's face but just couldn't think where. Then it hit him. "Yeah, I know you, shorty. You used to roll with Twenty-Gang!" Twenty-Gang was a group of all-girl criminals from Harlem, made famous by Evelyn

Panelli, aka Eve, when she wiped out an entire group of dealers from the West Side and got away with it.

"Yeah, I used to fuck with them a li'l something, why?" Frankie asked with an attitude.

Lakim closed the distance between him and Frankie and looked her in the eyes. "You don't remember me, do you?"

"No, should I?" Frankie took a defensive step back. She had done some wild shit when she was a young girl dancing in the shadow of Eve and Twenty-Gang, so there was no telling how Lakim was going to come at her.

"A few years ago a couple of chicks from Twenty-Gang caught me slipping and got me for some change. I remember you because it was your little ass who clocked me in the back of the head with the hammer. Small world, ain't it?"

Looking at Lakim, Frankie did remember his face. Big Kiki, who was one of the OGs of Twenty-Gang, had taken her out to bust her cherry on what was to be her first lick, and they rode down on a chubby young dealer from the projects and robbed him for some work and some money. Lakim had shed the baby fat and grown facial hair but she remembered his dark eyes and the murderous look he had given her, which was similar to the one he was giving her at that moment.

Frankie rocked back on her heels and threw her hands up defensively. "My dude, I don't want no problems with you over something that I did when I was young and dumb, but if you're looking for a problem then I got one, because I'm not really in the mood to play games." Frankie spat, which only made Lakim smile. She knew the brolic little man would tear her apart in a fistfight but she wasn't about to back down.

"Be easy, La." King placed a calming hand on his friend's shoulder.

The tension in Lakim's face drained away and he gave Frankie an amused look. "Shorty, I ain't got no problem with you over that shit. If I had caught you when it was fresh, I'd have tore ya fucking head off, but I'm over it. If anything, you taught me one of the most valuable lessons I could've ever learned in this game."

"And what's that?" Frankie was still standing there with her guard up.

"Never trust a bitch!" Lakim laughed. "On some real shit, though, that was a dumb-ass stunt but it took balls to try and pull off, especially for some females."

"Sometimes you gotta go all in and get it how you live," Frankie said seriously.

"And how you getting it now?" Lakim asked.

"Any way I know how."

"Well, considering the fact that you're out here getting locked up over dumb shit, it's obvious that you don't know much." Lakim laughed. "You got heart and I respect that about you, shorty. When you're ready to get with some *real* niggaz and see some *real* paper, you need to come holla at me."

"And what can you do for me that I can't do for myself?" Frankie asked defiantly.

"Upgrade ya life," Lakim said seriously. "But as ya girl Sahara can tell you, me and my niggaz ain't about a whole lot of talking, we let our actions speak for us, so make ya next move ya best move and see about me."

"Listen to you on ya Goldie shit," Sahara teased Lakim.

"Ma, you know I keep it G all day. Holla at ya girl and

let her know what the business is," Lakim told Sahara while keeping his eyes glued to Frankie.

"I don't need nobody to tell me something I can see for myself," Frankie shot back.

"Lakim, if you're done with your recruiting session, we've got business to handle, remember? Sahara, we gonna put y'all in a cab and bust a move," King said.

"That'll work, we about to make moves back to the projects," Sahara told him. "You ready, Frankie?"

"Nah, you go ahead, Sahara. I got something I need to do right quick and I'll meet you back at the crib," Frankie told her and started out up the street.

"Frankie, where the hell are you going?" Sahara called after her.

"I gotta go see a man about a dog," Frankie called over her shoulder and disappeared around the corner.

CHAPTER 22

After all that Frankie had been through that day, she wanted nothing more than to go home and crawl under the covers, but she knew that she couldn't while the clock was still ticking on their pending eviction. Their trip to see Debbie had not only been pointless, but it put them further in the hole with the fines they were going to have to pay because of the altercation. Frankie couldn't believe that for as crooked as Debbie was, she'd actually had the nerve to try to press charges on them. She wished she'd followed her first instinct and run up in her crib with the hammer instead of listening to Sahara and trying to handle the situation diplomatically. Snakes like Debbie didn't understand diplomacy and it was a mistake Frankie wouldn't make twice.

Frankie wandered through the streets of Harlem, thinking of a master plan. There were a few heads she could've gotten at to try to get up a few dollars to put toward the rent, but the majority of them weren't about to give up something for nothing and Frankie hadn't reached that point of desperation. That was the problem when running with thieves—there was no honor among them. She needed to get some quick cash and boosting wasn't going to cut it. She needed a lick, and as she looked up at the street sign and realized where she was, she knew just whom she could holla at about it.

She didn't get through on the first call or even the second, but Frankie was persistent. When she finally got through, she had to spend ten minutes explaining how she'd gotten the cell phone number in the first place before being granted a meeting and given the address to come to. It didn't take long for Frankie to reach her new destination. It was a quiet building on 133rd and Seventh Avenue. She tapped the intercom with the coded combination she'd been given and after a few ticks the lobby door buzzed open.

Frankie could've taken the elevator but she decided to jog up the six flights so she could see what she was walking into. She and the person she'd called knew each other through a friend of a friend so neither really knew how far they could trust the other. Quietly, she slipped from the stairwell and made her way to the apartment door, where she knocked and waited. A few seconds passed, then the peephole moved, followed by the sound of locks coming undone. When the door opened, Frankie was greeted by a beautiful body, attached to a more beautiful face.

She was five-nine or somewhere around there. The black stiletto heels she was wearing made it hard to tell. She wore a short-cut silk robe, but it did little to hide her undergarments. The black lace lingerie she wore had clearly cost a few dollars, but with a body like hers, only the best could drape it. She had the legs of a track star, leading the path to her curvaceous hips. Her breasts were just fuller than a handful, with rich brown nipples peeking out from behind her transparent bra. From the faint stretch marks and small pouch around her stomach you could tell she'd had kids, but other than that her body was a well-oiled machine. Her face was made up almost flawlessly, but Frankie could still see the bruising around her cheek that she was trying to cover. Even with the blemish she was still fine.

"How you doing, is—" Frankie began but was cut off by a roll of the girl's eyes.

"He's waiting for you in the living room." The girl stepped back for Frankie to enter. After replacing all the locks, she led Frankie into a carpeted living room. There was a nice-size television mounted on the wall over a surround-sound system that connected to several speakers through the living room. The small dining-room table in the corner was freshly wiped down and decorated with fake flowers and ornate mats. On the living room floor, a few toys were scattered from where the kids had neglected to pick them up. To anyone visiting, the apartment looked like it belonged to an average couple who might have had a few kids, but the hardened gangster sitting on the couch wearing a bathrobe and puffing an L said otherwise.

"Cutty, I wanna thank you for agreeing to see me." Frankie made to step forward but froze in her tracks. Cutty had produced the biggest machine gun she had ever seen and had it pointed at her face.

"Bitch, skip the pleasantries and tell me why you're really here," Cutty demanded. All Frankie could do was swallow.

It was the second time that night she had been caught without her gun, and from the looks of things, this was the time she wished most that she had it. If every drop of liquid in her body hadn't been frozen with fear, Frankie would've surely pissed her pants, looking down the barrel of that chopper. Cutty was known on the streets as a cold killer who was quick to violence. Back in the days he had been running partners with Frankie's cousin, but she and Cutty didn't really know each other, which made her coming to see him risky and borderline stupid, but she was desperate and knew that he was the man holding the bag that could potentially help her out of her situation.

"Little girl, I asked you a question." Cutty chambered a round in the machine gun.

"I—it's like I told you on the phone—I need a hookup," Frankie stuttered. Her lips were so numb that it felt like she was mumbling when she spoke.

"Hookup? What the fuck is a hookup? This ain't the phone company," Cutty barked.

The girl who had answered the door cut between Cutty and Frankie and moved the gun. "Why don't you stop playing before you scare this li'l girl to death? Sit down," she told Frankie, motioning toward the love seat while she sat on the couch next to Cutty. "Little girl, you must either be very stupid or very desperate to come up in here to ask Cutty for anything, so which one is it?"

"I guess a li'l bit of both," Frankie said honestly. "I kinda got myself into a li'l situation and need a quick come-up and I figured you could help me out, which is why I came looking for you when I heard you were home from prison."

"My reputation must precede me these days," Cutty said sarcastically, laughing. "And how did you manage to come across my contact information? I'm pretty sure I never fucked you because you're kinda on the young side, though you do have a phat ass." He looked her up and down. "So why don't you tell me who put you on my trail so I can pay them a social call after I'm done with you."

Frankie gulped. "I got your number from my aunt Eta. You told her to reach out if the family needed anything."

Cutty leaned forward and studied Frankie. "You one of Mel's li'l cousins?"

Frankie nodded. "I'm Frankie. Shamel used to bring you and Rio to my mom's barbecues at our crib in the Bronx back in the days."

At the mention of his old crime partner's name, Cutty immediately softened and placed the machine gun on the floor. "Oh shit, li'l Francine? Damn, girl, I almost shot you for nothing. Why didn't you say you was fam?"

"I tried," Frankie said weakly.

"Ah, man, this changes everything! Jada, go get me and cuzo something to drink while we talk." Jada mumbled something under her breath, which brought Cutty's scowls. "Did you say something?" He placed his hand on her thigh and squeezed tight enough to make her wince.

When Cutty finally released his grip, Jada sprang to her feet, rubbing her thigh. "I asked if y'all wanted light liquor or dark?" she grunted.

"Surprise us, just as long as you do it quick." Cutty smacked her on the ass way harder than he needed to. Jada gave him a murderous look before stalking off to the kitchen to do as she was told. She came back a few seconds later and placed two glasses of Hennessy in front of them. "That's more like it." Cutty sipped his drink. "Now you can go in the back and finished chopping up them cookies."

Jada rolled her eyes. "C'mon, Cutty, I been cutting up work for four hours. I've got razor cuts on my fingertips, my hands are cramping, and I'm gonna have to soak my nails for a week to get all this shit from under them." Jada raised her hands for Cutty to inspect.

Cutty took Jada's hand in his and kissed her fingertips lovingly. "My baby's fingers tired?" Without warning, Cutty bent Jada's fingers and brought her to her knees. "Do I strike you as someone who gives a fuck about your sticky-ass fingers getting tired? You should've thought about that before you tried to piss on my head and tell me it was raining when I was in prison, bitch!"

"Listen, if this is a bad time I could come back." Frankie attempted to get up but Cutty's voice froze her.

"You keep your li'l ass glued to that seat. This will only take a second." Cutty got up and hauled Jada off to the bedroom.

Frankie sat there nervous as hell, not really sure what to do. She hadn't made the connection when she'd first seen the girl that she was the notorious Jada Butler, the mother of Cutty's son Miles. Rumor had it that while Cutty was away, Jada had blown his stash partying and tricking off around Harlem. Jada and everyone else expected Cutty to be gone for a very long time but two years ago he had popped back up on the scene and had been none too pleased with Jada for how she had tried to shit on him, and he had vowed to get even. Seeing firsthand how Cutty treated someone whom he was supposed to love who ran afoul of him, Frankie had no illusions about what would happen to her if things went to the left. She had just made her mind up to forget the whole thing when Cutty reappeared.

"Fucking baby mamas." Cutty sat back on the couch, shaking his head. "You ain't nobody's baby mama, is you, Frankie?"

"Nah, I ain't got no kids and don't want no kids," Frankie said.

"That's a good thing, because when you have a kid with a muthafucka you're bound to them. No matter how fucking trifling they turn out to be, you're tied to them for the life of that kid, or at least until they're old enough to find out how much of a fucked-up individual the other parent is." He cut his eyes toward the bedroom. "Now let's deal with your little problem. How much work did you need and how much bread you got to drop up-front?"

Frankie didn't have an immediate answer, as it was the one thing she hadn't thought about when she'd come up with the plan. She was a thief and not a drug dealer, so she really didn't know what she was doing. She shrugged and said, "The thing is, I don't have any money, which is why I came to see you. I was hoping that we could work something out to where I hit you back after I flip it."

Cutty frowned and shook his head. "You kids kill me; you always want something for nothing, and use the name of a dead man to try and soften my heart. Normally I'd run your green ass outta here and give you a good slap for wasting my time, but on the strength of my man, I'm gonna give you enough rope to hang yaself." Cutty dug into the pocket of his robe and produced a baggie wrapped in a rubber band, which he unwrapped and held out for Frankie to inspect. It was only half full, hardly what she'd expected, but she didn't want to insult Cutty by saying so, so she just nodded like it was exactly what she'd expected.

"Let me save you the trouble of trying to bust your brain like you really know how to eyeball coke," Cutty continued. "That's eleven grams of some shit that ain't been stepped on, so you can do what you do and still get some change back."

"Good looking out, Cutty, that's love." Frankie reached for the baggie, but he pulled it back.

Cutty's eyes suddenly became dark and very serious. "Love ain't got nothing to do with this, baby girl. This here is a business arrangement. You take these drugs and the clock starts ticking on the payback and it's my money or your ass. Do we understand each other?"

Frankie's rational mind told her to tell Cutty to keep his drugs and get up outta there, but she desperately needed the money, so she took the devil's bargain. "I got you," she assured Cutty and stuffed the drugs into her pocket. Frankie got up to leave but Cutty stopped her when she reached the door.

"Francine," he called after her. "You try and burn me on this and it ain't gonna matter who you're related to."

Frankie just nodded and left.

CHAPTER 23

By the time Porsha got back to the hood, she was tired, aggravated, and had a splitting headache from where dude had slugged her. The liquor had him way outta pocket, and though she knew the bouncers had worked him over, she still felt cheated out of her personal revenge. Fools getting drunk and acting ignorant in strip clubs was one of the hazards of her profession. No matter where you worked and how tight security was, you always had the liquid thug who would let a few shots make him think he was the Mack.

The belligerent drunk was something most of the girls had to deal with at one point or another, but it didn't happen as often to the girls who were *with* somebody. Porsha had been approached plenty of times by men and women offering to manage her and watch her back, but none of them could ever sell her on the idea. She reasoned that since she was the one sweating and being damn near molested in the clubs, it would be insane to give someone else a piece of her take. Porhsa was opposed to the idea of a pimp or money manager, but in light of how close she had come to getting her ass whipped, she was giving some serious thought to hiring some protection. She had seen enough episodes of *Law & Order: SVU* to know that her life was worth more than the few dollars she was trying to save.

As she made her way down the pathway to her building she couldn't help but notice how quiet the hood was. Just a few hours ago it had been abuzz with activity, but now it looked dead. A few of the locals were in their usual spot on the last bench, drinking beers and smoking weed, but there wasn't a D-boy in sight. The only people outside who even resembled criminals were Levi and Bernie, who were shooting dice under the streetlight, under the watchful eyes of some of the local knuckleheads.

"Hold them dice until the lady passes," Levi told the group when he noticed Porsha coming their way.

"Wow, Levi, you never struck me as the gentlemanly type," Porsha said with a smile as she passed them.

"I ain't, I just wanted to watch yo ass shake when you passed," Levi said with a crooked grin.

Porsha sucked her teeth. "Boy, you could fuck up a wet dream."

"And I could care less as long as I was in it," he shot back.

"Whatever." Porsha rolled her eyes. "Hey, Bernie, where's your other half?"

"Boots is upstairs making dinner and getting the kids ready for bed," Bernie told her, shaking the dice in his palm.

"To be young and in love is a beautiful thing." Porsha smiled at Bernie.

"I know it, which is why I'm glad to have a down-ass bitch like Boots in my corner holding me down," Bernie said proudly.

"Love is overrated. Give me a nasty bitch who likes

to get drunk and have a good time and I'm happy," Levi capped.

"When you constantly shop in the gutter, all you'll ever come up with is trash, Levi," Porsha said over her shoulder, making her way to the building.

"I know it, and I'm good with garbage as long as it's got a hot mouth and a wet box," Levi called after her.

"Yo, that bitch can get it," Levi told Bernie when Porsha was out of earshot.

"You ain't never lied, but that's playing it too close to home for me," Bernie said.

"That's because you're afraid to take chances, my dude. Let me tell you something, if I thought there was even a chance that Porsha would let me hit that, I'd cheat God in a poker game to make it happen," Levi said seriously.

"Levi, you are too thirsty for words. Niggaz like you are constantly in the race, while niggaz like me already took first prize." Bernie poked his chest out.

Levi gave him a pitiful look. "My dude, if what you got is first prize, then I'll take runner-up all day."

"What you mean by that?" Bernie asked defensively.

Levi started to let him in on what everybody already knew, but he was in a decent enough mood that night so he let him live. "Nothing. I'm just saying I ain't the kinda nigga who can see myself locked down with the same piece of pussy night in and night out," Levi lied.

"Everything ain't for everybody, Levi, but at the end of the day we all play the game to find that one special person who we can trust with our lives," Bernie said.

Levi couldn't help himself. "So you're trying to tell me that you trust Boots completely?" One of the boys who was standing around listening started to snicker, but a stern look from Levi quieted him.

Bernie paused for a long moment. "Yeah, I trust Boots," he said, but he didn't sound as sure as he wanted to come across.

Levi wanted to fall in the grass laughing, but he held his composure. Instead, he placed a friendly hand on Bernie's shoulder and gave him a little squeeze. "Then you're a far better man than I am, brother. I wouldn't trust no bitch, especially one with Boots's pedigree." It was clear that Bernie didn't understand the word, so he elaborated: "It just means that Boots is a street chick, no disrespect, B."

"Oh, a'ight," Bernie said, with some of his confidence restored.

"Ayo," a voice called from the shadows of the path leading to the parking lot. All eyes turned to see who it was, but it was only Levi who smiled when he saw the thin young girl motioning for him to come over.

"I'll be back in a sec," Levi excused himself from the dice game. "Yo, Bernie, when y'all plan the wedding date I wanna be the first nigga to get an invite," he capped as he walked off.

"If you spent as much time trying to get a chick instead of worrying about the next man's, then maybe you'll be able to get some pussy without paying for it," Bernie called after him. "Sucka-ass nigga don't think I know he want my bitch." Bernie snorted.

Levi laughed at Bernie's parting remark. He'd tried to put Levi on blast, but anybody who knew him knew that he preferred whores to squares anyhow. For the same amount of money he would pay on a date, he could get a piece of grade-A pussy minus the headaches of conversation. Whores were definitely Levi's vice, but they were also Bernie's, whether he knew it or not. Boots's mouth was more rancid than the city dump and Bernie happily kissed her in it every night.

"What it do, Faye?" Levi greeted the girl. Faye was a slim goodie who had a decent enough shape, but it was nothing to write home about.

"I can't call it, a bitch out here stressed. I got into it with my moms again and she put me out," Faye explained.

"Damn, you and your moms are worse than Ali and Holmes. What y'all fighting about now?"

"Her stupid-ass boyfriend again. All that nigga does is lay around and drink all day, but she's constantly on me about when I'm getting a job. When I was getting a li'l bullshit money with Happy I always broke bread with her, and now she wanna act all funny about it. Me and her were arguing and her boyfriend tried to get in it so I swung on him. Instead of her taking my side she took his and told me I had to get out. I got the keys to my sister's crib in Yonkers, but she's not gonna be home until Monday so I would need the money to get there and for some food to hold me down for a few days."

Levi knew where Faye was going with it, but decided to play along. "How much you talking?"

"Maybe like fifty bucks. Do you think you can help me out?"

A plan immediately began to form in Levi's mind. "Well, I'm popped right now but somebody is supposed to be dropping me off some change in a few hours. Holla at me then and I can do something for you."

"Thanks, Levi, I promise I'll pay you back," Faye said sincerely.

"It's all good, Faye, you know you my li'l nigga. So where you gonna be?"

Faye shrugged. "I don't know, I guess I'll walk around out here until you holla at me."

Levi smiled. "Faye, you know I ain't gonna see you wandering around out here by yaself. I'll tell you what, why don't you come kick it with me at my spot. I got a blunt and a corner of Hennessy left from last night. We can sip and smoke until my bread comes through."

Faye's eyes lit up. After the day she had been having, a drink and some weed sounded like just what the doctor ordered. "Okay, I'll meet you on the corner of One-Hundredth Street in five minutes. I don't want these gossiping-ass niggaz to see us leaving together and start spreading rumors."

"Privacy is my middle name, ma. I'll see you in a few." Levi walked away. A broad smile crossed his face. Faye thought she was going to game him out of some bread, but Levi had a little game of his own he intended on playing with Faye.

After about ten minutes of waiting for the elevator, Porsha got tired of waiting and decided to take the steps. She hated going up and down the piss-and-graffiti-riddled stairs but she would be an old maid by the time the elevator came down, and that's only if they were actually working.

With her little roll-on in tow, Porsha began her hike. She was about to round the landing to the second floor when she heard movement. Retrieving her pepper spray from her purse, she placed her back against the wall and began inching up. As she drew closer, she was able to make out what sounded like faint moaning and slurping. Moving as stealthily as she could, Porsha poked her head around the corner and what she saw made her jaw drop.

Happy was sitting on the steps with his head back. His breathing was short and ragged in between his moans of pleasure. Between his legs a young woman knelt with her head moving up and down in a rhythm. His cubby fingers were wrapped in her dry weave as he tried to force himself deeper into her throat. From the way his bottom lip was quivering, Porsha could tell that the girl was good at what she was going. For as much as Porsha wanted to turn away, she found herself intrigued by what she was seeing. She wasn't into girls, but watching her expertly suck Happy off stirred something in her. Happy's grip on the girl's hair tightened as he gasped for her to go deeper and with a slight gag she obliged.

Catching brief glimpses of the girl's profile struck a chord of familiarity with Porsha, but she was so caught up in the show that she didn't place her right off. Happy winced and began to babble something unintelligible, signaling that he was about to come. The girl tried to pull her face away, but Happy used both hands to hold her in place and began ramming himself inside her mouth faster and faster. With a grunt, Happy exploded in the girl's mouth and all over her face and hair.

"Damn, that shit was great." Happy panted as he continued stroking his cock to empty himself.

"Nigga, I told you not to come in my fucking mouth." The girl jumped up and began wiping her face with the back of her shirtsleeve. When she turned around, Porsha got a good look at her and realized why she was so familiar. It was Boots.

"Wow, that was quite a show," Porsha announced herself, scaring the hell out of Happy and Boots.

"Bitch, what the fuck are you doing sneaking around in staircases?" Boots snapped. Her sharp words couldn't hide the embarrassment on her face.

"What am *I* doing in the staircase?" Porsha looked her up and down. "That's a question you better hope ya baby daddy doesn't ask you, boo-boo."

Boots got in Porsha's face. "Yo, on my kids, if you open ya mouth about this I'm gonna—"

"You ain't gonna do shit," Porhsa cut her off. "Let me tell you something, sweetie, I ain't one of these li'l bitches who get scared when they hear the stories about how you used to give it up, so watch how you talk to me, before we have a situation. I don't give a fuck about you, your dizzy-ass baby daddy, or whose dick you put in your nasty-ass mouth, so I stand to gain nothing by blowing you up. But let's be clear on something: the next time you roll up on me like you wanna do something, I'm gonna snatch that nappy-ass weave outta your bald-ass head."

"Ladies, ladies, there's no need to argue." Happy got in between them and draped his arms around both of them. "We're all adults here so I'm sure we can work this out like grown folks. Hell, there may be an opportunity here for us all to get better acquainted." He let his fingers brush Porsha's hair.

"Happy, if you don't move that slimy-ass hand you ain't gonna get it back," Porsha threatened.

"Damn, youz a cold bitch." Happy removed his arm.

"You keep trying to smut me like you do these bitches and you'll find out just how cold I am." Porsha bumped past him and made her way up the steps.

"I know that's right, only the best for Porsha. Well, you know my pockets run deep, baby girl, so whenever you're ready to stop playing hard-to-get, you know where to find me."

Porsha stopped and glared down at Happy. "Hap, your pockets can run from here to the other side of the world and it still wouldn't be enough to let your diseased little dick find its way inside these golden walls." With a roll of her eyes, Porsha disappeared.

"I can't believe this rotten bitch," Boots fumed as she fixed her hair as best she could. She could feel the come starting to dry at the roots and knew that she'd have to wash it soon before she ended up having to cut the weave out. "I swear to God, if she tells Bernie, I'm gonna stomp her out."

"Don't worry, she ain't gonna say nothing." Happy fixed his pants. He had a big smile plastered across his face and a far-off look in his eyes.

"I'm glad you're so damn confident that she's gonna keep her mouth closed, because I ain't. Bitches love to cause trouble. And what the hell do you keep smiling about?"

Happy let out a small giggle. "Because I think I'm in love."

Porsha was applying the finishing touches to her makeup when she heard Sahara come in. She knew it was Sahara and not Frankie because she wouldn't have heard Frankie. The girl moved like a cat burglar and had scared the hell out of Porsha on more than one occasion.

"How'd it go with Debbie?" Porsha asked Sahara when she came into the bathroom.

"Hold on," Sahara grumbled while she fumbled with the button on her pants and danced around trying to keep from pissing on herself. There was no way she was going to sit on one of the nasty toilets in the precinct so she had been holding it for hours and now her bladder threatened to burst. She finally got the button undone and plopped on the toilet to relieve herself. "Didn't you get any of the messages we've been leaving on the answering machine? We're just getting out of jail!"

Porsha's eyes widened. "Jail, how the hell did that happen?" Sahara went on to give her the short version of their altercation with Debbie while she cleaned herself up. "I told y'all going over there clowning wouldn't solve anything," Porsha reminded her.

"Porsha, miss me with that shit because I don't see you making no great strides on knocking out the rent. How much did you make shaking your ass this afternoon?" Sahara spat.

"I didn't make much but I didn't come back empty-handed," Porsha assured her. "And I don't know what you're getting mad at me for when my black ass is gonna be out in the street right along with y'all bitches if we don't get this rent paid."

"You're right, and I'm sorry if I was being short, Porsha, but I've had a really fucked-up day. I was gonna crack on King for some paper but he ended up having to pay a lawyer to get us out, so that cut into my action."

"What about Frankie, I thought y'all were together?"

"We were, but after King got us out she left me, talking about she was going to see a man about a dog, whatever the fuck that means."

"Knowing her, it was probably code for *I'm going to rob*

a liquor store." Porsha applied an extra coat of lip gloss. "So what are you gonna do for the rest of the night?"

"I'm probably gonna drown my sorrows in Hennessy until I pass out. This may be my last few nights sleeping on anything other than a cot in the shelter so I wanna enjoy them," Sahara said in a defeated tone.

"Well, we ain't out on our asses yet. I've got a B-plan." Porsha explained to her about the star-studded event she was working that night.

"Sounds like it's gonna be off the hook!" Sahara said excitedly.

"It is, ma. You should roll with me," Porsha suggested.

"Porsha, you know damn well my stripping days are over."

"I'm not talking about to work, simple-ass. Come out and keep me company while I do my thing. We can get shit-faced and laugh at the rest of them bitches while they try to keep up with me."

This made Sahara smile for the first time that entire day. "Fuck it, I might as well go with you. Let me wash my ass and change my clothes."

"A'ight, I'll be waiting for you downstairs. Our ride should be here in a few minutes." Porsha gathered her purse and keys and headed for the door. Before she left, she had a parting thought for Sahara: "Before you come down, please do something with that hair."

Levi lounged on his queen-size bed, blowing rings of ciga-rette smoke in the air, smiling like the cat that had eaten the canary. On the foot of his bed sat Faye, who was pull-ing her shirt back over her head. When they'd gotten back to Levi's apartment they'd smoked and drunk until they were both feeling nice, then Levi had cracked for the pussy. Faye tried to act like she wasn't with it at first, but it didn't take much convincing on the part of Levi to get her naked. She fucked and sucked Levi like the nasty little whore that she was and when they were done she let him blow his wad in her mouth for the promise of an extra fifty dollars. It never ceased to amaze him, the lows some chicks would stick to for cash, but as long as he ended up smiling when it was all said and done, he didn't pass judgment.

"You know, you're the first guy I ever let do that," Faye said.

"Do what?" he asked in a very disinterested tone.

"You know, come in my mouth."

"Is that right? I feel very special," he said sarcastically. "Listen, I know you got shit to do so I'm gonna call you a cab to take you where you gotta go." He had busted his nut and was ready to be rid of Faye.

"A cab?" She was confused.

"Yes, unless you planned on walking to the Metro North station."

"Oh yeah, thanks, Levi, I mean for everything."

"Nah, thank *you*, ma. That was some of the meanest top I ever had." He laughed.

"Shut up, Levi." Faye blushed. "But seriously, I had a good time with you and I was thinking maybe we could get together again soon."

"Sure thing," he said, only half listening. He was too busy scrolling through his phone for a taxi number so he could get rid of Faye's scheming ass. Levi told the cab where to come and ended the call. "Your cab should be downstairs in two minutes. Just hit the slam-lock on your way out."

"Okay." Faye continued to sit there like she had something else on her mind.

"What's the matter, did I forget to give you your money or something?" Levi sat up on one elbow and adjusted his glasses.

"Nah, you took care of me already. I was just sitting here thinking, what if this gets out? I know how you move, Levi, and I don't want my name to be mud in the hood."

Levi sighed. It was just what he'd feared—that he would have to have an actual conversation with her before he got the bitch to leave. There was nothing Levi loathed more than talking after sex. He slid to the edge of the bed and took Faye's hand in his. "Sweetie, I do what I do but I don't put it out there. You never hear me running around talking about who I did what with, and trust me, I've got some stories on some of ya favorite Hollywood stars, but I ain't on it like that. Any bitch you ever heard about me fucking is either lying, or trying to put me out there because she's bitter. It's the price of fame, baby."

Faye leaned her forehead against his chest. "That's why I fuck with you, Levi, you keep it gangsta."

"Of course I do." He patted Faye on the back of her head. "Now you better get going, you don't want your cab to leave you."

"Right." Faye got up off the bed and headed for the door. "I'll call you when I get to my sister's."

"You do that, sweetie." Levi reclined on the bed like he was about to settle down and go to sleep. As soon as the door closed, Levi was at his window. When he saw Faye get into the taxi, he rushed to his computer and fired it up. Levi took off his glasses and removed a small plate from one of the arms. From inside one of the hidden compartments he removed a small SD card and put it in his computer. An image of Faye's face in the throes of passion appeared on his screen. He had paid a grip to have his frames fitted with the spy-camera, but for the video quality they were worth every dime. He zoomed in on an image of him hitting her from the back and smiled. "The Internet is gonna love you, baby."

CHAPTER 24

Instead of taking a taxi home from Cutty's with her package, Frankie hopped on the train and rode the few stops back the hood. A taxi would've been more convenient and quicker, but it would've also been riskier. She had heard far too many horror stories about the police randomly stopping taxis and dudes getting caught with work, and she had no desire to be among that number.

Once she reached the safety of the projects she felt a little more at ease, but she still had a dilemma. Frankie didn't know her ass from her elbow about drugs. She had been around enough hustlers to have a general idea of what she should sell the drugs for and knew how to package it once it was rocked up, but she had no idea how to turn it from cocaine to crack. There were a few dudes on the block whom she could've gone to for help, but didn't want them in her business like that. With little other choice, she did the obvious and went to a crackhead for help.

Lulu was what you would call a throwback crackhead, someone who had started smoking in the eighties and had carried her oil burner over into the new millennium. Back in the days, she could be found in the company of some of Harlem's most notorious ballers and gangsters living the high life until the *high* became her life. She started out like most of the others, sniffing coke recreationally, until they started cooking it. Once Lulu had taken her first blast from a glass pipe, it was a wrap for her. The higher Lulu got, the lower she sank, until she went from ghetto beauty to another nameless face on a quest for a high; but for as much of a wreck as Lulu had become, she was still one of the best chefs in the hood, which is what had Frankie sitting at her kitchen table watching Lulu huddled over the stove working her magic.

"You got some primo shit here, girlie." Lulu ran her fingers along the edge of the coffeepot and smeared the excess coke on her gums. "Real high quality."

"I should hope so, considering what I had to go through to get it." Frankie fumbled with one of the loose baggies that were scattered on the table.

"Whatever you went through, it was worth it. This shit is gonna have the hood rocking," Lulu assured her as she dropped a few ice cubes into the pot and swirled them around. Once the cookie at the bottom of the pot began to harden, she used a fork to scoop it out and set it on a glass saucer, which she placed on the table in front of Frankie. Frankie went to touch it but Lulu slid it out of reach. "Don't fuck with it, it's still gotta dry."

"Lulu, I appreciate you looking out for me," Frankie told her.

"Shit, I ain't looking out for you, I'm looking out for me. This is a business arrangement, baby girl. You can move whatever you want outta my crib, as long as you hit me off, can you dig it?"

"Yeah, I can dig it. Lu, I'm kinda short on cash right now but as soon as I move a few of these pieces I'll hit you with something."

"Don't worry about it, li'l ma. I know how it is when you're first starting out, so I'm willing to work with you. How about you hit me with a li'l piece of one of them cookies as a show of good faith?" Lulu eyed the stack of crack cookies.

"That'll work." Frankie slid one of the already dried cookies to Lulu.

Using a kitchen knife, Lulu cut off a nice chunk of the cookie. Anybody hip to the crack trade would not have allowed her to help herself to such a large piece, but she knew Frankie was green and took advantage of that. She wrapped her piece in a napkin and stuffed it into her bra. "Frankie, for as long as I've known you you've been a thief; what made you wanna get caught up with this shit?"

Frankie shrugged her shoulders. "I'm trying to make a quick come-up."

"Shit, you picked a hell of a way to go about it. This is a dangerous game you've decided to play."

"Sometimes you gotta do what you gotta do, Lu," Frankie said honestly.

"I know that's right. You just make sure you be careful handling this shit here, girl. I done seen muthafuckas do some real brazen shit in pursuit of this li'l demon here." She nodded at one of the cookies. "It's worse when you're a female because a nigga is always gonna be looking to try you if you ain't got a team behind you."

"I'm good," Frankie said, sounding more confident than she actually was. There was a knock on the door, which startled both of them. Frankie grabbed a newspaper and placed it over the cookies on the table.

"Let me see who the hell this is." Lulu shuffled to the door. She looked through the peephole and, after confirming the identity, opened the door. In walked a kid named Mitch, who was one of Scar's newest recruits.

"Yo, Lu, Scar sent me up here to get that thing from you," Mitch told her.

"Okay, let me get it for you." Lulu went into the bedroom.

Mitch walked into the living room and noticed Frankie sitting at the table with a nervous expression on her face. "Frankie, what you doing here?"

"Nothing, just had to come holla at Lu about something," Frankie lied.

"You and me both," Mitch said, looking around curiously. He noticed the stained coffeepots and baggies on the table, so it was obvious what Frankie was doing there, and from the amount of paraphernalia he deduced that Frankie was handling some type of weight. He didn't question her further but he filed the information away.

"Here you go." Lulu came out of the bedroom holding a shoe box, which she handed to Mitch.

"Them shells still in there too?" he asked, peeking inside the box to inspect the gun.

"You know I ain't gonna tamper with nothing y'all leave me to hold unless it's drugs," Lulu said honestly.

"And that's why we fuck with you," Mitch said with a smirk and handed Lulu a twenty. "I'll see you around, Frankie." Mitch winked, leaving the apartment.

Frankie waited until she was sure Mitch was gone and immediately began gathering her drugs and paraphernalia. "A'ight, Ima see you later, Lu."

"Why are you rushing off, the last cookie ain't even dry yet?" Lulu asked. She wanted Frankie to stick around for a while so she could try to play her for another piece.

"I got something I need to do, so I gotta make moves," Frankie lied. Mitch's popping up like that had made her uneasy and she wanted to get her drugs out of Lulu's spot as soon as possible.

"Okay, baby girl. And remember, if you need to work outta here, it's all good as long as I eat," Lulu reminded her.

"Thanks, but I'm good. I think I'm gonna take it to the streets," Frankie told her and left the apartment.

Scar was sitting on the bench, smoking and checking the time on his phone impatiently. Earlier that day he had exchanged words with some kids from the other side of the projects, and though it might or might not lead to more than words, he didn't want to be caught slipping, which is why he had sent Mitch upstairs to get the hammer from Lulu's crib. He'd just decided to go and see what was keeping Mitch when Boots came out of the building.

"Boots, what's good?" Scar greeted her.

"Shit, about to go to the store right quick to get a Dutch," she told him.

"Put it in the air, I got something to puff on too."

"Nah, me and Bernie gonna blow this down after we put the kids to bed."

"Oh, y'all playing house tonight, huh?" Scar asked sarcastically. Boots responded by giving him the finger. "Stop acting like that, you know I'm just playing with you, Boots. Yo, I seen Bernie coming in the building a li'l while ago with a liquor-store bag so I know that nigga is gonna be sleep soon. You trying to get up later on?"

"I ain't fucking with you, Scar," Boots told him, already

peeping Scar's game. He was cracking for some ass, in not so many words.

"I don't know why you fronting like you don't like when I'm up in them guts."

Boots sucked her teeth. "Ya cock game is alright, but you got too many hangups for my taste."

"What do you mean by that?" Scar frowned.

"Scar, you know what the fuck I'm talking about. For one thing, you're cheap as hell, and for another, ya peeps got big-ass mouths. I don't need my business in the streets and y'all can't keep secrets." A few years back, Boots had made the mistake of letting Scar and his man Lloyd run a train on her and one of them had let it leak out. Thankfully, she'd been able to convince Bernie that it was a lie.

"Boots, you know that wasn't on me, I don't kiss and tell," Scar lied.

"Whatever, I ain't beat for the shit, homie, so save it." She started walking off.

Boots had some of the best head in the hood and Scar wasn't about to let her slide that easily. "Hold on." He caught up with her. "Yo, I was gonna go to the spot and spend some bread with one of the girls, but I'd rather spend it with you." Scar held up a hundred-dollar bill.

Boots hesitated. After what had happened in the staircase with Happy, she didn't want to be bothered, and Bernie was upstairs waiting for her, but there were quite a few things she could do with that hundred dollars. Besides, she knew from past experience that Scar always came quick, so it would be easy money.

"A'ight, fuck it," she agreed, "but I'm telling you now

that I want my money up front and if you take longer than ten minutes to come then you're just assed out."

"Fair enough, Boots. Let's go upstairs to my crib."

Eight and a half minutes later, Scar came out of his building grinning. Thirty seconds later, Boots emerged and made hurried steps up the block to the store. Boots was as trifling as whores came, but she was among the best when it came to sex. He knew he could've gotten her to fuck him for less than a hundred dollars, but the bill saved him the trouble of having to go through the motions of haggling with her. Some may have said that he had overpaid, but the money Scar had given her was *nothing*.

"Yo, Scar," Mitch called him from down the block. He had been so caught up with Boots that he'd almost forgotten about him.

"Damn, for as long as you took, a nigga could've came and blew my fucking head off," Scar barked at Mitch.

"Be easy, them niggaz ain't killing nothing and letting nothing die." Mitch downplayed it.

"And how the fuck would you know? Anyway, what took you so fucking long?"

"I was upstairs, chopping it up with Frankie," Mitch told him.

"Frankie? What the fuck was she doing in a rock house?"

Mitch laughed. "Dawg, you ain't gonna believe this shit." Mitch proceeded to tell Scar what he had seen in the crib. Scar, being a predator, immediately began thinking of a way to turn Frankie's good fortune into his own.

***

Boots was only supposed to be going to get a Dutch Master, but in light of her newfound wealth she decided to get herself something from the liquor store. She ordered a bottle of Moët and a pint of Hennessy. She knew Bernie was gonna beef about her taking so long, but once she got nice and laid her pussy on him he'd be okay.

"Fifty-two fifty," the man behind the glass told her as he bagged her bottles. Boots slipped him the hundred-dollar bill, which he proceeded to test with a special marker. He held the bill up to the light and frowned. "This is no good."

"What the fuck do you mean it's no good?" Boots looked at him as if he was trying to play her.

"Your money, it's no good. This bill is fake, miss, see for yourself." He slid the bill back to her.

Boots snatched the bill and held it up to the light. Sure enough, it was missing the watermarks embedded in real bills. "Fucking Scar!" Boots yelled when she realized she had been beat.

Part III

SEX, MONEY, MURDER

CHAPTER 25

Brick City, the newest strip club in Newark, New Jersey, was quickly building a name for itself for having some of the most premium ladies in the Garden State. It was located in Raymond Plaza, a quiet little strip mall off Raymond Boulevard, which had boasted a party-supply store as its biggest attraction before Brick City came along. Normally the Essex County zoning commission would've never allowed a strip club in the area, but the owner's father was connected to some very important people so they let it slide, provided that they kept the violence to a minimum. To ensure this, the owner had hired off-duty cops to work the door and the main area, but to handle the *real* headaches he employed some of Newark's most notorious gangsters. After the first two troublemakers were made examples of in the back alley of Brick City, word had gotten around that this was one spot you didn't want to come in and try to clown.

Ever since Brick City had opened two months prior, they had always been able to draw a decent crowd, but that night the parking lot was filled to capacity with people still trying to squeeze in. That night was supposed to be the official clap-off between New York and New Jersey—a dozen oiled and primed asses would be smacking together in competition for the ten-stacks that had been offered up for the contest. The event had drawn so much attention that a bunch of women's rights groups had banned together to try to shut it down, stating that it was morally appalling and painted a horrible picture of women. They were right, but at the end of the day it was all about supply and demand; the people demanded flesh and Brick City supplied it.

The clap-off was the main course, but the appetizers were no less exciting. Several rap and R&B acts would be performing that night but the big draw was a local kid who called himself Lord Scientific. The Newark native had been ripping shows left and right all winter and killing the Internet with his videos and free-style sessions. *F.E.D.S.* magazine had done a small write-up on him and the journalist was quoted as saying, "Lord Scientific has the energy and delivery of Method Man with the lyrical swiftness that Nas showed us on 'Halftime.' Hip-Hop . . . you have a problem!" The women had brought the ballers out, but it was Lord Scientific whom the goons came to see.

In addition to bringing out celebrities, the event had also attracted a slew of gangstas and underworld figures, most notably the infamous Shai Clark, boss of all bosses. The bulletproof town car carrying Poppa Clark's youngest son and his entourage pulled into the strip mall and was immediately guided by security to the front of the club, where the owner and several of his personal security staff stood waiting.

"Damn, look at this shit." Angelo peered out the window of the car at the crowd. He was dressed in a tailored gray suit and black tie.

"Yeah, this joint is packed, and I heard some of the most

primo bitches from two cities are supposed to be on deck tonight," Swann told them. His hair was neatly braided into plats tied off by red rubber bands. Swann was Shai's best friend and second-in-command of his organization.

"You better not let Marisol hear you say that," Shai teased him. He was tastefully dressed in a blazer, jeans, and a white T-shirt. Shai had put on a few pounds and sprouted some facial hair, but for the most part he still looked like the little boy who had come home from college to fill his father's shoes several years prior.

"Well, my baby mama ain't here and neither is your fiancée, so all bets are off, homie. What happens in Brick City stays in Brick City." Swann gave Shai dap.

"Well, I ain't got no girl, so I'm trying to put a gum in something. Point me at the bitch with the biggest ass and come back for me in an hour," Holiday capped, causing everyone in the car to laugh.

"While you three have got your faces buried in pussy, try to keep in mind that we're here on business too," Angelo reminded him. Of the quartet he was the most serious.

"Chill out, Angelo, you know we know how to conduct ourselves when we're out," Holiday told him.

"The only thing I know is that you better be the fuck on point. Having fun is okay, but you soldiers are here to be the eyes in the backs of our heads. There's going to be a lot of different crews in there and not everyone is a big fan of our family," Angelo reminded him.

Holiday pulled his twin nines from the shoulder holsters under his leather jacket. "I wish a nigga would try to play outta pocket. I'll put this whole fucking club to sleep, and that's on the big, homie."

"Put those fucking guns away before you accidentally

put us to sleep," Swann ordered. Shai was the boss, but Swann was his field general and all the soldiers respected him. When the town car pulled to a stop, two of Swann's handpicked shooters approached the back door and waited. "A'ight, let's do this," Swann said and pushed the door open.

People looked on in bewilderment as Shai was greeted with stern handshakes and smiles. You'd have thought the president had arrived, and in a sense he had. Shai and his people ran nearly every aspect of organized crime in the tristate area. Nothing was stolen, sold, or built without Shai's getting a taste. As he and his crew were fitted with VIP armbands, the owner walked over.

"Shai, I'm so glad you could make it." Paulie greeted him with a hug. He was a tall man who was always immaculately dressed with a movie star's good looks.

"You know I wouldn't refuse an invitation from a friend of ours," Shai replied. "The place looks good."

"It's better than good, Shai, it's a gold mine. Since we did the renovations, business has tripled and I have the Clarks to thank for it. Here, I got something for you." Paulie handed him an envelope. "Just a token of our appreciation."

Shai tested the weight of the envelope, then handed it to Swann, who put it in the inside pocket of his jacket. What few people knew was that the property where Brick City sat had been about to go into foreclosure until Shai stepped in. He had not only provided Paulie with the loan to save the property but had allowed Paulie the use of one of his contracting companies to do the renovations at half price. Of course, none of this was done out of the goodness of his heart. For his services Shai had become a silent partner in Brick City.

"Hey, Shai, I got a few more things to take care of so I'm gonna have my people show you to the VIP and I'll join you later." Paulie shook his hand again. "And remember, your money is no good in here tonight, not even for trim." He walked off.

"As if we were gonna pay for the pussy anyhow," Holiday said, snickering.

"Remember what I told you," Angelo said, elbowing Holiday as they were led into the recesses of the club.

King James sat behind the wheel of the big green Suburban parked in front of the party-supply store, watching the action in front of Brick City. He watched curiously as the man who had been pointed out as Shai Clark stepped from the town car to receive his praises. Though he had to admit that Shai wasn't quite what he'd expected, King James knew better than anyone else that looks could be deceiving. He continued to watch Shai until he was finally escorted inside and out of sight.

"How much longer we gonna sit in this ride, man? My legs are getting cramped," Dump complained. He was a huge man who took up almost an entire row of the truck seats on his own. He and King James had become friends in state prison, and when Dump touched down, King put him in position. He was as loyal as he was deadly.

"Until my nigga says we move," Lakim told him, expelling a cloud of smoke from the blunt he was toking on. He was just as eager as Dump to get to business, but would be patient and wait to see how King wanted to play it.

"Damn, I would live in that box." Alonzo watched two

girls walk past the truck wearing jeans that were way too tight.

"They probably working the spot tonight, so you may get your chance, baby bro. I told you it was a good idea to come out with us." Lakim passed Alonzo the blunt.

Alonzo happily accepted. "Yeah, I can't front, this spot looks like it's jumping!"

"Word up. Yo, Zo, you get to spend all that good supermarket money on whore pussy tonight," Ashanti joked.

"Fuck you, li'l bastard. That's why your young ass will be watching the whip instead of coming in to play with the grown folks," Alonzo shot back. Everyone in the car, including King, burst out laughing.

When King figured enough time had passed to get Shai and his crew situated, he decided it was time for them to make their entrance. "A'ight, let's do this." King got out of the whip and headed for the club, with his people following closely. The line to get into the spot was crazy, but King didn't do lines. With a fifty-dollar bill pressed in his palm, he walked up to the bouncer who was on the door.

"The line starts back there, homie," the bouncer told King.

"Yeah, can dig that, but I was hoping we didn't have to go through all that, feel me?" King shook the bouncer's hand, leaving the fifty in his palm.

The bouncer checked the bill and slipped it into his pocket. "A'ight, that'll work for one of y'all, but I see you guys are three deep, so, you know." The bouncer held out his hand.

"Word up, you're gonna rob me with no gun, huh?" King eyed him.

The bouncer shrugged. "I got kids to feed, homie. You know how it goes."

Lakim was frustrated with the bouncer so he stepped up. "Yo, what kinda bullshit is you trying to run, sun? You don't know who the fuck we be?"

The bouncer looked down at the shorter Lakim. "Check this out, fam: if you don't back up off me with that jail shit, we gonna have a problem."

"Chill, La." Alonzo pushed his brother back. "Check it, B," he addressed the bouncer. "My brother didn't mean no disrespect, it's just that we feel like you're being a little bit unreasonable with trying to make us pay fifty dollars per head plus the price of admission."

"First of all, I ain't ya B. So you can take that shit back across the bridge to Harlem, the Bronx, or wherever the fuck you're from in New York. It's fifty a head to me if you wanna jump the line and whatever you work out at the door is on you, take it or leave it," the bouncer said in a dismissive tone.

Alonzo felt his blood begin to boil the longer he stared at the smug expression on the bouncer's face. His initial instincts were to peel off one of the razors he had taped to the collar of his button-up and widen that smirk for the bouncer for talking crazy to him in front of all those people, but he didn't take it there. He was about to try reasoning with the bouncer one more time before he got physical, but he heard somebody calling his name.

"Alonzo, is that you making all that noise out there?" a female voice called from the darkened doorway of Brick City. Alonzo strained his eyes and saw a woman coming from behind a small podium just inside the foyer. It wasn't until she stepped outside into the light that he recognized Ms. Betty.

"Wow, what're you doing here?" he asked, surprised to see the older woman whose groceries he'd packed on numerous occasions, at a strip club.

"I'm trying to pay the bills, but what is your li'l tail doing here?" Ms. Betty shot back.

"Me and a few of the fellas were taking a friend out for his birthday and we heard this spot was good, so we came out. But as you can see, we're having a li'l trouble with your peoples." Alonzo glared at the bouncer.

Ms. Betty looked up at the bouncer. "Are you giving my nephew and his friends trouble?"

The bouncer now wore the expression of a kid who had just gotten a note home from school. "I'm sorry, ma, he didn't tell me that he was your family."

"Well, now that you know, you can step aside and let them through. Come on here." Ms. Betty grabbed Alonzo by the arm and led him inside the club. Lakim, Dump, and King brought up the rear.

King stopped short and glared at the bouncer. "And give me my fucking money back," he demanded. The bouncer sucked his teeth and gave King back his fifty.

Ms. Betty marched Alonzo and his people in like they were superstars, waiving the admission charge and instructing the girl who had taken her place behind the podium to fit them with VIP bands. She also gave them five drink tickets apiece and instructed them to come and find her if they wanted more. It was obvious that Ms. Betty had some serious pull in the establishment.

"Thanks for everything, Ms. Betty," Alonzo told her.

"This wasn't about nothing; you know you're family

to me, Alonzo. I always told you that if I ever was in a spot to help you out I would repay your kindness. Now let me get back to work." She gave him a hug. "Be sure to find me before y'all cut out so we can have a toast."

"You got that, Ms. Betty, and tell Lee I said what's up."

"I sure will. See you later, Alonzo." Ms. Betty sashayed back through the crowd and retook her post at the podium.

"Say, brah, where you know the old head from?" Lakim asked Alonzo once Ms. Betty had gone.

"I used to pack her groceries," Alonzo told him.

"Brah, a chick ain't showing you that kinda love for making sure her cans don't crush her eggs. What's really good?" Lakim pressed.

Seeing that Lakim wasn't going to leave it alone, Alonzo kept it real. "A'ight. When her son first came home he had a problem getting a job so I got him plugged in working a delivery truck to appease his parole officer. He went from loading trucks to driving them and eventually buying one and opening his own trucking company."

"You're a regular guardian angel, huh?" Dump joked.

"Nah, he did that off his own hard work, all I did was put him in position to have an opportunity."

King James took note of how Alonzo carried himself and was proud to see that he had grown into a humble young man. A lot of people gave Alonzo shit for squaring up, but King James held him in very high regard for turning his life around. "You're a good man, Zo-Pound"— King James draped his arm around Alonzo—"but right now we're in a bad place, so let's go do some bad things."

"What about the going to holla at Shai?" Lakim asked.

"It'll keep. Right now, let's just grab a few drinks and fuck with some of this pussy." King James smiled.

CHAPTER 26

Porsha sat in the spacious dressing room of Brick City, fixing her eighteen-inch pink wig. Jersey was foreign territory to her and she'd heard how fierce the comp could be, with girls willing to go above and beyond for a song and a dance, so she knew she'd need to step outside the box that night. Instead of a normal thong or bikini she decided to play dress-up, rocking a Warrior Princess outfit, equipped with a fake sword and bronze corset. Since she'd busted the outfit out she'd been getting compliments from the other girls and questions about where she'd gotten it, but of course Porsha wasn't fool enough to tell.

Fifteen minutes after they'd arrived at the spot, Kat had disappeared with some guy she knew, and Porsha hadn't seen her since. There was no doubt in Porsha's mind what Kat was up to, but she didn't judge her. A lot of chicks fronted like they had limits to what they would do for a dollar, but Kat didn't have those kinds of hang-ups. Kat was about her paper and didn't care who knew it or how they felt about it, which was one of the things Porsha admired about her.

The girls she had met at Brick City had come from all over the place for the event. Most of the out-of-town girls were cool, and just there to get their paper, but the chicks from Jersey were throwing major shade. There had been three fights that night between the chicks from Jersey and the out-of-towners, and the real ballers hadn't even started to show up yet, so the night promised to be eventful if anything. The girls from Jersey felt like just because it was their home turf it automatically made them the favorites to win the clap-off, but that's because they had never seen Porsha do her thing. She worked out four days per week and did Pilates every Saturday, so there was no way she planned on walking out of there without at least the rent money.

The door to the dressing room flew open and in walked a big-boned, light-skinned chick whom they called Brick House because of her statuesque build. She stood at just a hair over six feet in flat shoes, with huge breasts and one of the biggest asses Porsha had ever seen. She was a regular at Brick City so she walked around like she owned the joint, looking down on the new girls. Porsha had known her for only about a half hour and she already knew that she couldn't stand her.

"A'ight, you bitches listen up," Brick House's voice boomed. "Playtime is over and the real money has arrived. We got rappers, rock stars, and gangstas, all with rock-hard dicks and fists full of money waiting in the VIP area, waiting to blow both in no particular order. So if you're scared, keep your ass on the main floor, but if you're about that money, get your ass in gear and let's get it!"

"You ain't gotta tell me twice." A chunky stripper wearing a bad wig hopped up and shuffled toward the door. Her stretch-mark-covered ass was so big that if she was wearing a thong no one could see it.

"And where the fuck do you think you're going?" Brick House blocked her path.

"I'm going to get my paper, where do you think I'm going?" The stripper looked up at Brick House.

"The only paper you should be worried about is a paper bag to cover that nasty-ass weave you got going on. The VIP is off-limits to you, ma. We don't need you scaring these niggaz before we can milk them."

"And who do you think you are to tell me where I can eat at?" the stripper challenged.

"I'm the bitch that'll knock you unconscious if I catch you around any of my tricks," Brick House said with ice in her voice. "Now feel free to get whatever your fat ass can scare up on the pole or the main floor, but the VIP is off-limits. And if you don't like what I'm saying, then we can step into the bathroom for five minutes and discuss it. What you wanna do?"

The fat stripper looked around to see if anyone had her back, and of course they didn't. "I ain't beat for this shit, I'm going to get a drink." The fat stripper sucked her teeth and stepped around Brick House to leave the dressing room.

"You do that, but be sure to leave some liquor for the rest of us, you fucking whale," Brick House called after her. She walked down the aisle of benches and mirrors, examining the girls. No one would hold her evil gaze. "Some bitches just don't get it, only top-notch chicks eat here at Brick City. If you're a cow"—she looked at one stripper who was kind of on the chubby side—"or a skank"—she looked at another stripper—"then you play the main area and let the real hos show you how to get it up." She stopped and let her eyes linger on Porsha, who was still tinkering with her hair in the mirror. "Nice outfit, shorty."

"Thanks," Porsha said without turning around to acknowledge her.

Brick House leaned in close enough to invade Porsha's space. "I'll bet you look better out of it than you do in it," she whispered.

Porsha placed her hairbrush down and glared at Brick House in the mirror. "Unless you're tipping, you'll continue to wonder."

Brick House smiled, showing off the gold tooth on one side of her mouth. "By the end of the night I'll be toting a heavier bag than any bitch in this joint, so maybe we can arrange a private party."

"Sorry, I don't do fish." Porsha got up and brushed past her to leave, but Brick House grabbed her arm.

"I can dig it; you're new so you don't know how things work in the Bricks."

Porsha looked at Brick House's hand as if it had been dipped in shit. "I don't know how things work in the Bricks, but in Harlem people get hurt for touching women uninvited." Porsha tried to jerk her arm away, but Brick House's grip was like steel. She snatched Porsha back and shoved her against the wall, with her hand now around her neck. In her other hand she held a razor, which she ran threateningly down Porsha's cheek.

"Look here, li'l bitch," Brick House breathed into Porsha's face, "you're a long way from home so I suggest you get with the program. Brick City been mine since the day they broke ground, and I get a piece of whatever I want that comes in this muthafucka, including trump-mouthed pussy." She jammed her knee between Porsha's legs roughly.

"My, my, nobody told me that this was *jail night* at

Brick City." Kat strolled into the dressing room, still wearing her street clothes with her tote bag slug over her shoulder.

Brick House cut her eyes at Kat. "Don't worry, Big Kat, you can get next on this."

"Sorry to disappoint, Bricks, but the day li'l miss decides to swing the other way, I can assure you that I won't be going second. But from the looks of things she hasn't sworn off meat just yet. Why don't you ease up, Bricks?" Kat said in a easy tone.

"C'mon, Kat, you think you can just hog every stray bitch on both sides of the Hudson River?"

"Every stray needs a warm meal from time to time. I'm sure you of all people understand that, Bricks. Besides, this one ain't no stray, she's with me," Kat informed her.

Hearing this, Brick House released Porsha and took a step back. She and Kat weren't friends but they knew each other from the circuit and shared some of the same associates. Brick House was a thug, but Kat ran with certified gangstas so you had to be ready to bring it all to dance at her party. "My fault. Had I known she was one of yours I would've never tried her," she said sarcastically.

"I'm so sure," Kat said with a smirk. "You good, ma?" she asked Porsha.

"Yeah, I'm straight." Porsha finger combed the loose strands of her wig. As soon as she gathered her composure she rolled on Brick House and got in her face. "Bitch, you ever lay hands on me again Ima lay you."

"You got that, shorty." Brick House smiled and blew a kiss at Porsha.

Porsha was about to swing on Brick House, but Kat laid a calming hand on her shoulder. "Easy, li'l mama, I think the situation between you and Brick House is dead, right, Brick?" Kat turned to Brick House, who was still grinning and looking them up and down.

"Yeah, it's a dead issue as far as I'm concerned. I'll see y'all in the V.I.," Brick House told them and left the dressing room. When the bully was gone, all the girls breathed a sigh of relief.

"Dyke bitch," Porsha spat, still staring at the door.

"Baby girl, knock it off." Kat sat on the bench and began unpacking her bag. "This is a strip club, ma. You can't throw a rock without hitting somebody who likes pussy, has had pussy, or is seriously thinking about it. It comes with the territory, ma, so if you're squeamish, then this is the wrong line of work for you."

"I hear you, Kat," Porsha said.

"Don't just hear me, P, listen to me, because this is the second time in less than twenty-four hours that I've watched you walk into some bullshit that could've been avoided or handled different. Ma, I fucks with you all day every day because you a good chick, but at the same time I see what kinda chick you are."

"And what do you mean by that?" Porsha sounded offended.

"Calm down, I didn't mean no disrespect. It's like this." Kat stopped her unpacking and gave Porsha her full attention. "Some chicks do this as a way of life and some chicks do it as an means to an end and you fall into that category. Porsha, you ain't like a lot of these chicks: you don't have any kids and you ain't tied down to a man.

You do this to keep your bills paid, but you see how much bigger the world is."

"Hell yeah I do. I don't plan to shake my ass for singles for the rest of my days." Porsha snaked her neck.

"And that's exactly the point I'm trying to make here, ma. There are those of us who do this as a way of life and those of us who do it because we're too lazy or underqualified to work a nine-to-five. Now for as sweet as the bread is, we also gotta look at the flip side. If it ain't a trick who wants to take it beyond a lap dance trying to follow us home, it's a nigga trying to break the condom on purpose to pass us whatever he might be carrying, and let's not even dwell on the extra shit that goes on inside the club. How many bouncers at these clubs have tried to crack on you for a free blow job if you need a favor from them? This shit should come with hazard pay!"

"Yeah." Porsha laughed.

"True story, Porsha. You're laughing but I'm serious. This shit is high stakes, baby, and if you ain't playing until the end of the game, find another table to sit at, you understand me?"

"I understand, and thanks, Kat." Porsha nodded, absorbing Kat's wisdom. "But on another note, what's it looking like out there?"

"It's looking like the name of the club, Brick City, because damn near every nigga I seen was toting a brick in his hand. I'm about to throw it on and do what I do," Kat told her.

"You ain't said nothing slick to a can of oil. Ima see you out on the floor," Porsha told Kat as she prepared to head out.

"Yeah, Ima catch you in a few, but remember what I told you, Porsha. Once you crossed that state line you stepped into the big league, so be prepared for whatever it has to offer, be it good or bad."

"I got you, Kat, and I'll be sure to watch my ass out there," Porsha assured her.

"I'll watch your ass, you just watch your back." Kat slapped Porsha on the ass playfully and went back to her unpacking.

Porsha walked down the short, crowded hallways that led from the dressing room to the main area of Brick City. There was a bathroom on each side of the hall, one marked MEN and the other WOMEN, but both sexes floated in and out of each one. In a shadowed corner near a supply closet, a young man stood with his back against the wall and his eyes rolled back in his head. Kneeling in front of him was the fat stripper Brick House had run off earlier. She took the young man's penis into and out of her mouth slowly while fondling his balls in her hand. She paused briefly to spit on his dick, then went back to her business. Porhsa just shook her head and continued out into the main area.

Porsha was surprised when she saw all the people who had packed the strip joint. Four girls danced on the long stage behind the bar while at least two dozen more worked the room. It looked more like a nightclub, with people dancing, drinking, and fulfilling fantasies in private and in public. Porsha felt the telltale butterflies in her stomach that she hadn't felt since the first time she'd taken her clothes off in a room full of men. There was definitely more competition in Brick City than she had anticipated, but she was determined to get hers.

Porsha saw Sahara sitting at the bar, nursing a drink and trying to ignore some dude who was all up in her space. She looked considerably better than she had a few hours prior, having slicked her hair back and attached a long ponytail to it. With the way her black miniskirt clung to her wide hips, it was no wonder she was getting harassed. Sahara was a pretty girl and could've easily made a few dollars for herself at Brick City, but her heart wasn't in it. Instead, she had come along for the ride to keep her friend company and her mind off their pending money problems.

"Excuse you," Porsha said, sliding between Sahara and the young man. He turned his attention from Sahara to Porsha, but when she ignored him and gave him her back, he took the hint and moved on.

"Girl, thanks. I've been trying to get rid of that nigga for the last ten minutes, but the muthafucka acted like I was speaking a foreign language," Sahara told her.

"You know how some of these muthafuckas can be," Porsha said while waving to get the bartender's attention. She ordered two shots of Rémy and slid one to Sahara. "So, what do you think of the place?"

"This shit is off da hook," Sahara said, openly admiring the club. "And it's definitely some money in the building." She eyed a dude who had just walked in wearing an ice-flooded chain.

"I told you that you should've thrown something together and got down with me on this," Porsha reminded her.

"Thanks, but no thanks. I'll leave the ass shaking to you qualified bitches," Sahara joked.

"And there ain't too many as qualified as I am." Porsha lifted her ass off the seat and started popping it. A handful of singles seemed to fall from the sky, raining over Porsha and Sahara.

"Damn, you make that ass move like it's got a mind of its own." Sahara stared at Porsha in wonder.

"It does, and its mind is always on money." Porsha slammed her shot. "Look, I'm about to get to work, but I'll come back and check on you in a few, okay?"

"Yeah, do your thing, girl. I'm straight," Sahara assured her.

Porsha slid off the stool and disappeared through the crowd. Sahara downed her shot and called for another one as she began to loosen up a bit. She was watching the stage show when she felt someone tap her on the shoulder. "I ain't working, so get on like you've been spit on," Sahara said without bothering to look over her shoulder to see who it was.

"That's good, but it still leaves me wondering what the fuck you're doing here."

A ball of ice instantly formed in Sahara's stomach at the sound of the familiar voice. She knew whom she would see even before she turned around but it didn't make it any easier. Taking a second to finish the shot the bartender had just set in front of her, Sahara turned around and was face-to-face with a very angry King James.

After throwing back the shot, Porsha was feeling nice. It didn't take long for the wolves to descend on her, prodding and pulling Porsha this way and that. Part of her was disgusted by the aggressive touching, but her mind was on her money, so she played the game and accepted their offerings.

From the corner of her eye she spotted Brick House near the bar, whispering in the ear of a dude with long dreadlocks. Her eyes landed on Porsha and she watched her intensely as she made her way through the room. Kat had assured her that Brick House wasn't going to be a problem, but Porsha wasn't stupid enough to sleep on her. If Brick House tried to stunt on her again, Porsha would make sure that she drew her knife before the girl could get to her razor.

Watching Brick House watching her wasn't going to get the rent paid, so Porsha focused on working the room and trying to come up. Sitting at a table to her left was a group of Mexicans who were sipping beers and throwing money at anything in a thong that wandered near their table. She could tell by the way they were dressed—in jeans and cowboy boots—that they weren't hustlers, more than likely just a few friends out for a good time. Connected or not, they had money and Porsha needed it, so she made her way over to their table.

Without being invited, Porsha sat on the lap of one of the men and draped her arms around his neck. She hadn't been on his lap for ten seconds before she felt his dick stiffen in his jeans, so she knew she had him on the hook. He was so enthralled by Porsha that all he could do was smile and peel off singles as she rocked back and forth on his lap in time with the beat of the song that was playing. One of his friends reached over and tried to touch Porsha, but she slapped his hand away and rubbed her fingers together, letting him know he had to pay to play. By the time Porsha finished her rounds at the table she was two hundred dollars richer.

She was making her way to the other side of the room

to see what was popping when she noticed a commotion at the door. From the way some of the girls immediately slipped into chicken-head mode, she knew a heavy hitter had just entered the building. She started to ignore it and keep working the room, but her curiosity wouldn't let her. She slipped through the crowd and peered over to see what was going on, and when she saw who had just come in her eyes lit up like a kid on Christmas.

CHAPTER 27

The candy-red Hummer sitting on twenty-eight-inch rims drew more than just curious stares when it pulled into the parking lot. Two of the bouncers employed by Brick City guided the Hummer to a soft stop just short of the main entrance. The women stared in anticipation, planning their best courses of action to get next to whichever clique was riding in the Hummer, while the stick-up boys watched and plotted how they could relieve them of their valuables. Everyone took a cautious step back when they saw the man who climbed from the passenger side.

Devil rolled his broad shoulders to give himself some room in the black leather blazer he was wearing. It was a little warm for the jacket that night, but it concealed the two minimachine guns dangling under his arms. Devil was in his forties and though he had lived a very hard life, he still managed to keep himself in better shape than a man ten years his junior. In his line of work, which was busting heads, you had to make sure you were fit for war, especially when you were the guardian angel to one of New York's most-hated men. After giving a quick look around to make sure they were good, Devil opened the back door to let the passengers out.

Tone was the first to step from the Hummer. He had

traded his normally preppy gear for a pair of Nautica sweatpants and a thin hoodie. On paper he was the personal assistant/manager of the CEO and vice president of Big Dawg Entertainment, but in reality Tone was the man who made things happen. Tone had been birthed by the streets of Harlem and schooled in some of the most elite educational institutions in the city. By the time he graduated from St. Francis High School, where he'd broken almost every standing record for their Red Raiders basketball team, he'd found himself in high demand among college-basketball recruits. To everyone's surprise, Tone had chosen to stay close to home and enrolled at Rutgers, where he'd pursued a career in entertainment law while working part-time for his childhood friend Don B. at his start-up record label. By the time Tone had graduated, Big Dawg was on the radar of everybody in the music industry and he was Don B.'s right-hand man.

A few minutes later, Tone was greeted by a cat named Gotti from Irvington. Gotti was a large man who stood about six-foot-three with broad shoulders and a massive head, which he kept shaved. His eyes were hidden by dark sunglasses, but you could see the scar that started at the top of his forehead and disappeared into his thick beard. His huge medallion swayed like a pendulum as he approached the Hummer and shook Tone's hand.

"Gotti, what up, my nigga?" Tone embraced him.

"All is well, beloved. Thanks for coming out," Gotti replied.

"It's all good, my G. You know, the way you were going on about your boy, I had to come see what all the hype was about."

"Ain't no hype about it, Lord Scientific is the real deal,"

Gotti assured him. "So what's up wit ya man, he couldn't make it out?"

"Nah, he's right behind me. Yo, Don," Tone called over to the Hummer.

Don B. oozed out of the SUV, placing his crisp white Nike Airs soundlessly on the pavement. He took a second to shake the loose ashes from the blunt pinched between his lips, and adjusted the jeweled rottweiler head hanging from the end of his thick gold chain. When the people outside the club recognized him they immediately swarmed in for autographs and tried to hand him demo CDs. It took the combined efforts of the Big Dawg security team and the club bouncers to keep the mob in check. Don B. looked out at the dozens of adoring faces and sighed. Normally the self-proclaimed Don of Harlem would've welcomed the attention and made a good showing of it, but he wasn't feeling it that night. So much had transpired over the last few years and some of the wounds were still very fresh.

"Don, this is Gotti, the cat I was telling you about." Tone nudged Don B. out of his daze and drew his attention to Gotti's extended hand.

"My fault, what's good?" Don B. gave him dap.

"*You*, brother. It means a lot that you came all the way out here to check my li'l funk," Gotti said sincerely.

"Sooo woooo!" someone shouted from the crowd, which drew a ripple of calls from all the Bloods assembled, and there were quite a few of them out that night for Lord Scientific. Not wanting to be shown up in front of the NY rappers, the Crips, who occupied the other side of the parking lot, responded with a chorus of whistles. Don B.'s face hardened visibly as the tension between the two sides thickened.

"Don't worry, fam, ain't none of these li'l niggaz stupid enough to start tripping. B-Gang at least fifty strong in here tonight and most my li'l niggaz strapped, so murder is the order of business if it goes down," Gotti said loud enough for the Crips to hear. "Let's roll up in here and cop some bottles." Gotti started toward the entrance.

Tone eased up beside Don B. and whispered in his ear, "Stop whispering to them ghosts in your head and focus on the business at hand. Let's go greet your public."

Don B. nodded. There were a million and one things on his mind, but he was still the Don. Pushing away the shadows of the dead, Don B. slipped back into G-mode and made his way toward the entrance, with Devil on his heels.

The interior of Brick City was very tastefully decorated with its ice sculptures and marble-topped bars. Ladies of all shapes, sizes, and colors strutted around the joint in clear heels, thongs, and transparent sarongs that show-cased what they had for rent. When the overhead lights caught Don B.'s jewels, it seemed to send out a beacon to the money-getting chicks in the spot and drew them to him like moths to a flame. The men were kept at arm's length but Tone gave security instructions to let the ladies through so they could pay homage to the Don. Most of the chicks recognized Don B. from his music videos or repeat ap-pearances on the evening news, and the ones who didn't know him saw how he rolled and knew he had to be some-one important. Whatever their respective reasons, they all flocked to him with dollar signs in their eyes and hope in their hearts.

The smell of whore stink and weed raised the hairs on

the back of Don B.'s neck and stirred something low in his jeans as stripper after stripper closed in on him, tugging at his cock and playing with his jewels. A thick chick, wearing a pink wig and a costume that looked like something out of *Gladiator,* managed to break through the dozen other strippers who were trying to get Don B.'s attention. She stood on her tiptoes and whispered something to Don B. before letting her incredibly long tongue graze his ear and switching away. Don B. kept his eyes locked on her curvaceous body until she disappeared into a smoke-filled corner to make her pitch to the next mark.

"They love you, Don," Devil screamed over the music.

"They don't love me, they love my Big Dawg style," Don B. chuckled, giving Tone and Devil dap.

"Yo, it's gonna be a few minutes before the acts go on so let's hit the VIP and wet our beaks a li'l bit," Gotti screamed in Tone's ear over the music. Tone relayed the message to Don B. and the rest of their entourage and they made moves toward the VIP.

On their way to the back of the club, Tone spotted someone he recognized and stopped to chop it up with him for a few seconds. The dude he was talking to wore a pleasant expression on his face, but the cats he was with looked like some serious goons, which put Devil on point. After a quick exchange of numbers and the promise to get a drink later, Tone caught up with Don B. and Devil, both of whom were staring at him curiously.

"Who the fuck was them niggaz?" Don B. asked.

"That was my nigga Zo and his peeps. You remember Zo-Pound from back in the days, right?" Tone jogged Don B.'s memory.

"You mean that crazy li'l muthafucka who used to run around robbing everything moving? What the fuck is he doing in here, trying to stick the place up?" Don B. asked sarcastically.

"Nah, Zo ain't on it like that no more. After his last bid he squared up and got a job. He's legit now," Tone informed him.

"He can't be too legit hanging with King James," Devil said.

Don B. wasn't familiar with the name. "Who the fuck is King James?"

"A young boy from the Grant projects. I don't know him personally, but me and him were on the Island together years ago. He couldn't have been no more than eighteen at the time, but even the old heads ain't want no parts of his wild ass. Every time I turned around he was into some shit, cutting, fighting, arson—you name it and he's tried it. King James was a goon before these rappers made the term popular," Devil informed them.

"Shit, if he's on it like that, maybe we need to put him on payroll," Don B. joked.

"Good luck. The last nigga who tried to *offer* him a job ended up in the emergency room getting his jaw wired. Stay away from that kid, Don, because I'd hate to have to kill him. Violence is the only language an ignorant nigga like him understands," Devil said seriously.

"Well, I can't speak for that King James cat, but Zo is my li'l nigga and I invited him to the VIP to have a drink with us, so be easy, Devil," Tone told him.

"Your invitation, your problem, Tone, just remember what I told you about them dudes." Devil stalked off.

"That nigga is way too paranoid." Tone shook his head.

"Well, his paranoia has kept me in one piece all this time so I trust his judgment. Now let's go sip something." Don B. threw his arm around his friend and caught up with the group.

The more I see you work, the more I like you, kid," Kat said to Porsha. She had shed her street clothes and was now wearing a see-through one-piece that was decorated with black paw prints.

"What're you talking about?" Porsha gave her a devilish grin.

"Don't play stupid with me, I saw you all up on Don B. Good choice." Kat nodded in approval.

"I don't chose, I get chosen," Porsha capped.

"Whatever, bitch. I just know when you make your way up to the VIP to cut into that nigga you better take me with you. I heard all them cats from Big Dawg are handling major paper."

"We'll find out soon enough." Porsha gave her a high five.

"Say, what happened to your little friend?" Kat asked. "I haven't seen her since we got here."

"She's over there by the bar." Porsha nodded to where she had left her at the bar. Sahara was still sitting there, but there was a dude in her face, grabbing her by the arm and barking on her. Sahara looked scared shitless. "Oh hell to the nah," Porsha began, taking her earrings off.

"Calm down, P, and let's go get security to handle this," Kat urged her.

"You can go find security, I'm about to go see about my

homegirl." Porsha stormed off toward the bar. Kat sighed and fell in step behind her.

King, it ain't what it looks like," Sahara tried to explain.

"Do I look stupid to you, Sahara?" King James questioned. "I spend my bread to spring you and ya homegirl from jail and catch you shaking your ass at a strip club a few hours later, what the fuck do you think it looks like?"

"King, you're bugging. I keep trying to tell you that I ain't in here stripping, I just came with my homegirl to keep her company."

"Sahara, I ain't just start playing this game. Nine times outta ten, if a bitch is in a strip club, she stripping!"

"Well, I'm not, and while you're busy pointing fingers, what the fuck are you doing here? You told me you couldn't chill with me because you had business to handle, but your ass is in here tricking," Sahara shot back.

"First of all, this ain't about me, and second of all, you of all people know I ain't no trick, so knock it the fuck off. I am handling business; I got a meeting with some niggaz in here and once that's done, I'm out."

"Okay, cool. I'll just chill until you're done with your business and then we can leave together," Sahara suggested.

"Nah, that ain't gonna work," King told her.

"Why not?"

"Because I said so! As a matter of fact, why the fuck am I even standing here going back and forth with you? Take your ass home and I'll come by later."

"I caught a ride here with somebody, and besides that I can't just leave my homegirl like that," Sahara told him.

King James wanted to spaz on Sahara, but he knew that

if he did he'd end up spending half the night arguing with her, so he ran game. "Listen, this ain't a good place for you to be tonight. Some shit may go down and I don't want you getting caught up in it, baby girl." He stroked her cheek affectionately. "Check it"—he pulled out his bank-roll and peeled off two hundred dollars—"this should cover your taxi back to the city and be enough for you to pick up some piff on the way. Go home and I promise I'm gonna come spend the night with you, so we can bring in my birthday together."

This brought a smile to Sahara's face. "Do you mean it?"

"Of course I do, ma." King had almost sealed the deal when Porsha and Kat rolled up on him like the vice squad.

"Everything good over here, Sahara?" Porsha was speaking to her friend but glaring at King James.

"Who the fuck are you supposed to be?" King looked at her comically.

"You don't know me now, but if you keep trying to manhandle my friend you're gonna get to know me," Porsha shot back.

"Damn, baby, you're a feisty one, ain't you? Sahara, if you really wanna get me something nice for my birthday, then bring this li'l muthafucka home with you," King joked.

"Why don't you stop being such a dick." Sahara rolled her eyes. "Everything is good, Porsha. This is King," Sahara said, making the introduction.

"So this is the infamous King James, huh?" Porsha looked him up and down and her face said that she wasn't impressed.

"Yes, this is him. Listen, Porsha, I hate to flat leave you like this but I gotta go back to the city," Sahara told her.

"Why, is everything okay?" Porsha asked.

"Yeah, everything is cool, she's just gotta get my birthday present ready," King James answered for her. "Ain't that right, boo?" He slapped her on the ass.

"I'm sorry, P," Sahara said. She was clearly embarrassed by the whole situation and the way King James was openly eyeballing Porsha and Kat.

"Don't sweat it, I know how it can be when duty calls," Porsha told her. "How are you gonna get back to the city?"

"King gave me some bread so I'm gonna hop in a cab." Sahara held up the hundreds.

"You sure, ma?"

"Yeah," Sahara said, sounding unsure of her decision.

"Okay, I'll see you back at the crib." Porsha gave her friend a tight hug. "You make sure you text me to let me know you made it in safe, okay?"

"I got you," Sahara assured her.

"C'mon, li'l ma, I'll have one of the bouncers make sure you get in the cab safely." Kat took Sahara by the arm and led her toward the exit, leaving King and Porsha alone at the bar.

"So you're Sahara's other roommate, huh?" King James eased closer to Porsha.

"Something like that," Porsha said, while she busied herself straightening out her singles.

"Maybe I'll see you around, then?"

Porsha stopped her counting and looked up at King. "Just because you're a trifling asshole doesn't mean that I am too, so I seriously doubt that." She flipped her wig and sashayed off, with his eyes glued to her ass the whole way.

CHAPTER 28

After what felt like a trip OT, Sahara had finally made it back to the projects. The driver of the Green Cab that had brought her from Newark tried to charge her a hundred dollars and she told him to eat a dick. He looked like he wanted to get out of the taxi and argue about the money, but thought better of it when he saw the dark project building looming. He spat something at her in a language she didn't understand, and Sahara flipped him the bird and kept it moving into the projects.

For the most part, the block was quiet for the weather to have been so nice at that time of night, when Sahara got out of the Green Cab on Columbus Avenue. There was a sprinkling of people still out and about but nobody that she fucked with like that, which meant that her night was officially dead, and she wasn't happy about it.

She'd been having a good time at Brick City until King rolled in on his possessive bullshit. Sometimes Sahara thought it was cute when King laid down the law. It made her feel special that he was actually concerned enough about what she did and where she went, instead of like a jump-off, which is what she felt like sometimes. Like most men, King did his thing on the side, but he respected her enough not to flaunt it. She knew that she wasn't King's main chick, but she was making a strong push to earn that position, and nights like those came with the territory.

She'd been impressed and proud of Porsha at Brick City. They had worked together at a few clubs on the New York circuit so Sahara knew Porsha was no slouch, but there was something that stood out about her at Brick City that Sahara had never noticed before. In addition to being a bad chick, Porsha had the ability to capture the attention of a whole room without even trying, which made her a natural at the art of seduction. Sahara had done well for herself on the circuit too because of her exotic good looks, but she had never had the confidence that she saw in Porsha. Sahara knew her girl was having a ball at Brick City while she was going to find a DVD to watch, so she'd have to be content with getting all the dirty details from Porsha when she came home later that night.

As she was going into the building, Levi was struggling to get out. He had a computer monitor in his hands and a plastic bag hanging from his wrists with a bunch of wires hanging out. "Damn, what's all that?" Sahara asked, holding the door for Levi.

"Thanks." Levi stepped out. "Just some stuff I bought off Scatter from the ninth floor."

"Levi, every time I see you you're buying or trying to fix something electronic. What do you do with all that stuff?" Sahara asked.

"Come by the crib one of these days and I'll show you," he said slyly.

"Nigga, you got me fucked up thinking you're gonna get me back to the crib so you can get my goodies. You must think I'm Boots," she shot back.

Levi balanced the computer monitor on the fence. "Now of all the names to pull out of a hat, why that one?"

Sahara looked at Levi as if she couldn't believe he was even asking. "Please, Boots is like a doorknob and all you niggaz have had a turn. Everybody except Bernie is hip to what time it is with her. Don't act like you ain't never been up in them guts."

"Being the gentleman that I am, I can neither confirm nor deny your accusations. Catch you later, Sahara." Levi scooped up his electronics and left.

"Only in the projects." Sahara shook her head and went into the building.

She rounded the corner just in time to see Mitch slipping out of one of the first-floor apartments. He had a small pair of binoculars in his hand and a suspicious look on his face, which was nothing new. When he saw Sahara he stuffed the binoculars into his pocket and tried to act natural.

"What you doing creeping around in the middle of the night, Sahara?"

"I'm grown and grown people don't creep, but I could ask you the same thing. What's up with the binoculars?" she asked.

"Nothing, just fucking around," Mitch lied.

"Coming outta Snoop's apartment, I can believe that."

Mitch looked at her as if she were crazy. "Don't play yaself, I wouldn't fuck that girl with my enemy's dick."

"Yeah, right. You and Scar will stick your dicks in anything wet."

"Ain't neither one of us stick our dicks in you yet," he said slyly.

"And you never will, Negro," Sahara capped and got on the elevator.

Sahara walked into her apartment and was greeted by silence, which was rare considering the hours her room-mates kept. Of the three of them, Sahara was the only one who had a normal job, if you called working in a braid shop normal. It wasn't the most glamorous job in the world, but she was good at it and for the most part she kept her bills paid. There was a half-empty bottle of Jack Daniels on the kitchen counter, so she knew that Frankie had been there. She didn't understand how Frankie turned her nose up at champagne but could down straight whiskey.

She went down the hall to give Frankie the rundown on what had happened but when she tried the knob to her bedroom door it was locked, which was unusual. Frankie never locked her door unless she was entertaining com-pany and it had been months since she had come home with a man. Sahara knocked, but there was no answer. She listened to the door, but all was quiet. It was the middle of the night and there was no sign of Frankie, nor had she called, which made Sahara begin to worry.

"Where the hell is this girl at?" she wondered aloud.

Frankie leaned against a parked car in the parking lot behind her building, smoking a Newport and nervously watching everyone and everything around her. She had been a drug dealer for only a few hours and already her nerves were shot. How some people did it day in and day out was a mystery to her, and as soon as she scraped up the rent and Cutty's money she was retiring.

After Lulu had finished cooking the coke for Frankie, she had taken it back to her apartment to start bagging it up, which turned out to be more work than she expected.

Though the work Cutty had given her didn't seem like much in its powder form, it was quite a bit once it was rocked up and chopped. Bagging it up had been a chore in itself, so she'd packaged half and stashed the rest in her bedroom. Armed with her product and a mission, Frankie took it to the streets.

Frankie wasn't the only dealer in the hood, but she was the newest so she had to be mindful that she didn't step on anyone's toes. She knew from experience that hustlers could be very territorial over turf, and her being a woman didn't help to tip the scales in her favor, so she had to keep a low profile about it. Her initial plan was to go to the other side of the projects and set up shop, but that plan went out the window when she heard that one of the buildings got raided. She knew the jump-out boys would be crawling all over the Amsterdam side so Columbus was probably the easiest place to do it. She chose the parking lot because it was familiar territory to her and it'd be hard for the police to trap her off if they rolled up. For an extra piece of rock Lulu had agreed to route some of her friends to Frankie's location, so she was all set. Now all she had to do was get her product off without getting locked up.

Frankie spotted the shadows moving behind a parked car to her left and three words popped into her mind: *stick-up kids*. She quickly moved to the grass where she had her pistol hidden and prepared for battle. Her fingers had just wrapped around the grip of the gun when the person who had been creeping came into view. It was fiend from the next building over named Scatter. As usual, he was dressed in a wrinkled business suit and overcoat.

"Dude, you almost got popped creeping up on me like that," Frankie said seriously.

"My bad, baby girl, but you know you gotta tread light when you walk on the wild side." Scatter flashed a checkered grin. "You know, I thought Lulu was bullshitting me when she told me you were out here trapping."

Frankie shrugged. "I'm just trying to do me."

"So I see," he said, scratching the side of his face. "Check it, though: I need some of that butter you laid on Lulu. She let me taste it and that shit is outta sight!"

"You like that, huh?" She smiled.

"'Like' is an understatement. Frankie, there ain't been no rock out here like that in years. You got some boss shit on your hands, girlie. Play your cards right and you're gonna be one rich muthafucka."

"I ain't trying to get rich off this shit, Scatter. I'm just trying to get where I need to be and I'm leaving this shit alone."

"Well, if you ain't out here trying to come up, what the hell are you doing out here hand-to-handing poison?" he asked.

"It's like I told you: I'm trying to get where I need to be. I'm in and out like the Flash."

"That's what they all say." Scatter laughed. "Frankie, normally I charge muthafuckas for my infinite wisdom, but since I like you I'm gonna lay some free game on ya ears. Selling drugs is an addiction that burns at both ends of the candle. The same way the addicts get addicted to the product, the pushers get addicted to the money."

"Well, I don't plan on doing this long enough to test that theory," she told him. "Now are you gonna keep running your mouth or do you wanna get served?"

"Sho ya right, sho ya right. Let me get two of them thangs." He rubbed his hands together in anticipation.

Frankie dipped into her bra and handed Scatter two baggies, while taking his money with the other hand. When he held them to the light his eyes got wide. "Damn, these is some boulders. I like how you do business, Frankie."

"No doubt, and make sure you spread the word to ya peoples that I'm out here. Offer only good while supplies last."

"I got you." He stuffed the baggies into his pocket and started to walk off, but stopped short. "Frankie, I know you gonna do what you do regardless of what I say, but let me leave you with something: if you playing for a quarter instead of the whole game, then you might as well stay on the bench, because if them people come calling you're gonna get the same amount of time as a full-time player. I'm out." Scatter shuffled back the way he had come.

Frankie was glad to see Scatter go. She had brushed him off, but she couldn't deny the truth in his words and they bothered her more than she let on. Frankie knew she had no business out there in the trap, but she felt like it was the quickest way to get what she needed. Suddenly the hairs on the back of her neck began to stand up and a nervous feeling settled in the pit of her stomach. She turned around but didn't see anybody else in the parking lot. She thought she saw the curtain in Snoop's apartment window flutter, but all the lights were out. Before she could investigate further, another fiend rolled up to get served. She chalked it up as her nerves and went back to trapping.

CHAPTER 29

There were two VIP areas at Brick City, the upper and lower levels. The lower level was open to anyone who had enough money or clout to get in, but the upper level was reserved for the *special* guests. With its velvet curtains and fancy decor it was reminiscent of an opera-house balcony. The upper level overlooked the main floor, with three forty-two-inch flat-screen televisions that normally showed sporting events, but that night the screens showed four different close-up angles of the main stage, where the girls peeled off clothes and the patrons peeled off bills.

Unlike the lower-level VIP, there were no restrictions upstairs. Girls fucked, sucked, and made conversation according to what the men wanted and could pay for. In a dark corner, a hip young hustler wearing a chain that looked like it weighed more than he did drank champagne from the bottle while two young women, one white and one Asian, took turns pleasuring him. The Asian girl amused herself trying to see how much of his thick cock she could force into her throat while the white girl crawled behind her and began eating her from the back. The young man poured champagne down the Asian girl's back and watched as the white girl sipped it from the crack of her ass.

"Do you see that shit?" Holiday asked, staring at the

spectacle. He, Shai, Angelo, and Swann had a private table in the rear of the VIP, right under one of the flat screens.

"Why don't you mind your own business, you fucking pervert," Angelo scolded him.

"Fuck that, it ain't like they're putting shade on it. Them bitches is going at it in plain sight. I'm about to go ask if it's a private party." Holiday made to get up, but Shai grabbed him by the arm.

"Chill," he said coolly. His voice was barely above a whisper but Holiday felt the weight of it and retook his seat. "There's nothing wrong with having a good time, but we have an image to maintain, feel me?"

"I got you, big homie." Holiday nodded. He still spared the occasional glance over to the corner where the freak show was going on. "I wonder where the fuck this nigga Paulie is?"

"Judging by the crowd in here, he's probably got his hands full. He'll be along," Shai told him. Holiday and his youthful impatience could be frustrating but Shai tried not to be as short with him as Angelo was, because he understood him. It wasn't that long ago that Shai had been the impatient youngster of the crew who needed a guiding hand.

"Look at this nigga here." Swann cracked a smile when he saw Don B. and his team enter the VIP.

Angelo frowned. "What the fuck is this, an episode of *Gangland*?"

"Chill out, Angelo." Swann stood up as Don B. neared their table. "What's popping, homie?"

Don B. peered over his sunglasses and smiled when he recognized Swann. "Oh shit, what it do, blood?" Don B. greeted him with a complex handshake.

"It do whatever I tell it to, that's the life of a boss nigga," Swann boasted.

"Sho ya right, B. Yo, Devil, you remember Swann, right?"

Devil scrolled through his mental Rolodex and placed the name with the face. "What's popping, li'l homie, or should I say big homie now?" Devil cut his eyes to Shai.

"Ain't shit, B, out here trying to live like everyone else," Swann told him.

"The way I hear it, you're living real good." Devil gave Swann the once-over, paying special attention to the heavy chain around his neck.

"Putting in work eventually pays off for some of us," Swann shot back. He and Devil were from two different generations of the same set, but had never quite seen eye to eye. Swann represented the new regime while Devil was a walking reminder of a bygone era.

"You're Shai Clark, right?" Gotti asked.

Shai looked up at him with a blank expression. "That all depends on who's asking. Do we know each other?"

"Nah, we don't know each other but we know some of the same people. My homies Li'l Red and Dee put in some work for ya peoples a while back," Gotti name-dropped, trying to cut into Shai.

Shai shrugged his shoulders. "Sorry, but I don't know them cats or what you're talking about. It was nice meeting you though, fam." Shai turned his attention to the screen to watch the floor show.

Gotti felt slighted and it showed on his face. "It's like that, huh?"

"Straight like that," Holiday answered for Shai. For a long moment he and Gotti glared at each other across the table.

Sensing where it was about to go, Swann interjected. "Don, it was good seeing you, my G. We gotta hook up soon."

Don B. immediately picked up on what Swann was doing. "Fo sho, fo sho." Don B. dapped him up. "C'mon, fellas, let's head over to our table." Don B.'s group fell in step behind him. Gotti and Holiday continued to shoot daggers at each other but nobody made a move.

"I don't like that one-eyed muthafucka," Angelo said once Gotti was out of earshot.

"Neither do I," Shai agreed. "He was either wearing a wire or dumb as hell. Either way, I don't want him around us."

"Say no more, Shai. He step wrong and Ima give you his kufi as a birthday present." Holiday patted his waist.

Where'd you disappear to?" Lakim asked when King resurfaced. One minute he had been with the group and the next he'd vanished and they'd all been worried.

"Had to handle something right quick," King said in an easy tone.

"You was getting a lap dance from one of these fine honeys, huh?" Dump smiled.

"Nah, I saw one of my shorties in here and had to set her straight," King told him.

"You fuck with one of these strippers?" Alonzo asked, surprised. He knew that King James was very particular about the kind of women he dealt with.

"You know better than that, Zo. Just some li'l joint from the P's in here playing herself, so I sent her home."

"Go so we ain't gotta worry about none of ya li'l chicken heads following you around while we in here trying to get our swerve on," Dump teased him.

King twisted his lips. "C'mon, sun. This is my court and everybody in the kingdom knows their places, ya heard? Zo, where you know that kid from that you were talking to?"

"Oh, that was my man Tone. He runs with Don B. and them Big Dawg niggaz," Alonzo said.

"Pussy-ass rappers," Lakim spat. He disliked the new breed of rappers like Don B. because he felt like they were movie stars trying to play the roles of gangsters.

"Nah, Tone is cool. He invited us upstairs to get a drink later on," Alonzo said.

"Whatever," King said. He wasn't big on handouts, or on Don B. He didn't know Don B. personally but had heard enough about his exploits to know that he didn't like him or what he represented.

Lakim tapped King's arm. "You peeped ya man?" He nodded upstairs to the balcony, where Shai and his entourage had just been seated.

"Yeah, I see him." King James zeroed on Shai. He was flanked by several men and from their body language he knew they were strapped. Getting close enough to Shai to confront him would be a little trickier than he had expected. Suddenly an idea sprang into his head. "Ayo, Zo, let's go take ya man up on that drink offer." King marched through the club, ignoring the strippers who were trying to get his attention, focusing on the man he had come to parlay with. One chick jumped in front of him and tried to drape her arms around his thick neck, but King swatted her aside with a sweep of his powerful arm. They climbed the stairs to the VIP entrance and their way was blocked by a beefy bouncer.

"Sorry, fellas, this is a private party. The public VIP is downstairs so you're in the wrong place," the bouncer told them.

King James locked eyes with him. "Nah, we're in the right place. We were invited. My name is King James, ask about me."

"I wouldn't care if your name was Prince Albert, I can't let you in here, fam."

King James shook his head. "I gotta give it to Brick City for their equal opportunity employment program, because all y'all niggaz act like you just fell off a yellow bus."

The bouncer puffed up. "How about if I bust you in the jaw, funny man?"

"My nigga, if you even think about laying hands on my fam, I'm gonna snap you like a fucking twig." Dump stepped up. The bouncer was big, but Dump was bigger.

"Now, you can let us in so we can spend some bread and pop some bottles, or keep being a dick and we can pop you." King James folded his arms. "How you wanna do it, sun?"

Fuck is good wit ya peeps?" Gotti asked Don B. once they were settled at their table.

"Who, Swann? He's a good nigga, a real street nigga," Don B. told Gotti.

"Nah, not him. The pretty boy, Shai."

"I can't call it, B. I met his pops a few times, but I don't know Shai."

"Well, he might wanna show a li'l respect with him being so far from home," Gotti said.

Devil laughed. "Shai is a pissy li'l fuck, but he's still the boss of bosses. The boy is protected from on high. He's untouchable."

"Everybody is touchable," Gotti said.

"Fuck all that suicide talk, where's ya man Lord Scientific?" Don B. cut in.

"He should be here in a few. I spoke to him a li'l while ago and he said he's on his way from East Orange. While we're waiting, let's get some drinks." Gotti waved one of the waitresses over and put in an order for five bottles of champagne, a fifth of Rémy, and some waters. His attention wandered over to the entrance of the VIP, where he noticed security exchanging words with a husky cat rocking a big chain. "Fuck is good with these niggaz?"

Tone looked over and recognized the man as King James. "Oh, that's my man and his homies. Give me a sec." He got up and walked over. After a few quick words, security allowed King James and his crew into the VIP. Tone led them over to their booth and made the introductions. "Fellas, this is my man Zo and his team."

"Peace, peace." King gave everyone at the table dap.

"We got some bottles on the way, y'all wanna join us?" Tone offered.

Alonzo opened his mouth to accept the invitation but King cut him off. "Nah, it looks like y'all are in the middle of something and we ain't trying to intrude."

"It's all good," Tone assured him.

"We appreciate the offer, but we're gonna grab a table and fuck with some of these bitches. Good looking out on that business with security, though. Let's motivate," King ordered his crew, and moved toward an empty table not far from where Shai was sitting.

Alonzo stood there for an awkward moment, not quite sure what to say. "Sorry about that, Tone."

Tone made a dismissive gesture. "It's all love, Zo, don't worry about it. If you decide to take me up on that drink offer, I'm here."

"Fo sho." Alonzo gave him dap. "Lap dance on me though, ya head?" Alonzo promised before leaving the men to their business.

"That kid Zo is a'ight, but King James ain't got no class," Don B. capped before putting his feet up on the table.

The waitress came over and set the bottles and some ice buckets on the table along with some plastic cups. "Can I get you guys anything else?" she asked.

"Nah, we're straight, baby," Gotti said, handing her several hundred-dollar bills. The waitress thanked him, but continued to linger around. "Something else I can help you with, sweetie?"

"Ah, I'm sorry . . . I don't mean to come off as a groupie but I was wondering . . . could I have your autograph?" she asked Don B.

"Bitch, get on with that shit," Gotti snapped.

"It's all good, my nigga, the Don always has time for his adoring public." Don B. smiled. "You got a pen, baby?"

The girl handed him the pen she had been using to write down drink orders. "Thank you so much," she squealed. "Make it out to Tasha."

"No problem." Don B. looked around for something to write on, but she saved him the trouble when she popped her breasts out of the bikini top she was wearing.

"You can sign right here." She squeezed her breasts together. All Don B. could do was laugh while scribbling his name on her ample breasts. "You have no idea how much this means to me."

"It's nothing, baby," Don B. told her.

The girl leaned in to whisper to Don B., "I go on break in twenty minutes. Meet me in the parking lot and I'll show you that Superhead ain't got shit on me." She grabbed Don B.'s dick through his jeans. The girl moved on to the next table, leaving the group shocked and Don B. smiling.

CHAPTER 30

Porsha had finally found her groove. After Sahara had left, she and Kat played the bar for a while, throwing back shots courtesy of their adoring public. The Jersey cats in Brick City acted like they had never seen a chick like Porsha before. Granted, the chicks from Jersey who were dancing that night were far from slouches, but Porsha had a swag about her that set her apart.

After their drink session, Porsha and Kat hit the floor to get their trap on. There was a heavyset kid sitting at a table with a group of his boys, draped in more ice than Colorado in December, who was waving Porsha over. She started to ignore him but when he raised a brick of singles she changed her mind. Motioning for Kat to follow, Porsha went over to the table.

The fat kid and his friends were very generous, showering Porsha and Kat with bills of different denominations for their raunchy routine. By the time they were finished, Porsha had most of the fat kid's money and his life story. He was a hustler named Vern who moved weight in South Jersey, and from the weight of his jewels she could tell he was doing well for himself. He tried to get Porsha to slide off with him, but she declined the invitation and took his number instead. She might not have been down to fuck him that night, but Vern was someone she definitely planned to follow up with.

"Damn, I should've brought my ass to Jersey to get it in years ago," Porsha said, counting her money. She was already up almost a stack and the night was still young.

"I tried to tell you, ma. Money in New York is good, but out-of-town cats spend it more freely," Kat told her. Then she leaned in to whisper to Porsha, "Don't make it obvious, but look up." She nodded over her shoulder.

Porsha acted like she was fixing the shoulder strap on her corset and cut her eyes up toward the balcony. Don B. was leaning on the rail with a drink in his hand, watching her like a hawk. He must've known she was looking at him because he smiled and raised his drink.

"That nigga has been watching you all night," Kat told her.

"Good, I need him all worked up when I cut into that ass," Porsha said seriously.

One of the guys working for the DJ came over and whispered something to Kat. She nodded and held up two fingers, before sending him back off to the DJ booth. "Well, Ms. P, I think he'll be good and worked up in a few minutes."

"What the fuck are you talking about?" Porsha asked. Just then she heard the DJ's voice.

"Alright, you muthafuckas, get ya money right and belly up to the bar. Coming to the stage, live from Harlem World, the lovely Ms. Porsha!"

Porsha stood there with a confused expression on her face after hearing her name. "What the fuck? I planned on working the floor, I didn't sign up to hit the stage, so how the hell are they calling me?"

"Because I signed you up," Kat said with a sly smile. "You talk the talk, now let's see if you can walk the walk."

"Porsha, where you at?" the DJ shouted.

"I told you, if you're in, then be all in. What you gonna do, rookie?" Kat challenged.

"Kat, I'm gonna kill you after I finish rocking this muthafucking pole," Porsha said, and sauntered off.

Kat took a seat at the bar and ordered a drink while she waited for the show to start.

Porsha walked out onto the stage timidly, hoping that she didn't bust her ass in her six-inch heels. The bright overhead lights stung Porsha's eyes, making it hard to see the crowd, but she could feel every eye in the room on her. She spotted Kat sitting at the bar watching her, smiling, and wanted to dive off the stage and start choking her. Kat had put her in an awkward position, but Porsha had come too far to turn back. She had danced on her fair share of poles in her day, but she'd always had a planned routine.

"Fuck it," she said to herself and nodded for the DJ to start the music, hoping it was something she could rock to. She didn't recognize the song at first with its heavy guitar riffs. This definitely wasn't a rap song. As the drums began to pound, the song struck a chord of familiarity in her and her lips parted into a smile. Her brother played the song so much that she hated it, but was glad for his obsession with George Thorogood & The Destroyers. The way the chicks at Brick City had been hating on her all night, she knew the DJ's playing that song was a sign for her to let it all hang out and show them who the boss bitch was.

Shaking off her butterflies, Porsha let everyone watching know why she was truly "Bad to the Bone."

Once they were settled at their table, Lakim broke out one of the blunts he had stashed in his sock. Security downstairs had been on some bullshit about weed smoking, so his lungs were on the gate. As soon as he lit it, the smell of Sour Diesel stank up the room. "Much better," he said, exhaling a cloud of smoke.

"That weed smells like you rolled it in shit." King fanned the smoke.

"That's how you know it's good." Lakim took two more pulls and tried to pass it to King.

"Stop playing with me, man. You know I don't smoke when I'm on the clock."

"Then let me hit that muthafucka." Dump reached across the table and snatched the weed.

"Can I get you guys anything?" the waitress asked, coming over to their table.

"Yeah, bring us a bottle of Crown and a shot of whatever you got hiding up under them booty shorts," Dump told her.

The waitress twisted her lips. "I don't know if your paper is long enough for what I got under these shorts, but I'll be back with your bottle." She turned to leave but King stopped her. He whispered something in her ear and slipped her some bills. The girl gave him a confused look, but eventually nodded and went off to get their drinks.

"I'd suck a baby outta her snatch," Dump said, eyeing the waitress.

"Nigga, you'll put your mouth anywhere. As a matter

of fact, keep that blunt, I'll spark another one." Lakim laughed.

"Fuck you, La." Dump blew out a cloud of smoke.

Lakim and Dump traded jokes, and even managed to drag Alonzo into their shenanigans. The trio was like kids in the schoolyard, smoking weed and tossing money at the strippers as they came and went, but King's mind was elsewhere. His eyes were fixed on Shai Clark. You could tell he carried weight from the way those around him hung on his every word, but to King James he didn't appear to be much more than a kid. If they were up north, King would've flat-out confronted him about what had happened to his worker, but they were in the world and the rules were quite different. The situation would have to be handled with diplomacy instead of fists. Approaching Shai like a common thug wouldn't work, so he bided his time and contemplated an angle to approach him.

Alonzo nudged King. "You good?"

"Yeah, all is well, God. I'm just checking the scene." King laid his eyes on a chick with balloon breasts. "What about you, you having a good time, Zo?"

"I'm good; it's just been a minute since I've been out so I'm getting adjusted."

"Well, you're amongst family, so feel free to let your hair down, my G." King put his arm around him.

The DJ's voice came over the loudspeaker, announcing the next dancer to take the stage. Alonzo thought he was bugging when he heard the name, or it might've been a coincidence, so out of curiosity he fixed his eyes on one of the flat screens that gave them a view of the stage. When he saw the pretty brown thing take the stage he had to do a double take. She was wearing a wig and a costume that made her look different, but Alonzo would have known that figure anywhere. He sat there, mouth agape and speechless, as he saw the longtime object of his affection in a whole new light.

Alonzo found himself both turned on and repulsed as he watched Porsha work the stripper pole like she'd been born to do it. She whipped her hair wildly to the rock-and-roll song blaring through the DJ's speakers. She bent her body at impossible angles as men and women showered her with money and cheered. She dropped flat on her stomach and popped her ass cheeks in time with the saxophones on the track. One dude jumped onstage and tried to kiss her, only to have security yank him down and toss him out on his ass. The crowd loved Porsha and she loved them back.

Alonzo couldn't watch anymore. He had known that Porsha was no angel, but seeing her dancing at a strip club for dollars was something he wasn't ready for. Something swelled in Alonzo's chest after watching Porsha on the stage and he realized it was jealousy, which was absurd. Alonzo had had a crush on Porsha for as long as he'd known her, but she kept him in the *friend zone* so the romantic attachment was one-sided. Still, he'd always held on to the hope that one day she would come around, but after what he'd seen he didn't know how he felt about her anymore.

"She bad, huh?" King startled him. Alonzo hadn't realized he'd been watching the show too.

"She a'ight," Alonzo said as if Porsha was nothing special.

"She a'ight?" King looked at him funny. "Sun, I don't know if we looking at the same chick, because that bitch on the screen is bad! My nigga, I'd try to break my dick

off between them pretty-ass lips if she gave me the chance."
King laughed, but Alonzo got quiet. "My fault, you know
her or something?"

"Nah, I thought I knew her." Alonzo turned his back
on the flat screen.

King had been around enough liars to know one when
he heard it. "Let me tell you something about chicks, Zo.
When you're young and first discovering your heat, it'll be
the ones you care about the most who treat you like shit,
but it's a necessary road to travel on your way to figuring
out how to appreciate a good chick. That's my jewel on
you for the day."

"Forever the teacher." Alonzo nodded.

"That's my job, to open the eyes of the blind. Now let
me open your eyes to some of this fine trim in here." King
motioned around at the women moving about. "Shake that
shit, Zo, and have a good time."

CHAPTER 31

Brick House sat fuming in the corner as she watched Porsha rock the stage. She had been watching the little bitch make her rounds for most of the night, smiling and winking at dudes but not really giving up anything worth watching. She knew by the end of the night she was going to be able to stunt by making the most bread that night, but it looked like Porsha was gonna be a problem.

"These niggaz in here spending tonight," a stripper named Peaches interrupted Brick House's thoughts. She was a short chick with a pretty face and a decent body from Newark whom Brick House sometimes ran with.

"Yeah, a bitch like me might end up at the dealership tomorrow," Brick House boasted, showing her a purse full of money.

"I don't know if I'm doing all that, but I'm gonna be straight when it's all said and done," Peaches said. "Yo, did you see that new bitch up there killing it?"

Brick House sucked her teeth. "She did her thing, but I wouldn't say she was killing it."

"Say what you want, but she had me ready to try and get at her li'l ass," Peaches admitted.

"You better stay away from her, because Kat is playing

it and you know how that crazy bitch gets down," Brick House said.

"I ain't fucking with Kat. You been up to the VIP yet?" Peaches asked.

"Nah, it's probably the usual suspects up there and I'm trying to wait for it to thicken out."

"Well, I heard Don B. is up there with some of his peoples."

Brick House's head snapped around. "When the fuck did he get here and why are you just now telling me?"

"I don't know when he got here, but I thought for sure you'd have known before anybody else." Peaches gave her a knowing look.

Brick House and Don B. had history. She had met him when she was working outta New York and given him the blow job of his life. For three straight weekends he had shown up at the strip club, and she'd gone home with him every night and he had thrown bread around like it was water. Just on the three nights she had slid with him she had cleared more than what she'd have made working in the club all night. If Don B. was in the building, then she still had one more card to play.

"Come on, let's go upstairs and see what's good with the real players." Brick House motioned for Peaches to follow her. Brick House crossed the room and cleared the stairs to the VIP in record time in her high heels. The bouncer was leaning against the banister, smooth talking one of the other girls, when Brick House approached. "What it do, Flea?"

Flea shook his head, "It's a real gangster party in there, ma. It ain't for the faint of heart tonight."

"Then I should feel right at home." Brick House strutted inside. When Peaches tried to follow, Flea stopped her.

"C'mon, baby, you know the rules. A dub to me and some neck later on." He held out his hand.

"Flea, you ain't charge Brick House nothing to get in and you gonna hit me up for twenty?" Peaches snaked her neck.

"Brick is family and you're an employee. Now up that dub. As a matter of fact, give me twenty-five for trying to dry snitch."

Peaches wasn't happy about it, but she gave him the money. "You're a real asshole, Flea." She pushed past him.

"I'm an asshole who is twenty-five dollars richer thanks to you," he called after her.

Don B. was feeling good. He had a drink in one hand, a blunt in the other, and a chick on his lap. Gotti had really laid it out for the New Yorkers, making sure their glasses and their lungs stayed full all night. There were fine women, good weed, and good drink, which was the only way the Don knew how to party. It had been a while since he had been out in the spotlight and being back on the stage felt good.

"So how're you enjoying the Garden State's hospitalities?" Gotti asked Don B.

"This shit is lovely." Don B. blew smoke into the stripper's waiting mouth. "I could get used to this."

"And this is only the beginning, my nigga. Once we start getting money together it's gonna get even sweeter. It's been a long time since Jersey had a rapper step out in the limelight and I know Big Dawg can do that for my man Lord Scientific."

"You don't do nothing but create starts at Big Dawg, homie." Don B. took a toke of the blunt. "From what I heard on the CDs y'all sent over, he's definitely got some lyrics, but in this game you need more than lyrics to make it to the top. It's about your presentation. The ability to captivate people is the one thing all true stars possess."

"I think after you see his stage show tonight you'll agree that my man leaves a lasting impression," Gotti assured him.

Before the conversation could go any further, Brick House walked up. Every man sitting at the table had his eyes glued to her ass when she moved. "What's popping, Big Dawg?" She stood over Don B. and the girl who was giving him a lap dance.

Don B. took a second to peer over the shoulder of the girl who was sitting on his lap. He looked at Brick House over his shades and nodded in greeting. "Chilling," he replied, and went back to his lap dance.

Brick House felt slighted and her face said it. She tapped the stripper on her shoulder. "Shorty, take a break for a minute." The girl looked like she wanted to protest but thought better of it and left. "What's good, Don B.?"

"Everything was good until you broke up my groove, what's good with that?" Don B. adjusted his pants.

"I'm saying, I thought you could've at least called a bitch if you were coming to Jersey; you know these are my stomping grounds," Brick House said.

"Oh, you're from Jersey? That's what's up," Don B. said in a very disinterested tone and poured himself another drink.

"What's good, shorty, you shaking or running ya mouth? You're holding up traffic." Tone motioned toward the other girls who were circling them like vultures.

"Be easy, me and Don B. know each other," Brick House told Tone. Tone looked to Don B. for confirmation but he just sat there like he had no clue what she was talking about, which angered Brick House. "Word, you just gonna sit there like you don't know a bitch on your Hollywood shit?"

"Shorty, I meet a lot of women in my travels. Your face looks familiar, but I can't remember your name." Don B. shrugged.

Brick House folded her arms and looked at Don B. in disbelief that he was playing her to the left. "Oh you don't know my name? You were screaming my fucking name when I was riding you at that motel in the Bronx."

"Oh, okay. I fucked you at a motel in the Bronx? That really narrows it down." Don B. laughed and so did his crew.

"Ay, ma, come over here and let me see what you're working with and I'll scream your name all night long." Devil waved some singles at her.

"Listen, boo, me and my mans is over here handling business and trying to have a good time, so if you ain't trying to shake, you need to keep it pushing," Gotti said, not bothering to hide his irritation with Brick House.

Brick House felt like a wet food stamp, the way she was being brushed off by the celebrity and his crew. She wanted to plead her case and try to jog Don B.'s memory but she wouldn't play herself like that in front of Peaches. "I hear you talking that shit, Mr. Boss Baller," she said, her eyes narrowed to slits. "I'm gonna remember this shit, Don."

"Baby, you can write it down if you need to," he shot back.

"I'm gonna see you around, nigga," she warned as she walked away with Peaches in tow.

"I doubt it," Don B. called after her. He shook his head and turned back to his group. "You slip a bitch a li'l cock on a drunk night and they act like they got standing. Fuck outta here. Yo, one of y'all niggaz roll something up and bring me a bitch. I'm trying to keep this party popping."

CHAPTER 32

I can't believe he tried to play you like that, Brick," Peaches said, fighting back the urge to laugh in Brick House's face. She couldn't wait to put the word out about how Don B. had shitted on Brick House.

"Fuck him, li'l-dick muthafucka. He better hope I don't call Li'l Flame and them and get his ass robbed when he leaves here," Brick House fumed.

"If I were you I would. It would teach them New York niggaz about trying to come on this side stunting," Peaches instigated. She got off on drama and encouraged it whenever she could.

"I ain't even beat for that whack-ass nigga. He ain't the only nigga in here holding," Brick House said, looking around at the various ballers in the VIP. Her eyes landed on a rough-looking group toward the back who clearly weren't from Jersey, but their money looked just as green. The two strippers worked their way over to King's table and began sizing the men up openly.

"What's popping, ladies?" Dump asked.

"You, big daddy." Peaches invited herself to a seat on his lap. She ran her hand up Dump's leg and grabbed a handful of his crotch. "You're a big one, huh?"

"You better believe it. Dump don't do small," he boasted.

"Why do they call you Dump, because you like to eat?" she asked, rubbing his large belly.

"Nah, because all I do is dump on muthafuckas. Now stop wasting time and handle ya business." Dump picked her up by her waist and placed the stripper on his lap.

"I think I'm gonna like you." She beamed.

"You want a dance, boo?" Brick House approached Alonzo.

"Nah, I'm good," Alonzo said, still mulling over Porsha.

"No, he ain't." Lakim slid over next to his brother and pulled out a roll of singles. "My li'l brother is shy, so why don't you drop that big ass on him and bring him out of his shell."

"I think I can do that." She lowered herself onto Alonzo's lap, pressing her breasts against his chest. "Don't be shy, baby." She took Alonzo's hands and placed them on her ass cheeks. "Doesn't that feel better?"

"Yeah," he said, panting. Alonzo tried to be cool about it, but shorty was turning him on. "What's ya name?"

"They call me Brick House, but you can call me yours as long as you're spending." She pushed her breasts up toward his mouth.

"You let us worry about the money, you just keep working that ass, ma." Lakim started dropping singles on her head.

Brick House was truly a beast. She ground back and forth, flexing her ass cheeks on the bulge in his jeans every time she moved. She proceeded to pop her huge breasts from her bikini top and shove them in Alonzo's face. Before he knew it, he was sucking on her brown nipples like a starved child. Brick House locked her fingers behind his head and threw both legs up on his shoulders, grinding her box on his chest. Without missing a beat she spun around, planted her palms on the ground, and started bouncing her ass up and down on Alonzo's lap.

Brick House turned back around so that she was facing Alonzo again. With nimble fingers she undid his zipper and had his dick out and in her hand before he even realized what was going on. "Damn, that's a lot of dick." She stroked him firmly. Pre-come ran from the head of his dick and over her knuckles. "You wanna fuck my li'l pussy with all this dick?" she asked, her voice husky.

Alonzo's depression over Porsha had faded and he was now thinking with his loins. "Fuck it, how much?"

"Give me two hundred and I'll get you right."

"That's kinda steep, sis." Alonzo had only about two hundred dollars on him and he hadn't intended on blowing it all in one shot.

Brick House took Alonzo's hand and slipped two of his fingers into her pussy. She was dripping like a faucet. "Stop acting like you don't wanna tear these walls down." She then took his fingers and licked her juices off them.

"A'ight, you've tortured my man enough," King James interjected. He counted out two hundred dollars and gave them to Brick House. "Go take care of my family."

Brick House grabbed Alonzo by the hand and led him deep into the recesses of the VIP, where there were thick black curtains hanging from the wall. Alonzo gave King James the thumbs-up sign before disappearing behind the curtain.

Brick House led Alonzo through the curtains and into a smaller room that was connected to the VIP. It was too dark for him to really see what was going on, but from the stench of sex and the moans he could hear in the shadows, he didn't need his eyes to see what was going on. He thought Brick House was going to fuck him in there, but she led him farther still into the recesses of the room to a door marked EMERGENCY EXIT. She pushed the door open and a cool gust of wind washed across them from somewhere at the bottom of the stairs.

"What's good, I thought we was gonna get it on?" Alonzo asked suspiciously.

"We are," Brick House assured him. "We can handle our business out back so I ain't gotta worry about none of these nosy bitches in my mix." She tried to pull him by the hand but Alonzo jerked away.

"Shorty, I ain't trying to fuck outside."

"Look, the muthafucka who owns the club be on some bullshit trying to tax us for fifty percent if we get caught turning tricks in the club, so sometimes we go out back. It's a dead-end street so we ain't gotta worry about no traffic coming through and interrupting."

"I don't know, ma."

Brick House pressed up against him and grabbed his hand, slipping it into her wetness. "C'mon, baby, I need you to put this fire out. Don't do me like that." She sucked on his neck.

Every ounce of common sense Alonzo had told him that it was a bad idea, but like most men his age, he was thinking with the wrong head. "A'ight, let's go. But you need to come down off that price some, being that you making me fuck you outside."

"Since I like you, we can negotiate. Don't worry, boo, I'm gonna make sure you remember this pussy for a long time." She led him by the hand through the door at the bottom of the steps and out into the alley. Brick House wasted no time getting down to business. She shoved Alonzo against the wall and began licking his ears and around his neck, while prying his dick from his pants. "That feels good, don't it." She jerked his dick.

"Yeah, that's nice." Alonzo closed his eyes.

"The best is yet to come." She dropped her purse to ground and knelt on it so as not to scuff her knees on the concrete. She circled her thumb and index finger around his shaft and stroked it gently while fondling his balls with her free hand. She clamped her lips around the head of his dick and inhaled gently, drawing a low hissing from Alonzo. Gradually she opened her mouth wider and slid it farther down his shaft. When she came back up she let her saliva run freely down his dick until it was good and wet. Every time she bobbed down on him, she let his dick slip farther and farther into her mouth until his dick had completely disappeared and her tongue touched his balls.

"Damn, you're trying to make me nut," Alonzo said, moaning.

"Nah, you ain't getting off that easy," she told him while stroking his cock aggressively. Brick House produced a condom and rolled it onto his rock-hard dick. Brick House got off her knees and braced herself against the wall with one hand. She moved her thong to the side and hiked her ass up. "Get in this pussy." She spread her lips.

Alonzo looked around cautiously to make sure nobody was looking before sliding up behind Brick House. She was so wet that he missed his target three times before hitting his mark. Brick House's pussy was so warm and tight that Alonzo stood completely still, letting her soak him. "Damn," was all he could say as he spread her ass cheeks and pushed himself into her as far as he could, grabbing two handfuls of her ass, forcing her up and down faster and faster. Alonzo was trying to force himself into the depths of her guts.

"That's right, get all in this pussy." She pressed both hands against the wall and threw it back as he pumped.

Alonzo grabbed a fistful of her weave and started going to town on her, slamming his dick in and out of Brick House as hard as he could, but no matter how hard he stroked, she begged him to fuck her harder. Alonzo had been with quite a few women in his day, but Brick House's pussy was hands down the best he'd ever had. He felt his legs start to buckle as he came closer and closer to climaxing. Abandoning his grip on her hair, Alonzo locked both his forearms under her and lifted Brick House off her feet. His face twisted into a horrible mask of pleasure and pain as he emptied himself into the condom. He felt like the come would never stop spilling out of him, and when it finally did, he slumped against her with his forehead on the wall. The night was silent except for the sounds of their heavy breathing, but the silence was interrupted by the sound of someone chambering a round into a pistol to his rear.

"Now that you've got yours, give me mine," a voice demanded from behind him.

Alonzo didn't have to turn around to know what was happening to him. "Rotten bitch." He grunted as Brick House slid from beneath him, leaving him standing there with the condom hanging off his dick.

"Ain't nothing personal, boo, but it's like I told you

earlier: I need *all* my chips." Brick House went to stand near the robbers.

"Turn around real slow and don't try nothing stupid," a gunman ordered him. Alonzo turned around to face his robbers. There were two of them, both wearing masks and both armed.

"Just be easy, my nigga. Y'all can have all this." Alonzo went to reach into his pocket and his head exploded in pain as the gunman hit him with the hammer. Alonzo stumbled into the wall, but kept his footing.

"Didn't I tell you not to do nothing stupid?" The gunman pressed the hammer to Alonzo's forehead. "Yo, Brick, get this nigga's pockets."

Brick House cautiously moved to Alonzo and began rummaging through his pockets.

"Shitting where you live is never a smart thing, baby girl," Alonzo warned her.

"Shut up before I shit on *you*." Brick House pulled his money out and began counting it. "Nigga, all you got is two hundred dollars and you was up in there like you was balling out with ya peoples? I should've tried to get ya man with the ice on out here instead of your broke ass."

"King would've killed you on the spot. A nigga like me, I'm gonna wait until later so I can take my time with you," he said seriously.

"You pop a lot of shit for a nigga on the wrong side of a pistol." The gunman jabbed the gun into Alonzo's chest. When he did, it hit against something that sounded like metal. The gunman yanked the front of Alonzo's shirt down and saw the thick link around his neck. "Run that too."

"A'ight, just be easy. I don't want no problems, B." Alonzo slowly reached for his neck. Seeing that he had Alonzo under pressure, the gunman relaxed, which was a big mistake. Instead of removing the chain, Alonzo went for the two razors he had taped to his collar. In one motion Alonzo jerked his head to the side and brought one of the razors down across the man's forearm, opening a vein. The gun went off, missing Alonzo's head but damn near deafening him, being fired so close to his ear. Ignoring the pain, Alonzo lunged, swinging the razors. His hands were a blur as the two small blades opened up gashes on the gunman's face, neck, and chest. Unfortunately, none was a killing blow, but they were enough to take him out of commission long enough for Alonzo to try to reach the second gunman.

The second gunman fumbled with the slide on his gun nervously as Alonzo closed the distance. From the looks of things, he was an amateur, which was good for Alonzo but bad for him. Alonzo swung the razor with the intention of taking the gunman's face off, but Brick House snuffed him, throwing off his aim. When Brick House saw Alonzo's angry eyes turn to her, she hightailed it back to the fire-exit door, which she had left propped open with a bottle. She had just reached the door when Alonzo caught her across the back with the razor, opening up a wide gash. He tried to take her head off with the second strike, but she managed to get to the safety of the door and slam it behind her.

Remembering his unfinished business, Alonzo turned back to the second gunman, who had finally managed to figure out how to work his pistol and was about to fire on Alonzo. Thankfully, a metal pipe busted his head to the white meat before he had the chance. The second gunman dropped like a brick at Ashanti's feet, who was standing there holding the pipe in question.

"Bitch-ass nigga." Ashanti brought the pipe down across his head once more for good measure. "Man, I've heard of getting caught with your pants down, but you've taken this shit to a new level." Ashanti looked down at Alonzo's exposed dick.

"Very fucking funny." Alonzo fixed himself. "You were supposed to be with the truck, what are you doing back here?"

"You're welcome," Ashanti said sarcastically. "I had to take a leak so I wandered back here, and from the looks of things it's a good thing I did. What happened?"

"I came back here to get some pussy and the bitch set me up. These niggaz tried to rob me." He motioned at the two men on the ground. The first gunman, whom he had cut, was rolling around on the floor in pain. "Come here, muthafucka." Alonzo dragged the gunman out into the alley. He snatched the mask off and saw that the face underneath couldn't have been more than seventeen or eighteen, but by then he was too far gone to care. All he'd wanted to do was come out and have a good time, but the petty thieves had awakened the sleeping giant. "You tried to take my money so I'm gonna take your face." He hit him with the razor. Alonzo didn't stop cutting the kid until his arms were tired and the boy's face looked like an old pack of hamburger meat.

"King ain't gonna like the fact that we dropped two bodies outside his meeting," Ashanti said, looking over the bloodied men.

"Right now I don't care who likes what, them niggaz violated."

"So what do we do now, clean the mess up?" Ashanti asked.

"Fuck them, nigga, leave 'em for the rats." Alonzo spat on the robber. "Let's go get the whip and scoop our peoples."

CHAPTER 33

You see my kid brother on his shit?" Lakim smiled.

"Looks like kid brother is about to get into some grown-man shit. I can't front, shorty had an onion," King admitted.

The waitress had finally found her way back with the liquor King had sent her for. She was carrying a fifth of Crown Royal and a bottle of champagne. She placed the Crown in front of King and headed over to Shai's table with the champagne. King watched her closely as she placed the bottle down in front of Shai and spoke in a hushed tone. Swann said something to her, to which she just shrugged her shoulders and walked away.

"So what's good, we gonna step to this nigga or what?" Lakim was staring daggers at Shai and his team.

"We gonna take care of business in a minute," King told him.

"God, you been saying that all night and so far all we've done is sat here and stared at them. I say we step to them cats and speak our piece." Lakim was getting impatient.

"Nah, I think we'll let them come to us," King said coolly.

"A'ight, now I know you bugging. What reason would Shai's people have to step to us?"

"Lakim, sometimes you don't need a reason when you have a well-laid plan." King cracked a devilish grin as he watched Holiday walking toward them.

Here you go, fellas." The waitress set a bottle of champagne on Shai's table.

"Sweetie, we didn't order this," Shai told her.

"Compliments of the gentleman over there." She nodded across the room.

Shai looked to see where she was pointing and saw a brolic sipping a bottle of water. He was watching Shai, but it was more of a curious stare than threatening. "Tell him thanks, but no thanks." Shai pushed the bottle away.

"Look, dude gave me a hundred dollars to make sure that I didn't bring it back, so unless you're giving me two hundred that's on y'all," she said and walked away.

"Bitch," Swann spat.

"What's good with that kid? He's been watching us all night," Angelo pointed out.

"I don't know. Do you know the nigga, Shai?" Holiday asked.

"I've never seen him a day in my life," Shai said.

"Then let me roll over there and ask him what the fuck he's looking at." Holiday got up.

"Chill the fuck out." Shai's voice froze him. "Take the bottle back and tell them niggaz we good, but don't cause a scene."

"I got you, B." Holiday grabbed the bottle off the table aggressively.

"I'm serious," Shai warned.

"Okay, Shai." Holiday headed across the room. "What's good?" he addressed King James.

"I see you received my gift." King nodded at the bottle.

"Yeah, good looking out but I can't accept this." Holiday held the bottle out toward King but he didn't move.

"That's cool, because I didn't send it to you, I sent it to Shai," King said coolly.

"Well, right now I speak for Shai and we good." Holiday slammed the bottle on King's table.

Dump and Lakim moved, but King raised his hand for them to be still. "You know it's bad form to insult someone by returning their gift, but being that you're just a solider I'll overlook it. Tell Shai that I sent the bottle over as a peace offering so that maybe we could sit down like men and discuss my grievance."

"Your what?" Holiday had no idea what the word meant. "What the fuck you mean you wanna discuss something with my dude? My nigga, I don't know who think you are, but you ain't him."

King placed his water bottle on the table and calmly stood up. He was taller than Holiday, so he was looking down on him when he spoke. "First of all, I ain't ya nigga, sun. As far as who I am, my name is King James."

At the mention of his name, the word *enemy* flashed through Holiday's brain. "Muthafucka." Holiday reached for his gun, but King's hand clamped around his wrist, preventing him from clearing the gun. He struggled but King's grip was like steel.

"You simple-minded-ass li'l nigga." King slapped Holiday viciously across the face, dazing him with the powerful impact. "I told you all I wanted to do was talk, but you gotta make a movie, huh?" King slapped him again. Holiday's head whipped back and forth limply with every slap.

A bouncer who had been standing nearby tried to intervene, which was a mistake. Dump swung one of his clublike fists and knocked him out. Seeing the commotion, Swann and Angelo sprang into action, guns drawn and murder in their hearts. Lakim broke two beer bottles and tossed one to Dump as they jumped between King James and the approaching killers. They were outgunned but it didn't matter to them. They were brothers and the fate of one would be the fate of all.

King stood there, still manhandling Holiday, watching the plan he had so carefully laid being dashed to hell because the youngster couldn't control himself. Looking at his men wielding their broken bottles and Shai's men wielding their guns, it was obvious how it would play out. He wrapped one of his massive hands around Holiday's neck and began to apply pressure. If they were going to die, at least he would take one of theirs with them to hell.

"Enough," Shai's voice boomed out. He stood there like the calm in the middle of the storm of violence. He walked up to King James, who was still strangling Holiday. "My dude, you see what it is, so you know that this can only end poorly. Tell your people to fall back and I'll do the same."

"All I wanted to do is holla, but ya man was outta pocket," King snarled.

"And that's for me to discipline the young boy, not you. I don't want my people going to prison or your people going to the morgue, but that's exactly how it's gonna play out if we get it on in this club. Let go of my man and tell your people to stand down. This is the last time I'm gonna ask you."

King weighed it. For as much as he wanted to kill Holiday, he wanted his men to live more. "A'ight." He shoved Holiday away roughly.

When Holiday caught his breath he tried to rush King, but Shai caught him by the back of his shirt and spun the young man to face him. He spoke in a hushed tone so that only Holiday could hear him. "You defy me in public again and you won't have to worry about this nigga killing you, because I'll off your li'l ignorant ass myself, understand?"

"Yeah, Shai," Holiday said fearfully.

"Good." Shai smoothed the wrinkles in Holiday's shirt. "You'll get your chance, but not here and not like this." Once he had calmed Holiday, he turned his attention to King James. "Dude, what the fuck is your problem?"

"Shai, it's like I was trying to tell ya li'l man, I only wanted to talk. There was no disrespect intended," King told him.

"Who the fuck are you to want to talk to me about anything? You cause a scene in my friend's club that could send us all to prison if the police were called and then talk some *no disrespect* shit? This shit goes beyond disrespect, my man. If this club didn't belong to a friend of ours I'd have you and your whole team taken into the alley and shot, then ship your heads to your mothers as a lesson as to why they should've used birth control."

"Is that right?" King asked defiantly.

"Muthafucking right." Shai got in his face, trying to intimidate King, but all he did was smirk. "You're smiling like what I'm saying is funny. Am I a joke to you?"

"Nah, you ain't no joke, Shai, you're the boss," King said in a less-than-sincere tone.

"Then wipe that fucking smile off your face," Shai ordered.

"Look, Shai, I ain't trying to go back and forth with you, sun. I got something I need to holla at you about right quick, then we'll be on our way," King said, finding himself increasingly irritated with the way Shai was talking to him. He wasn't sure how long he'd be able to keep himself from taking a swing at him and making the situation worse.

"Blood, you got a problem understanding English?" Swann stepped up. "Ain't shit to talk about. Now why don't you and these project niggaz you brought in here with you get the fuck outta here while you still can." He cast a casual glance at the entrance of the VIP, where several men had just come in. They took up positions behind Swann and glared at King James and his crew.

King James looked from Swann and his small army back to Shai. "So it's like that, Shai?"

Shai raised his hand in the air and closed it into a fist. When he did so, his men formed a circle around King James and his crew. "It's like that and then some. Good night," Shai said, dismissing him, and walked back to his table.

Three bouncers who worked for Brick City closed in on King James and his crew and without words let them know that they had overstayed their welcome. Lakim and Dump looked to him for their next move, and he motioned that it was time to go. King lingered behind to bring up the read as the bouncers escorted them out. Holiday was hunched over Shai's table, shooting him daggers. King gave him a knowing nod as both of them knew that their business was far from concluded.

"Bitch-ass niggaz." Dump bumped the bouncer at the VIP entrance on their way out. As they made their way down the stairs, the stripper with the pink hair they'd seen on the screen was making her way up. "Baby, that was a hell of show you put on out there," Dump told her.

"Thanks." Porsha smiled.

"Dump, come on, we ain't got time for that shit right now," King barked.

"A'ight, nigga, damn." Dump reluctantly followed.

"Yo, God, we can't leave Zo," Lakim said to King.

"We ain't leaving him, we're just getting out of harm's way. We got a pass because we're in a public place but ain't no telling if the treaty will hold when we're off the club's property. I'll feel a lot safer once we get back to the whip and arm up. Hit Zo on the jack and have him meet us out front," King told him. "I don't even think Shai and them knew Zo was with us, and even if they did, they ain't gonna try nothing in here. Zo will be good until we regroup." King was relieved when they were out of the club and in open space, but that feeling quickly faded when he realized that the truck wasn't where they'd left it. "Fuck did this li'l nigga go with the whip?" King looked around nervously. "La, I told you I ain't wanna fuck with that li'l nigga, he ain't even on point!" No sooner had the words left King's mouth than the big truck screeched to a halt a few feet away from them. Alonzo was behind the wheel and Ashanti was in the backseat. King hopped in on the passenger side while Lakim and Dump sandwiched Ashanti in the back.

"Fuck y'all niggaz was at, it almost went down," Lakim snapped once they were all back in the whip.

"My fault, I had a li'l situation, B," Alonzo told them,

peeling out of the parking lot. When they passed under the streetlight, King saw the blood on his hands.

"What's good, you hit?" King asked nervously.

"I'm good, it ain't my blood," Alonzo told him.

"At least not all of it," Ashanti joked from the back-seat. None of them would get the joke until Alonzo filled them in on the way back to New York.

After King and his rowdy bunch were cleared out of the VIP, it was back to business as usual. The confrontation between Shai and King James spread through the club like wild fire, and everyone was buzzing about the mysterious cat who had the balls to challenge New York's under-world boss. It had even reached the ears of Paulie, who had rushed upstairs to offer Shai his apologies.

"Shai, I'm sorry about that whole thing," Paulie said for the seventh time.

Shai waved him off. "Paulie, I keep telling you that wasn't on you so don't worry about it."

"Yeah, but this is my club so everything that goes on in here is on me. I don't even know how those guys got up here, but trust me, the guy who let them slip by is gonna find himself on the soup line tomorrow."

"That ain't necessary, Paulie. I don't blame him for this; I blame myself because I should've nipped it in the bud earlier." He cut his eyes at Swann, who was still fum-ing. "Paulie, you've done a great job with this place and I'm glad to be in on the ground floor."

"Thanks, Shai, but I couldn't have done it without your help. Hey, let's toast to it!" Paulie suggested.

"I'd love to, but we gotta cut out."

"C'mon, Shai, don't let that street shit ruin your night. Stick around for a while, I'll have some more bottles and a few of the girls sent up here for you."

"Thanks, but no. I got some things I need to take care of early in the morning anyhow. Thanks for the offer though." Shai shook Paulie's hand.

"Anytime, anytime. Listen, you gotta come by on Sunday. We're kicking off amateur night and I'd love to have you on hand as a special guest judge."

"I'll let you know, Paulie. Let's go, fellas," Shai told his crew.

"I don't like those cats, Shai. People like King James don't have the good sense to be scared of anything," Angelo said.

"Word, I'm with Angelo. That nigga King James was out-of-bounds. I say we blast on them niggaz ASAP," Holiday said.

"You don't *say* shit, Holiday. I'm still running this candy shop," Shai reminded him. As much as he hated to admit it, Holiday was right.

"Still think this beef is gonna stay in the streets?" Swann asked.

Shai gave Swann a knowing look. "These niggaz seem to be forgetting their places and need to be taught a lesson. Tighten that muthafucka up."

Swann knew without his having to say so that Shai wanted King James dead. "Say no more, my nigga."

CHAPTER 34

Damn, I can't believe it almost went down in here," Tone said after King and his crew had been escorted out.

"I told you that nigga King James was bad news," Devil reminded him.

"More like stupid." Don B. snorted. "Who in their right mind is gonna try and style on Shai Clark? For as heavy as we are in the streets, even we know better than that. Moving like that, ya man King James has got a life expectancy of about twenty minutes. Speaking of time"—Don B. looked at his watch—"what the fuck is up with ya man Gotti? We been waiting for this nigga Lord Scientific to go on all night."

"It shouldn't be too much longer. Gotti went downstairs to get him set up a few minutes ago," Tone told him.

"Well, he better hurry the fuck up. The Don doesn't like to be kept waiting, so I'm about ready to bounce," Don B. said, crushing some weed up in a blunt on the table. He skillfully rolled it up and sparked a lighter on the end of it. Through the flames he saw the stripper with the pink hair walking toward him. "Then again, I may have a few more minutes to kill."

"What's goodie, big time?" Porsha sauntered over.

"That's Big Dawg, and now that you're here, everything is good." Don B. looked her up and down. "Don't just stand there looking all good, take a load off, ma." He patted his lap. Porsha took the seat next to him instead. "Damn, mama, I ain't gonna bite you, at least not yet."

"I don't like to be bitten. Spanked, maybe, but I don't do the biting unless I'm biting my lip in pleasure when I'm getting dicked down," Porsha teased him.

"We might be able to arrange that."

"Slow down, speedy, and let's start with a drink first." Porsha helped herself to a glass of champagne. Her cockiness turned Don B. on.

"It took you long enough to come check for a nigga, ma."

"I was a li'l busy, as if you didn't see my show," Porsha told him.

"Shit, every nigga in the joint seen ya show. I wouldn't be surprised if it was airing on pay-per-view too," Don B. joked.

"They can show that muthafucka on the moon as long as I get my cut, ya heard?" Porsha said seriously.

"I like a chick that's about her paper," Don B. told her. "But on some G shit, I dig ya style, ma."

"That makes two of us, because I dig my style too."

Don B. laughed. "You a funny chick. Check, after I conduct this li'l business I'm gonna slide outta here. Why don't you go get dressed and we can go get something to eat."

Porsha took a sip from her glass and calmly set it on the table. "That definitely sounds like something we may be able to discuss, but let's be clear on a few things, my G. Just because I shake my ass don't mean I'm selling it, so if you think throwing a li'l bit of paper in the air is gonna get you in my panties, you can save ya bread for one of these slums-ass hos sucking dick in the bathroom down-stairs; that ain't my bag."

"I didn't mean it like that," Don B. lied.

"Of course you didn't," she said sarcastically, "I'm just letting you know what it is with me. You can't put a price on what I got down here." She patted her pussy. "If I fuck a nigga it's gonna be because I dig him, not for paper."

"I can respect that," Don B. said, not really knowing how else to respond. "Do you dig me?"

Porsha thought on it for a minute. "You a'ight, but then again I'm just meeting you. Who knows how I might feel about you down the line." She took another sip from her glass.

All Don B. could do was shake his head. It seemed like she had a snappy comeback for everything he said. He was used to chicks throwing themselves at him, but Porsha was a horse of a different color, which meant he would actually have to put some effort into fucking her. Normally he wouldn't bother, but he was intrigued by the sharp-tongued young lady.

A big-boned dark-skinned chick strutted over to their table and motioned that she needed to talk to Porsha. "Excuse me for a second," Porsha said, getting up. She made sure to throw something extra in her walk for Don B.'s viewing pleasure. "What's good, Kat?"

"We gotta bust a move, baby," Kat told her.

"Bust a move? Girl, you tripping. I'm in here making a killing and I've got this nigga spinning right now." She motioned over shoulder to Don B., who was whispering something to his people.

"Well, you're gonna have to take that meal to go. Shit is going down in here and it ain't good. They found two dudes in the alley out back carved up like two birds on Thanksgiving, and on top of that I heard one of these niggaz tried to rape Brick House. Best believe before the night is over the police are gonna be crawling all over this joint, and with the type of shit they got going on in here, I don't wanna be around for it."

"Damn, that's horrible, I hope she's okay," Porsha said sincerely. Brick House was a royal bitch, but rape was something Porsha wouldn't wish on her worse enemy.

"Fuck her, it's gonna be poor us if we get caught in here when it hits the fan. I called my brother Marcus already and he said he'll be here in twenty minutes to pick us up. I'm leaving. What you gonna do, P?"

Porsha weighed her options. If what Kat was telling her was true, then she definitely needed to shake the spot, but she had her hooks in Don B. and didn't wanna lose him just yet. She looked back at his table, where the waitress had just set two more bottles. "I'm outta here in a few minutes too but I think I'm gonna catch a ride with Don B."

"Porsha, don't be a fool for no dick," Kat warned.

"Of course not. He was just saying that he was ready to bounce anyway, so by the time I get dressed he should be ready to roll out. With or without Don B., I'm outta here in the next forty-five minutes or so."

Kat knew the look in Porsha's eyes all too well. She wanted to drag her out of the club and harm's way, but Porsha was grown, or so she thought. "A'ight, do you then, ma, but make sure you hit me and let me know that you got outta here in one piece."

"I will." Porsha gave Kat a parting hug. Then she went back over to Don B.'s table and reclaimed her seat next to him.

"What's up with your homegirl, she ain't wanna party?" Tone asked. He would've loved to get a piece of Kat.

"Nah, she had to make a move. I'm probably gonna leave too because she's my ride back to Harlem," Porsha said. She knew that if she put it out there, Don B. would take care of the rest.

"Oh, you live in Harlem? Don't even worry about it, I'm going the same way so it's nothing to drop you off after breakfast," Don B. offered.

"You're persistent as hell, aren't you?"

"I wouldn't be where I am today if I knew how to take no for an answer. Go get ya clothes and whatever else you gotta do so we can get outta here," Don B. told her.

"A'ight, give me like twenty minutes." Porsha went off to get dressed.

"I know you gonna let me taste that, my nigga," Tone said as soon as Porsha was out of earshot.

Don B. smiled. "You can always ride in my whip, Tone, as long as I get to test-drive it alone first. I'm gonna bust that slick-mouthed bitch wide open!" One of Gotti's minions appeared at the table and told Don B. that Lord Scientific would be performing in about fifteen minutes on the main stage. "About fucking time." Don B. grabbed a bottle off the table when he got up. "Let's go downstairs and watch this shit so we'll be close to the door, because as soon as shorty is done getting dressed I'm trying to get outta here."

Don B. led his crew downstairs into the swarm of people. Devil and the bouncers kept the groupies back as best they could, but it was still a task. Don B. had long ago lost interest in the hype of Lord Scientific, and his thoughts were on Porsha and the things he planned on doing to her. If Lord Scientific wasn't all that they'd hyped him up to be, Don B. was outta there.

Don B. and his people met Gotti by the bar, where he was talking to the young cat who worked for the DJ. He was confused because he'd expected him to be on stage with the mysterious Lord Scientific. Instead, there were some kids up there who looked like they were the Wu-Tang Clan in their early days. There were about a dozen of them, dressed in oversize T-shirts, khakis, and capri shorts and waving red bandannas as proudly as if they were American flags and they were doing their patriotic duty. They were some of the dingiest cats Don B. had ever seen and some of the surliest. The group parted like the Red Sea and from their midst a lone figure stepped forward. He was topless, showing off his well-defined body and the golden revolver that dangled at the end of the thick chain around his neck. His long dreadlocks swayed back and forth as he bobbed to a beat that only he could hear. The crowd became deathly silent as he surveyed them from under hooded eyes.

"Jersey!" he bellowed, and the crowd went wild just before the music exploded through the speakers.

The reaction was like nothing Don B. had seen since they heydays of Bad Blood, when his li'l homies were tearing down every club in New York City. The crowd fed off the rapper's energy liked starved children, singing the lyrics along with him. The rapper had them eating out of the palm of his hand, and even Devil was caught rocking to the ill beat. Everything was going well until someone threw an empty water bottle onto the stage.

"Hold on, hold on. Cut the muthafucking music," the rapper ordered the DJ. There was some grumbling throughout the crowd as the performance was halted. "Who threw that?" the rapper asked, surveying the crowd.

At first there was no response, then someone pointed out a smug-looking cat who was standing off to the side with about a half-dozen dudes, all wearing hard faces.

"Oh, you niggaz think you funny, huh?" the rapper said, zeroing in on the man and his crew. "Well, Ima show you how we deal with comedians in Newark, muthafucka." The rapper looked at his crew and gave them a knowing nod. "Feeding time," he said and pointed at the bottle thrower.

The young boys leaped off the stage and swarmed in on the bottle thrower and commenced to beat him like an unruly child. His team tried to jump in and found themselves swarmed by every Blood gang member in the club. Chairs were thrown, people were trampled, and Brick City was being torn apart. The performance had turned into a full-scale riot and the party was officially over.

"Fuck this, we gotta get Don B. outta here," Devil yelled over the crowd, knocking out some drunk who had gotten too close to them.

"True," Tone agreed, ducking a bottle that sailed over his head. "Yo, Gotti, we'll hook up another time so Don B. can see your boy do his thing."

Gotti laughed. "You just did." He nodded across the room. The rapper with the dreads had come down from the stage and was in the thick of the fight, attacking everything that moved. He jumped on one kid and started strangling him with the microphone cord while his crew kicked the kid in the face repeatedly.

"You can't be fucking serious." Tone looked at him

and shook his head in disappointment before turning to Don B. "Don, my fault for wasting your time on this."

Don B. laughed. "Wasting my time? My nigga, I ain't had this much fun in years. Gotti, y'all niggaz come to the city and see me tomorrow afternoon so we can discuss this paperwork."

Tone thought that Don B. had finally lost his mind, but his thinking was quite clear. Lord Scientific and his crew were wild as hell and it would probably end up costing Don B. more to clean up after them than to actually make a record, but their brand of ignorance was just what Big Dawg Entertainment needed to reassert itself at the top of the food chain. The whole world would look at Lord Scientific and see a thug, but Don B. saw a dollar sign.

Part IV

TRUTH AND CONSEQUENCES

CHAPTER 35

By the time Porsha made it back to the block the next day she was damn near out on her feet. As Kat had promised, Brick City was live, but Porsha didn't think either of them was prepared for how live it would get before it was all said and done. She came out of the dressing room just as the fight was about to pop off. Lord Scientific and his crew tore the places to pieces and security was powerless to stop the swarm of Bloods who laid siege to the establishment. It got so crazy that they had to call in the task force to shut it down.

The Bloods were good ass kickers, but the boys in blue were professionals. They were handing out ass whippings, pepper spray, and charges like free toys on Christmas. They were lenient with the celebrities but all the regular folks were treated to rides to various precincts in and around Essex County. Porsha almost broke down in tears when they slapped the handcuffs on her. She was already strapped for cash, and knowing that the few dollars she had managed to scrape up in Brick City would have to go toward her bond was the icing on the cake. Just when things seemed bleakest, Don B. came to her rescue. She wasn't sure what he said, and honestly she didn't care, but by the time he got finished whispering in the right ears and greasing the right palms, Porsha was released along with the rest of his entourage.

After they left the club she rode with Don B. and his crew back to the city in their Hummer. From the outside, all the windows were tinted so dark that you couldn't see the inside, but once Devil opened the door for Porsha to climb in and she got a good look, she was thoroughly impressed. Like the exterior, the interior was candy red, including the steering wheel and carpet. There was a standard row in the back of the extended truck but Don B. had ripped the rest out and replaced them with airplane seats that you could heat or cool to your liking. The leather was so soft that Porsha felt like she would rip it if she moved the wrong way, so she tried to stay still for most of the ride. She had been in some nice rides before, but Don B.'s Hummer took the cake.

Don B. and Porsha sat nestled in the rear row of the Hummer, sipping cognac and blowing Kush as they got to know each other a little better. From what she had heard about Don B. he was supposed to be some sort of ignorant-ass thug, but he was actually quite intelligent. She was thoroughly impressed as he took her through the history of jazz music and hip-hop, breaking down how the two were so closely related. He was so passionate when he spoke about music that Porsha could tell he had a genuine love for it and wasn't just another rapper who was out to get paid.

By the time they crossed the George Washington Bridge the sun was just about up. Don B. and Porsha had been so wrapped up in their conversation that neither of them had noticed how fast the time was flying. Don B. offered to take her to breakfast, which sounded like a great idea to Porsha, who had the munchies like you wouldn't believe from all the weed they had smoked. They stopped at City Diner on Broadway, where they gorged on steak and eggs and continued talking until the sun was well up. Of course, when they left, Don B. cracked on Porsha for sex, but she shut him down. She expected him to show his true colors and get mad, but he was surprisingly cool about it. By the time he dropped her off in the projects, Porsha found herself head over heels in *like* with the superstar.

Before going upstairs to take it down for the day, Porsha decided to hit the supermarket up for some milk and a box of Cap'n Crunch. She was still full from breakfast but knew that by the time she woke up she was going to be starving all over again. She was making her way down the cereal aisle when she spotted Alonzo in the back, stacking canned goods. When they made eye contact she smiled and waved at him, but to her surprise he gave her his back and kept working as if he hadn't seen her.

"What up, Zo?" Porsha approached him.

"Chilling," he said over his shoulder, not bothering to look up from the crate of cans.

Porsha stepped around so that he had to face her. "Damn, what are you looking all sour about?"

"Ain't nothing, had a rough night is all." Alonzo's tone was flat.

"Not the workhorse. I didn't know you actually hung out, for as much time as you spend in here."

"I get around, just like everybody else." He looked her up and down, then went back to his cans.

"Alonzo, why are you acting like I kicked your dog or something?" Porsha asked.

"I'm good, shorty. Like I told you, it was a rough night. I went out with my brother and some of his friends last night and things got a little crazy."

"Really? Where'd you go?"

"A li'l spot in Newark called Brick City. By the way, that was some li'l show you put on," he said with an attitude.

Porsha now understood why he was throwing shade her way. "So you saw me dance, huh?"

"Among other things," he capped. "I didn't know you were that flexible."

"There's a lot you don't know about me, Alonzo."

"Yeah, I'm starting to see that."

Porsha folded her arms. "Alonzo, I know you ain't got an attitude because you saw me dancing?"

"No, I don't have an attitude about anything. If you dance, sell pussy, or whatever the fuck it is that goes on in there, that's your business. I ain't got no papers on you," he said a little sharper than he'd intended to.

Porsha's eyes narrowed to slits. "Nigga, you got me fucked up. First of all, I don't sell ass, I give it away freely to whomever I choose. And second of all, how dare you disrespect me like I'm some lowlife whore."

"I didn't call you a whore, I was just saying . . . Forget it." Alonzo attempted to go back to stacking shelves, but Porsha spun him around to face her. There was a fury in her eyes that he had never seen before and it made him take a cautionary step back.

"Let me make a few things clear to you so there's no misunderstanding between us. I don't give a damn how broke I am, I would never degrade myself by selling my body for a few punk-ass dollars. Maybe you're used to associating with those kinds of bitches, but I ain't the one or the two. Yeah, I strip and I make no apologies for it. It isn't the most respectable job, but that doesn't give you a right to knock my hustle, especially when your ass is in here working in the supermarket. For as intelligent as you are, you're in here wasting your life working in a super-market instead of shooting for something bigger. I may be a stripper, but at least I'm out there trying, instead of set-tling. I do what I have to do to keep a roof over my head and food in my stomach, simple as that. And if you ain't helping me pay those bills or feed myself, then it ain't none of your fucking business." She knocked over the cans he had just stacked. "Now judge that." She stormed off down the aisle.

"Porsha," he called after her, but she was long gone. Alonzo flopped down on the crate and sighed, watching the cans rolling around his feet. He hadn't meant to come at Porsha so harshly, but his emotions took over his mouth and it ended up all bad. The twisted part about it was that he wasn't sure if he was angrier at Porsha for being a strip-per or at himself for what he had been dumb enough to walk into at Brick City.

He hadn't slept a wink all night because every time he closed his eyes he saw blood. Allowing a stripper to lead him into an alley alone was a novice mistake and he knew better. Being away from the streets for so long had dulled his instincts, but that situation had been a case of not exercising common sense. Had it not been for Ashanti, he would've been the one bleeding out onto the cracked New-ark streets instead of those two kids.

The boy's face was still as vivid in his mind as it had been the night before in the alley. Once the gun had been removed from the equation, the tough-guy exterior had faded and he'd been little more than a frightened kid. Alonzo tried to feel bad for what he had done, but he couldn't. Alonzo had carved him up so bad that he wasn't sure whether he had killed him or not, and at that point it really didn't make a difference. The truth of the matter was that the moment that boy had picked up a gun and decided to try to rob Alonzo, he had ceased to be a child and stepped into the realm of grown men, so he'd been dealt with accordingly.

"Alonzo, those cans aren't gonna pick themselves up." The manager, Mr. Green, hovered over him.

"I'm on it, Mr. Green," Alonzo told him.

"Then get to it, chop, chop." Mr. Green clapped his hands and walked away.

As Alonzo stood there looking at Mr. Green's departing back he was tempted to hurl one of the cans at him, but getting fired wouldn't help things. While he knelt to pick up the cans, Porsha's words came back to him and he couldn't help but wonder if he really was just settling.

CHAPTER 36

You plan on sleeping all day, or are you ready to rejoin the land of the living?" Sahara stuck her head into Frankie's bedroom.

Frankie removed the pillow from her head and looked around groggily. She felt like she had just gone to sleep. "What time is it?"

Sahara checked her watch. "Two thirty. What time did you creep in here last night?"

"Late," Frankie said, sitting up.

"Must've been superlate because I came in about one and you still weren't here. Where were you?"

"You don't even wanna know." Frankie wiped the cold from her eyes. She had been in the parking lot for most of the night selling crack, but it had been a slow grind. Fiends had come sporadically to cop from her, but she hadn't been able to get that steady flow. No matter, when the sun went down today she planned to get back to it. When Frankie yawned, her nose was assaulted by the smell of something frying, which made her stomach growl. "Damn, what you cooking?"

"Just some wings and fries. I made enough for you if you want some," Sahara offered.

"Hell yeah." Frankie stretched.

"Then get your ass up and come in the living room because I sure as hell ain't serving you," Sahara told her.

"A'ight, let me roll up first."

"Ew, at least brush your teeth before you put your mouth on the Dutch," Sahara teased her.

"Fuck you, Sahara. Ain't no telling what you had your skank-ass mouth wrapped around last night."

"Wherever I had my mouth, please believe it was minty fresh." Sahara let out a breath.

"Girl, you stupid." Frankie laughed. "Speaking of skanks, is Porsha up?"

Sahara shrugged. "The hell if I know. I ain't seen her since I left her in Brick City last night."

Frankie frowned. "Brick City, ain't that a strip joint or something?"

"'Or something' is right. Girl, we had it popping in there last night!"

"You went to a strip club with Porsha? I have got to hear this story." Frankie tossed off the covers and sat up. It was then she realized that she was still fully dressed. She was so tired she must've crashed without getting undressed.

Sahara looked her up and down. "Did you sleep in your clothes? Shit, looks like I ain't the only one with a story to tell. C'mon, let's get high so we can exchange gossip and bust these wings down."

The first thing Porsha noticed when she walked in was the smell of fried chicken, which told her that Sahara was home. The girl had her flaws, but knowing her way around the kitchen wasn't one of them. She propped her roll-on against the wall near the front door and made her way into the living room, where Sahara and Frankie were eating chicken wings and engaged in a deep conversation. From the way they both went silent, Porsha knew that she had been the topic.

"I knew my ears were ringing for a reason," Porsha greeted her roommates.

"Wasn't nobody talking about you," Sahara lied.

"Where ya been, Penny?" Frankie did her Chip Fields impersonation.

"Girl, I had a wild night." Porsha flopped on the couch.

"And a wilder morning from the looks of your hair," Sahara joked.

"I know you ain't talking." Porsha looked at the mop on Sahara's head before snatching one of her chicken wings. "So is King still here sleeping it off, or did he bounce already?" When Sahara didn't answer, Porsha knew what it was. "Don't tell me he stood you up again?"

"It wasn't like that, Porsha, he called me and told me he couldn't make it. Something came up," Sahara lied. She hadn't seen or heard from King since she'd left Brick City. She'd been calling and texting him all night and morning and he still hadn't hit her back.

"Um-hm." Porsha saw right through the lie. This wasn't the first time King had left Sahara hanging and she was sure it wouldn't be the last.

"So how was Brick City?" Frankie asked.

"Girl, it was off the chain!" Porsha went on to tell them of her adventures at Brick City and her morning with Don B.

"I can't believe you spent the morning with Don B." Frankie was surprised.

"And didn't fuck him," Sahara added.

"Sahara, why does everything have to be about sex with you?" Porsha rolled her eyes.

"It ain't just about sex, it's about sex and money, and ya boy Don B. has got plenty of it," Sahara said. "So are you gonna fuck him?"

"Sahara!"

"I'm just saying, P, I'd fuck him if I had the chance."

"You'd fuck anything with a pulse, loose ass," Frankie cracked.

"At least my pipes ain't clogged. When was the last time you got dicked down again?" Sahara rolled her neck.

"Okay, okay, you two cats retract your claws. I'm in a good mood and I don't need y'all blowing it."

"Listen to you sounding like a love-struck puppy." Sahara pinched Porsha's cheek.

Porsha swatted her hand away. "Quit playing. Ain't nobody loving nothing. I just think Don B. is cool peoples."

"With a healthy bank account," Sahara added.

"Yes, gold digger, with a healthy bank account. I can't even front them dudes was in the spot blowing wild paper, and don't even get me started on his ride. I ain't never seen a Hummer tricked out like his. I felt like I was riding in a spaceship on the way uptown."

"Well, don't let yourself float too far into orbit fucking with Don B.," Frankie told her.

"And what do you mean by that?"

"I mean have fun, but don't get too caught up with that cat. I heard some real foul stories about Don B. on the streets," Frankie warned.

"Like what?" Porsha questioned.

"Like he's a dog, treats women like shit. My homegirl's

sister used to fuck with him back in the days before he blew up and she said he treated her like the shit on the bottom of his shoe."

Porsha sucked her teeth. "You know how bitches be hating. She's probably just mad that she missed the train when he was on his way to the top. Don B. was a perfect gentleman when we hung out."

"And so was Jeffery Dahmer until he got them mutha-fuckas in his crib and started snacking on them," Frankie countered. "Porsha, I ain't trying to tell you not to fuck with him, just go into the situation with your eyes open, feel me?"

"Yeah," Porsha said, not really paying her any mind. She had heard her share of stories about Don B. too, but he was a star so a little baggage was to be expected. She wasn't stupid enough to go into the situation with Don B. expecting some great love affair, but she liked his company and would see for herself what he was about instead of letting rumors and haters influence her decision. "I'm tired as hell, I just wanna put something on my stomach and lay down."

"Yeah, get your beauty sleep because the party contin-ues tonight," Sahara said excitedly.

"What the hell is going on tonight?" Frankie asked.

Sahara rolled her eyes. "King's surprise party, remem-ber?"

"Shit, you did mention something about that. I don't know if I'm gonna be able to make it though, Sahara. I got something to do," Frankie said, thinking about the rest of the crack she had stashed in her bedroom.

"That makes two of us," Porsha said.

Sahara looked back and forth between them. "I know

y'all ain't serious? What do y'all have to do that's so damn important?"

"I'm working on getting my end of the rent money up. We only got a few more days before they try to toss us out on our asses," Frankie reminded them.

Sahara turned to Porsha. "And what's your excuse?"

"I've got a date with Don B."

"So bring him with you. He'll probably know half of the criminal muthafuckas in there anyway."

"I don't think that'd be a good idea."

"And why not? Your little rapper boyfriend too good to hang out with us common folk?" Sahara asked with an attitude.

Porsha thought about keeping it real with her friend and telling her how King had tried to push up on her, but she didn't want to hurt her feelings so she lied. "It's not like that, but he's taking me to a movie screening and then dinner and I'm not sure what time everything will be over. I'll call you and see if the party is still popping after we eat."

"You bitches are so whack." Sahara got off the couch and pouted like a child. "That's alright, I don't need y'all to have a good time. I can party like a rock star by my-self." Sahara stormed into her bedroom and slammed the door.

"Damn, now I feel bad," Frankie said.

"Shit, I don't." Porsha took the blunt clip out of the ashtray. "King is an asshole and I ain't feeling him." Por-sha lit the clip and went on to tell Frankie the story of how King had tried to hit on her in the club.

"That's some dirty shit." Frankie shook her head sadly.

"Tell me about it; but you know if I try to bring it to Sahara she's gonna get mad at me instead of him, so I'm gonna sit back and watch it unfold." Porsha exhaled the smoke and passed the weed to Frankie. "I'm about to check my e-mails before I lay down." She fired up the laptop that was sitting on the coffee table. As she was scrolling through her e-mails she accidentally opened one that she was trying to delete. It was a pop-up from a pornographic Web site called BrownGirls.com, which boasted that it was one of the most widely watched African-American amateur porn sites. "Some people have too much free time on their hands."

Frankie looked over Porsha's shoulder at the video image of a girl getting fucked in the ass. "Damn, that looks painful."

"I tried it once and never again," Porsha told her. As she stared at the video she couldn't help thinking that she had seen the girl somewhere. "I think I know this chick, Frankie. I might have seen her dancing at one of the clubs."

Frankie studied the girl's face and she recognized her too. "Nah, that ain't no stripper, that's a ho." She laughed, but Porsha didn't seem to get the joke. "Porsha, look real close and tell me where we know that skinny bitch from."

Porsha stared at the video, racking her brain trying to place the girl. It wasn't until the girl faced the camera to receive the come-shot that it hit her. "Oh shit, that's Faye!"

"It sure is, in all her skank-ass glory."

"Damn, I knew she was a jump-off, but I didn't know she'd taken it this far." Porsha leaned in closer to the screen. "The way she was taking that dick, I don't know if I'm mad at her or proud of her."

"That bitch is just nasty." Frankie shook her head.

"Ain't no doubt about that, but who put her ass on this Web site?"

Boy, Levi, I wish you could've seen her face when Porsha rolled up on us. I thought the girl was gonna shit her pants," Happy said, taking another bite of his egg roll. He and Levi sat on the bench in front of 875, enjoying the weather and trading war stories.

"I can only imagine," Levi said, lighting a cigarette. "What I can't understand is why Boots thinks that the fact that she's a jump-off is a secret."

Happy shrugged his broad shoulders. "Beats the hell outta me. Everybody and they mama knows that girl's snatch is open for business twenty-four/seven. Well, everybody except Bernie."

"Let me tell you something." Levi blew a cloud of smoke into the air. "The day that nigga finally figures it out is the day he's going to jail for the rest of his life."

"You ain't never lied, because he's sure as hell gonna kill her, if he don't kill himself first." Happy laughed.

"I'd pay good money to see her finally get her sneaky ass beat, B."

"Fuck all that, I'd pay good money to see Porsha butt-ass naked," Happy said seriously.

"Word, that's a bad bitch. I've tried every angle I could think of to crack that and she just ain't going for it. I just don't understand it, Hap."

Happy shoved the last of the egg roll into his mouth and wiped his hands on his pants. "Ain't too much to it when you understand the nature of a bitch, Levi. See, they all fall into categories and Porsha is what you would call an on-the-wagon ho."

"What the hell is that?"

"An on-the-wagon ho is the same thing as an on-the-wagon drunk: they get clean and pretend that liquor is the devil, but in the back of their mind they still crave it. A bitch like Porsha moves in these big-money circles, but she's gonna always crave a street nigga hip-deep in her box. Eventually they all fall off the wagon and so will Porsha, and when she does ol' Hap will be there waiting on her."

"Hap, you're shot out," was the only response Levi could think of. He didn't know which was more amazing, the fact that Happy had actually voiced his warped theory or the fact that he actually believed it. He had seen some girls stoop to unimaginable levels for Happy and his deep pockets, but Porsha didn't strike him as that type or that desperate.

"Man, that ain't nothing but the truth," Happy declared. "All these bitches fall into a category, Porsha is just one of many."

Thankfully, before Happy could continue with his foolishness, Levi spotted the FedEx truck pulling up on the avenue and a broad smile spread across his face. "Be right back, Hap." Levi got off the bench and met the delivery-man. He had been waiting for the package for weeks and it had finally arrived. Levi's hands trembled as he tore open the package and read over the paperwork. The more he read, the bigger his grin got.

"What's you got that got you cheesing so wide?" Happy asked suspiciously.

"My ticket outta the ghetto," Levi said in a half-joking tone.

"That's a riot! Nigga, unless it's a check for a million dollars in that bitch, your monkey ass will be sitting right her on these same benches with me next summer." Happy snorted. "I don't know why muthafuckas is always talking about getting out of the hood. Shit, I love the hood. You know, some people . . ."

Happy went on and on, but Levi wasn't listening because in his mind he was already plotting his next move. People like Happy liked to try to dash the dreams of others because they didn't have dreams of their own, but even his negative energy couldn't put a dent in Levi's armor that afternoon. Happy and the rest of the sorry muthafuckas in the hood might still be sitting on the benches next summer, doing the same shit, but not Levi. He planned on being somewhere warm with a drink in one hand and a titty in the other.

CHAPTER 37

Once the sun had set, the streets returned to life and so did Ashanti. It had been quiet that day for him. After partying all night with King James and his crew, Ashanti was exhausted. It had been a long time since he's had a night like that and it was good to have some good criminal fun again.

Ashanti sat on the benches in front of 3150, thumbs clicking away on his PSP. His face was contorted into a mask of concentration as he tried to go for thirty with Kobe in 2K. He had never been big on video games, as he was always in the streets committing crimes, but ever since he'd *appropriated* the handheld game he'd been glued to it.

At the other end of the bench, a group of girls were talking about how it had gone down at a strip club in New Jersey the night before. Ashanti smiled, because he knew they were talking about wh'at had happened at Brick City. Alonzo had put it down on the kid in the alley and Ashanti was impressed. He had always known Alonzo as a clean-cut working dude, but in that alley Zo-Pound came out and Ashanti had been impressed by what he saw. He had heard plenty of stories of how the kid gave it up, but seeing him in action was something else altogether.

With his curiosity killing him, Ashanti inched down a

bit so he could hear the girls clearer. As they told the story he became confused. According to them, there was a huge riot and the place had to be shut down, but when Ashanti and the rest had pulled out the club was in full swing. Something must've gone down after they'd left, and he was kind of upset that he had missed it. There was nothing Ashanti appreciated more than a good riot.

"Psst, pssst," he heard behind him, causing his head to snap around. On the other side of the fence was a young white dude, dressed in skinny jeans and a Ben Folds Five T-shirt. "Anybody working?" the dude asked him.

Ashanti started to bark on him, thinking he might've been an undercover, but as he looked closely he saw the telltale signs that the dude was a genuine addict. Ashanti didn't have any drugs on him so he started to send the dude away, but an idea formed in his head. "What you need?"

"An eight ball," the dude told him, wiping his nose with the back of his hand.

Ashanti knew that look. The dude was jonesing and would be easy prey. "A'ight, come around the fence and meet me in the lobby," Ashanti told him, slipping his video game into his pocket next to the small .22 he was carrying. The dude started up the path toward the building and Ashanti fell in step a few seconds behind him. Ashanti slipped into the lobby and motioned for the dude to go into the staircase.

"I was looking for Shark, but I didn't see him. Is this the same stuff he's pushing?" the white dude asked Ashanti once they were in the stairwell.

"Yeah, yeah, that's my man," Ashanti told him, casting an occasional glance through the window in the staircase door to make sure the lobby was still clear.

"Cool, because the last time I came through to cop from someone other than Shark I got burned," the white dude told him.

"Nah, I ain't gonna burn you, but I am gonna fuck you." Ashanti pulled his .22 and pointed it at the white dude. "Run that bread, blood."

The white dude made a face as if he couldn't believe he was about to be robbed. "Are you fucking serious?"

"As a heart attack. Now come up off that change and don't make me ask you again." Ashanti pressed the gun into the dude's chest. The dude dipped his hand into his pocket and fumbled around for a minute before producing some bills, which he handed over. Ashanti stuffed the bills into his pocket and then clubbed the white dude in the head with the gun, opening a wide gash and dropping him to one knee. "Nigga, do I look stupid enough not to peep game when a muthafucka is trying to piece me off?"

"Hey, cool out, man." The white dude used one hand to try to stop the flow of blood coming from his head and the other to hand Ashanti the rest of his money. "Dude, the least you can do is leave me bus fare to get back downtown."

Ashanti paused for a minute as if he was considering it before he kicked the white dude in the gut. "Fuck yo bus fare, pussy. You should've thought about that before you brought you ass up to Harlem to buy drugs."

The sounds of footsteps coming down the stairs drew their attention. Knowing that Ashanti wouldn't shoot him in front of witnesses, the white dude tried to use it to his advantage. "Help, he's robbing me!" he screamed.

"Shut the fuck up." Ashanti grabbed him by the front of his T-shirt and gave him a few whacks to the chin with his gun.

"What the fuck is this?" King James rounded the corner of the second-floor landing. He was flanked by Lakim and a young dude who ran with them named Wise. "I know you ain't on ya stick-up shit in my building?" He glared down at Ashanti.

"Yes, he's trying to rob me," the white dude said frantically, clawing at King's pant leg.

"Fuck off me, devil." King kicked him away. He turned his attention back to Ashanti. "I asked you a question, God."

"This shit ain't about nothing. He came through trying to cop and I'm just trying to show him that crack is whack." Ashanti smiled, but King didn't.

"Wise, take this cracker outside and get him right," King ordered.

"Thanks, man." The white dude held his hand out to King, but the big man looked at it like it was a rattlesnake.

"Don't take my kindness for weakness, pussy. Get your poison and get the fuck outta my hood," King snarled at the white dude. The addict nodded and scrambled out of the staircase behind Wise. King descended the last few steps and stood directly in front of Ashanti. "When niggaz come to my hood to buy drugs, they get drugs. You wanna rob addicts, then you do it outside these projects, you understand?"

"I got you, King, but I don't know why you tripping off me trying to stick that cracker," Ashanti said.

"I could give a fuck who you rob or kill, li'l one, unless it's done on my turf," King told him. "Had you robbed that devil, the police would've been all up and through here cramping my style and that's no good. Like I said, just be mindful of where you conduct your business, Ashanti."

"A'ight, I got you, King," Ashanti agreed.

"Yo, we was just talking about ya li'l ass," Lakim told Ashanti. "Take this walk with us right quick." He held the stairwell door open for Ashanti to step out.

Ashanti hesitated. King James and his crew were like a pack of wild dogs, vicious and unpredictable, so you never knew what to expect from them. He had been with their inner circle and witnessed a crime being committed, so he knew very well that he could be walking into a setup. He tightened his grip on the .22.

King picked up on his hesitance. "Be easy; if I wanted to rock you, that li'l-ass gun wouldn't do much to stop me," King assured him. "Come on." Ashanti was still hesitant, but he did as he was told. When they were outside, King started talking again. "When Lakim told me to let you ride with us I was skeptical, but after everything that happened I'm glad we did. Not only did you carry yaself like a stand-up dude the whole time, but you saved Zo's life."

Ashanti shrugged. "I was just holding it down, that wasn't about nothing."

"Maybe not to you, but it spoke in volumes to me," King said. "What're you doing with your life these days?"

"I don't know, just trying to live like everybody else."

"Robbing crackheads ain't living, li'l nigga." Lakim laughed.

"It's better than starving," Ashanti shot back.

"He's got a point there," King said with a smirk. He then got serious. "Ashanti, do you remember a few years ago when I bumped into you and your boy Animal and we had that talk?"

"Yeah," Ashanti said with a little sadness in his voice. That day was the last time he had seen Animal.

"I tried to warn you against getting caught up in this lifestyle, and even though you acted like you were listening I could tell by the look in your eyes that you had already made up your mind."

"What are you, some kinda mind reader?" Ashanti asked.

"Nah, I was you a few years ago," King said seriously. "Ashanti, you're your own man and though I may not agree with how you live, I can't knock you for it either because Allah knows I'm no angel. You've already made your choice and I can't change your mind, but what I can change is how you live."

"King, what're you talking about?" Ashanti was confused.

"He's talking about putting you down to get some real money," Lakim cut in. "What's good, sun, you ready to see how a *real* nigga moves?"

"No disrespect, but I came up under the realest nigga to ever touch a Harlem street, so I think I know how *real* niggaz move," he said, reflecting on Animal and how it used to be for their little team.

"Animal was a beast, but he's gone and we're still here," King pointed out. "I know you're out here living pillar to post and trying to keep food in your belly as best you can, but the world is so much bigger than that, and the game is so much sweeter when you're playing for a winning team. I ain't gonna twist your arm about it, but the offer is on the table, next move is on you."

Ashanti weighed it. Since his team had been broken up and he'd been left on his own, things had been hard on him. He was living, but barely. Without Animal's or Brasco's backing he didn't have the resources or muscle to take it to the next level, and King James could change that. When he measured the way he was living against how he could be living, it was a no-brainer. "I'm wit it."

"That's peace." Lakim hugged him. "We gonna look out for you, sun. No more rainy days, feel me?"

Ashanti nodded.

"Word up, this is a family here, baby." King gave Ashanti dap. "Everybody eats as long as a nigga pulls his own weight, and I know that ain't gonna be a problem with you."

"You see me out here so you know how I move," Ashanti said confidently.

"Indeed." King stepped directly in front of Ashanti and looked down at the youngster. His eyes were cold and his face deathly serious as he spoke. "All we ask of you is loyalty, my G. Stick to the script and we'll go to the top, deviate and I'll return you to the essence. I spent too much time in prison already to go back for another nigga, ya heard?"

Ashanti never batted an eye. "Once given, my loyalty is unquestionable. That's something I learned from the big homie."

King stared at him for a long moment, looking for a crack in his armor, something that would show the tell-tale signs of uncertainty, but he found none. Where the eyes of an average teenage boy were full of life and won-der, in Ashanti's he saw nothing. Riding with Animal all those years at such a young age, he knew Ashanti had seen far more than most grown men and the fact that he was still knee deep in it said a lot for his character. He was the last of a dying breed and would be a strong piece on the chessboard by the time King was done grooming him.

CHAPTER 38

And what are you doing here?" Ms. Ronnie said when she walked into her apartment and found Gucci lying on her couch, watching television. The house reeked of weed and there were empty Chinese food containers on the coffee table.

"Jesus, I thought you'd be happy to see me, Mom." Gucci sucked her teeth.

"I'm always happy to see you, but not unannounced. What if I had a man up in here waiting on me to get in from work?"

"Ma, you know you allow no men to be laying up in your house, especially when you're not home, and what the hell are you wearing?" Gucci looked her mother up and down. She was rocking a one-piece gold catsuit with gold shoes that went almost perfectly with her metallic-gold wig.

Ms. Ronnie twirled around so that Gucci could see the whole outfit. "You like it? I bought it on sale from Walmart."

"You should've left it in Walmart."

"Li'l girl, you don't know shit. I be resting and dressing since before your li'l ass was born so I know what's fly and what's not."

"Ma, that outfit might've been rocking in the eighties

but in the new millennium you look kinda crazy." Gucci laughed.

"Crazy is me shooting your ass and telling the police I thought you was a burglar," Ms. Ronnie said with a roll of her eyes. "And where the weed at and don't lie and say you ain't got none because I smell it all up and through here."

"Your ass is like a bloodhound." Gucci pulled the clip from beneath a magazine on the table and tossed it to her mother. "And don't take my blunt to the face because it's the last of it."

"Girl, when you're in this house ain't no such thing as 'my' unless it's in reference to 'mine,'" Ms. Ronnie told her before lighting the clip. "Now"—she blew out some smoke—"what are you doing here?"

"Nothing, I just needed to get low for a while, that's all," Gucci said as if it were nothing, but Ms. Ronnie knew better.

"Gucci"—she sat on the couch next to her daughter—"you came outta this womb so I can tell when something is bothering you. Now you can either tell me what's wrong or I can make you tell me." She began tickling Gucci. Gucci had been extremely ticklish since she was a little girl and Ms. Ronnie often used this tactic to get the truth out of her.

"Okay, okay, stop before you make me pee on myself." Gucci laughed. "If you wanna know the truth, I'm hiding from Tionna."

"Why, did you girls have a falling-out or something?"

"No, it's nothing like that. I just promised her that I would go to this party with her tonight, but I really don't wanna go. She's been blowing my phone up for hours and I haven't picked up."

"Now you know that ain't right. You and Tionna have been thick as thieves for as long as I can remember and I'm sure you've dragged her to more than a few places that she didn't want to go to, the free clinic being one that I can think of off the top of my head," Ms. Ronnie joked.

"Ma, you ain't even right for that." Gucci shook her head.

"Stop it, you know I love Tionna like she was one of my own, but the girl has some issues."

"Yeah, but she's getting it together."

"Thank the Lord." Ms. Ronnie raised her hand to the sky and passed the weed to Gucci. "So why don't you wanna go to this party?"

"I don't know, Ma. I just don't feel up to it." Gucci curled her legs under her and dug a chicken wing out of one of the greasy bags. Before she could bite it, Ms. Ronnie plucked the chicken wing from her grasp.

"Gucci"—Ms. Ronnie took a bite of the chicken wing—"your ass has been moping around for God knows how long like the ghost of damn Christmas Past, and to be honest I'm getting sick of it."

"That's not true, Ma," Gucci denied.

"The hell it isn't. When is the last time you went out somewhere?"

"I go out all the time."

"I'm not talking about going shopping or taking trips by yourself, I mean really gone out and had a good time with your friends?"

"There's more to life than clubbing, Ma."

"You would have to actually be living to be able to tell somebody about life, honey, and this shuffling around you're doing ain't living, it's making you old before your time. You used to be such a vibrant girl but ever since what happened to Animal you've been a shell of yourself."

"This has nothing to do with Tayshawn," Gucci said, getting defensive.

"This has everything to do with him, Gucci. At first I was sympathetic to your pain and understood that you were in mourning, but years later and you're still walking around in a daze? Baby girl, I'm starting to worry about you," Ms. Ronnie said seriously.

"I'm cool, Ma," Gucci lied.

"No, you're not. Gucci, I had love for Animal too, but he ain't here no more, baby. You can't keep loving a ghost."

"You sound like Tionna now."

"Then Tionna was telling you right and the girl has more sense than I gave her credit for. Brooding ain't gonna bring Animal back or mend that broken heart."

"So I'm just supposed to act like he never existed?" Gucci snapped.

"You better watch that tone, because you ain't too old for me knock you on your ass," Ms. Ronnie threatened.

"Sorry, Ma. I didn't mean to snap at you like that, I just get so tired of people telling me to get over him. Nobody knows what we had and nobody knows what I'm going through with not having him around."

"I know, baby. The heart is a funny thing and we can't dictate how fast it heals when it's been broken, but at the same time you have to want it to heal."

"I do," Gucci whispered, staring at the carpet.

"Then do something about it," Ms. Ronnie challenged. "Put on some clothes and some makeup and go have a good time with your friend. You owe it to Tionna, but more importantly you owe it to yourself."

"You're right, Mommy, and thank you for always keeping it one hundred with me." She hugged her mother.

"You know I don't bite my tongue for nobody. Right is right and wrong is wrong." Ms. Ronnie snatched the blunt back. "Now call that girl and handle your business." She walked into the bedroom, blowing smoke rings in the air.

Gucci walked down the hall to the bathroom and looked at herself in the mirror. Her hair was pulled back into a ponytail and she wasn't wearing a drop of makeup. She was still a very pretty girl, but the face staring back at her wasn't the Gucci she knew, who had once demanded the attention of every baller in Harlem. Her mother's words rang in her head, and as much as she hated to admit it, she was right. Life was too short to live it reflecting on the things that had happened and what could've been, especially when the future looked so bright. She was young, pretty, with no kids and a healthy bank account. She had too many things to be thankful for not to take the time to appreciate her blessings. She picked up her cell to call Tionna and hoped it wasn't too late.

"Hey, T," Gucci said when the girl picked up on the other line.

"Don't *hey T* me, do you know how long I've been trying to call you?" Tionna shouted.

"I know, I know, but I was going through something and turned my phone off. Look, are you still trying to go to that party tonight?"

"Yeah, I was going with or without your stinking ass, because I had a feeling you were gonna flake on me and pull this grieving-widow shit."

"I can't front, I started to, but I wanna go."

"Really? What brought on this change of heart?" Tionna was surprised.

"Sometimes you have to live in order to understand what life is about," Gucci said, reflecting on the talk she'd had with her mother.

"Huh?"

"Never mind, T. Give me a few to go home and get dressed and I'll be through to pick you up."

CHAPTER 39

Look at you, getting all sexy." Frankie leaned in the doorway of Porsha's bedroom, watching her finish dressing. She had on a tight-fitting red dress that dropped to her navel in the front, showing off an ample amount of cleavage.

"You know I gotta do it big for our first official date and I wanna leave an impression on him." Porsha winked, doing the last strap on her three-quarter ankle boots.

"You're gonna leave more than an impression, ma. That nigga is gonna be all over you, girl. I hope you got your pepper spray."

Porsha stopped her buckling. "Frankie, why do you keep trying to throw Don B. under the bus?"

"Because the boy is scandalous," Frankie said simply.

"I'll bet you wouldn't feel that way if I told you he had a friend for you to hook up with," Porsha accused.

"Yes, I would, because any nigga who hangs with Don B. is probably scandalous too. Just because a guy has money doesn't mean he has morals. Besides, I never really dug hustlers. I've always been more partial to the gainfully employed, like Alonzo. Now that's who you should've hooked up with."

"Fuck Alonzo," Porsha spat.

"Damn, what's that all about?" Frankie wondered. Alonzo had always been a cool dude, even letting them get free stuff from the supermarket when they were low on cash.

"I don't like how he came out his mouth earlier when I was in the store. Him and his boys were in Brick City and saw me doing my thing and this nigga gets an attitude, acting like I got the plague or something because I dance. I'm like, are you fucking serious?"

"Maybe his feelings were hurt," Frankie suggested.

"Hurt over what? I didn't do anything to him."

Frankie shook her head. "Porsha, you can't be that fucking dense. Alonzo has been head over heels in love with you since you first moved around here, so seeing you out there shaking your ass in front of all them dudes was probably a shock to his system. He's a man in love, so you should try to be a little more understanding. Who knows, if you actually took the time to notice him, you guys may actually hit it off."

"Ain't nobody stunting Alonzo." Porsha walked to the small mirror hanging on the wall and checked her hair. "I need a man who is gonna take care of me, not struggle with me."

"Youz a damn fool." Frankie laughed.

"Call me what you want, but if things go the way I plan, you won't be calling me broke." Porsha blew herself a kiss in the mirror. "Speaking of fools, where's Sahara?"

"That chick been up and outta here. I think her and King was going out to eat before the big party."

"Now if anybody needs your words of wisdom it's that bitch. It'll be a matter of time before the other shoe drops with that cat, and Sahara is too blind to see the writing on the walls."

"You're one to talk." Frankie raised an eyebrow.

Porsha rolled his eyes. "Please, those are two different situations. She's chasing a petty-ass crack dealer and I'm chasing a legitimate businessman."

"Ha, that's funny. Don B. has seen more than his fair share of courtrooms. That boy has been linked to more murders over the last few years than swine flu," Frankie said.

"And he ain't spent a day in jail, so what does that tell you?"

"That he's slicker than a pig in shit."

"Hater," Porsha said, grabbing her purse off the bed. "So what're you gonna do tonight?"

Frankie shrugged. "Probably just hang around here and see if I can get a few of these pieces off. You know the moment of truth is right around the corner and if we don't have that money, the kind of dudes we're dating will be the least of our concerns."

"I don't know why you're saying *we're* like your ass has had a date since Jesus turned water to wine," Porsha joked.

"Whatever, I'm just picky about who I go out with. A big bank account don't move me, ma."

"Which is why you're home alone tonight. Toodles." Porsha winked and headed out.

"Skank," Frankie said when she heard the front door slam. Now that everyone was out of the house, it was time for Frankie to get ready for her date . . . with the trap.

* * *

Porsha stepped out of her building shining like new money. She was greeted by smiles, waves, and compliments from the people she knew as well as people who had never spoken to her before. A few of the locals tried to holla, but she looked right through them. She wasn't about to waste time with commoners when she had a date with royalty.

She made her way down the path toward the avenue, trying her best not to break her ankles in the high heels. She scanned the street for Don B.'s Hummer but there was no sign of it. Porsha found that strange, as he had called her ten minutes ago and told her to be downstairs in five minutes. "Where the hell are you?" She looked at her watch.

"Damn, is that America's next top model?" Scar slithered out from whatever rock he'd been hiding under. Following him like lost puppies were his henchmen Mitch and a lanky kid everyone knew simply as Spoon. "Where you off to, the track?" He laughed and so did his boys.

"I'll bet your mama wished she would've swallowed you," Porsha capped.

"Mama ain't swallow me, but you can. What's up, I got twenty dollars for you to let me and my boys take turns dumping in your mouth." Scar waved a twenty-dollar bill at her.

"Scar, youz a real punk-ass nigga. You're always out here talking to chicks, but when them niggaz from the other side came over here you were too busy running to pop shit," she spat. This stuck a nerve in Scar.

"What you say to me, bitch?"

"You heard me, coward."

"I think it's time for me to teach your tramp ass some manors." He took a menacing step toward her.

"Scar, on my mama, if you put your hands on me I'm gonna have you locked up, after I cut you," Porsha threatened. She was scared to death but wouldn't give him the satisfaction of showing it.

"I'll have knocked you out and woke you back up before the police make it here." He grabbed her by the arm. "You're gonna learn to respect me, bitch." Scar raised his hand. Before he could swing, they were all bathed in the bright headlights of a red Bentley Coupe.

"What's popping, we got a problem here?" Don B.'s voice boomed as he hopped out of the driver's side. He was draped in a red Pelle jacket, dark jeans, and a red California Angels cap. "We got a problem?" Don B. repeated, lifting his jacket to expose the butt of the gun in his pants.

"I don't know, do we?" Porsha looked at Scar.

Scar wisely released Porsha's arm and took a step back. "Nah, we ain't got no problem." He glared at Don B.

Don B. stepped up and stood toe-to-toe with Scar. "Are you sure, because the way you're mugging me I'd think we had a problem." The gun dangled in his hand at his side.

"Nah, no problem, Big Dawg." Scar gave him a sarcastic smirk.

Don B. matched his smirk before slamming the gun into the side of Scar's head. Scar crumbled in a heap, clutching his head. Mitch and Spoon took a step toward Don B., but when he turned the gun on them they froze in place. "I wish you niggaz would." He cocked the hammer. "You good, boo?" he asked Porsha.

Porsha kicked Scar in the ribs. "I am now."

Don B. tucked his gun. "Let's get outta here before one of these niggaz makes me go up top on them." He extended his arm.

Porsha hooked her arm around his. "Ready when you are, daddy." She smirked at the angry boys as she and Don B. walked to the Bentley.

Scar lay on the ground, fuming, as he watched the couple enter the Bentley. His head throbbed from where Don B. had cracked him with the gun, but his pride was hurt worse than anything else. He was so mad that he wanted to cry, but he held his gangsta face. Scar had been embarrassed in his hood and in front of his team. It was an offense that he couldn't let slide. He would settle up with Porsha and eventually Don B., who before that night had been his favorite rapper.

Mitch reached down to try to help Scar off the ground. "You good?"

"Fuck from round me, nigga." Scar swatted him away and got to his feet on his own. "That punk stole me and y'all just stood around and let it go down!"

"But he had a gun, Scar," Spoon tried to reason.

"You've got a gun too, jackass." Scar yanked up Spoon's shirt and snatched the gun out of his pants. "Gimmie my muthafucking strap, pussy. That bitch Porsha thinks she can just style on me and I ain't gonna do nothing? Laugh now, bitch, but you gonna cry later. Y'all bring y'all asses on and let's put in this work."

It was blocks before Porsha finally stopped trembling. She and Scar had never quite seen eye-to-eye, so there was no love lost between them. They had exchanged heated words on more than one occasion but it had never gotten physical. There was no doubt in her mind that Scar would've opened a can of whip ass on her if it hadn't been for Don B. Porsha felt like a ghetto princess being rescued by her knight in crimson armor. She knew what other girls said about him, but at that moment she felt blessed to be by his side.

"You okay?" Don B. asked, steering with one hand and trying to light the blunt clip dangling between his lips with the other.

"Yeah, I'm good. Just a little bit shaken up." Porsha ran her hand over the spot on her arm where Scar had grabbed her. "Me and Scar are always arguing, but I can't believe he was about to hit me."

"It's a good thing for me and him that he didn't, because he'd be dead and I'd be fighting a body," Don B. told her.

"Boy, you're wild for the night. I appreciate you stepping up for me like that, Don, but I don't want you getting in no trouble for getting caught up in my beef."

"Shorty, I wasn't getting caught up in nothing. I seen homie about to jump outta bounds with a lady I love, so I put him in his place."

Porsha did a double take. "How you figure you love me and you've only known me twenty-four hours?"

"Don't flatter yourself just yet, ma. I wasn't speaking particularly; the Don loves all the ladies, even the ones I don't know yet." He took her hand in his and kissed it. "Now enough with the small talk. Are you ready for the first night of the rest of your life?"

"Lead the way, baby." Porsha settled into the soft leather

seat and enjoyed the ride. As she watched the lights and tall buildings streak by her, Porsha couldn't help but think that she could finally see the silver lining in her dark cloud, but elsewhere the storm was just brewing.

CHAPTER 40

Old San Juan, Puerto Rico

Animal smelled it miles before it even came into view. La Perla, also known as the slums. It was a six-hundred-meter stretch that snaked down the Atlantic coast, established around the husk of an old slaughterhouse and inhabited by some of the most dangerous criminals in the area. This was the place Cruz had chosen to hide in, and this is where he would die.

Once Grovaldo had fallen, Cruz's men on the streets had started running around like chickens with their heads cut off. A rash of infighting had broken out between the individual crews to see who would take Grovaldo's place as street boss and Cruz's right hand, but they were so busy killing one another that Cruz found himself vulnerable and bolted for higher ground until the mess could be cleaned up. Everything was happening just as K-Dawg had predicted it would.

K-Dawg had pulled out all the stops on this one. An entire hit squad comprised of Los Negros Muertes and some of Poppito's soldiers were dispatched to finish the dance and bring home the prize, which was Cruz's head. Poppito was very specific about having Cruz's head, and he had even offered an extra million dollars to the soldier who brought it in. Every killer on the mission was either talking about or preparing himself to claim the head and the million dollars, but not Animal. He just wanted to knock Cruz out of the box and be done with Puerto Rico as well as Los Negros Muertes.

"Do you hear me talking to you?" Chris nudged Animal. He had been so lost in his own thoughts that he hadn't even noticed the young man. They were sitting shoulder-to-shoulder in the back of a cargo van. "I asked if you were gonna try for the head and that million-dollar bounty?"

"I hadn't really given it too much thought," Animal said.

"Then what's that for?" He nodded at the machete hanging from Animal's pants.

Animal unsheathed the blade and turned in over in his hand. "Don't wanna wake the neighbors." He smiled. Of everyone he had met while in Puerto Rico, he had become the fondest of Chris. Sonja's baby brother was a cool young dude whose only flaw was being reckless in his efforts to please his father, which is what had landed him in the van next to Animal on their way to commit a murder.

"You crazy." Chris laughed. His smile soon faded and the worried expression he'd worn most of the trip returned.

"You good?" Animal asked him.

"Yeah, just got the jitters, that's all. Animal, can I ask you something?"

"What up?"

"I ain't trying to sound like no pussy or nothing, but do you ever get . . . you know . . . nervous before you do something like this? I mean, don't get me wrong, I've blazed at niggaz and I may have even hit a few, but this is just a flat-out slaughter and I ain't never been on a ride like this."

Animal turned to him. "Chris, ain't no shame in being afraid. I'd think something was wrong with you or you were just plain stupid if you weren't. Every time I put a gun in my hand I'm afraid, because carrying guns opens the possibility of having to use them. I can understand you being nervous, homie, because this murder thing ain't for every-body, which is why I tried to get you to fall back when we were arming up to come out here."

"I gotta hold my pop's name down and show him that I can be just as helpful to him as Sonja," Chris explained.

"Dawg, I know that's your sister and there's the sibling rivalry thing and all, but Sonja is a trained killer and more qualified to be out here than you are. I don't like her being out here either, but she was the voice of your father long before I came along, so I don't tell her about her business. I would've loved for Sonja to be somewhere else instead of rolling to this shit hole, but she's here and the only thing I can do about it is watch her back and make sure she gets out the same way she came in," Animal said seri-ously.

"You really like my sister, don't you?" Chris asked with a smirk.

"She's a'ight," Animal said, downplaying it.

"It's cool, dawg. I actually think you and my sister would make a nice couple. You're a cool cat, Animal, Dad likes you and I know my sister does so I'm cool with that. Who knows, maybe when this is done it'll free up some time for you guys to hang out."

"Maybe," Animal said and turned his attention to the

streets of La Perla. It was something out of *New Jack City*. Addicts roamed the streets in heavy numbers while the dealers served them out in the open. People stood on corners or sat on stoops, brandishing guns freely and watching the van pass. The van pulled down an alley that was only a half block or so from the building where Cruz was hiding out. They would walk the rest of the way for fear of one of Cruz's lookouts spotting them too soon. A few seconds later, they were joined by a second van, which had entered La Perla from the other end of town. Nearly a half-dozen men and a woman got out of the vans, dressed all in black and carrying assault rifles. Two men, carrying binoculars and sniper rifles, headed to the roof of the building they were parked behind. Everyone was in position and waiting for K-Dawg's instructions before they moved in. He knew that this would be their first and last chance to get at Cruz, so he had planned everything down to the letter.

Animal was helping Chris adjust the strap on his bulletproof vest when he saw Sonja coming their way. She was leading the team that would take the point and clear a path for the assassins. Dressed in black and carrying a MAC-11 in each hand, she looked every bit the beautiful angel of death. Sonja's team was to burst through the wedge and clear a path for the second team to take out Cruz. She glared at Animal for a second, then turned her attention to Chris. "You okay?" She stroked his cheek.

Chris moved her hands. "I'm good, why do you keep asking me that?"

"Because you're my li'l brother and I'm always gonna worry about you," she told him.

"Don't worry, Red, Animal has got my back and that muthafucka is bulletproof," Chris boasted.

Sonja rolled her eyes. "Let me tell you something, Christopher. This"—she laid her hand on the rifle he was carrying—"is the only thing you can depend on when we go inside, so you better tighten up and get serious about this," she barked.

Chris was embarrassed because Animal had seen him getting disciplined by his big sister. "Sonja, you out here trying to bark on me like I'm some punk kid who doesn't know what's going on? My gun goes off just the same as any one of these other niggaz'." He looked around at everybody.

"You need to watch that, Christopher," Sonja warned.

"No, you're the one who needs to watch it and show some respect. You need to be home wearing a skirt and taking care of Daddy, instead of out here playing soldier!"

Moving faster than anyone's eyes could register, Sonja slapped her little brother viciously across the face. "How dare you disrespect me like that?" Chris raised his hand like he wanted to swing, but Sonja's raised machine gun gave him second thoughts. "Christopher, I love you to death, but you know I'd kill any man, including you, before I let them put their hands on me."

"Fuck this shit. I'm gonna show you just how I give it up." Chris stomped off, bumping through the snickering soldiers. Sonja made to follow but Animal stopped her.

"Let him cool off," he whispered to her, leading her away from everyone else.

"I used to change his fucking Pampers and he's gonna act like he wants to raise his hand to me? I'll kill that li'l muthafucka first," Sonja fumed.

"Sonja, be cool, because you were wrong," Animal told her.

Sonja looked at him like he was crazy. "How do you figure I was wrong? I'm only trying to look out for that ungrateful bastard."

"C'mon, ma, you slapped that man in front of men who will one day have to follow his lead. That's like saying it's okay to disrespect him. I know you're angry, but think about how he's feeling."

"And what do you know about feelings?" she hissed. "You know what, fuck the both of you. I've got bodies to drop." Sonja walked away. Animal wanted to follow her, but it wouldn't have done any good. Sonja and her brother had the same temperament; it was best to give them their space instead of arguing.

"There's too much at stake here to bring drama to the table, li'l bro." Justice walked over, cradling an M16, with a pair of binoculars hanging from his neck. "Keep your head in the fight."

"Justice, you don't know what the fuck you're talking about. That didn't have nothing to do with me," Animal told him.

"Looked like you were in the middle of it to me."

"Whatever, man. So when do we move in?" Animal changed the subject.

"We're supposed to wait for K-Dawg. Should be any minute now."

"Our fearless leader is about to get his hands dirty? This I gotta see," Animal said sarcastically.

No sooner had the words left his mouth than they heard the roar of an engine. K-Dawg came rumbling around the corner, riding a black motorcycle with a sidecar attached. Sitting in the sidecar was a chick whom they had seen around but didn't recognize as a member of Los Negros

Muertes. Her gloved hands gripped the handle of the carbine machine gun that was mounted on the front of the sidecar.

"Where the fuck did you get that?" Justice looked the motorcycle over, paying special attention to the mounted machine gun.

"I had this baby imported especially for today." K-Dawg patted the barrel of the machine gun. "Everybody check your weapons and your reservations. This is the last ride." K-Dawg revved the engine of the motorcycle. "Y'all niggaz ready?" he asked the group, but he was looking at Animal. In answer to his question, Animal cocked the two silencer-equipped Desert Eagles he was carrying. "A'ight, into positions and let's bang."

Justice and his group went to their van and Sonja and her group started for theirs. She was just about to climb into the passenger side when she realized that her brother hadn't returned. "Where's Chris?"

Justice and the others looked around but nobody could find him. "This fucking kid," Justice snapped.

"Justice, he was a part of your unit; get this shit under control so we can handle business," K-Dawg ordered.

Justice took out his Boost phone and chirped the lookouts on the roof. "Yo, can you guys see Chris from up there?"

A few seconds passed, then a voice came back: *"Yeah, but you ain't gonna like it."*

"Stop playing and tell me where the fuck he is!" Justice barked.

"Moving in on the target."

"Muthafucka." Justice threw his phone against a wall.

"Fuck it, we'll roll without him," K-Dawg said.

"Wait, we can't ride in there blasting and we don't know where Chris is," Sonja said frantically. She cursed herself for embarrassing him and making him run off. Sonja wouldn't be able to live with herself if something happened to him because of her.

"Chris knew protocol and he broke it, that's on him. Move in," K-Dawg ordered, and peeled off on the bike.

"My brother's gonna get killed because of that maniac." Sonja began to sob.

"Don't worry, we'll get him," Justice assured her. "Animal, I need you to . . ." He had turned to say something to his little brother, but he was gone.

CHAPTER 41

Chris was so mad that he could barely hold back the tears that welled up in his eyes. Chris's whole young life had been spent trying to impress his father and prove that he could walk a mile in the shoes left by his late brother, Juan.

When Poppito started to get up in years he trusted the day-to-day operations of his business to Juan. The streets both loved and feared Poppito's oldest child. Some feared him enough to want him dead, which is what had led to Juan's murder. After the death of his older brother, Chris had expected to be groomed to take his place, but instead Poppito had passed the mantle to Sonja. The slight didn't go unnoticed by Chris or the soldiers, and the youngster found that he had to work three times as hard to earn the respect that he should've been given. After what Sonja had pulled in front of the troops, he knew that he would have to do something to save face, so he decided to go after Cruz on his own.

Chris knew from one of the maps they had all been provided with for the mission that there was a collapsed laundry room connected to the back of the building where Cruz was hiding. K-Dawg had decided against using that as a point of entry because the entrance had long been cemented over and the only way in was through small boarded-up windows on the back. It would've been no good for the all-out attack but it could work for Chris.

Chris wasn't prepared for what he saw when he hopped the fence that separated the back of the abandoned tenement from the street. The once sprawling yard looked like a modern-day apocalypse, with its mounds of rubble that stood nearly as high as the three-story building itself. The stench of dead animals and human excrement was almost overwhelming to his senses as he picked his way through the debris. Looking up at the abandoned building, he began to wonder if he was making the right decision.

Suddenly gunfire erupted, causing Chris to reflexively drop to his belly, landing just a few feet from what looked like the decomposing corpse of a dog. A wave of bile rode up his throat but he was able to force it back down. He fumbled with his assault rifle as another wave of gunfire rang out. Chris lay there for a full five minutes before he realized that no one was shooting at him. K-Dawg had begun the assault, and instead of being on the front line, Chris was crawling on his belly through garbage.

"Fuck this." Chris got up and crept toward the structure. What was left of the laundry room, like the rest of the rear of the building, was boarded up tight. Just above the laundry room were several small windows, one of which had the glass broken out. Chris scaled the short building and knelt in front of the window. It was just large enough for him to squeeze through.

Chris lowered himself into what he could only assume was the basement of the building. It was dark so he couldn't see, but the inside of the building smelled worse than the outside, if that was possible. Shutting out the increasing sounds of gunfire coming from outside, he made his way toward a sliver of light that had to be one of the exits marked on the map. He thought it was strange that the rear of the building wasn't guarded, but he wasn't about to look a gift horse in the mouth. Chris pulled the door open and began climbing the darkened stairwell leading to the upper levels of the building. He made it up three steps before he was blinded by several flashlights. When his vision cleared he saw three men holding the flashlights as well as some very big machine guns. For all Chris's ingenious planning, he had never taken into the consideration the surveillance cameras that had been watching his every move.

The leader of the gunmen stepped forward with his rifle trained on Chris's forehead. "We hear your piece-of-shit father put a million dollars on Cruz's head. I wonder how much he'll pay for yours."

"Most likely quite a few pennies more than yours is worth," a voice called from behind them. The three gunmen turned at once and saw Animal standing at the top of the stairwell, grinning menacingly. They never even got a chance to scream as the bullets tore through their bodies.

Chris took one look at the corpses at his feet and vomited.

"Now that's just fucking nasty." Animal shook off the loose chunks of food that had splattered on his boot.

"They were gonna kill me." Chris gasped, holding on to the wall to keep on his feet.

Animal grabbed Chris and slammed him roughly against the wall. He pressed the hot barrel of the gun against Chris's chin, searing the soft flesh of his throat. "And I should've let them, you dumb little shit," Animal snarled. "You could've gotten yourself as well as the rest of us killed by going lone wolf. What the hell were you thinking?"

"I'm sorry, I just wanted to show you guys that I could pull my weight," Chris said.

"How, by getting your fucking head blown off? Li'l nigga, this ain't no video game so there's no reset button. When you're dead, you're dead, and you better learn that real quick before you end up getting yourself or somebody else hurt. Now come on, there's killing to be done." Animal started back up the stairs.

Nearing the lobby level of the tenement Animal could hear all hell breaking loose. Gunshots and the screams of the dying could be heard all around him. The stairwell door swung open and one of Cruz's shooters spilled through it, followed by a hail of bullets that shredded the door. When he spotted Animal he tried to raise his gun, but the killer was already on the move. Wielding the machete like a samurai sword, he delivered two sharp cuts to the shooter's chest and abdomen, dropping him to the ground, but he was still alive.

"Finish him," Animal told Chris.

"But he's dying already," Chris said.

Animal pointed the bloody machete at the young man. "Blood on my hands, blood on yours."

Chris stood over the fallen man and pointed his gun at his head. The man looked up at him with pleading eyes, begging for his life. Seeing the wild look in Animal's eyes, Chris decided he feared the young killer more than the stain of a murder on his soul and pulled the trigger. The man's head splattered like a rotten tomato. Chris turned away, refusing to look at the corpse.

"Don't turn away now." Animal grabbed him by the

back of his neck and forced him to look at the bloody corpse. "You wanted to be a gangsta, so take a good look at what your choice of lifestyle has to offer. Just be glad that you're on the proper end of the bullet . . . this time. Now let's go, kid. Stick close to me and you may actually live through this." Animal led the way up the stairs.

Through the window in the stairwell door Animal caught a glimpse of what was going on outside. K-Dawg and the team had turned it up on Cruz's men, lighting up the front of the building like the Fourth of July. From the intelligence they had gathered, Cruz was holed up in an apartment on the top floor, so the plan was to cut off all the exits so he couldn't escape, which K-Dawg and the rest had taken care of. From the looks of things, Los Negros Muertes had most of the soldiers occupied, so he and Chris would have to deal only with the stragglers left behind to guard the police chief. They soon found that it would be easier said than done, as more men came spilling down the stairs, all armed and ready to die in defense of their leader.

Animal resheathed his machete and drew both guns. "Watch my back and try not to get in my way," he told Chris as he bounded up the staircase to meet his enemies. Watching Animal in action was like watching Michelangelo paint a masterpiece in blood. Had they been trained soldiers they might've stood a chance, but these were street punks and mercenaries hired by Cruz in a last ditch effort to save him from the inevitable.

The idiot leading Cruz's charge was the first one to get it. He had an extremely large machine gun, which he tried to bring around to spray the crowd, but the stairwell was too narrow so the gun scraped off the wall and slowed his motion by a fraction of a second, which was all Animal needed. He grabbed the barrel of the gun and pulled with everything he had, knocking the shooter off-balance and putting him in a reverse choke hold. As Animal applied pressure to his neck, the shooter's finger involuntarily squeezed the trigger, ripping through his team with a hail of bullets. The rest of them retreated farther up the landing for fear of being shot.

The man struggled in Animal's grip as the choke hold got tighter. "Sucks to be you right about now," Animal whispered in his ear before snapping his neck. The shooter's body went limp and Animal let him drop to the floor.

"Down!" Chris roared. Animal hit the floor as bullets whizzed over his head and buried themselves in the body of a man who was trying to creep on them from the second-floor-stairwell door. "Animal, these muthafuckas are like roaches, the more we squash the more of them come. Something has got to give if we wanna get to Cruz."

More gunshots erupted around the corner where Cruz's soldiers had retreated, causing Animal and Chris to get low and prepare for another attack. A lone solider staggered down the stairs with a far-off look in his eyes. Animal was prepared to fire on him, but before he could, the soldier pitched forward and fell down the stairs. When he landed they could see the smoking holes in his back. A confused look passed between Animal and Chris but it all made sense when K-Dawg appeared, holding a smoking rifle.

"We got Cruz trapped in his apartment. Let's finish this," K-Dawg told them and disappeared back around the corner.

CHAPTER 42

The damage Animal had done in the stairwell was nothing compared to the mess K-Dawg and the others had created on the third floor. The peeling brown walls were now red, stained with blood and brain matter donated by the dozen or so bodies strewn throughout the hallway. Most had been killed instantly in the hail of bullets, and those who were unfortunate enough to still show signs of life were finished off by bats and pieces of wood as Poppito's soldiers made the rounds, bashing their skulls in. The floors were so slick with blood that they could barely walk without slipping. It was a massacre.

Sonja stood at the end of the hallway, giving last-minute instructions to some of the soldiers. When she saw Animal and Chris emerge from the stairwell she rushed to them and hugged her brother. "Thank God you're alright." She sobbed.

"I told you Animal had my back," Chris said, smirking.

Sonja pushed Chris away and punched him in his chest. "You scared the shit out of me. Don't you ever pull a stunt like that again!"

"I'm sorry, for what I said and for running off," Chris said.

"It's okay, just as long as you're safe," Sonja told him.

She turned to Animal and wrapped her arms around his neck. "Thank you so much for saving my brother's life. I don't know what I'd have done if we'd lost Chris."

"You know I couldn't leave my li'l man on stuck like that. It would've hurt me to lose him too." Animal squeezed her. "See, even monsters have feelings," he whispered in her ear.

"I could never see you as a monster." She planted a soft kiss on his lips. "I've seen the man beneath the mask, which is why you'll always own part of my heart, even if you don't want it."

"Fucking pathetic," Sincere grumbled loudly enough for them to hear.

Animal turned to him. "You got something you wanna say to me, homie?"

"All my talking is done with heaters." Sincere patted the gun on his hip.

"Then let's stop the subliminal shit and have a grownup conversation." Animal drew one of his Desert Eagles.

Sincere drew his pistol. "That's cool with me. I'm ready to dance when you are." He and Animal circled each other like two wolves about to square off over a kill.

"Stow those weapons," Justice ordered.

"Fuck that, this is long overdue." Sincere kept his eyes on Animal. He knew you didn't draw down on a man like Animal and not kill him, so he was ready to go all the way with it.

Justice cocked his M16 and aimed it at Sincere. "I ain't gonna ask you again, Sincere."

Sincere cut his eyes to Justice. "You would shoot me, Jus? What happened to the oath we took, Los Negros Muertes above all?"

"That shit goes out the window when it comes to my family," Justice said seriously. "I don't wanna do it to you, Sincere, but I will."

"Everybody stand down." K-Dawg stepped in among the three of them. The rest of the soldiers formed a circle around Justice, Sincere, and Animal, ready to take them down on K-Dawg's command. "I say who lives or dies, and right now it's Cruz's time."

None of the trio wanted to back off, but none of them wanted to challenge K-Dawg's authority. Sincere was the first to lower his weapon, followed by Justice. Animal was still clutching his pistol, glaring at Sincere.

K-Dawg moved to stand directly in Animal's line of vision. "You really wanna try me on this?"

Animal reluctantly put his gun away. "You got that, Boss Dawg, but this ain't over."

"I don't doubt that, Animal, but it ain't gonna go down now." K-Dawg lowered his voice so that only Sincere and Animal could hear him. "Family business is never aired in front of outsiders. You two wanna throw down, then we'll do it the right way when we get back to the farmhouse. Get me?" Both Animal and Sincere nodded. "Good, now let's finish this and get the fuck outta the slums."

At the end of the bloodied hallway there was an apartment fitted with a steel door that stood out among the rest. Several members of their hit squad knelt, keeping a watchful eye on the door with orders to shoot anyone who came through it. A young dude whom Animal didn't know by name, but knew his face, knelt in front of the door, working on the lock with a blowtorch. Beyond the door was the prize they had been working for so many months to claim: Cruz.

"What's the story?" Animal asked K-Dawg.

"This is the hole the rat has crawled into to try and avoid judgment, but it ain't gonna help him. One of the oldest lessons we learn is that you can't cheat death," K-Dawg said.

The lock finally came away under the heat and everybody got on point. The unit moved forward and took up positions outside the door. They were supposed to wait until the extraction squad moved in to clear them for entry, but young Chris had other ideas.

"You muthafuckas can stand around if you want, but I'm trying to see about those million dollars." He broke ranks and rushed the door. Everyone shouted for him to fall back, but Chris ignored them. He saw it as an opening for him to save face for his earlier blunder as well as collect the bounty on Cruz's head. With his gun raised, he kicked open the door to Poppito's haven and stepped inside. As soon as he crossed the threshold he was greeted by a chest full of buckshot.

It all seemed to happen in slow motion. Animal heard Chris's statement but was too slow to stop him as he breezed by. At almost the same moment as his foot forced the door open, the man standing on the other side opened fire with the shotgun. The blast hit Chris in the chest, lifting him off his feet and sending him sailing down the hall, skidding to a stop just behind where they were positioned. Sonja looked at the prone body of her little brother and Animal knew what she was going to do even before she started moving.

"Muthafucka." Sonja jumped to her feet with tears blinding her. She advanced on the apartment, dumping with the twin MAC11s. Everything in her line of fire was torn to shreds as the machine guns whined and breathed death into the apartment. Even when both clips were empty she continued to squeeze the triggers.

Animal approached Sonja cautiously and placed his hand on her forearm. "It's okay, baby girl," he whispered, trying to pull her away. She stood stock-still, tear-filled eyes fixed on the doorway for a long moment before finally allowing Animal to pull her away. Together they walked over to where Chris had landed. The young boy lay on the ground, writhing in pain and gasping for air. Animal knelt beside him and ripped open his shirt, exposing the smoking and ruined bulletproof vest beneath.

"Damn, this shit hurts." Chris gasped.

"Pain is good, because the dead can't feel shit," Animal told him while undoing the straps on his vest. Chris's chest was badly bruised and he had a few minor cuts, but he was okay.

"Man, if you hadn't made me put this vest on I'd be dead. I guess you saved my life again, huh?" Chris tried to muster a smile.

"Don't get too used to it. I'm in the business of taking lives, not saving them," Animal joked. "Tend to your brother," Animal told Sonja and went to join the others in the doorway of the apartment. The smell of smoke and gunfire was so overwhelming that the men began to cough. The doorway and walls of the apartment were shredded and they could barely see anything through the cloud of gun smoke.

Justice went into the apartment first, sweeping his M16 back and forth for signs of trouble. Animal came in behind him, Desert Eagles raised, ready to back his brother up. Lying on the floor of the foyer was the man who had shot Chris. He was still alive, but that was only a temporary setback. Animal knelt down and smacked the man to make sure he was coherent. The man looked up at Animal with glassy eyes. "You still with us?" Animal asked. The man nodded. "Good." He shoved the barrels of both guns into the man's mouth. "This is for Chris." He pulled both triggers and put the man's brains on the stained wooden floor. Wiping the brain matter off his face with the back of his hand, he joined his brother.

The apartment was a wreck. Everything in it was decorated with bullet holes and was smoking. Slumped over in a chair near the window was a man with a rifle on his lap. He had never even gotten a chance to pull the trigger before Sonja had turned him and everything else in the apartment to Swiss cheese. The soldiers fanned out through the apartment but there was no sign of Cruz.

"Search the whole building. Under no circumstances is Cruz to leave here alive," K-Dawg ordered the soldiers. A handful of them went off to do as they were told, leaving K-Dawg, Justice, Sincere, Animal, and one of Poppito's soldiers in the apartment.

Animal went to search the bedroom again, accompanied by Poppito's soldier. The bed was unmade and there were two Styrofoam containers with half-eaten food in them. Animal touched a piece of chicken and noticed it was still warm. Cruz couldn't have gone far. He turned his attention to a large dresser in the corner. Something about it nagged at him so he went to give it a closer inspection. When he looked down at the floor, he noticed fresh scuffs, as if the dresser had been recently moved. He motioned for the soldier to cover him while he moved the dresser. Sure enough, there was a trapdoor in the floor. Animal slipped his fingers in the grooves to pull the trapdoor open while the soldier stood with his gun ready. He had barely gotten the trapdoor up when he heard a gunshot. The soldier pitched backward when the bullet connected with his forehead.

Animal reflexively let go of the heavy door, which dropped on the hand holding the gun that was peeking out. Someone below shrieked as the hand was trapped between the door and the floor. Animal stomped on the trapdoor repeadedly until the hand released the gun, which he kicked away. He then pulled the trapdoor away, revealing Cruz hiding in the hole, clutching his broken wrist.

"Come here, you sneaky little fuck." Animal dragged Cruz out of the hole and tossed him to the middle of the floor. It was his first time ever seeing the so-called boss of Old San Juan, and frankly he wasn't impressed. Cruz was a worm of a man who couldn't have weighed more than 150 pounds on a good day. He had thinning black hair, which he wore combed over his massive head. Trembling as he was, he hardly looked like the tyrant the people had made him out to be.

"So this is Cruz, huh? He don't look so badass to me." Justice raised his M16, causing Cruz to curl up into a ball fearfully.

K-Dawg placed his hand on the barrel of the gun and pushed it away. "Chill." He stepped between Justice and Cruz. "Little man, you've caused me quite a bit of trouble over the last few months."

"Listen, I'm sure we can work something out. I've got millions of dollars stashed at one of my safe houses and you can have it all if you let me live," Cruz pleaded.

"We don't deal in money, we deal in death." K-Dawg dropped a tarot card at Cruz's feet.

Cruz picked up the card and looked at the image of the Grim Reaper in horror. "Los Negros Muertes," he said in shock. It was then that Cruz realized the dire situation he was in and did what came naturally—he ran. He made it almost to the window before Animal shot him in the leg and dropped him a few feet away from freedom.

"I want his head and that million cash." Sincere started after Cruz, but K-Dawg's voice stopped him.

"Back off," K-Dawg told him, watching Animal move in on Cruz.

"C'mon, dawg, it's supposed to be up for grabs," Sincere argued.

"You heard what I said." K-Dawg's tone was icy. Wisely, Sincere left it alone. "Take him, Animal," K-Dawg ordered. Animal looked at him hesitantly. "We've been out here all this time chasing this muthafucka. Only his death can end this mission. Finish him."

Animal stalked Cruz, who was still crawling for the window in hopes of escape. He was pathetic, but Animal felt no sympathy. In Cruz he didn't see a police official or crime lord, but the man who had been the cause of his being trapped in Puerto Rico and away from the woman he loved. His death would bring an end to K-Dawg's sick little game and put Animal one step closer to reclaiming what he had given up, his life.

Animal grabbed Cruz by the front of his soiled silk shirt and pressed him against the window. "Yea though I walk through the valley of the shadow of death . . ." Cruz began praying, but Animal shoved the Desert Eagle into his mouth, silencing him.

"God has long ago turned a deaf ear to the prayers of men like us," Animal said before pulling the trigger. Cruz's brains leaped from his skull and out the window. Cruz was as dead as a doornail before he hit the floor, but Animal wasn't done. With a powerful stroke he swung his machete and lopped off Cruz's head. Animal held Cruz's head in his hands like a basketball and tossed it to K-Dawg. "I'll be expecting my million cash when we get back to the house," he told him, wiping the machete clean on Cruz's shirt.

"You earned it," K-Dawg said proudly, stuffing the head into a shopping bag. "A'ight, we're done here. Let's move out," K-Dawg ordered.

"Hold on, there's still some fun to be had," Sincere said as he plunged his hands into the hole Cruz had been hiding in. He came up dragging a girl by the hair who they had missed on the first look. She didn't look to be more than sixteen but from the lingerie she was wearing it was obvious what she had been doing with Cruz. "Looks like we got one of the boss's mistresses."

"Please don't hurt me." The girl trembled.

"I'll bet Cruz was up here fucking the lining outta that tight pussy of yours." Sincere pinched one of her breasts. "What do you think, should I fuck her first or cut her head off? If they offered a million for Cruz's head, I know hers has got to be worth something." He waved the fire ax he had been carrying at the girl. Everyone watching laughed, but Animal didn't.

When Animal looked at the young girl he couldn't help

but think of Mimi. Mimi had been one of the few people left in the world, outside of Justice, whom Animal called family. She was a down-ass broad who wanted nothing more than to prove herself to Animal and the family who had cast her to the side like trash. At the end of the day it was her loyalty to Animal that had caused her death when the men who had came for his life ended up taking hers.

"Leave her," Animal told Sincere.

"What the fuck do you mean leave her? Poppito says everybody in the building dies and she's in the building. You've had your fun, now let me have mine." Sincere tossed the girl onto the bed and pressed the ax blade to her throat. "What do you want first, baby, the blade or the cock?"

"No!" the girl screamed as Sincere ripped her panties off. He had freed himself from his boxers and was about to penetrate her when pain shot through his skull. Animal grabbed a fistful of his hair and tossed Sincere onto the floor. Sincere drew his gun, but Animal shot him in the shoulder before he could get off a shot. Sincere rolled around on the floor, clutching his shoulder in pain.

Animal stomped Sincere in the gut before straddling him and shoving the barrel of his Desert Eagle into his eye. "What kind of man would rape and murder a little girl? You sick muthafucka, I should splatter your brains all over this place." Animal rained spittle on him as he spoke.

"Okay, you've made your point, kid," K-Dawg told him. Animal didn't respond. "I said let him up!" K-Dawg barked.

Animal wanted to shoot Sincere so bad that his hand was trembling. Slowly he got up off Sincere, but the urge to kill remained. "I'm done," Animal said in a shaky voice.

"Just relax, bro." Justice went to place his hand on Animal's shoulder but he slapped it away.

"Fuck you and fuck relaxing!" he shouted. "I didn't sign on for killing no kids and I ain't gonna stand by and see nobody else killing no kids." He turned to K-Dawg.

K-Dawg tried to stare Animal down, but he wouldn't turn his eyes away. "Fuck it, let the girl be."

Sincere looked at him in disbelief. "What kinda shit is this? Poppito paid us to wipe everybody out and we just gonna let this bitch live? Fuck all this." Sincere struggled off the floor, holding his shoulder. "This muthafucka Animal been causing problems between us since he got here and now he's calling the shots for Los Negros Muertes?"

"Calm down, Sincere," Justice warned.

"Nah, because I'm only saying what everybody else is thinking. K-Dawg laid out a bunch of rules for the rest of us, but his pet Animal seems to be exempt from those rules. You know, shit like this can make muthafuckas start to question who's running Los Negros Muertes."

The whole room went quiet. K-Dawg approached Sincere and stared him down. "You're way outta pocket right now."

"K-Dawg, miss me with that shit. Don't tell me I'm outta pocket for voicing my grievance when all this nigga Animal does is challenge your authority. What happened to that shit you were talking in the hall about being the one who decides who lives and dies?"

Without warning, K-Dawg shoved the barrel of his gun into Sincere's gut and pulled the trigger. Sincere flew back onto the bed next to the girl he had been trying to rape, staring at her with dead eyes. "I do," K-Dawg told his corpse. "Anybody else feel like challenging my authority today?" He looked around at everyone in the room, but let his gaze linger on Animal. Animal remained silent and walked out of the apartment. "Good, now let's get the fuck outta here." K-Dawg tossed the bag containing Cruz's head to Justice and left.

CHAPTER 43

Gucci drove up, down, and sideways at least five times before finally finding a parking spot. Unfortunately, the spot was three blocks from the club, so they would have to hoof it the rest of the way. The walk didn't bother Gucci too much because she had brought her breakdown flip-flops in her purse, but Tionna hadn't had that kind of foresight so she would have to do the walk in heels.

"Girl, the way my left shoe is pinching my pinkie toe, I'll barely be able to walk, let alone dance when we get to the spot," Tionna complained. She was wearing a fierce black spaghetti-strap sequinned dress and black needle-toe heels.

"I wouldn't know nothing about that." Gucci wiggled her toes in her flip-flops. She looked stunning in a green off-the-shoulder dress that hugged her hips enough to give off sex appeal but not scream *slut*.

"Sometimes I really hate your ass." Tionna sucked her teeth.

"I would hate me too if my dogs were barking. So what kinda place is this? I've lived in Harlem all my life and have never been there, let alone heard of it."

"I've never been there, but I guess it's nice for Marlene and those stiff-ass lawyers to be partying up in there.

She's cool as hell, but some of her friends are bourgeois as hell."

"Jesus, that's all I need, some Oreos in tight-ass suits singing Biggie verses in my ear all night long. The things I do for my friends." Gucci shook her head.

"Gucci, you need to stop acting like that. It'll be good for you to get some culture in your life once in a while."

"Shit, you're one to talk. You just stopped dating nig-gaz fresh outta prison, so don't make me go there, T." Gucci rolled her neck.

"Fuck outta here, after Duhan I learned my lesson." Things between Tionna and Duhan, the father of her two sons, had ended poorly when he found out she was doing her own thing instead of holding him down. They decided to call it quits by way of a fistfight in the visiting room on Rikers Island.

"Speaking of Duhan, have you heard from him lately?" Gucci asked.

"Hell no and I don't wanna hear from him. He called me a few times when they shipped him upstate to try and make it right, but I ain't beat for that shit. I changed my number and had the collect calls blocked."

"That's fucked up, T. I know shit went sour with y'all, but that's still Duhan and Duran's dad. He should at least be able to speak to his kids."

"Shit, they know how to read and write. If he was that worried about being in his kids' lives, then he wouldn't have gotten his simple ass thrown in jail in the first place."

"But you didn't feel like that when you were balling out of control," Gucci pointed out.

"Listen, I didn't put no gun to Duhan's head and tell

him to take it to the street, that's something he chose to do on his own, and I just reaped the benefits of that. After I laid up and had them babies for him, what I got was owed to me."

"You sure did get what was owed to you." Gucci snickered.

"Very fucking funny."

The two girls hiked the rest of the way, reminiscing and trading insults. Though Gucci and Tionna argued more often than they didn't, neither of them could deny the fact that it felt good to be hanging out with each other again. They rounded the corner of the block where the club was located and were pleasantly surprised by what they saw. Because of the location they had expected it to be a hood spot, but the club actually looked pretty nice. There were a few luxury cars double-parked out front with guys and girls mingling before they headed into the club. When Tionna and Gucci came into view, everyone did a double take.

Tionna checked her makeup in her small compact mirror while Gucci put her shoes back on. "So what's up, you ready to turn this joint out or what?"

"Honey, I was born ready. Let's go show these bitches that the queens of Harlem have returned." Gucci flipped her hair and led the way inside.

Alonzo sat at the bar, nursing a Hennessy and Coke and wondering for the hundredth time what the hell he was doing there. He had had one of the worse days at work, starting with the argument with Porsha. He hadn't meant to come off on her like he had, but once he'd opened his mouth the words had started spilling out and he couldn't stop them. He knew he had hurt her feelings and felt horrible about it, but there was nothing that he could do about it at that point. He intended to apologize to her when he saw her again, but Porsha had been MIA since then.

Just when he thought things couldn't get any worse, two crackheads decided to start fighting in the supermarket. They managed to knock over a whole rack of jelly and of course Mr. Green called on Alonzo to clean it up. He had to mop the aisle four times before he finally managed to get the floor to stop sticking. On top of all that, one of the cashiers called in sick so Alonzo had to work through lunch, covering for her on the register. By the end of his eight-hour shift, which had turned into ten hours, Alonzo was too through. He needed to blow off some serious steam and Lakim had just the trick: King James's birthday party. At first Alonzo was going to pass, but he figured it beat sitting in the house all night. So once again he found himself in the company of wolves, feeling like a German shepherd.

Lakim rolled up behind Alonzo and draped his arm around him. "What up, kid, you good?"

"Yeah, I'm straight. Just came over here to get a drink." Alonzo nodded at the half-full glass.

"Nigga, why you over here blowing your bread and we got all kinda bottles popping in our section?"

"I just wanted to get some space for a minute, ya know?"

Lakim sucked his teeth. "Man, fuck all that, you amongst family, my G. It's a party going on and you over here looking all stressed out. What's good with that, somebody fucking with you or something?"

"Nah, it ain't nothing like that. I just had a rough day at work," Alonzo explained.

"The man still got his foot knee deep in your ass, huh? I keep telling you fuck that supermarket shit. You need to come get this money with us."

"Lakim, I'll leave the trap to y'all, you know I ain't off that no more," Alonzo reminded him.

"C'mon, sun. You think I'd have my baby bro in harm's way? I ain't talking about putting you on no fucking corners, I'm talking about upper management. We'll give you your own spot and you run it as you see fit."

"I'm good, La."

"A'ight, but when you get tired of lugging boxes for that cracker you know big bro got you, fam."

"Break yoself, blood." Ashanti interrupted their conversation. His eyes were glassy and he reeked of alcohol and weed. Because of his age he had never been in a club before, and shouldn't have been in that one, but Lakim had pulled some strings and gotten the manager to look the other way.

"I keep telling you about that 'blood' shit," Lakim warned.

"Chill, B, you know I don't mean no disrespect by that. I call you blood cuz you my family," Ashanti half slurred. "Man, I ain't never seen this many hos in one spot at one time." Fascinated, he looked around at the women moving about the club.

"I told you, fucking with us, your lifestyle was gonna change. This ain't shit, wait until we really start balling and then you'll see why we're the winning team," Lakim promised.

"Shorty, let me get another shot of Patrón." Ashanti banged on the bar top.

Lakim pulled him away from the bar. "Chill the fuck out,

sun. You need water more than you need a drink right now." Lakim slid away the shot the bartender had just set down and requested a bottle of water for Ashanti. "Here, nigga, flush that li'l kidney of yours." He handed Ashanti the water.

Ashanti reluctantly accepted the water, but once he began chugging it he felt his head start to clear. His eyes wandered around the club and he spotted two familiar faces coming down the stairs to the club area. "Oh shit, look at these muthafuckas." He nodded at the two girls.

Lakim's eyes zeroed in on the girls and he began licking his lips. "Damn, shorty in the green can get it!"

"Show some respect, nigga. I know her." Ashanti put the water on the bar and made his way across the room.

This spot is a'ight." Gucci nodded in approval, taking in the stylish decor of the place.

"I told you that it had to be something special if Marlene and them were partying here. Speaking of Marlene, I wonder if she's here yet." Tionna looked around. "Fuck it, I'll text her in a minute to see where she's at. You wanna get a drink?"

"Sure, if you're paying," Gucci said.

"That's a bet. First round is on me." Tionna led the way to the bar.

It didn't take long for the vultures to swoop in, trying to invade Tionna and Gucci's space. Most of them were locals so they didn't get any play. After swatting hands, sidestepping guys, and cursing a few out, they finally made it to the bar. There were no seats, but two dudes gave up theirs, thinking that it would earn them the favor of the young ladies, but all it did was get them dismissed once the ladies were planted on their seats. Tionna ordered two Hennessy and Red Bulls for them and enjoyed the scenery.

"Damn, I'd almost forgotten how thirsty niggaz uptown could be," Gucci said, ignoring a dude at the other end of the bar who was trying to get her attention.

"That's the price we pay for being young, fly, and pretty." Tionna winked.

"You ain't never lied," Gucci said. She felt someone touch her arm and spun around, ready to curse out whoever it was who had touched her uninvited. The frown on her face turned into a smile when she saw that it was Ashanti. She almost didn't recognize him all clean-cut in his button-up and soft-bottom shoes. But for as grown-up as he was dressed, the red bandanna tucked into his shirt pocket said there was still a lot of kid in him.

"What's good, ma." He greeted Gucci with a hug.

"Hey, Ashanti!" she said happily. "I haven't seen you in a minute, what you been up to?"

Ashanti shrugged. "Not much, just trying to make it."

"You staying out of trouble?"

"As best I can, but you know how that goes."

Gucci laughed. "Still the same li'l badass Ashanti, huh?"

"I'm a trap boy for life," he said honestly.

"Ain't you a li'l young to be in here?" Tionna asked.

"Age is a small thing when you're rolling with big boys," Ashanti boasted.

"So you're getting your weight up, huh?" Tionna looked him up and down. It had been a while since Tionna had seen Ashanti and he was growing up to be quite handsome.

"Back off, cougar. Fifteen will get you twenty," Gucci said playfully.

"Stop hating, Gucci. I'll be eighteen in a few months. So what's good, T?"

"Ashanti, you need to quit. Tionna's old ass will eat you alive," Gucci tried to tell him.

"Gucci, we're less than a year apart so if I'm old, what does that make you?"

"Still younger than *you*," Gucci shot back.

Ashanti shook his head. "Y'all are still crazy as hell."

"And you're still in places that you have no place being," Gucci told him. "Who are you in here with, Brasco and them?"

"Nah, my nigga B-Sco locked up and I don't see Nef too much no more," Ashanti said in a saddened tone.

"Brasco stay locked up."

"You know how it is when you're in the life, Gucci. We take the good with the bad."

"Yeah and it's mostly bad," she pointed out. "Ashanti, I sure wish you would get up outta these streets and go back to school. You're still young enough to do something with your life."

Ashanti laughed. "What life? My family doesn't want me and the system can't hold me. The one nigga who did love me is gone." When Ashanti said it he saw hurt flash across Gucci's face. "I'm sorry, Gucci, I know that's still a sore spot for you. How are you holding up?"

"I'm working through it one day at a time. Some days are easier than others."

"True story." Ashanti looked down at his shoes. "You know"—when he raised his head, his eyes were misty—"I ain't never known no good in my life. From my mama pimping me out when I was a baby to having to fight every day of my life because I'm so small, people have always treated me like shit unless I was able to benefit them, but it wasn't like that with my nigga Animal. Even when that dude didn't have shit I could still get half of it, ain't too many niggaz built like that no more. On the real, if I ever found the niggaz who got at him . . ." His emotions overcame him and he couldn't find the words.

"It's okay, Ashanti." Gucci rubbed his back. "I know, trust me I know."

The guy who had been at the other end of the bar trying to get Gucci's attention finally got up the courage to come over. His timing couldn't have been worse. "What's good, can I holla at you for a minute?" He was a dark-skinned kid with bad skin, dressed in a fake Polo shirt and some ugly brown shoes.

"Now is not a good time," Tionna told him.

"My fault, I didn't mean to intrude. I was just trying to see if I could buy the lady a drink. She looks like she could use it," he said pleasantly.

"Can't you see we're having a moment? Have some fucking respect," Ashanti snapped.

"Chill, shorty, I wasn't trying to come over here and fuck up your groove," the guy told him.

When Ashanti heard the word *shorty,* his Napoleon complex and the liquor kicked in. "Who the fuck you calling shorty, you trying to play me?"

"C'mon, B, you bugging right now. Calm that big-man shit down." The kid waved Ashanti off.

"You're a tough guy, huh?" Ashanti folded his hands behind his back. Nobody but Tionna saw that he had just pulled a gun out of his pants. "How about if I smack the shit outta you for talking slick?"

"What?" The kid moved in on him. Ashanti's arm had

started inching from behind his back when Lakim grabbed him by the wrist.

"I think you've had a little too much to drink. Maybe you should go kick back for a minute," Lakim whispered in Ashanti's ear.

"A'ight, La," Ashanti said, but kept his eyes on the kid he'd been arguing with. "Gucci, Tionna, Ima catch up with you later on." He backed through the crowd, still glaring at the kid.

"That li'l boy just got saved for a good ass whipping," the kid boasted.

Lakim took a sip of his Corona and made eye contact with the kid. "You having a good time at my man's party?"

"Yeah, this shit is real live." The kid smiled. The smile faded when Lakim broke the bottle on the bar and placed the jagged end to the kid's throat.

He grabbed the kid roughly by the face and pressed the broken end into the kid's Adam's apple. "You fucking faggot, I should open you up for trying to disrespect my li'l man!"

"I'm sorry." The kid gasped.

"One sorry muthafucka." Lakim poked him. "Get the fuck outta here before I kill you." He shoved the kid. Lakim grabbed a napkin from the bar and began wiping the excess beer from his hands. He felt Gucci's and Tionna's eyes on him. "You ladies enjoy the rest of the party." He tossed the napkin onto the bar and walked off.

Gucci had a mortified look on her face, but Tionna was smiling from ear to ear. "I know you don't think that shit is funny?" Gucci asked.

"Nah, I was just wondering if he was seeing anybody."

Gucci shook her head. "I can't take yo ass nowhere."

"Hater." Tionna sipped her drink. She looked over near the entrance and saw Marlene walk in accompanied by several men dressed in business suits. "There's Marlene. Come on, let me introduce you." Tionna grabbed Gucci by the hand and led her across the room.

CHAPTER 44

Porsha's night with Don B. felt like a dream. Don B. treated her to dinner at a French restaurant uptown that she'd had no idea even existed. It was a cute little spot not far from St. Luke's Hospital and had a beautiful view of the park. The menu was in French, so Porsha had some difficulty figuring out what she wanted to eat, but to her surprise Don B. was able to translate it. His French wasn't very good, but he knew enough to place their order.

After dinner they headed downtown to the movie screening. It was a modest theater on the Lower East Side that showed mostly foreign films and critically acclaimed independents, but they shut it down for the night for the screening. It was a forty-minute short called *From Harlem With Love,* which was written and directed by a young writer from Harlem whom Don B. had grown up with. When Porsha saw the melting pot of people who turned out for the screening, she assumed it was going to be some Euro-type film that she couldn't get into, but it was actually pretty good. It was centered around a dude from the neighborhood who had gone on a killing spree. Porsha cried during the scene when the main character's girlfriend fell to an assassin's bullet that was meant for him.

After the screening there was a meet and greet for the

cast and crew a few blocks away at a small restaurant. Porsha felt slightly out of her element, listening to the conversations about movies that she had never seen and books that she had no interest in, but she did her best not to embarrass Don B. with her ignorance. She got roped into a discussion with a group of producers from Europe, who seemed to have more than a passing fascination with her. One guy in particular, who had had one too many glasses of wine, fawned over Porsha, telling her how pretty she was and how he wanted to use her in his next film. She knew he was talking out of his ass, but it felt good to hear.

When asked what she did, Porsha said simply that she was in the entertainment field and didn't elaborate any further.

Don B. seemed right at home seemingly so far out of his element. It was amazing to her how he could turn his hood persona on and off as needed to blend in with the different crowds. Porsha mostly played the sidelines but it seemed like every few minutes Don B. was introducing her to this one and that one who was involved either with the film or with some other aspect of the industry. When Don B. announced that they were leaving, no one wanted to see them go, including Porsha. She was having a good time, but Don B. promised that the night would only get better, so she went along.

"What'd you think?" Don B. asked when they were back in the car.

"I had a great time. Your friends were so nice and they really seemed supportive of your friend's film," Porsha said.

"Stop fronting. Those were a bunch of dry-ass crackers who wouldn't have wiped their asses with that script if the Don wasn't backing it. They don't give a fuck about us or the stories that come out of our communities."

Porsha was confused. "So if you really don't like these people, why were you in there all smiley and stuff?"

"Because it's good business. For as big of cocksuckers as those guys are, they're also very influential. The connections they have can open doors that might otherwise be closed to me and help take Big Dawg to the next level, so I play the game."

"Sounds like the game is phony to me."

"As a three-dollar bill, but business ain't about keeping it real, it's about keeping it profitable. After you've been around for a while you'll have figured it out."

"Oh, so you plan on keeping me around for a while, huh?"

Don B. looked at her. "I'd be a fool to let a catch like you get away, ma. You've been chosen; now let's see if you make the cut."

"I hear that hot shit." Porsha cut her eyes at him. "So, where are we off to now?"

"A friend of mine is having a li'l thing out in Brooklyn Heights. I figured we'd slide through there for a hot sec and have a few drinks. Besides, I need to holla at him about something."

Porsha frowned. "Brooklyn Heights? Ain't no clubs out there so what is it, a house party or something?"

"Or something," he said and turned his attention back to the road.

What Don B. took Porsha to was anything but your average house party. His friend Tone owned a beautiful three-story house with a view of the bridge. When Don B. pulled up with Porsha on his arm, people treated them like the king and queen of the music industry. He led her through the long hallway to the living room, giving her the 411 on all the plaques that lined Tone's wall. People milled about in the spacious living room with its high ceilings and glass furniture, drinking and smoking weed and engaging in a few other activities. There were a few heavyweights from the New York music scene there, and she thought she might've recognized an athlete or two. No matter who they were, they all paid homage to Don B. and the lady on his arm. Porsha caught a little shade from a few of the video hos in attendance but that just made her throw it extra hard as she crossed the room.

"Glad you came through, my nigga." Tone walked up to greet Don B. He was wearing jeans and a wife beater with a pair of Gucci slippers on his feet. A blunt of some of the most potent weed Porsha had ever smelled dangled from his lips, dropping ashes on the carpet every time he said something.

"You know I had to let my presence be felt, B." Don B. gave him dap.

"I see you brought li'l miss thing from the other night with you." Tone looked Porsha up and down, licking his lips. His eyes were beet red and narrowed to slits. "What's good?"

"Chilling," she told him. "This is a nice place you have here."

"It's a'ight, just someplace to lay my head when I'm in New York," he stunted. "Yo, y'all come on in and re-lax. Don, you probably know everybody already but if not you'll get to know 'em before the night is over." Tone walked to the other side of the living room, plucking two of the video hos from the group and disappearing around the corner with them.

"Yo, Don, let me holla at you for a minute. I got somebody I want you to meet," someone called from across the room. Porsha recognized him as a popular R&B singer who had had a few number-one singles.

Don B. looked at Porsha for approval. "Go ahead and handle your business," she told him.

"A'ight, I'll be back in a sec. Why don't you grab us a few drinks." Don B. nodded at a gallon of Hennessy and some plastic cups that were on the mantel. He bopped over to the corner and began speaking with the singer and his entourage.

Porsha made her way across the living room to the makeshift bar, taking in the scene as she went. She had been to some wild parties before but this ranked up there with the wildest of them. In the corner on a love seat next to the patio door, two girls took turns snorting lines of coke off an album cover, while a man and a woman were squeezed in next to them, kissing and petting heavily. Porsha watched curiously as the man's hand disappeared beneath the woman's skirt and began fondling her sex. A small crowd had gathered to watch, but the couple didn't seem to mind. Porsha managed to tear herself away from the show and continued toward the bottle.

She reached for the bottle but someone else beat her to it. She was a pretty Spanish girl with a big weave and pants that were so tight they looked like they'd split if she bent the wrong way. "My bad, you go ahead," Porsha told her.

"How about you hold the cups and I pour," the girl suggested.

Porsha balanced all three cups in her palms while the girl poured the drinks. "Thanks," Porsha said, handing the girl her cup.

"So, I've never seen you around before. Are you signed to Big Dawg or just part of an entourage?" the girl asked.

"Neither," Porsha said, not bothering to elaborate further.

"I'm sorry, I didn't mean it like that. I'm Macy," the girl introduced herself.

"Porsha."

"Wow, I love your haircut." Macy reached out and touched Porsha's stylish cut. When she pulled her hand away she let it brush against Porsha's cheek.

"Excuse you." Porsha pulled away.

"Relax, mama. It's all good here. This must be your first time at one of Tone's parties." Macy smiled.

Porsha set her drink on the mantel and looked at Macy seriously. "Check this fly shit, I don't know what you thought you were trying to do, but I ain't that bitch, so if I were you I'd be the fuck easy."

"Damn, you ain't gotta be all stink about it. Bitch, if you ain't with the program then what the fuck are you doing here?" Macy snapped.

Just then Don B. walked up. "What the fuck are you doing?" He glared at Macy.

"Chill, Don, I was just kicking it with ya li'l plaything. Maybe later on we can all play together." Macy tried to wrap her arms around Don B.'s neck but he pushed her away.

"Macy, get your drunk ass outta here before I have you thrown out."

"Fuck you, Don B. You always want a bitch to share her goodies but you never wanna share yours. I can't stand a cuffing-ass nigga." Macy stomped away.

"What the fuck was that bitch's problem?" Porsha asked.

"Pay her no mind. Macy doesn't know how to hold her liquor," Don B. said, downplaying it.

"So is she one of your shorties or something, because she seems awful familiar?"

Don B. lowered his shades and looked at Porsha over the top. "If you're asking me if I fucked her, yes. If you're asking me if I'm still fucking her, no. Now are you gonna stand here giving me the third degree about how many of these skanks I ran through or are we gonna enjoy the party?" Porsha was still frowning, so Don B. tilted her chin up so that she was looking into his shaded eyes. "Listen, there ain't gonna be too many places we go where I haven't fucked a broad, but when I'm with you it's not about my past, it's about *our* future, smell me?"

"Okay." Porsha's face lit up a bit.

"That's the pretty smile I like to see." Don B. kissed her on the forehead. "Here, I brought you some wine in case that Hennessy is too strong for you. I don't know if you can hang or not," he teased her.

"Nigga, please. I say, why waste it." Porsha took the Hennessy shot down. It felt like liquid fire going down her throat but she held her game face.

"That's what I'm talking about, baby. Let's go in the den, it's too fucking noisy out here." Don B. took her by the hand and led her through the house. As soon as they stepped into the den, Porsha found her eyes stinging from all the weed smoke in the air. The den was a little less hectic than the living room. Macy sat on a couch, whispering into the ear of a white girl with green eyes and red hair who wore a see-through blouse and no bra. Macy fondled the girl's pink nipple through her shirt while giving her shotguns from the blunt in her mouth. Porsha was glad she had found someone else to focus her attentions on. Tone lounged on the floor on a bearskin carpet between the two girls he had disappeared with. They took body shots off him while he watched *Scarface* on the big-screen television mounted on the wall with the volume muted. One of Don B.'s unreleased tracks played through the surround sound speakers mounted on the walls.

"Damn, your crew goes hard, don't they," Porsha said, watching the two girls on the floor licking the excess liquor off each other's lips.

"That's the only way Big Dawgz know how to party," Don B. told her, leading her to an unoccupied couch on the other side of the room. Once they were comfortable, he fired up a blunt. The smell of the weed was so tart that it made Porsha sneeze. "This is that good shit." Don B. passed her the blunt. Porsha took two baby pulls and started coughing. "Slow down, mama. Don't want you to hurt yourself."

"That shit is harsh," Porsha said between coughs.

"Sip some of that wine to wet your whistle." Don B. pushed her cup toward her.

Porsha took a gulp of the wine and frowned. It tasted especially bitter, even for red wine. "How long are we staying here?"

"Only for a li'l while. We gonna blow a few Ls, then get up outta here," Don B. promised.

The few minutes turned into a few hours. Porsha and Don B. smoked weed and did shots while sipping the bitter wine and listening to Don B.'s CD. Between the liquor and the weed, it felt like the temperature had jumped up by two hundred degrees. She got up to go to the den's bathroom to throw some water on her face and stumbled.

"You okay?" Don B. asked, blowing smoke rings into the air. Somehow Macy had made her way from the couch where she had been sitting with the white girl over to the couch Don B. was on.

"I'm fine," Porsha lied and shut herself inside the little bathroom.

When she was gone, Macy gave Don B. knowing look, to which he smiled and began stroking her thigh.

Porsha sat on the toilet seat and put her head between her legs to try to get it to stop spinning. Every time she tried to lift it, the room seemed to move. She finally managed to stand up and walk to the bathroom sink, where she planted her palms and tried to catch her breath. Her heart was beating so fast that it made her nervous. Porsha splashed cold water on her face in an attempt to clear her head. The bathroom door clicked open, making Porsha's head snap up, which turned out to be a mistake. She had barely made it to the toilet before the wine and the French food they'd eaten earlier came shooting out. Every time she heaved she felt like she was trying to push her lower intestines out through her mouth.

"Looks like somebody went a little too hard." Don B. helped her to her feet and over to the sink.

"I am so sorry, Don," Porsha said, flushing her mouth with water. "It must've been something I ate at the restaurant because I never call earl."

"There's a first time for everything when you're party-ing with the best. Don't worry, the Don's got you," he said, rubbing her back.

Porsha looked up at herself in the mirror. Her eyes were red and swollen and her pupils were dilated. "I look a hot fucking mess."

"Nah, you look just fine to me." He began planting kisses on the back of her neck. Don B. turned Porsha around to face him and began kissing her tenderly along her jawline.

The feel of his lips on her skin sent unexpected waves of pleasure through Porsha and it became hard for her to think. "Wait a minute, let me get myself together." She laid her hands on his chest with the intention of pushing him away, but her arms felt like noodles.

"You good." He slipped his tongue into her mouth. Don B. kissed Porsha passionately, kneading her breast like pizza dough. She was barely able to stand on her own, let alone resist his advances. When Don B. had slipped the crushed pill into her drink he'd known it would hit her be-fore long, but he'd had no idea it would hit her that hard.

"I don't feel so good," Porsha moaned as he slipped his fingers in and out of her.

"I'm about to make you feel great," Don B. rasped in her ear, trying to get his dick out of his pants. He lifted her skirt and began fumbling with her panties. Porsha tried to push his hands away, but he ignored her weak attempts and kept at it. He was so hard that he almost scraped him-self on his zipper trying to get it free.

When Porsha felt Don B. slip himself inside her, she gasped. His thick cock split her lips and tapped the deep-est part of her walls. "Damn, I want you but not like this," she said almost incoherently, moaning.

"When opportunity knocks, you gotta answer the door, ma." Don B. reached over and cut out the light, still buried inside Porsha. She felt so good that he wanted to live inside her.

Porsha's head continued to spin as Don B. stroked her on the bathroom counter. He thrust himself inside her so hard that she leaned over and threw up in the sink, but that didn't stop his pumping. Porsha's head knocked up against the mirror as he dug into her faster and faster. She heard the bathroom door click open again and the last thing she saw was someone else slip into the bathroom just before she passed out.

CHAPTER 45

King James had been unusually quite that night. Sahara met him uptown and they went for a bite at Applebee's before hitting Harlem Lanes for some bowling. It was supposed to be an intimate night with just he and Sahara until the big surprise, but to her disappointment he brought Dump along. He gave them a wide berth, not interfering with their date directly, but the fact that he was around irritated her. When Sahara asked King why Dump was there, he brushed her off, promising to tell her later. Something was going on with King but Sahara wasn't sure what it was.

King had found himself reflecting on his confrontation with Shai for most of the day. He had gone through his plan a million times before actually stepping to Shai, but in the blink of an eye it all had gone to shit and he'd found himself with a potentially volatile situation on his hands. Until then he had had the advantage of knowing his opponent without Shai's even realizing that he existed, but that was gone and the crime lord was well aware of King James and his position. Now the question remained as to what Shai would do with the information.

"It's your turn, baby," Sahara said, snaping him out of his daze.

"Sorry." King got up and grabbed the bowling ball as it

came out of the shoot. He tried to focus on the pin that was second left from the center, but his roll was totally off and the ball bounced into the gutter. "Fuck."

"Damn, baby, your game is suspect tonight. What's good with you?" Sahara asked.

"I got a lot of shit on my mind right now." He picked up her vodka and cranberry and took a sip.

"Now I know something is up because I've hardly seen you drink and never clear liquor. What's good, baby?"

"Nothing, babe." King kissed her on the forehead. "Just stressing over some niggaz I got into it with last night."

"King, what happened yesterday will still be there for you to dwell on tomorrow. It's your birthday and I brought you out so you can have a good time, even if we do have a third wheel with us." She looked over at Dump, who was leaning against the shoe-rental counter.

"You're right," he told her, but his mind was still firmly wrapped around the situation with Shai. "I'll be back, I gotta take a leak." He got up and started off to the bathroom. The bathroom was empty when he first walked in, but as he un-did his pants over the urinal someone else walked in. He was a heavyset kid who had a very familiar face, but King couldn't place him right off.

"What's good?" the kid said to King as he took the urinal next to his.

King just nodded, as he had never been a fan of talking while he had his dick out. The whole time he pissed, he could feel the kid's eyes on him. He was either gay or up to something, and the staring made King uncomfortable. He shook himself and walked over to the sink to wash his hands. The kid moved to the sink directly beside him.

Through the mirror King could see the kid staring at him more openly now and his heart began to pound.

"You're King James, right?" the kid asked.

"Yeah," King said, already calculating the best counter for whatever came at him.

"You don't remember me, do you?" The kid started to raise his hand and found himself in a bad way.

King caught him with a quick right hook and immediately grabbed the kid's Adam's apple between his index and middle knuckle, cutting off his air. The kid gasped frantically as King slammed him against the wall and then the mirror, shattering it. "Who sent you?" King snarled into his face.

"No . . . nobody." The kid gasped.

King slammed him against the mirror again. "I seen how you was looking at me, God. Who the fuck are you and where you know me from?"

"Downstate," the kid blurted out.

When he called the name of the prison it rung a bell in King's head as one of the many fine establishments he had visited, so he released his grip a bit, but not enough to let the kid move. "What about Downstate?"

"It's me, Sammy. We were in Downstate together in 2001. You left me all those books when they moved you. I was just trying to say what's up. You don't remember me?"

King studied his face, looking for signs that he was being deceived. He did recognize him! Sammy had put on about twenty pounds of muscle but his face was still the same. "Oh, shit, my bad, sun." King released him. "I thought you were somebody else. When did you touch down?"

"A few weeks ago." Sammy tried to catch his breath.

He balanced himself on the sink and looked up at King fearfully. "I was only trying to say what's up."

"Sammy, I'm sorry about that, man." King reached out to help him, but Sammy jumped back. "Hey, at least let me buy you a drink."

"Nah, I'm straight. I got some people waiting on me." Sammy skirted around King to the bathroom exit.

"Well, it was good seeing you, Sammy, holla at me," King called after him but Sammy was already gone. He looked at himself in the cracked bathroom mirror and sighed. He was letting Shai turn him into a basket case and he still wasn't sure if they even had a problem. To Shai, someone like King James was too insignificant to even put the energy into. "Fuck this," he said, determined not to let Shai ruin his birthday. "We out," King said to Sahara when he came out of the bathroom.

"Wait a second, we haven't bowled all of our frames," Sahara pointed out.

"Fuck that game, boo. This is my birthday and I'm ready to start getting it in. Let's go hit a club or something and get crazy."

"I know a nice place we can go," Sahara offered.

Holiday sat behind the wheel of the Honda Accord parked across the street from the bowling alley, right next to the State Building. He was dressed all in black with a pair of gloves tucked into the top pocket of his fatigue jacket. In the backseat were two young boys who were desperately trying to get down with Holiday. When Shai had given the word to handle King James, he'd decided to give them the opportunity to make their bones. What King had done wasn't a major infraction, but Shai wanted him to serve as an example of his new *zero tolerance* policy.

Holiday watched King James, Sahara, and Dump come out of the front and get into a green Suburban that had been parked at the curb. He waited until they pulled through the light on 125th Street and Seventh Avenue before following.

Frankie checked the pockets of her hoodie and realized that she had more money than product on her, which meant she had to take another trip to the crib. This would be the third trip she took that night. Once word had gotten out that Frankie had some bomb-ass work, the fiends had started coming steadily. In two nights of hustling she had managed to get up her end of the rent money, what she owed Cutty, and still have some bread left over for herself. If Scatter had never been right about anything else, he was right about how sweet drug money was. Frankie had promised herself that it would be a one-shot deal, but the more she trapped, the more she considered getting some more coke from Cutty.

After selling off the next few pieces she had on her, Frankie decided to go and re-up. On her way to the building she noticed that the block was quiet, which was unusual for a weekend. Frankie entered the building and rode the elevator to her floor. She was hungry and starting to get tired. She had made enough money to call it a night, but she figured, why quit when she was on a roll. After she moved another package she would grab something to eat and call it a night. The entire walk down the hall to her apartment she felt like she was being watched, but there was no one else around. She figured it was her next-door neighbor being nosey again, looking through her peephole, as she often did when she heard someone coming or going from their apartment. Frankie had just unlocked her door when the staircase door burst open and three masked men came charging at her.

She tried to run into the apartment and close the door, but one of the masked men managed to wedge his foot into the doorway before she could. Frankie shoved as hard as she could, slamming the door on his foot and drawing a painful scream from him. The two other masked men reached the door and together they overpowered Frankie and forced their way into the apartment.

Frankie tried to make a mad dash for the bedroom but one of the gunmen grabbed her by the hair, sending waves of pain through her body. "Where the fuck you going." He spun her around. Frankie socked him in the jaw, forcing him to lose his grip on her. The second masked man swung on her, but Frankie weaved it and caught him with a two piece to the face, dropping him. One thing they hadn't counted on when they ran up in her crib was that Frankie was a skilled boxer.

Frankie tried for the bedroom again, but the masked man she'd dropped tripped her up and she fell to the floor. She found herself being yanked roughly to her feet and thrown against the wall. She was about to start swinging again, but the masked man froze her when he shoved a gun in her face.

"Where is it?" he demanded.

"Where's what?" Frankie played dumb.

"That's how you wanna do it, huh?" The man hit her

in the face with a gun and opened up a gash on her cheek. "Now stop playing with me, bitch, and tell me where the drugs are."

"I don't know what you're talking about," Frankie said, sticking to her story. She was rewarded for her defiance by a crushing blow to the nose that sent her crashing to the living room floor. Tears welled in her eyes, clouding her vision. She knew even before she felt the blood gushing down her face that her nose was broken.

The masked man stood over Frankie with his gun aimed at her. "I'm gonna ask you one more time, where are the drugs?" Frankie remained silent. "Y'all two niggaz tear this place up. I'm gonna deal with this tough li'l bitch," he ordered his crew. The two men went about the task of tearing up the apartment, looking for the money and stealing anything that appeared to be of value.

"Bingo," one of the masked men said as he reentered the living room. In his hand he held the shoulder bag that had been hidden in the closet. The sight of the bag made Frankie's heart sink. They had the drugs and the money.

"See, all you had to do was give it up, but you wanted to be a smart little bitch like your homegirl," the man with the gun snapped.

"You got what you want, now get the fuck out!" Frankie screamed at him.

The man with the gun kicked her in the face viciously. "Who the fuck you screaming at, ho? I can see I gotta teach you some manners." He kicked her in the ribs. The man with the gun punched and kicked Frankie violently in the face, ribs, and back. From the way he was whipping on her, she knew that she was going to die in that apartment.

"Fucking whore." He spat on her, out of breath from the beating.

Frankie lay there, bleeding and half conscious, while the man with the gun paused his beating to give last-minute instructions to his team. One eye was swollen shut and the other was caked with blood. The pain in her ribs was so intense that she could barely move, let alone breathe. Unconsciousness tried to claim her but she knew that if she went out it was over. Ignoring the pain, Frankie inched her hand under the cushion of the couch where she kept her gun stashed, and came up blasting.

She closed her eyes and kept pumping the trigger, firing off shot after shot. She could hear the men screaming and glass breaking but she didn't dare open her eyes. The gun finally clicked empty and all was silent except for the sound of her heart pounding in her ears. Frankie forced her good eye open and surveyed the damage. One man lay bleeding by the front door, mouth opening and closing as he tried to gasp for air. Lying a few feet away from her was the man who had been beating her. There was a quarter-size hole in the center of his ski mask and blood pooling under his head. Frankie tried to reach for the phone to call the police but everything was going black. Her last thought before she passed out was that at least she had taken one of them with her.

CHAPTER 46

Sahara's heart was beating almost out of her chest with excitement as the club came into view. When she'd told King where she wanted to take him he had scoffed at it, saying that the club was too close to the hood and he wanted a change of scenery for his birthday. His stance on the issue had begun to soften when she'd started sucking him off in the backseat of the truck. Dump's thirsty ass almost crashed twice, trying to watch the show through the rearview mirror.

When the girl at the door saw King approaching, her face lit up. "Happy birthday." She draped her arms around him and gave him a kiss on the cheek. Sahara didn't like the way the girl was hanging on King but she let it slide so as not to ruin the night by arguing.

"Thanks, baby," he said and walked into the club. Sahara looked the girl up and down and rolled her eyes before falling in step behind King. "Damn, it seems like the whole world knows it's my birthday."

"You know Harlem loves you." Sahara kissed him on the cheek and looped his arm in hers to let the girl at the door, and anyone else who might've been watching, know that she was claiming King.

The dining area was empty at that hour of the night,

but it sounded like the club was in full swing downstairs. Dump led the way, giving dap to the few heads he knew who were loitering on the stairs. It was darker than usual in the club area, but they could still see that it was packed. King saw some dudes he knew from Queens posted up by the bar, drinking and having a good time. He knew those dudes didn't stray too far from their hood, so to see them uptown meant something was afoot. He was just about to point it out to Dump when suddenly the lights of the club flicked on and King was greeted by everyone yelling, *"Surprise!"*

After a few hours of doing shots with Ashanti, Alonzo was more feeling groovy and on his way to becoming shit-faced drunk. He had never been much of a drinker, so letting Ashanti goad him into the shots probably wasn't a good idea, but it took his mind off his problems for a time.

When King had arrived, the party officially kicked off. Everybody had turned out for the event, from friends to family to associates; they were all in the building. Bottles were popped, blunts were fired, and people crowded around to wish King the best on his born-day.

Lakim and Ashanti were on the dance floor, getting it popping in a circle of chicks who cheered them on. They were both drunk and having a blast. Lakim seemed especially attached to a thick chick in a black dress whom Alonzo didn't know. She had *sack chaser* written all over her, but his brother seemed smitten. Watching her made Alonzo think back to Brick House and how she had tried to set him up, so he made a note to himself to warn his brother to watch his back.

King sat at the table that had been reserved for his party, sipping champagne and greeting his guests. It was the most at ease Alonzo had seen him in a long time and he was glad to see his homie having fun. King had been through more at his age than some people who had been around twice as long. He'd come home from jail to nothing, but through grinding and sticking to the script, he was carving out a nice slice of the pie. He made sure everyone around him ate too, which was one of the things Alonzo admired most about King.

When the song was over, the girl Lakim had been dancing with excused herself to go chop it up with her partner in the green dress. Alonzo had had his eyes on the honey in the green since she'd walked into the joint. He could tell that she was a hood chick, but there was something about the way she carried herself that made her stand out among the rest. The two girls talked for a few, then the one in the black led the one in the green over to where Lakim and the others were chilling to make introductions. Alonzo figured that now would be as good a time as any to introduce himself to the girl and try to put his bid in before the rest of the vultures swooped in on her.

Alonzo gave himself the once-over in the bar mirror to make sure he looked okay, then checked his breath before heading to the table. There were so many people packed in the club that he had to squeeze and bump his way through the crowd. Everywhere he looked, people were having a good time and smiling . . . almost everyone. On the far side of the room his eyes picked up three dudes who were screw facing and acting like they were drinking. At first he thought they were just some partygoers who weren't having a good time, but there was something about the way they were dressed that bothered him. Who wore army fatigues to a club?

The shortest of the three men was familiar to Alonzo. Not familiar like he knew him, but familiar like he had seen him around before. He said something to his boys and then began making his way through the crowd, his eyes fixed on something on the other side of the room. Alonzo followed his line of vision and saw that he was staring at King James. King was so preoccupied by his guests that he never saw the three men or the guns they produced from the insides of their fatigue jackets.

Gucci was having the time of her life. She had heard through the grapevine that Marlene was a bitch, but she was actually a pretty cool chick and even knew some of the same people that Gucci did in Harlem. Marlene was smart, funny, and inspirational, which was more than Gucci could say for the other lawyers who showed up from the office. One of them got drunk and kept trying to sing to Gucci, which annoyed her to no end. Thankfully, a young attorney she had been introduced to earlier named Franklin came to her rescue. He didn't work for Marlene's firm; he was a criminal attorney who had come to the party with one of the other lawyers. Franklin was tall, dark, handsome, caked up, and interested in Gucci. He had been watching her all night, but she'd pretended not to notice.

"Thanks," Gucci told Franklin after he had persuaded the singing lawyer to find someone else to pester.

"No problem. I know how Jerry can be when he's had too much to drink, and he would've been over here doing his best Bobby Brown imitation all night. Personally,

I would've gone with Al B. Sure," he joked, causing Gucci to smile. "You know, I've been watching that smile from across the room all night."

"Then how come you're just coming over here?"

Franklin shrugged. "I dunno, shy I guess."

"I find that hard to believe with the way you've been charming these ladies in here all night."

"Nah, I wasn't trying to charm them. I was just making small talk."

Gucci chuckled. "So is that what you're doing over here, making small talk?"

"No, you I'm actually trying to charm." He winked.

"Well, it'll take more than a pretty face to charm me."

"But you do admit I'm handsome, right?"

"You're okay, I guess," Gucci said, downplaying it.

"Bullshit, I'm sexy and you know it." He smiled.

"I see there's no shortage of confidence with you."

Tionna staggered over with a drink in her hand and a dreamy look in her eyes. "Girl, this party is off the chain!"

"Your ass is off the chain. How many drinks have you had, T?"

"Just a few." She hiccuped. "Stop being such a killjoy, it's a party!"

"Girl, you're too funny." Gucci tried to laugh it off to hide her embarrassment at the spectacle Tionna was making of herself in front of Franklin.

"And I'm just getting warmed up. Gucci, come over here for a minute with me, I want to introduce you to La-kim and his boys." Tionna grabbed her by the hand and tried to pull her out of her chair.

"Tionna, be easy. Don't you see me talking?" Gucci was clearly annoyed.

"Girl, he'll still be here when you come back and it'll only take a second. You don't mind do you, chocolate?"

Franklin shrugged. "Do your thing, chicken wing."

"I'll be back in a second," Gucci said, excusing herself.

"And I'll be here waiting when you do," Franklin assured her.

"Your timing couldn't have been worse," Gucci told Tionna when they were out of earshot of Franklin.

"Fuck that square, I'm trying to introduce you to some real niggaz."

"Weren't you the one just saying how I needed to get some culture in my life and that I needed to stay away from thugs?" Gucci reminded her.

"These ain't thugs, these are gangstas. There's a difference. Now shut up and be cute," Tionna told her, pulling Gucci through the crowd of King's adoring public. "Hey, did you miss me?" She approached Lakim.

"Of course I did, ma," Lakim said coolly, exhaling weed smoke into the air. "Tionna, this is my nigga King, the birthday boy."

"Nice to meet you, King." Tionna shook his hand.

"Likewise," King told her, looking past Tionna at Gucci. "Who's your friend?"

"Oh, this is my girl, Gucci." Tionna almost shoved Gucci into King's lap.

King admired her openly and Sahara picked up on it. He had been staring at her since she walked up and Sahara didn't like it. She knew right then and there that she would have to get rid of the pretty brown-skinned girl before King's nose got too open. "And I'm Sahara," she cut in.

King gave Sahara a look that said she was approaching

crossing the line, then turned his attention back to Gucci. "Pardon me for staring, but you look so familiar. Are you from Harlem?"

"Born and raised," Gucci said.

"Then that's probably where I've seen you at. We probably know some of the same people."

"You do, she was my homie Animal's old lady," Ashanti spoke up from the chair where he was sitting. He had been so quiet that Gucci hadn't even noticed him. The look on his face said he wasn't pleased about what was going on.

King picked up on it and fell back. "I'm sorry for your loss. Animal was a good dude and a friend of mine. Anyhow, you ladies are more than welcome to join us. We've got bottles and weed and your money is no good here."

"Why thank you." Tionna squeezed in next to Lakim and helped herself to a drink. "Don't just stand there, G, sit down."

Reluctantly, Gucci took a seat. She really wasn't feeling King and his crowd, but didn't want to be rude, especially since Tionna had put her on the spot. She helped herself to a glass of champagne and tried to look like she was having a good time.

Ashanti's mood darkened when Gucci and Tionna came over, and he didn't try to hide it. It sickened him to watch King fawn over Gucci and her soak it all up. Even though Animal was dead and gone, he felt like she was disrespecting his memory by being all up in King's face.

"I'm about to go take a leak." Ashanti got up to keep himself from saying something he might regret later. He spotted Alonzo bulldozing his way toward them, screaming and flailing his arms. He couldn't hear what he was saying over the music so he raised his hands, asking what was good. Alonzo pointed frantically at something to the left of him and when Ashanti turned his head he saw the men step through the crowd with guns raised. "It's on," Ashanti shouted, diving out of the way and drawing his pistol at the same time as the men started firing.

Dump was the first to react. He pushed the girl he had been talking to out of the way and drew his hammer. The cannon thundered in the club, causing everyone to scatter and duck for cover. A patron, who had made the mistake of stepping into the line of fire, caught a bullet in the back and dropped. Dump tried to shove the frantic people out of the way so he could get a clear shot, but panic had set in and the club had turned into a madhouse. A bullet ripped through his chest, knocking him back, but the big man stayed on his feet and fired back. A second bullet whizzed through the air, slamming him in the gut and sending him down.

King James managed to flip the table over just as the bullets meant for him slammed into it. He had left his gun in the house, which was turning out to be a mistake that might cost him his life. Sahara, who was frantic, tried to grab on to him for safety, but he shoved her off roughly while he tried to get out of the way of the shooters. He tried to run, but one of the bullets caught him in the shoulder and sent him crashing to the floor face-first. He rolled over onto his back and saw the faces of one of the shooters and Holiday standing over him.

"You ain't so tough now, are you?" Holiday snickered, raising his gun to finish King off. Just then a battle cry rang out over the screams of the frightened club goers.

"Die, pussies." Ashanti was charging them with his gun spitting. The shooter who had been standing next to Holiday caught one in the head, raining pieces of skull and brain on Holiday. The next bullet struck Holiday in his leg, dropping him to the floor a few feet away from King. The third shooter who had been with Holiday came out of the crowd, trying to get the drop on Ashanti, but all he ended up getting was a bullet to the face. When he fell, Ashanti put two more in his chest for good measure. He turned back to Holiday to finish him off, but he had slipped away in the confusion.

Lakim rushed to King James's side, gun in hand and ready to claim his pint of blood. Alonzo was hot on his heels. "How bad is it, God?" Lakim asked.

"Nigga caught me in the shoulder." King grunted as Lakim and Alonzo helped him to his feet. "How's Dump?"

"He's hit up pretty bad, but still alive. I tried to move him, but he's too heavy," Alonzo said.

"I seen the shooter, it was that nigga Holiday. Word is bond, I'm laying all them Clark niggaz down," Lakim said angrily.

"We won't be laying shit down if we're all locked up. Let's get up outta here before the police come," King told them.

"What about Dump?" Alonzo asked.

"We gotta leave him. I'll get my lawyer on the case as soon as we're clear of here," King said. He hobbled over to Ashanti and placed his hand on his shoulder. "You did good kid, real good. I ain't gonna forget this."

"Thank me later. Let's just get you outta here, big homie."

A bloodcurdling scream caused Ashanti to jump, gun raised and ready to start shooting again. He looked for the source the scream and saw Tionna leaning over Gucci's prone body. The front of her green dress was soaked with blood. "No." Tears sprang to Ashanti's eyes. He tried to go to her, but King stopped him.

"What are you, fucking crazy? You're standing in the middle of a massacre with a murder weapon in your hand," King reminded him.

"I gotta go to her," Ashanti said, sobbing.

Lakim grabbed Ashanti by the front of his shirt and shook him. "She's gone, Ashanti, there's nothing you can do for her now. You wanna make this right, we get back at the niggaz who did it."

"He's fucking dead, him and his whole family," Ashanti vowed.

"Don't worry, my nigga, you'll get your chance to make good on that promise. You have my word on that," King told him.

Lakim and Alonzo helped King to the door. Ashanti hung behind for a few seconds more, watching Tionna break down over the body of her friend. He felt so weak and helpless at that moment that it made him physically ill. At that moment he swore on the life of his friend Animal that no matter how long it took he would track down and kill both Shai and Holiday for what they had caused, or die trying.

CHAPTER 47

It was well into the next afternoon when the police finally released Sahara. They had questioned her through the night and most of the morning about the shooting, but she had stuck to her story: "I don't know what happened." Several witnesses had claimed to see her enter the club with one of the shooters, but without more than hearsay they couldn't prove it, so they'd had to turn her loose.

The shooting at the club had her terrified. One minute they were drinking and having a good time and the next she was covered in blood. That was the closest she had ever come to dying and it made her start to take a long, hard look at the company she kept and the lifestyle she was living. With all that had been going on, she hadn't had a chance even to start working on getting up her end of the rent money, but at that point she didn't care. She was just glad to be alive.

As the taxi was pulling up in front of the projects, she spotted Porsha stepping out of another cab. Sahara jumped out of her cab and caught up with her roommate, anxious to hear of her night with Don B. and if she had come any closer to getting the rent money, but the questions died in her throat when she got a good look at Porsha. She looked disheveled and tired, and her eyes were swollen like she had been crying.

"Are you okay?" Sahara asked her.

"I don't even wanna talk about it," Porsha said, fighting off the urge to start crying again as she had been for the last few hours.

"Did that muthafucka Don B. do something to you?" Sahara pressed.

"I said I don't want to talk about it," Porsha snapped.

"Damn, you ain't gotta bite my head off. I was just trying to make sure you were good," Sahara said in a hurt tone.

"I'm sorry, I just had a fucked-up night." Porsha sighed. When she had woken up that afternoon in the bed between Tone and Don B. with no recollection of how it had happened, she'd flipped out. She had pressed Don B. about what had happened and all he'd done was laugh, saying that he didn't know she liked to walk on the wild side. Porsha tried to tear his eyes out and would've succeeded had it not been for security restraining her. Don B. had them throw Porsha out on her ass without offering her so much as cab fare to get home. If she hadn't been smart enough to bring her own money she would've been stranded out in Brooklyn. The whole ride back to Manhattan, all Porsha could do was think of Frankie and her warning about the notorious Don B. When she got into the house she was going to tell her that she had been right, but not before she took at least an hour-long shower to wash the stink of Tone and Don B. off her.

"Your night couldn't have been any worse than mine."

"Really, what happened, Sahara?"

"Everything." Sahara went on to tell her of the shooting at the club and the girl in the green dress who had lost her life.

"That poor girl." Porsha shed a tear.

"I know, and I just kept thinking how that could've been me to catch a bullet meant for King," Sahara reflected. "I think I'm good on thugs for a while."

"You and me both, ma."

The girls walked to the building, talking between themselves, both tired and in need of a good shower. They couldn't help but notice that people were staring at them strangely. It wasn't until they saw Levi that they would find out the reason for the strange looks.

"Y'all okay?" Levi asked in a sincere tone, which was unusual for him.

"Yeah, we're good, but what the fuck is everybody staring at?" Porsha asked.

Levi gave them a surprised look. "You didn't hear?"

"Hear what?"

"Frankie, she's in the hospital."

"In the hospital, why, what happened?" Sahara was becoming frantic.

"The nigga Scar and two of his homies tried to run up in your crib and tried to rob it," Levi said, shocking the girls. "Frankie tried to fight them off but they beat her up pretty bad."

"That muthafucka Scar, I'm gonna kill him," Sahara said, fuming.

"Too late, Frankie beat you to the punch. One of the neighbors called the police because of all the noise and they found Spoon bleeding like a stuck pig and Scar dead on your living room floor. Apparently Frankie put one in his monkey ass. I can't say that I'm sorry he's gone either."

Porsha's head was spinning as she tried to process what Levi was telling her. "That doesn't make sense. Scar is a dirt bag, but why would he try and rob us and we ain't got shit?"

Levi looked at the confused faces of Porsha and Sahara and shook his head. "For y'all to live under the same roof y'all sure don't know much about each other. For the last few days Frankie has been out here moving more cracks than a road worker."

"That doesn't make any sense. Frankie is a thief, not a drug dealer," Sahara said.

"Man, for the past few days every crackhead in the hood been buzzing about them boulders she been out here serving. If you don't believe me, ask the police. In addition to them bodies they found quite a bit of drug paraphernalia in your crib."

Porsha shook her head in disbelief. "This shit don't make no sense, we gotta get to the bottom of it. What hospital did they take Frankie to?"

"I don't know, but my guess would be St. Luke's. If I were you I'd hurry up, because the way I hear it they'll be carting her ass outta there to go to court come Monday morning."

"Court, what the hell for?" Sahara asked.

"Murder."

When Frankie finally came to, she felt like she had just gone five rounds with Mike Tyson. Her head was throbbing and she couldn't see out of one eye, but she was thankful to be alive. From the sterile smell and bright lights she knew she was in a hospital, which one she didn't know and didn't care, she was just glad to be alive. When she tried to sit up, pain racked her ribs. She tried to move her hand to assess the damage, but to her surprise her right arm was handcuffed to the bedpost.

"What the fuck?" Frankie yanked at the shackle but it wouldn't give. "Is anybody out there? What's going on?"

A doctor came into the room, accompanied by a man in a wrinkled brown suit. He had *cop* written all over him. From the look on the doctor's face, Frankie already knew she wasn't going to like what she had to say. "How are you feeling?"

"I feel like shit on a stick, thanks for asking," Frankie said. "Can somebody please tell me why I'm chained to this bed?"

"I think the detective will be better suited to answer that question." The doctor stepped aside and the detective approached the bed.

"Good afternoon, ma'am. I'm Detective Brown," the tall black man introduced himself.

"I wish I could say I was pleased to meet you. Do you mind telling me what's going on here? Am I under arrest or something?"

"Unfortunately you are," Detective Brown told her.

"What kinda bullshit is this? Three dudes kicked the shit out of me and I'm under arrest? You have got to be kidding me."

"Afraid I'm not, ma'am. Last night units were dispatched to your home at 845 Columbus Avenue on a domestic dispute. They found one man dead and one critically wounded, and the murder weapon with your fingerprints on it."

Slowly the pieces started coming back to Frankie. She

remembered grabbing the gun from under the couch cushion but everything after that was fuzzy. "Shit."

"Shit is right, and you've stepped into a big pile of it, li'l lady," Detective Brown told her.

"They were going to kill me, I had no choice," Frankie tried to explain to the detective.

"I don't doubt that, miss, but you still shot and killed two men with an illegal handgun."

"Two? I thought you said one was critically wounded?"

"Yes, but Mr. Payne expired this morning," Detective Brown explained to her. "I'm just here to advise you of your rights and what you've been charged with. Now is there anything you can remember from last night that might help me to help you?"

"You want me to help you fuck me? I don't think so. I'm not saying anything else until I speak to a lawyer." Frankie turned her head away so that the detective wouldn't see her crying.

"I think that might be best," Detective Brown told her before reading Frankie her rights.

CHAPTER 48

Old San Juan, Puerto Rico

Animal knelt in one of the pews of the dilapidated church located just outside of town. The building was so ancient and unkempt that it threatened to fall in on itself. The city wanted to tear it down, but it had been declared a landmark by the people of Old San Juan, which meant that they couldn't. To spite the people, the government let the church go, refusing to make repairs, and the people were too poor to do it themselves, so the church continued to crumble one brick at a time. Hardly anyone came there to worship anymore, but it was one of Animal's favorite places to go in Old San Juan when he wanted to commune with his soul.

The last few days had been restless for him. Every time he closed his eyes he saw visions of the men he had massacred in La Perla. Usually killing didn't bother him, but for some reason he couldn't shake the images of the massacre. When they had gotten back to the farmhouse, Animal had received a hero's welcome for the work he had put in on Cruz and his men, but he didn't want their praises, he just wanted to be left alone. In the still of the night Animal had slipped off the property and come to the church, where he had been holed up for the last two days.

There was something about being in the church that

soothed some of the unrest going on with him. He had never been a religious man, but believed in the higher power—how else could anyone explain all that he had lived through? Animal had stood in the shadow of death on many occasions and no matter how many times it had looked like his number would finally be called, he always managed to walk away. It was as if God had a plan for him that hadn't been revealed to him yet.

His grandma used to tell him that they were all God's creatures, put on earth to do God's work to earn their place in heaven, but for as much of the devil's work he did, he couldn't help but wonder how far in the other direction the scales had tipped. Animal cast his tired eyes up to the image of Jesus on a cross that hung above the altar and felt like the eyes of the statue were looking down at him accusingly. "If you have something you want me to do, just tell me, don't leave me in the dark to wonder," Animal said to the statue, but there was no response. "Just like I thought." He got up and brushed his knees off. He heard a rustling to his rear, but didn't bother to turn around. "You can come out, Sonja."

Sonja materialized from the shadows. She was wearing ripped jeans and a T-shirt. "How did you know?"

"I smelled your body wash." He sat on the bench. "What are you doing here?"

"Looking for you." She sat next to him. "You've been missing for two days and K-Dawg is having a shit fit. They thought you bolted back to New York."

"Don't worry, when I decide to leave this island and Los Negros Muertes I'll give boss dawg proper notice," Animal told her.

"You know, I'm completely baffled by you, Animal.

You could stay here and live like a king, but you'd rather go back to New York and live like a fugitive." Sonja shook her head. "Fucking men."

"So how's Chris doing?" Animal changed the subject.

"He's good, thanks to you. I know I keep telling you this, but I can't express enough how grateful I am for everything you done, no just for my brother but for my dad too. This war wasn't going to end until he or Cruz was dead and I'm glad it was Cruz."

"No thanks needed, I was just doing what I was paid to do, and speaking of payment, tell your dad I haven't forgotten about my million dollars." Animal laughed.

"Already taken care off, Animal. I deposited your money in an account that I opened up for you under a false name. All the information is in here." She removed a small leather booklet and held it out. When Animal reached for it she pulled it back. "Can I ask you something, Animal?"

"If it's gonna get you to hand over that little booklet, sure."

"Why do you torture yourself like this?"

"What do you mean?"

"Every day I watch you grieve over a life and a woman that you can never get back. I think you know that you can't get them back, yet you torture yourself with thoughts of what-if. Why is the life you left behind more important than the life you can have?"

Animal sighed. "It ain't necessarily the life, but the people who were in my life. I mean, of course I miss being a big rap star and all, but I miss the loved ones I left behind more than any of that. I came up on free lunch with Brasco and them, so not having them around anymore is hard on me."

"And what about Gucci?" Sonja asked.

"Yeah, I think I miss her most of all. Not being able to have at least said good-bye has hurt me the most," Animal said sadly.

"Your really love her, don't you?"

"With everything that I am. When they ripped me away from her it created a hole in my soul that will never heal." When he looked up at Sonja there were tears in the corners of his eyes.

Seeing Animal like that made Sonja's heart hurt. She had wrestled with the decision the whole ride over to the church. Sonja had always held on to the hope that over time Animal would forget about Gucci and come to love her, but seeing the pain in his eyes she knew that she had been selfish. "Animal, there's something I need to tell you."

"You know you can tell me anything, Sonja. What's going on with you?"

"It's not about me, it's about Gucci."

She now had Animal's full attention. "What about her?"

Sonja tried to find the right words. "The other day I overheard K-Dawg and Justice talking about a shootout that happened at this club, where a lot of people got hurt. I don't know for sure, but I heard K-Dawg say something to Justice; telling him about the girl would only screw Animal's head up worse. I assumed they were talking about Gucci. I'm sorry, Animal."

Animal barely heard her apology. It felt like all the breath had been stolen from his body after hearing the news. He had promised that he would always be there to protect Gucci but he had broken that promise and something had happened to her. When he tried to stand, he found that his legs wouldn't support him. Animal dropped to his knees in the shadow of the cross and cried like a baby.

"I'm so sorry." Sonja knelt beside him and rubbed his back. "I never wanted to hurt you, but I felt you had a right to know."

"Thank you, Sonja," he said, sobbing. "I'll be okay. Is she dead?"

"This I don't know because K-Dawg never said."

"I've got to go to her." He staggered to his feet.

"You can't." Sonja grabbed him by the arm. "Animal, you know the fact that you're under K-Dawg's protection on the island is the only reason that you're not dead or in jail. If you try to go back into New York, all bets are off."

"It doesn't matter. I at least have to try. If there's even a snowball's chance in hell that Gucci is still alive, then I need to find out."

Sonja's eyes became misty. "You would really walk into what could be your death for this woman?"

"In a heartbeat," he said seriously.

Sonja was quiet for a long moment. She knew that Animal's mind was made up and there was nothing she could do to change it, so the least she could do was try to help him. "Here." She handed Animal the booklet.

Animal opened it up and when he saw what was inside he was confused. In addition to his banking information there were some credit cards and a fake ID in the name of John Collins with his face on it. "What is all this?"

"Your freedom," she said sadly. "My mother always told me that if you truly love something, let it go. If it was meant to be, it'll come back. Leave now, and don't go back to the farmhouse for anything. K-Dawg has got people at all the airports but I have a friend named Pablo in San Juan who owes me a favor. He'll get you off the island in his boat, but after that you're on your own."

"Sonja, if anyone finds out you helped me . . ."

"I'm not worried about it, Animal. The only thing that matters to me is that you're happy, even if it isn't with me." Tears rolled freely down her cheeks.

"Thank you so much, Sonja." He hugged her. "I'll never forget you for this."

"I hope not. Now get outta here before I come to my senses and realize how stupid this is." She shoved him. Animal went for the exit, but Sonja's voice stopped him. "Animal, no matter how this plays out, just know that I'll be here waiting for you with open arms if you decide to come back."

Animal smiled at Sonja and left the church.

Animal was in such a rush to get back to New York that he almost tripped over his feet, trying to get out of the church. He had no way to know if Gucci was still alive, but it didn't matter. The hope that she was alive was enough for him to run through the gates of hell with gasoline underwear on.

Animal had made it a few yards away from the church when he was suddenly blinded by headlights. When his vision cleared he was confronted by Justice and several armed men, and his big brother didn't look happy.

"That bitch set me up," Animal snarled.

"No, she didn't. We had no clue where you were, but K-Dawg knew if we stuck close enough to Sonja she'd lead us to you. Come with me back to the farmhouse and let's get this all sorted out."

"I can't do that, Jus. You know what's happened so you know I gotta go," Animal said. He was unarmed except for the knife he was carrying in his boot, and that would be no match for the high-powered machine guns.

"Listen to yourself, li'l bro. You're about to walk into the gas chamber over a broad that's probably dead anyway. I can't let you do that to yourself."

"And you can't stop me either." Animal pulled the knife from his boot.

Justice hoisted his M16 and aimed it at Animal. "Put that fucking knife down and come back to the farmhouse with me, Animal. Me, you, and K-Dawg can work this out."

Animal laughed maniacally. "K-Dawg has got that leash around your neck so tight that you'd draw down on your own family? As much as I hate to say it, Jus, prison seems to have robbed you of your balls and your loyalty. You ain't my brother, you're just a nigga wearing his skin." Animal stalked toward him.

Justice chambered a round into the machine gun. "Animal, I don't want to hurt you."

"That's too bad, because I damn sure plan on hurting you, Justice. Let's dance, nigga." Animal lunged at the same time as Justice pulled the trigger.

EPILOGUE

The deadline to pay the back rent came and the girls had failed to come up with the money. The marshals were kind enough to let the girls grab as much of their stuff as they could before they padlocked the door. Anything else they needed out of the apartment they would have to get from whatever storage facility the city dumped it in, and that's if there was anything left after the movers got done picking over it.

Sahara and Porsha held each other and cried as the lock was placed on their door, signaling the end of an era. They had had some good times and bad in that apartment, and also learned some life lessons that would stick with them for a long time. They had tried to visit Frankie while she was in the hospital but the police wouldn't let them, saying that they would have to wait until after her arraignment and visit her on Rikers Island. They still couldn't believe that the DA was prosecuting her when Frankie had been the victim. It was another example of how the system wasn't designed for people of color.

Porsha and Sahara packed the things of Frankie's that they were able to salvage and took them out to her aunt's house in New Jersey before going their separate ways and promising to keep in touch. Sahara had family in the Bronx that she was able to stay with. It was overcrowded with all her relatives in the apartment, but it was better than sleeping in the streets, so she didn't complain. Her experience with King James taught her what she should've known all along—that she wasn't built for the street life. With a new lease on life, she devoted her time to working extra hours doing hair at the shop and trying to stack enough bread to open her own spot.

The transition hadn't been so easy for Porsha. After being evicted from the projects she had gone to stay with her sister for a while and fell back from stripping to try to put more of her energies into school and her degree, but that didn't work out. It seemed like every day her sister was on her back about one thing or another and constantly bringing up the mistakes that she had made in her life. It was like living with her mother all over again, so she left. Porsha floated around for a while until she was able to find a small apartment in the Bronx that fell into her budget. It wasn't much and the neighborhood was suspect, but it was hers. She often found herself thinking about Alonzo and what might've been if she hadn't been so hard on him. One day she decided to go to the supermarket and check in on him, and was surprised when Mr. Green told her that Alonzo had quit a few weeks prior. This made Porsha smile because he had finally decided to dream bigger for himself. She would see him again someday, but for now she was just going to focus on herself.

A week after she'd been arrested, Frankie finally had her day in court. She had expected to see the legal aide she had been going over her case with, but she didn't recognize the man who had introduced himself as the counsel for the defense. He and the DA argued back and forth about the seriousness of the charge and what the punishment should be. The defense counsel wanted the judge to rule that it was self-defense but the DA kept bringing up the fact that it was an unregistered handgun and that there were drugs found at the scene. He finally agreed to throw the drugs out and reduce the murder charge to involuntary man-slaughter, but he still wanted Frankie to do time, so she took it to trial. The judge set a trial date and ordered that Frankie be held on twenty thousand dollars' bail. She pre-pared herself to go back to the island and get comfortable because she knew damn well she didn't have that kind of money, but when she got back in the tank she was informed that her bail had been posted. Frankie had no idea who had posted her bond and she really didn't care, if it meant that she could get back on the streets.

A few hours later, Frankie was released from 100 Cen-tre Street and took a deep breath. It had only been a week but she felt like she had been locked up for months. As she walked down the courthouse steps she saw the lawyer who had represented her sitting on a double-parked car, star-ing at her.

"So it was you that posted my bond?" Frankie asked.

"Don't be stupid, little girl. Somebody wants to talk to you." He knocked on the back window. The window rolled down and Frankie saw Cutty's coal-black face looking out at her.

"Get in," Cutty ordered.

"Listen, Cutty, if it's about your money—" Frankie began, but he cut her off.

"Stop talking and get in." He pushed the door open.

Frankie was scared shitless but she didn't have a choice so she got into the car. "You know, I had to do quite a bit to track you down, girl."

"Yeah, I ran into a little situation." Frankie wrung her hands together nervously. She thought about coming up with a story and trying to spin him, but figured she'd do better telling the truth. "Cutty, I know I owe you some bread from that work you gave me but I got robbed."

"I know all about it, Frankie. I handled that li'l situation personally." He pulled a folded-up handkerchief from his pocket and handed it to her. Frankie looked inside the handkerchief and almost threw up when she saw that there were two fingers wrapped in it. "That's the one who got away," Cutty explained. "Dumb muthafucka was spending my money around Harlem like it was water. Nobody steals from Cutty."

"So I guess this makes us square, huh?" Frankie mustered a weak smile, but Cutty's face was serious.

"The hell we are. By the time I caught homie the money was almost gone, so that debt is on you, and so is that bail money I just dropped to get your li'l ass out."

"Hold on now, Cutty. I can understand about the money from the coke, but I didn't ask you to bail me out," she tried to reason.

"I know you didn't. The way I see it, had I left you in jail, then you wouldn't have been able to get my bread, right, you see how that works?"

"Not really, because I'm ass broke. Shit, I ain't even got no place to live," Frankie said.

"I've considered all that, which is why I've decided to let you work the debt off. Until you get my bread, your li'l ass belongs to me." Cutty rested his hand on Frankie's thigh.

Frankie slapped Cutty's hand away. "I ain't no whore."

Cutty shook his head. "First you fuck up my money and now you insult me; that's no good, Frankie. And for the record, if I wanted your li'l pussy I'd take it and there wouldn't be shit you could do about it. I don't want your pussy, Frankie, I want your services. You're gonna come and work for me."

"Doing what?" she asked suspiciously.

"Don't worry about that just yet. All you need to know for now is that when I call on you, you'd better answer."

Happy sat on the living room couch in Snoop's apartment, listening to the new stereo system he had brought for his shortly and demolishing a Big Gulp. The projects had been full of drama and he got off on every second of it. He was partially glad that the girls had gotten kicked out of their apartment, but sad because he had never gotten a chance to fuck Porsha. Had he known they were in danger of getting evicted, he would've offered her the money a long time ago in exchange for a taste of her sweet love. A desperate woman was prone to do things she normally wouldn't have, and Happy loved a down-on-her-luck broad. No matter, there were plenty more flowers to pluck in the projects as the times got harder and when they needed something, Happy would be right there to give it to them.

As he sat there plotting on his next victim, Miss Info came on with her celebrity drama report: "From the projects to the penthouse, it's been the Cinderella story that's had the Internet buzzing. Check out my latest video blog entry as your girl got a chance to sit down and chop it up with the owner, Brown, LLC, and his widely popular Web site, BrownGirls.com. You've read about his incredible story, now hear it from the man himself. Mr. Levi Brown."

Happy spit his Big Gulp all over the table when he heard the girl say Levi's name. Happy and Levi were as thick as thieves and there were two things he knew about Levi that made the story impossible to believe. For one, he didn't know his ass from his elbow about computers, and two, Levi was broke. Happy had just loaned him a hundred dollars the other day so that he could buy a bus ticket down South to visit his relatives. There was no way in hell that he could've been sitting on a million dollars and Happy not have known about it. The story had to be some kind of mistake.

He jumped off the couch and went over to the computer on the dining room table. As fast as his fingers could type, he went to Miss Info's site. When Happy saw the picture of Levi dressed in a business suit and holding up a laptop, he found that he suddenly didn't feel too well.

Tionna sat by Gucci's bedside, watching her sleep and trying to keep from crying. She had been doing quite a bit of that since Gucci had been shot. It took four surgeries before they were finally able to stabilize Gucci. The bullet had hit her in the stomach and done a number on her small intestines before exiting through her back. The doctors said that she was very lucky because if it been a fraction of an inch to the right it would've hit her spine and she would've been paralyzed. She had avoided paralysis but still wasn't out of the water yet. Gucci had slipped into a coma and no one knew when or if she would come out of it.

Tionna had taken it the hardest of everyone, including Ms. Ronnie. She felt like if she'd never pressured Gucci into going to the club in the first place, then she wouldn't have gotten shot. Everyone tried to tell her that it wasn't her fault, but no matter what they said, Tionna would always feel like it was, which is why she was at the hospital day and night watching over her friend. On more than one occasion Ms. Ronnie had tried to persuade Tionna to go home and get some sleep, but she refused to close her eyes until Gucci opened hers.

Tionna felt a cold wind on her back that sent a chill down her spine. The window was closed, so she figured it must have been a breeze coming from the open door. Tionna got up and closed the door. When she turned to go back to Gucci's bedside, someone grabbed her from behind. She opened her mouth to scream, but a gloved hand covered her mouth.

"I'm going to move my hand and you are not going to scream, do we understand each other?" a familiar voice whispered in Tionna's ear. She nodded. "Good." He released his grip. As soon as he moved his hand, she shrieked and broke for the door. Before she could get it open, she was grabbed roughly from behind and forced against the wall. "Dammit, Tionna, shut up before hospital security comes," Animal told her.

Tionna turned white as a ghost when she saw Animal. "But you're dead, everybody said you were dead." Tionna blinked, thinking her eyes were playing tricks on her.

"No, I'm very much alive, which is more than I can say

for the men who did this to Gucci." He approached her bedside and stared down at her. She was just as beautiful as he remembered her, if not more so. "How long has she been like this?"

"For over a week now. The doctors say she had a mild stroke during the last surgery," Tionna explained.

Animal took her hand in his and kissed her cold fingers. "My poor baby"—tears dripped from his eyes and splashed on her arm—"look what they did to you. Don't worry, I'm here now and I'm gonna make this right, I promise." Animal leaned in and kissed Gucci on the lips before turning to make his exit.

Tionna followed Animal to the door. "What are you going to do?"

He looked over his shoulder at her. "What do you think I'm going to do?"

Tionna nodded. "Can I ask a favor of you, Animal?"

"I'm all out of goodwill, T," he said seriously.

"It ain't for me, it's for Gucci . . . well, kinda. I know I might be wrong for saying this, but I don't care. When you find the ones who did this, punish them." Tears welled in Tionna's eyes. "Make them suffer for what they did to my girl."

"That I can do." Animal nodded. "Get word to your friends and loved ones, T. Tell them that they might wanna stay off the streets for a time. The sky is gonna rain blood over Harlem, and I don't care too much who gets wet."

K'WAN KEEPS THE STREET FICTION GAME ON LOCKDOWN

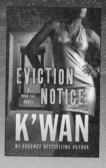  

Visit the-blackbox.com and sign up to receive GANGSTA WALK, a never-before-released free short story from K'wan

 St. Martin's Griffin